THE HUMAN STRUGGLE
BOOK THREE

The

RACE
of
MEN

EVE OTTENBERG

America Star Books
Frederick, Maryland

America Star Books has allowed this work to remain exactly as the author intended, verbatim, without editorial input.

Softcover 9781680907209
PUBLISHED BY AMERICA STAR BOOKS, LLLP
www.americastarbooks.com
Frederick, Maryland

Fiction by Eve Ottenberg

Series: *The Human Struggle*
Book I: *Realm of Shadow*
Book II: *Zone of Illusion*

Novels
Sojourn at Dusk
Dark Is the Night
The Walkout, a Tale in Three Parts
What They Didn't Know, Stories and Essays
Reluctant Reaper
Suburbia
Dead in Iraq
The Unblemished Darlings
Glum and Mighty Pagans
The Widow's Opera

"…it was too sad to count our numbers and find fewer each time, and to see each other ever more deformed and more squalid. And it was so tiring to walk those few steps and then, meeting each other, to remember and to think. It was better not to think."

Primo Levi, *Survival in Auschwitz*

"Each generation has to fight for its life. Each generation has to struggle against darkness. Each generation finds itself in a life and death war for survival, whether all individuals know it or not. Each...that's what I've learned at the end of a long, laborious and often futile series of battles. I am Pavel Saltwater, anti-fascist fighter since childhood, recently liberated from one of the enemy's killing centers, one run by non-humans, defeated and destroyed not by us, the dying inmates, but by angels, though I'm happy to say we hung every human collaborator, every guard, every official of that center, the first chance we got. Now I'm in a hospital at the front, where He who does not wish to see the race of men destroyed is bombing the shit out of His and our enemies. But something is wrong, because they haven't been routed. Even here, in my cinderblock infirmary room, I can hear their tank fire, their machine guns, the white-hot fireballs released by the angels who strive to protect us. Oh, sometimes this seems like an endless war. It's been going on for millennia and will probably continue for millennia, and I have nothing to look forward to but a life of struggle, suffering, loss and fighting at the front, until the enemy kills me. Only one thing is sure, he won't capture me again. I'll blow my head off first. No more killing centers for me. Never again." The pockmarked man stopped writing and laid his dreadfully frail frame back on the pillows. Soon a nurse came to him, with a bowl of steaming soup, a thick slab of white bread, well-buttered, and two small beverages—a glass of juice and one of milk. "I'm hungrier than this," he snapped.

"If you eat more, it will make you ill," she replied with marked composure. "You're making great progress. Let's not spoil it now."

"What about my anti-psychotics?"

"You don't need the meds now."

His hazel eyes glittered angrily at her. "Lady, I just got out of a killing center, where, for months, I was in contact with the enemy. Prior to that I suffered a lifetime of enemy attacks. I've lived on those meds for decades. Don't tell me I don't need them. They're what kept me and my deceased wife alive, when we were taking in and raising the orphans of fighters, all chased by the enemy, all of whom were followed by death sweeps. Those meds kept us alive and sane. Don't you tell me something you know nothing about. The enemy's been all over me. Na to. There it is. You get me my medicine!" He hollered.

"Shh, shh," she gently pushed him back on his pillows. "I'll ask the doctor, okay?"

But Saltwater had commenced coughing and could not reply. The nurse glanced anxiously at the pills on the night stand.

"You didn't take you TB antibiotics," she reproved him worriedly.

"They make me feel sick."

"You need them."

He resumed coughing.

"You have tuberculosis, Mr. Saltwater. You must take your medicine," whereupon she shook out a tablet from the orange bottle and extended it to him in one hand, the cup of juice in the other, oblivious to his pleading gaze. "I don't want it," cough, cough.

"You have no choice. You want to survive, don't you, Mr. Saltwater? Survive and return to you home world, planet four?'

"I want to survive and never encounter this enemy again."

"Well, I can't guarantee the second part of your wish, but these antibiotics will save your life."

"Are you married, nurse Wren?"

"Yes, married to a fighter."

"Where is he?"

"Last I heard, someplace called sector one thousand, which is under enemy attack."

"The poor bastard."

She looked away.

"I'm sorry. That was thoughtless."

She shook her head and the motion gilt her chin-length blond hair. "It's true. He's very unlucky. Apparently the enemy is winning in sector one thousand. There's even talk of a possible sector collapse."

Saltwater sat upright. "A whole universe may collapse?"

"That's the rumor."

Something flickered in the pockmarked man's eyes, something canny, something dark and light at the same time. He reached over to the pad of paper he had been writing on, tore off a sheet, scribbled a few words, folded it in two and handed it to the nurse. "This is for Ivan."

"Ivan? Ivan on the council?" Astonishment filled her voice.

"Yes," Saltwater replied, finally swallowing his medicine. "Take it to him now. At once. Before sector one thousand undergoes a reality collapse and your husband and all the rest of our fighters and all the billions, possibly trillions of inhabitants are destroyed, murdered by our enemy."

She turned to leave.

"Oh, and nurse Wren? Please get me some solid food, something besides white bread."

In the next few moments the pockmarked man reclined back against the pillows and gazed at the painting of a window with sun and trees outside, which adorned the far wall. Then he sighed, spoke out loud a few words to the mental image of his dead wife, and commenced slurping his soup. As he did so, in strode the tall, gray form of Ivan Smironovich, leader of the fighters' council. "What's this?" He snapped, waving the paper that Saltwater had scribbled on. "You can get us AI?"

The survivor nodded, his hazel eyes glittering with hatred, as he replied: "then we'll be ahead of our enemy for once."

"Not so," the council leader sighed and sat heavily on the bed next to Saltwater's.

"They have it?" Pavel cried in alarm.

Ivan nodded miserably.

"But this is terrible! They'll destroy us."

"That appears to be the aim." Ivan paused and studied the pockmarked man for a moment. "What I'm about to tell you stays between us. Too high a price was paid for it. Too much heroism. Too much sacrifice."

Both men fell silent for a moment, Ivan gazing down at his big, knobby hands, clasped in his lap. "We obtained most of the codes, the computer codes, of this…monstrosity, the enemy's artificial computer life."

"You *obtained* them?" Saltwater sat upright. "You mean you sent some luckless fighter behind enemy lines, you were telepathically linked to him, he relayed the codes to the techs, and then he was captured, tortured and killed."

"He killed himself before capture," Ivan sighed again. "As I said, we have paid a high price for this knowledge. But our techs are having trouble…"

"I'll help. Get me those codes today. And when I get you AI, we'll learn everything we need to know about this enemy's killing machine."

"We need you to get us AI," Ivan continued, "so that we can use it to find out what exactly we're dealing with. All we know now is only very sketchy—they have AI and it's homicidal."

The pockmarked man resumed slurping his soup, and bit savagely into his piece of bread, muttering, "the sons of bitches, may they all rot in hell."

"I couldn't agree more. But are you well enough for this work?"

"Never better. Get me those codes."

"The programs are deadly and will infect all computers in all the human worlds, using them for human destruction," Ivan began. "We've turned to the Argans to devise a counterattack, they being the most technologically advanced of all the peoples we have ever encountered."

"It won't be enough," Saltwater said. "Even the Argans with their fantastic weaponry, computers and technology generally won't be able to cope with this."

"Still, we want you to go there."

"To their sector?"

"Yes, to work with them on these codes and on getting us AI, as you said you could do."

Ivan sat silently for a moment, turning the paper over and over in his big, bony hands. It was a sudden, unguarded instant and in it, he was the picture of defeat.

Saltwater sat forward alertly. "What aren't you telling me?"

The leader of the fighters glanced up, collected now, determination not to collapse under the dreadful weight of his knowledge now visible in his sharply sparkling green eyes. "Our techs haven't been entirely frustrated."

"Oh, what have they been able to learn?"

"The enemy's artificial life form?"

"Yes—what?"

"It's basically a very powerful extermination computer."

Saltwater leaned back. "And the targets of these extermination programs," he began.

"Men and women," Ivan said, attempting though failing to extinguish every trace of despair in his voice. "All of us."

The tall, bony, angular woman with the badly cut, short dark hair and the hard, flat, aggressive gaze, clad in cheap clothes, tromped through the underbrush, her appearance bringing to mind the possibility that she was a homeless person lost in the wilds of the Canadian woods. Like a homeless person, her face was visibly worn with care and exposure to the elements, but unlike such an unfortunate, there was nothing unfocussed or meandering about her presence. She was hard and strong and looked very much like someone who came directly to the point, which, after a moment she did, stopping in front of a stone hut with one window and one door and shouting, "guardian of earth, where are you?"

The door opened, out stepped a hale though ancient, white-haired hermit, who glanced at her and exclaimed, his brown eyes glimmering with delight, "Antoinella Lontra! What brings you back here?"

"I've had a relapse," she said.

Sudden concern creased his already lined face. "You were in contact with the enemy," he said.

"I am a fighter. I am always in contact with the enemy. I cannot afford a relapse."

He stepped out of the hut, snatched a handful of a spidery green herb that grew under the window and held it toward her. "Enter, and have some of this. I'll make it into a tea for you. But first tell me, what was different about this situation that might have caused your relapse?"

"I was at a new front."

"A new front!" He gasped.

She gave a grim little smile. "You guardians who never leave earth are very behind-hand. New fronts have been exploding like popcorn on a stove, for oh, at least the past decade, since the late '80s."

"Worse and worse," the old man muttered. "Where is this new front?"

"Someplace called sector one thousand. Don't ask me where it is, I couldn't tell you. All I know is that it is a reality through which the enemy has been rampaging like a wildfire, and it is very probably doomed."

"A whole universe! Oh that I never have to leave this protected planet, praise God for that!" He paused, sniffing the herbs he had picked. "If they've been popping up so frequently, what made this front different?" He asked, gazing now, off through the dense trees and then, before she could answer, he cried: "this particular articulation of the enemy! That's what did it."

"How do you know?" She demanded, then paused, her hard dark eyes wide in astonishment. "I saw it! I saw your vision, the burning cities, the non-human interrogator in his battleship in orbit above a planet, a whole planet in flames."

"This is terrible," the old guardian said.

"No kidding. Come. Make me that tea. I must return to the front as soon as possible."

And with that, the two strange figures, guardian and fighter, walked into the dimness of the little stone hut.

"That non-human interrogator in the battleship?" The old guardian began, setting the herbs on a worn, wooden plank table.

Lontra gazed at him questioningly.

"He is in sector one thousand."

"So I gather."

"But that is not his usual purlieu. Ordinarily he is to be found deep behind enemy lines, at a certain supermax enemy prison, the very one from which two fighters sprang you some years back."

11

They stared at each other, then the ancient man continued. "He was your interrogator."

"How do you know?" She demanded.

"I cannot say how I know. I do not understand it. But I know. And this is why you've had a relapse. You must not return to sector one thousand."

"I'm needed there."

"No. I'm sure they could use you at the main front just as well."

The hard woman seemed to relent. "Well perhaps."

"No perhaps. Definitely. For you to return to sector one thousand would precipitate a disaster, and not just for you."

"How so?"

"Just as we have become aware of him,"

"Yes?"

"So he would become aware of you, your whereabouts, your healing, your stay on this planet. In short, he would learn about earth."

***

"You know, on some worlds, those," the medium-height, nondescript man with the fringe of brown hair pointed a weak, puffy hand at the laptop, "those have not been invented yet."

"Yeah, but we're not interested in those worlds," the pockmarked man replied, sitting up in his hospital bed, tapping on the laptop. "We're interested in those that have advanced as far as possible, as far as is known."

"That would be the Argans."

"Where I'm headed, brother."

The pale, medium-height man sat heavily on the next bed. "I'd sort of hoped you'd stay."

Saltwater gave a dry little laugh. "At the front? Thanks a lot, Lindin."

"We need fighters like you."

"You're just lonely for an old friend from your home world."

Lindin shook his head. "No, there are plenty of fighters from our solar system here. It's just…the Argan universe is so far, and their civilization is so vast. It spans thousands of galaxies. We'll lose you, Pavel, you'll never come back."

"Nonsense. I have a project I need their help with. I won't fall in love with Argan supertechnology and never return."

"Famous last words."

"True last words."

The two fighters sat silently for a moment, and their eyes, virtually the same, sharp hazel tint met.

"Remember the plain of oblivion?" Lindin asked at last.

"How could I forget?"

"You saved my life."

"You would have done the same for me."

"Yes," the nondescript man nodded. "That's why I put in a request. That's why I'm coming with you."

"To Argas?!" Saltwater shouted in surprise and then, in some little annoyance, "I don't need a baby sitter."

"You're frail and ill, Pavel. Yet you've insisted on leaving soon. That shows bad judgment, as I argued to the council."

"To the council," the pockmarked man looked dumbfounded.

"Yes, and they agreed." Lindin leaned forward, weak, puffy hands clasped, eyes sharp, alert behind steel-rimmed glasses. "I'm coming with you, to make sure you take your meds, to prevent you from the inevitable overwork, to insure your recovery. I'm coming, Pavel, to make sure you stay alive."

***

Detective Rafael Orozco sat in his squad car with the thick-set, kindly-faced priest in the passenger seat in the great but run-down, second-rate city of D____, on the mid-Atlantic East Coast, staring up at the sign that read Catafalque Street.

"So Anders," the policeman said, "you zoom across the Milky Way on the back of an angel for what? To tell me I'm not going to this sector one thousand, wherever in heaven that may be. I don't get it."

"They want you here, on earth, hunting death-worshippers and running the transuniverse orphanage in the same old routine way."

"The same old routine way?! A whole reality's collapsing. There will be millions of orphans to place. I don't see how a few thousand of us can manage it, and I don't understand why I've been sidelined."

"This comes from the top, Rafael."

"So I gather."

"Very few fighters from earth are to be involved in sector one thousand, because apparently this articulation of the enemy is particularly virulent to earth, and you know Who wants to keep him ignorant of earth."

"What—He's afraid this enemy will read our minds?"

"No. It's in the event of capture and interrogation."

The light of sudden recognition flickered in Orozco's dark, doleful yet canny eyes. "Oh, so this is a master interrogator."

"I never heard of such."

"I have, and I've seen them at the front. You don't want to get anywhere near one of those. They are very nasty pieces of work."

"Well, He who does not wish to see the race of men destroyed is taking no chances. Only very few, very select fighters from earth will journey to sector one thousand, and most will be far from the front."

"To eliminate the possibility of capture."

"Correct."

"This is a dreadful situation, Vivaldi. Es muy malo, siempre malo."

"Worse and worse," the priest sighed.

"We're losing, brother. We've been losing and losing, and we shouldn't be, and we don't know why." Orozco paused pensively, then asked, "how many enemy commanders, you know, the kind that can barbecue a city with the wave of a hand, how many of those in this sector one thousand?"

"Lots. The sector's apparently overrun with them."

A look of terror entered the policeman's dark and doleful eyes, a look that flickered like a very rare and unwanted guest. "We could lose that reality," he said softly.

"Let's not jump to the worst conclusions."

"You, Anders, ain't never seen one of those black-clad, fascist commanders in action. I have. Dios mio, this is terrible."

The priest remarked that he assumed his friend had witnessed the destruction caused by such commanders at the front.

"Yes I have," Orozco replied somberly. "And it's terrible. The battlefields of Elsewhere are soaked in the blood of fighters slaughtered by those sons of bitches. It happens like clockwork. Whenever we send a squadron in, if He isn't directly involved or if we ain't got help from some angel, we're in for a bloodbath."

"The front sounds terrifying," the priest commented.

"It's a nightmare. The only thing, the *only thing* that keeps us fighters alive and sane there is Him. We hear Him directly in our minds—that reasonable, rational voice of hope, that

15

voice that's always right, always correct—without it, we'd have lost the war years ago, because it's been goin' against us since the 1970s, and here it is 1997, and in all that time, we who fight, who actually fight on the side of the angels, we've been losing. And we don't know why. And now, this new cataclysm in sector one thousand just means that things have gone from bad to worse." The policeman pounded a mighty fist on the steering wheel. "If only we knew what was wrong!" He exclaimed. "Then we'd fix those death-worshipping sons of bitches once and for all."

"Our knowledge is always limited," the priest began.

"Yeah, but in this case, it's a disaster. A little information could save a lot of lives, but it ain't forthcoming. You'd think the guardians could be of some help with this."

"Your visionaries, you mean."

"Earth's visionaries, earth's last, best, deepest, most secret line of defense against the enemy. Yes, you'd think they'd have some inkling of what's wrong, and I'm going to see one after you leave, to put that very question to him."

"He's old and wise?"

"He's old. I don't know about wise. He's been battling insanity for the past five years, but then so have three fourths of all guardians recently. Whatever's wrong for us, on the battlefield, seems to be afflicting them too, in a different way."

The two men lapsed into gloomy silence and sat, staring out the windshield at a gray day now grayer due to the light patter of rain. Around them, the towers of mid-town loomed indistinctly in the downpour, the sky was enshrouded with clouds, passers-by hurried along under umbrellas.

"I'm glad you're not returning to the front," the priest said at last, quietly.

"Oh? Why's that?"

"Because every time I hear that that's where you're headed, I can't help thinking that it could be the end for my great friend, the fighter, Rafael Orozco. And if there's one thing I pray for, my brother, it is that you will die of old age, comfortably, in your bed."

"Give that up," Orozco growled, "because, not to put too fine a point on it, regrettable as it is, I won't."

"You never know."

"I'm sure of it. No, Anders. I won't die of old age in my bed. I been a fighter long enough to know that that ain't my destiny."

***

Some hours later, rain still falling, the policeman, alone now, parked his Impala on Lincoln Street and gazed out the windshield at the dreary day, the long, sweeping sheets of rain enveloping sky and air and the many crooked, gray tombstones of the little churchyard behind a tall, black, dripping and gleaming wrought-iron fence, right near where he had parked. Orozco glanced across the street at the high, narrow, but stylish townhouse, wrapped in rain, and thought, fondly, of the inhabitants, Lydia and Howard MacKenzie, two old friends from way back, from the time when Howard had been a state representative, who listened thoughtfully to everything the leathery old Mexican policeman had to say about their decaying and crime-ridden city of D____. They knew, or rather believed, nothing of fighters, guardians or the war, off-world. But Howard did have a younger brother, Horace, who, like many guardians, suffered from a relentless psychotic depression, who had tried repeatedly to kill himself and who currently resided on the psych ward of a local hospital. Orozco sighed as he thought of how desperately he needed Horace's help and stepped out of his car, into the rain, then jogged across the street and up the slippery steps. He pressed the doorbell, and heard the faint chime echo up through the house, soon followed by the heavy tread of footfalls and thereafter the thunk, thunk of deadbolts being unlocked.

The door opened, and there loomed the tall, portly, sharp-eyed presence of the former legislator, his rather stern visage creasing into something approximating delight at the unexpected appearance of his old friend. "Lydia!" He called over his shoulder to his wife. "It's Rafael Orozco, our friend the detective!" Then, turning to his guest, "step in out of the rain, you're drenched." Rafael did so, pushing the front door shut behind him. "It's been what? Almost two years?" Howard cried, reaching forward and lustily shaking his old friend's enormous hand, with his, almost equally large one. "About that," Rafael conceded. "It was a mayoral campaign rematch, Lozzo versus Terrazini, and you, in your capacity as leader of local Dems, wanted to make sure that would-be Mussolini, Lozzo, played by the rules."

"And we forced him to," Howard chuckled. "And he lost—again. Hopefully he's off the political stage for good. Well," he clapped his hands and rubbed them together. "It's too early for a martini, but I can offer you a cappuccino with our new cappuccino machine, a gift from Carla, our oldest, who is, as you may know, running for city council."

"So I heard. Yeah, I'll take a cappuccino."

"Lydia!" Howard hollered.

"I heard, I heard," that gray-haired, alert and sharp-eyed woman said, coming down the hall behind her husband. "Great to see you, Rafael," and she clasped his hand and kissed his lined, leathery old cheek. Then the two men decamped to the living room, with its hyper-modern Mies van der Rohe chairs, which looked far more uncomfortable than they were, causing the policeman to hesitate and his host to gesture magnanimously at the couch—"sit there."

To Howard's inquiry about what brought him, Rafael replied, "your brother, Horace."

The former legislator sighed. "He's on the psych ward at Salk Hospital, where he was moved last month from a long-term facility. He's preparing to exit and return to his house here in Uptown, on Apocalypse Avenue. I certainly hope your business with him is not of a nature to set off any, any—"

"Psychological fireworks? No, I don't think so," Orozco replied.

Howard, leaning forward, rested his elbows on his knees and clasped his hands between them. "You two were always close in a way I could not understand."

"Just good friends," the policeman said roughly. "And he helped me out once, on a case."

The attorney nodded. "His grasp on reality is very shaky," Howard continued. "He still talks about the war—that war in another reality that obsesses him and that, I'm convinced, is the most florid outgrowth of his psychosis. His is a very deep depression, a psychotic depression."

"Is he on meds?"

"Of course, has been for years. That didn't stop him trying to kill himself, though."

"Just so he don't succeed."

"He won't. We've hired a live-in housekeeper, most of whose job, unbeknownst to Horace, will be keeping an eye on him."

"Oh, he'll figure that out, real quick."

"Too bad," Howard snapped. "He'll have to live with it. It's one of the conditions of his release."

This testiness, along with a slight wobble of the head, shocked Rafael into the realization that in a mere two years, his friend Howard MacKenzie had become old. He now fully looked the part of the senior citizen; he was…elderly. The policeman sighed at the sudden awareness of a time when he would no longer have this friend, and mentally chided himself for allowing two whole years to elapse between his pow-wows with the wise though quite cynical old attorney.

"Who is this housekeeper?" The policeman asked.

Howard chuckled, receiving the proffered cappuccino from his wife. "A young Israeli expat, name of Gideon."

"Why the chuckle?"

"Oh, Horace's reaction. He says Gideon's a fighter."

Something deep and darkly bright flickered in the old policeman's eyes. "You mean," he said with elaborate blandness, receiving his own cappuccino from Lydia in turn, "Horace considers him tough."

"No, no, not merely that," Howard corrected him. "An actual fighter from this…this war that Horace believes in. But no matter," he waved a hand airily. "They've bonded."

"Ah," Orozco breathed. "So when does Horace return to Apocalypse Avenue?"

"Tomorrow. Gideon picks him up tomorrow."

"I'd like to be there."

"Suit yourself."

"And I'd like to speak with him today."

"No problemo," Howard smiled. "Visitors allowed until seven p.m."

The old investigator sipped his cappuccino with satisfaction.

"You certainly look like the cat who swallowed the cream," thus keen-eyed, gray-haired Lydia, sitting now in the chair next to her husband.

"That's exactly what I am," and doleful Orozco almost smiled.

"Would you mind enlightening us?" She demanded.

"Yes. Yes I would."

"You and Horace," Howard sighed. "It's like you're part of a secret society."

"A secret society of lunatics," Lydia said.

"Thanks a lot," Orozco snapped.

"Well, look where this alternate world crap has got him—thirty milligrams of zyprexa a day and thousands of dollars in mental health care bills. To say nothing of multiple suicide attempts. Lucky he's so damn clumsy. Never could tie a knot."

"He tried to hang himself?" Orozco asked.

They nodded. "In his basement," Howard enlightened him. "Part of Gideon's job will be keeping him out of the cellar. We don't want any second attempts." The old attorney pulled at the knees of his summer, khaki pants, making himself more comfortable. "This Gideon's smart. I briefed him myself, gave him Horace's whole long history."

"You told Gideon everything Horace has said about the war?" Orozco asked slyly.

"The whole delusional kit and kaboodle. He took it all in. He's a very bright guy, was quizzing me on details of Horace's last vision."

"Oh," the policeman remarked casually, "what was that?"

"Something about a reality collapse in some place called sector one thousand. I told Gideon the only reality that had collapsed was Horace's, that he was lost in a land of delusions. Sector one thousand! What next?"

"I'll tell you what next," Lydia put in, "one of his quote doubles unquote had been captured by the enemy."

Orozco's hand shook, but he managed not to spill his beverage. "One of Horace's doubles?"

"Yes," Lydia snapped, "as if we didn't have enough trouble with the one we've got, he's convinced he has not just doubles but multiples."

The phone rang, and the wife rose to answer it, then called from the kitchen: "Howard! It's Mayor Terrazini on the line for you."

"Ooof," Howard lumbered to his feet. "You'll have to excuse me, Rafael. Dante only calls in emergencies." And with that he left the room, as the policeman placed his cup on the coffee table and his head in his enormous hands. Lydia returned. "Dissolving in a puddle of despair over Horace's lunacy?" She asked.

"Where did he say his captured double was?" Orozco nearly snarled in anger and hopelessness.

She started. "He wouldn't say. He said he'd only tell a fighter, because fighters would have to rescue him." She paused. "Look, Rafael, his psychosis is…florid. There's very little hope of him ever being in touch with reality."

"That's what you think, sister."

"What's that supposed to mean?" She snapped.

"He's in touch with reality all right. It's just one he ain't supposed to be in touch with."

"What's he supposed to be in touch with?" She asked clear and curious.

"Earth, not sector one thousand. Earth, and only earth."

"Well, he ain't," Lydia laughed grimly. "He's in the stratosphere."

"I never heard of anything like this before. What a disaster!" And with those words, the old detective rose to leave.

"You can say that again," his hostess agreed.

The policeman tromped back out into the gray rain, which whooshed down in sheets now, sheets that curved to drape the buildings, graveyard, parked cars, passers-by under umbrellas, in long, gray, damp folds.

"Ain't never heard of no guardian in touch with some other reality," Orozco grumbled to himself. "They belong to earth, only earth. How could this be?" He slid back behind the wheel of his Impala, and slammed the door shut. "I'm gonna have to file a report," he muttered to himself, "that there's a Horace MacKenzie, prisoner behind enemy lines, who knows where, and he has to be rescued, pronto."

"You will discuss this with Gideon," a voice spoke in Rafael's mind.

"He's just another fighter. That won't do no good," Orozco snapped back mentally.

"Listen, Rafael, you will tell him everything. You will hold nothing back. The law of the minimum does not apply here. He needs to know all you know about the MacKenzies, about Horace's illness, about you."

"Me?"

"Yes. Your work with the orphanage. How you and Carmella Marquez teamed up to drive back the enemy on the plain of oblivion. Your secrets, your past."

"Nunca! Never! This is madness. I ain't tellin' some fighter I never met all that."

"You must and you will. He will need your help, and you will be linked to him."

"Linked? Telepathically? I fail to see the necessity for that."

"You may, but you know Who does not. He doesn't want any surprises causing Gideon to stumble."

"What's so special about this Gideon?" Orozco grumbled mentally.

"He has been chosen."

"Chosen? That don't sound good."

"For him it is not, but it is necessary."

"What is?"

"For him to journey behind enemy lines to rescue the captured fighter, Horace MacKenzie."

"Oh," Orozco spoke out loud, dully, flatly. "Now I get it."

***

The old Impala sloshed through the silvery rain, the hypnotic rhythm of the windshield wipers glazing the fighter's eyes.

"Snap out of it, Rafael," he heard in his mind. "Stay alert. You're going to be in the presence of a very unusual guardian in a moment and one who is, though remotely, nonetheless definitely, in contact with the enemy." The old investigator did as he was told: focused his doleful brown eyes and parked near Salk Hospital. This time he remembered his blue umbrella on the floor before the front passenger's seat.

He trudged through the rain pondering—how would he and this Gideon ever locate the other Horace MacKenzie? He could not imagine; short of divine revelation, it seemed an unsolvable mystery and obstacle. He ground his teeth in frustration. Somewhere in the kingdom of night, a fighter, double to one of earth's guardians, was enchained in one of the enemy's thousands of supermax prisons. He, Orozco, did not even know what reality, what alternate universe, this territory lay in. "And I don't want to know, I have to admit." He thought.

"Too bad. This is your job. You have your work cut out for you. You too have been chosen."

"Great. Just friggin' great."

"Stop complaining. It could have been you, not Gideon, chosen to go."

"Dios mio!" The policeman exclaimed aloud and stopped, in a suddenly intense downpour, under his umbrella.

"Pick up the pace, Rafael."

"I know," he thought. "Time's awasting." After a moment, he asked mentally, tentatively, "so that was under consideration?"

"Yes it was."

"Phew," the old policeman sighed. "That was close. I guess I dodged a bullet."

"Your age counted against you."

"How old's Gideon?"

"Thirty-three."

"Lucky man."

"Hardly."

"You got that right," Orozco snapped aloud and stepped into the hospital's lobby. It was crowded with visitors leaving but hesitating to step out into the downpour and so, it took longer to get to the man behind the information desk. But soon he stood in the elevator, on his way up to the sixth floor, a floor of locks, secure doors and some patients shackled to their beds. The old policeman shuddered grimly, as an orderly led him to a room with a door standing open.

"Rafael, I've been expecting you," boomed the bass of Horace MacKenzie's voice. "What took you so long?"

"Resistance."

"Ah, now as ever the unwilling servant of the Lord," and, to the orderly's astonishment, the mental patient smiled—something he had not been seen to do since he arrived on the ward.

"You can leave us," Orozco told the orderly, who objected but finally complied upon sight of the detective's badge.

"Idiots," Horace breathed. " Catastrophe all around, whole sectors collapsing, and they shackle the people most able to help to their beds."

"I'd keep quiet about sector one thousand if I were you."

"Why should I?" Horace demanded, brown eyes blazing fiercely.

"To stay out of the loony bin, for one reason," the detective snapped.

"Oh," Horace waved a hand. "I could give a shit about that."

"You better. You better give a shit, and you better keep quiet. There's a master interrogator in sector one thousand, and we do not, I repeat *not* want him becoming aware of you."

"It may be too late," Horace cried disconsolately and flung himself into a green plastic chair.

Alarm overcame the detective's leathery old visage. "How so?"

"They've captured another Horace MacKenzie, a fighter."

Orozco relaxed. "That won't lead back to you."

"You know that for sure?"

"The other Horace is unaware of your existence, right?"

"We may be telepathically linked."

"Shit!" Orozco hollered, and the orderly promptly appeared. "Go away, young man. I'm conducting an investigation here." The orderly disappeared, as the policeman, suddenly calm, popped a mint into his mouth. "But this fighter, your double who's been captured—he don't know you're a guardian, or what that is, does he?"

Horace shook his head.

"Phew," Orozco exclaimed and rubbed the back of his massive hand across his forehead. "How in heaven did you get linked to a fighter in sector one thousand?"

"I'm as dumbfounded as you are. And even Gideon, who's spent the past fifteen years at one front after another, says he never heard the like of it."

"Something's wrong somewhere," Orozco intoned. "I've said it before, I'll say it again. Humanity's on the run, we're losin' and we shouldn't be. Things are going haywire, kerfloouie, like you gettin' linked to a double in another reality. That ain't supposed to happen to guardians. Do you see through his eyes?"

"No. I hear his thoughts, and words."

"So you know where he is?"

"Yes. He's no longer in sector one thousand."

"Good, 'cause that place is about to collapse, brother, that's for sure. Please don't tell me he's in the realm of shadow."

"He's not."

"Hallelujah!" And Orozco breathed a noisy sigh of relief.

"He's in the kingdom of night's gulag. It's a world of concentration camps."

The policeman stared at the mental patient. Finally he said, "never heard of it, but it don't sound good."

"It's not."

"Where is it?"

"In the remains of someplace called sector ten, very near the absolute front, walking distance."

Orozco sighed, leaned forward and put his face in his hands.

"I take it that's bad?" Horace asked.

"It's bad," the detective spoke through his fingers. "The enemy conquered sector ten some years back, when he beat us on the plain of oblivion. I kind of thought it had ceased to exist."

"It's a fascist reality," Horace explained. "All the natives are in chains."

"Those poor indigenous people—Jesus Christ."

"They were primitive?"

"Yes, and doubtless judged by their death-worshipping conquerors to be of a subhuman strain."

"The misery there is dreadful."

Orozco sighed again. "It never ends," he murmured at last. "Just when you think you've seen the worst of it, that it couldn't get any worse, you find out there's some new crappy reality, the kingdom of night's gulag in sector ten, where they've shipped some luckless fighter and doubtless others."

"A good number of others."

"How many?" Orozco growled.

"Hundreds at the very least. But look on the bright side."

"There's a bright side?"

Horace smiled: "They didn't get shipped to the realm of shadow."

***

At about the time of this conversation, a youngish, muscular man with black, curly hair, dressed in faded jeans and a green T-shirt, sloshed through the rain under a black umbrella in the swanky precincts of Garibaldi Square, which he paused to gaze at, utterly empty in the downpour. It was his first time in this neighborhood, and he seemed to be reconnoitering it, rather in a military manner. He glanced from the deserted, elegant, wet square with its empty benches, back to the gleaming facades of the buildings that faced it, and studied them until his gaze settled on a sign, about knee-high, indicating a bookstore below street level. The sign read: The Sun, The Moon and The Stars. He gave a grim little smile, then made for it through the streaming rain.

Down at the entrance, a strong young woman with cropped hair, glanced up from the cash register. "Your name?" She demanded boldly.

"Gideon Cohen."

She slammed the register shut. "What news from the front?"

"Nothing good," he replied. "We struggle to survive."

She grimaced, then pointed to the path through the warren of dim rooms and stacks of books at the back of the store. "I'll take you to him." With that, she rounded the register and locked the front door. Then she led him through a bibliophile's haven, passed crammed, floor-to-ceiling bookcases, past the offices of a small press and on, until at last they reached the publisher's and book-seller's office, seemingly far underground and far, far back from the front of the store.

"Galen," she called. "Gideon is here."

With that, an ancient though still spry octogenarian, with longish white hair, sandals, khaki pants and a white, button-down shirt, shuffled out from behind the desk, his hand extended to the new arrival. They shook, as Gideon's sharp, dark-eyed gaze explored the office—its desk, with the computer to the side, the one narrow, high window, the wooden chair facing the desk, the floor-to-ceiling bookcases, all full.

"You see how I live," the old man remarked.

"I see how you live," his visitor repeated.

The old publisher nodded at the strong young woman, and she left, then he reached behind the newcomer, pulling the door shut and gestured at the empty chair.

"Why me?" The young man asked, seating himself, as his host did the same behind the desk. Galen ran his knobby, gnarled hands through his white hair. "That's the same question I asked myself over forty years ago, in the concentration camp. Give it up. It's a waste of time. Besides, I can't answer it. I am merely the messenger."

"A messenger who's also a guardian. You saw that vision of this dreadful place—this world of gulags in the kingdom of night?"

Galen nodded, and his dark eyes glimmered deeply and with life. "Doubtless it was not the last such vision, either."

"Well, it better not be. I'm going to need some very specific information—what planet, what continent, what supermax facility, before I even consider going off-world."

"You are very brave."

"I do as I'm told, because I understand what's at stake. How did this double come to be linked to one of earth's guardians?"

Galen sighed and rubbed his eyes. "That I do not know, though as far as I do know, such a thing has never occurred before and certainly not spontaneously, not of its own accord."

"That vision of that fascist reality has flooded the minds of fighters from earth to Elsewhere and back. I suggest, Galen, you put in a request for it to stop. We got the picture. We understand."

"But I don't. I'm still…befuddled. Like you, I'm stumped—how could this happen?"

Gideon sighed, as his sharp, dark eyes studied the old concentration camp survivor. "I wonder too, but in the end, does it matter? We have a job to do; that's all that counts."

"Does it matter? Everything connected to the enemy matters. Somehow this, this…defensive development was brought on by events in sector one thousand."

"Events directed by a non-human master interrogator."

"He must have come in contact with a fighter from earth at some point—that is my surmise."

Something dark and light at the same time flickered in Gideon's eyes. "Your explanation makes some sense. Remember the story of the ghost?"

"Yes, they tortured her, the non-human ones, and when she escaped, when Lontra returned to the battlefield, something was unleashed, something quite able to hit the enemy, merely through her gaze. This may be a similarly mysterious unleashing of a defensive force. It's a guess, but it seems probable."

"In other words," Gideon spoke softly, intently, "this Horace MacKenzie, the imprisoned fighter, not the guardian, may well have become a…a weapon in His hands."

"Well put," Galen smiled, and something deep, dark, ancient and retaliatory glimmered visibly in his eyes.

The visitor brought his hands with the stubby but muscular fingers together. "Now I understand the rescue. We need him. We need the weapon he has become."

"We also must save as many fighters from the kingdom of night as we can."

"I am not Moses. I cannot free and lead tribes of fighters through a world of gulags. We will be caught, tortured and killed."

"I didn't say tribes."

"How many, Galen? Because as I see it? Just getting this man Horace out will be hard enough."

There was silence, which Gideon finally broke. "I assume you've had a vision?" Then he fell silent again, dark eyes wide.

"Now you see?" Galen asked, the life of another Being visibly flickering in his eyes.

"A woman and three men, one sick, and three of these fighters in the prison are talking. She believes they can escape. They are close to the front." Gideon paused. "The two male fighters, one sick, one healthy, are Horace's cellmates."

"All four," Galen suddenly announced, and as he did, Gideon thought he heard a distant trumpet. "All four must make it back alive. Their work is not done."

Despite the faint trumpet, Gideon chaffed. "People *do* die before their work is done."

"Not in this war," the old man quietly contradicted him.

"Whatever," the young man dismissed this response, thinking, quite logically of the heaps of fighters' corpses on the blood-soaked battlefields of Elsewhere. He regarded the old man with a mixture of awe and anger, for it was Galen who had dragooned him, Galen who was sending him to the kingdom of night—and he did not want to go. He said so. The ancient guardian apologized, repeating that he was only the messenger.

"I doubt that," Gideon grumbled, and then, no contradiction forthcoming, demanded, "you were consulted, no?"

"By the council? No."

"I mean above the council."

"What makes you think seraphs would consult me?"

"Above the seraphs," the young man continued stubbornly. "You're a friend of His. It's obvious. You could have got me off the hook."

"I, too, do as I'm told—because I understand what's at stake."

Gideon grumbled, scarcely audibly to himself, then leaned forward. "First I'm told to come take care of a guardian. Then you know Who sees me through his eyes. Next thing I know I'm a hero on a suicide mission behind enemy lines."

"Not a suicide mission."

"Really? Really? Because it sure looks like one to me."

"My understanding is that for the first half, getting to the prison, you will be telepathically linked to another fighter, here in D____, a fighter who, I'm assured, really is a friend of His."

"Like you're not," Gideon sighed, then resumed. "So that'll keep my feet on the right path."

"Correct."

The young man's gaze wandered over the crammed bookcases. "So you're a scholar."

"I've got a little learning, yes," Galen waved a self-deprecatory hand. "That's the most one can hope for."

"I doubt that," his visitor repeated. "A lot of learning looks more like it." He sighed. "My grandparents were survivors like you." He said.

"Then you know we don't like to talk about it."

"Understandably enough…I've been in this war since I was 15."

"I too, exactly the same age."

"I want out. I want to live."

"Many fighters feel as you do, but you and they forget—it is not up to us. It is not us guardians who sent you to the front. You were driven there, and not by us."

"By who then?"

"By our enemy, your enemy, who has persecuted you mercilessly since childhood."

***

The next day they felt the full heat of July. Howard MacKenzie, stepping out of his house early morning on his way to the office, saw waves of calefaction already billowing up from the sidewalk. Detective Orozco, exiting his Impala at Salk Hospital noticed that the asphalt on the street was soft, melting slightly in the tremendous heat. The city birds were silent, reluctant to exert themselves in what felt like an oven. Lydia MacKenzie stepped up to the thermostat in the hall and turned the central air-conditioning on high. Galen did the same in his bookshop, while Gideon, staying with a web-designer friend in the River District, stepped out of a cold shower, refreshed and ready to face his fate, in the form of a mad guardian and a divinely favored fighter, waiting for him at the discharge desk of the psych ward.

The city of D____ lay prostrate. Everywhere was evidence that the heat was too much for it. "Shut the door, hurry shut it," shopkeepers everywhere addressed their customers, while only the bravest drivers rolled their car windows down. The young Israeli turned the key in the ignition of his little gold Honda and in minutes with the air conditioning, the sweltering interior, the steering wheel too hot to touch, had all become ice cold. "That's better," he said aloud, as he tore through the Vicinato Italiano, then down Insane Asylum Avenue in the direction of Uptown. Parking in front of Salk Hospital, he regarded the hot sidewalk with evident distaste. At last he decided to sprint to the entrance, rather than drag out what would only be an uncomfortably sweaty arrival.

Up on the psych ward, Gideon saw Horace in the company of a tall, lean, grizzled man, who he judged to be in his mid-fifties, with gray hair, a lined face and doleful, yet somehow canny dark eyes.

"Hello brother," this man addressed him. "We're just checking out."

"And you would be?"

"Detective Rafael Orozco. I take it you're Gideon Cohen."

The younger man nodded. The old detective gave him a sidelong glance. "We got our work cut out for us," he said softly.

"You certainly do," snapped the nurse. "Mr. MacKenzie here needs his medications every day at the same time, after dinner. And he is not to be left alone for any great length of time."

"Define great," the detective snapped back.

"Over a half an hour."

"I'll go mad," Horace lamented.

"You already did," Orozco retorted.

"I need privacy, time to myself."

"You jettisoned the right to that when you tried to hang yourself in your cellar."

"That's passe" and Horace airily waved a hand.

"That's what you think. It made an indelible impression on everyone who knows you. Nope. If the nurse here says no more than thirty minutes, that's the rule."

Favorably impressed with this fighter, Gideon nodded in agreement, came around behind Horace and grasped the rather tall, portly and balding would-be suicide under the elbow. The trio walked to the elevator, as the nurse departed. "So who will live with Horace while I'm away?" Gideon asked. "Me and an investigator I know who does a lot of work from home, name of Starfield," Orozco answered. "We'll alternate shifts, since we both gotta put in occasional appearances at our respective offices. In the beginning, till you reach the prison, most of the babysitting will devolve to Starfield. Once you liberate those four fighters, you and I will part ways—at least that's the scenario I'm hoping for—you'll get them to the front, pronto, and I'll be taking care of our psychotically depressed friend here."

"I can hear you," thus Horace.

"So?" Orozco slurped on a mint. "You think I don't know that?"

"Did it ever occur to you that it's rude to refer to me in my hearing as a lunatic or a psychotic?"

"No," slurp, slurp. "'Cause it's the truth."

Gideon chuckled, the wonderfully air-conditioned elevator opened, they stepped in, and down they zoomed to the lobby.

They drove their two cars through the now very uncomfortable heat to Apocalypse Avenue, Horace in the Impala, then parked and waited on the front step, as the mental patient sorted through his keys. Then they entered and set about making brunch, with the food that Lydia had shopped in a day or two previously. Since Horace was a merciless kibbitzer who did actually nothing, the young

Israeli banished the two older men to the living room, while he whipped up mushroom and scallion omelets, toasted bagels and set some kippered salmon on a plate. Though warm at first, the tall, old townhouse cooled off quickly after the policeman flipped on the central air-conditioning. Then he flung himself into a comfortably padded armchair in the living room, across from his host, seated on the blue couch and glowering at him from under bushy, knitted eyebrows.

"So where did you say your double, this other Horace was captured?" The policeman asked.

"Someplace called sector one thousand. Don't ask me where that is. There's a front. He was at it. He was captured and beaten, but luckily he was not wounded, because from what I heard through his ears, the wounded were summarily shot."

Orozco ran the back of one of his big hands across his forehead. "And then they moved him?"

"Yeah, they shackled him and the other unwounded prisoners and transported them to a prison."

"Near the front?"

"Very near. Just over on the enemy's side."

"What's this prison like?"

"Horrible. They infect the inmates with diseases we've never heard of before. They rape some of the women."

"But not all."

"Not all. And they don't beat them too much."

"The women or all the prisoners?"

"All. They're content to…make them sick."

Orozco ran his hand down over his face, then asked worriedly, "this prison, is it run by non-humans?"

Horace shook his head. "No. It's run by death-worshipping men."

The policeman heaved a large sigh of relief.

"They're still horrible," the mental patient warned.

"But it's not as bad as it could be, brother," the policeman replied. "Not by a lot." He paused to take a plate with an omelet that Gideon, having entered the room carrying three, extended to him.

"If they're not beaten," the young man said. "they won't have broken bones. No broken bones makes fleeing easier."

"When did you first become…telepathically linked to this double?"

"About a month ago. He was fighting on a front in sector one thousand. I started hearing through his ears and hearing his thoughts—all of which forced me to conclude that I better shape up, get the fuck out of the mental hospital and get help to these people any way I could."

All three men ate their omelets in silence, until Orozco spoke: "you drew the right conclusion, brother."

"Thank you. I've never been connected to people off-world before. I'm a guardian of earth. I see what the enemy does here and transmit that knowledge to fighters, who are here. This connection to a double in another universe, well, it's a whole new ball of wax."

"It's something new under the sun, to be sure," the old Mexican said. "Whether good or ill, only time will tell."

"But time has already told one thing that I don't understand," Gideon said.

"What's that?"

"Why do these four fighters have to be rescued? I mean generally until now, it was my understanding that once you fell into enemy hands, in an enemy prison, well, the game was up. I never heard of rescuing fighters like this before."

"Then you, young man," Orozco snapped, polishing off the last of his eggs, "you haven't been paying attention."

***

Two days had passed. During that time, the pockmarked fighter had downed his pills promptly, almost religiously, had eaten a little more at each meal, without the complaint, on the tip of his tongue, that he could have eaten a *lot* more, and had commenced stretching exercises in the morning. He received the same two visitors each day—Ivan and Lindin— and the leader of the council repeated the words, "we need you to get us AI, so we can learn what we really are up against. Frankly, we don't know a thing. We're waiting for you invention, Pavel, to enlighten us, to discover for us what this really is and how and where it works." By contrast, Lindin just sat quietly and, in the silence that enfolded the two old friends like yet another friend, waited for Saltwater to say something, anything, about his deceased wife Hannah, whom Lindin had known so well. But on the second day, he made a delicate inquiry and received an abrupt reply: "They shot her right in front of me, at the separation station, because she was ill. Never allude to it again, Lindin. That's enough." And the two men lapsed back into a silence that lasted thirty minutes, until the medium height, nondescript fighter was called away, and Nurse Wren arrived with a spaghetti and meatballs dinner, with a salad, soup and buttered white bread on the side.

"I could use a drink."

"Alcohol?" Nurse Wren exclaimed. "Absolutely not! Not with those antibiotics you're on. Alcohol is strictly forbidden."

"Even beer?"

"Yes, even beer. Here, have a tall glass of iced tea."

Grumbling, the patient sipped his beverage, then asked if she had received any word of her husband. She sadly shook her head, and the very straight, blunt-cut blond hair waved like one solid piece of gold in the dim light of early evening.

"No news is good news," Saltwater consoled her.

"Is it?"

"Absolutely." He paused. "The separation and the waiting and the not knowing are terrible, but news of disaster is far worse, because then you have to give up hope, and hope, Nurse Wren, whether you know it or not, is what keeps us all alive."

"I know it," she said quietly.

"It is the last thing to die," he continued. "And when it does, you've lost the whole world, the world that was wrapped up in that person who you know is dead. And when it dies for yourself, when you come face to face with the immediate and irreversible fact of your own impending death, then you lose everything."

"That's what you saw in the killing center?"

Saltwater grimaced. "That's what I saw. More meatballs, please." As she extended another plate of meatballs and removed the old one, he asked nonchalantly: "any more word on when I may get out of here?"

Her attractive features, most especially her mouth, pulled down in disappointment, as if she had just realized the true reason for his sociability, he who was usually either withdrawn or all business. But she answered, "I believe the latest word from the council is two more weeks. Your doctor said he was called in,"

"Doctor Levi was *called in before the council?*" Saltwater was astonished.

The nurse nodded. "He told me that he told them the earliest he could release you was two weeks, and even then it depended on your appetite and exercise."

The pockmarked man's hazel eyes glittered angrily. "But I'm ready to go now."

"You're not well enough yet. You haven't gained enough weight. Even two weeks," she soothed, "is pushing it. Two weeks will be over before you know it."

39

"Not before *I* know it. Each day is an eternity of boredom and a day wasted. Did you bring me more of those codes?"

She pointed to a sheaf of papers on the next bed. "Where are the ones you've finished?"

It was his turn to point—to the stack on the night-table. "The techs say your work is invaluable," she remarked, reaching for the papers.

"Yeah? Well, why don't they step up and help me get out of here before two weeks?"

"Because they don't want you to die," she snapped. "And they respect the doctor's opinion."

"Do I look like someone who's ready to die?" He demanded belligerently.

"Yes. You look like you could hardly walk, you're so frail."

"Bah, you're all in this together," and he turned his head away in disgust.

"Eat your food, Mr. Saltwater. Then work on those codes. As long as you do that, no day is wasted." She turned to go, as he opened his mouth to retort, then shut it, deciding instead on silence.

Pavel Saltwater passed two miserable weeks, eating as much as he could without getting sick and doing stretching exercises beside his bed. After a week, he took to walking around the ward, and then down the long, cinder-block corridors of the bunker; he would walk for a half an hour, then return to his bed, exhausted, and nap. When he woke, invariably Lindin sat next to him, a somewhat sad expression on his rather nondescript face. Then the two old friends would chat about home and gossip about mutual acquaintances. This garrulousness was invariably cut short by the arrival of Nurse Wren with dinner, over which Lindin would hover, hanging, as it were, on his friend's every bite, like a mother worried about her child's nutrition. After this meal, the two old friends would stroll around the bunker,

Lindin invariably saying "you look better, today, Pavel," and the pockmarked man rejoining, "you say that every day, brother." Then the fighter led his friend the convalescent back to bed and practically tucked him in, turning off the lamp on the night-stand and admonishing him not to dwell on unhappy thoughts but to "sleep, sleep." And so would pass another day, bringing the killing center survivor closer to that long-dreamed-of morning of departure for Argas.

The other patients were less obstreperous than Saltwater, except for one twenty-year old Argan, who had survived an exploding shell with two broken legs, two broken arms and a sprained back. He lay, immobilized in his bed, cursing anyone who approached and demanding information from the medical staff about the timing of his release from the front. The pockmarked man ignored the ferocious profanity and persisted in his attempts to extract information from this patient, named Lillo, who eventually stopped shouting and demanded to know "what the hell you want from me?"

"I'm going to Argas," Saltwater began.

"Well, I'm glad to hear someone around here has some luck."

"How will they send me?"

"Probably in one of our ships."

"Those thin silver things, hovering on the horizon, toward the back of our side of the front?"

"Yes, of course. The needles. I wish they'd send me back on a needle. Goddammit, it's fucking impossible to get any information out of anyone around here."

"You're lucky to be alive."

"Don't give me that. I got four broken limbs and an excruciatingly sprained back. There's nothing lucky about me."

"I wish I were going home to planet four, not to sector three thousand three hundred thirty three."

"Planet four? Never heard of it. Must be a backwater."

"Oh, it is, which is precisely why I love it. Our enemy is not interested in backwaters."

"Well, our enemy would be wise to avoid Argas."

"How so?"

"Our techs have been working on a secret weapon, to mimic the effect of a fireball, you know, the kind the angels shoot."

Saltwater sat up straight in the little chair beside the Argan's bed. "You mean they could kill an enemy commander?"

"That's the point, brother."

"But how?"

"Don't ask me. I'm not a military scientist. But that's what they're doing."

The pockmarked man got to his feet, murmuring, "to mimic a fireball! Geeze, I never thought I'd live to hear that. We humans, we could actually win the war."

"That's the idea," the Argan snapped. "Now since you'll be traveling to my world, would you mind pulling the strings you're obviously capable of pulling and find out when I'll get sent back there?"

"I'll do what I can, Lillo. But don't expect much. I'm pretty low-level."

"Ha! I'd like to be low-level enough to get sent to Argas, that's all I got to say."

The next day a tall, hawk-nosed fighter with thick, frizzled, gray hair, accompanied Lindin to the convalescent's bedside.

"Jonas Emmanuel!" Saltwater exclaimed. "I thought you were done this tour at the front."

"I am," the fighter smiled. "I'm back to planet four tomorrow."

"And your sister, Omega?"

"She stays here. They don't seem at all inclined to release her." He replied rather grimly.

"They're never inclined to release anyone," the pockmarked man grumbled. "Once they got you here, they want to keep you indefinitely."

"Not me!" Lillo hollered from two beds away. "I'm gettin' the fuck outta here."

"You can't even move," Saltwater retorted. "I doubt you're going anywhere." Then to his two visitors, he said in a low voice: "He's an Argan, and he's been giving me some very encouraging info on the state of their military technology."

"Well, it's the most advanced there is," Lindin spoke softly. "What sort of information?"

"A project to mimic fireballs."

The two guests looked at each other

"Then we could kill enemy commanders," Saltwater elaborated.

"We, uh, figured that out, Pavel," Jonas said. "How far along is this project?"

"A good ways. There may be hope for the human race yet."

"Well, if any of us are ever going to destroy a commander," the nondescript man murmured, "it would be the Argans, certainly not the rest of us."

"It would give me untold satisfaction to see a mere man, a mere human being, incinerate one of those arrogant sons of bitches," Saltwater said. "Especially since all you ever do see is them barbecuing our troops. The master race! They make me sick."

Lindin reached over and flicked on a small lamp with a shade on the night-table; its yellow light illumined the lines in the weary faces of the three old friends, seeming, for just a moment, like the warm light that might shine on them after a meal together at a favorite restaurant, or at the end of a well-played card game at one of their homes. But this could only be a fleeting impression: the walls were cinder-block, there were no windows, beds filled the vast room, beds in which the injured lay, recuperating, and to complete the disassociation, from time to time the rumble of a fireball or another explosion vibrated through the floor and ceiling. No, they were not anywhere familiar, normal, anywhere that partook of ordinary human rhythms; they were Elsewhere, on the edge of livable reality, on the border, the very frontier that faced down another reality, proud, inhuman, barbaric, murderous, and the two utterly opposed realities were at war, and the three men knew it, and knew where they fit into it, but still they let the warm yellow light, emanating from the lampshade, lull them with thoughts of home, and diurnal routines and normal, unscarred life far away from the war that had burnt through their lives and the lives of millions before them, a war that had lasted for millennia and looked, from what they could see of its progress, most likely to endure for millennia to come. A thought that sobered and oppressed them.

"I envy you, traveling in a needle," Jonas remarked. "Do you have any idea how they work?"

"Lillo explained it," the pockmarked man replied. "It's like sewing, hence the name. It gathers up multiple realities, opens a wormhole at the front of the ship, to another universe and another and another, till it has gathered a bunch, then it shoots through. In no time, you move from the front to Argas."

"And it's equipped with those fusion weapons?" Jonas asked.

Saltwater nodded.

"I envy you meeting the designers of those," the hawk-nosed man continued. "Boy, I'd like to copy those plans for our system, just in case death-worshippers ever come our way."

"They won't," Lindin reassured him. "We're too remote, too insignificant. They'll leave us alone."

"But to be prepared," Jonas reiterated.

Nonetheless, the trio sat in satisfied silence, contemplating the safety afforded by the obscurity of their home-world, each bending his thoughts to some warmly loved aspect of home, and Saltwater finally voicing their shared wish: "If only I were back on planet four right now. I'd hike up to the Great Northern Forest, near the angel's stronghold, forage for mushrooms, scallions and moss and sleep on a bed of pine needles between towering evergreens. God, how I miss my home."

"But you're so eager to get to Argas," Lindin demurred.

"That's because it'll give me a chance to get even with the monsters who did this to me," and he pointed both hands at his skeletal frame, at his generally starved self, while both friends nodded. "No contradiction there," Jonas murmured, then after a moment, "where in sector three thousand three hundred and thirty three will you go?"

"Argas itself," Saltwater replied, "the home-world, which is, as I understand it, one vast military installation, more advanced, technologically than anything any of us have every encountered in any human sector."

"You'll be working with their scientists?" Jonas asked.

The pockmarked man nodded.

"Maybe you could get some defensive weaponry for our system."

"Jonas! Leave it alone!" Lindin snapped. "The enemy is not even aware of our world. We'll never come under attack."

Jonas' eyes gleamed with sudden sadness, two deep, dark wells of grief. "I think otherwise."

"Based on what?" Lindin snapped again.

"That's it," the hawk-nosed man sighed. "I can't say, except that...that, well, I had a vision."

"Better hit the meds, brother. Only certain fighters have visions, and they don't come from our world," Saltwater said.

"I know," Jonas sighed again. "But all the same, I had a vision, and I wish we had better weaponry."

"What exactly did you see?" Lindin demanded.

"An enemy commander in our system, swarms of death-worshipping men, and two of our five inhabited planets in flames."

"That's not a vision," Saltwater concluded. "That's a nightmare. You dreamt it."

"No," Jonas insisted. "I saw it—I see it, because I've seen it more than once—during the day. Billions will die, brother, billions. In our home world."

***

The woman in the jeans and black tank top, with the curly black hair rubber-banded into a ponytail, merged into the stream of prisoners in the little concrete yard, penned in by the high walls of the prison, beneath an ugly, yellow sky. Discreetly she scanned her companions, her gaze finally settling on one, a tall, older, rather heavy-set, gray-haired man with a weary face but brightly alert eyes. She drifted swiftly in his direction.

"Horace," she began, "they released Albert today. He'll be back in your cell when you return."

"Good," the older man mumbled.

"Not if he's infectious, it's not good. They had him in a lab, injecting him, then taking blood samples, then injecting him. He's sick, Horace, good and sick."

"I'm not leaving him behind."

"Did I suggest that?" She snapped.

"No. Good. You did not."

"Tell Eel what I told you. You two are his cellmates and you'll have to tend to him. If he gets too sick, these death-worshippers may just kill him for the fun of it."

"No, Carmella, they won't, not if they've gone to all this trouble to infect him. They're running some kind of test."

"They're monsters," she hissed, "and I'd like to break every one of their filthy necks."

He nodded and they moved forward in a circle, in the crowd around the circumference of the dreary little yard. "How are your symptoms?" Horace inquired, after a moment.

"They've let up, but I've still got the bug. I can feel it. I know it, and it knows I know it. But it's hiding a bit now to trick me. This is one smart bug."

"It's infected fully twenty percent of all fighters," the tall man said. "Our side needs an antibiotic to kill it and fast."

"For what it's worth, it's infected the human death-worshippers too. They were the original guinea pigs. I guess that's how highly regarded they are by the master race they so slavishly imitate."

"They are completely expendable," Horace said. "But they don't believe it. They think once their side has won, the fiends will spare them, even elevate and reward them. They are delusional. If we are destroyed, they are next."

"Where's Eel?" She asked suddenly.

"Sleeping."

"I thought he had nightmares, and avoided sleep."

"Listen, Marquez, he's human. He's not an enemy commander who thrives on insomnia. He thought if he slept during the day, the nightmares might abate. I said, give it a shot."

"Whatever works. That last dream he told me about, where there was sunset at dawn? That gave *me* nightmares."

"He believes he's telepathically linked to someone at the front, to a fighter Elsewhere, or in some contaminated reality."

"Such links are only ever deliberate."

"That's what you think."

She stopped, put her hands on her hips and stared at him defiantly. "What's that supposed to mean?"

Horace stopped and turned to face her, drawing the whole, large length of himself up: "That you are mistaken."

***

She did not rise early, but slept in most days until seven thirty or eight, and when she did get up, felt wonderfully rested and eager for her herb tea and the mixed vegetables that the old man had fried for her. Many she didn't recognize, so he explained that they were merely humble wild plants, sorrel and such, but that their salutary effect derived from their combination. He did not ever ask if she took anti-psychotic meds, he assumed it and, she noted to herself, he was correct. "You think you'd die without them," he finally said one morning, as he saw her place a little white pill in her mouth.

"I don't merely think, I know."

"Cut the dosage in half, starting tomorrow."

"Are you nuts? I'll jump out of my skin and, in all probability attempt suicide."

"Not while you're in my care," he replied.

She shrugged, then agreed, as he explained, "it could speed up your healing."

"Tu es un grand curandero," she murmured.

"Yes I am a great healer, one of the last of my kind. Few guardians have time for this work anymore, though there are some who dwell in the rain-forests of Brazil. But most are too busy losing their minds to think about reconnecting with earth, with the plants of earth and with how they can be combined to repulse the enemy's mental inroads. Here," he pushed a plate of fried greens across the plain wooden table to her. "Eat and then we'll forage in the forest."

As they picked their way through the underbrush and trees, the ancient guardian inquired about her dreams, specifically the sensation of the nearness of the enemy. No, that was, mercifully, gone, and had been gone for some days.

"Then you have begun to heal," he said and stroked his white beard. "This may not be as bad and as dangerous as we thought," he concluded, while uprooting a thistle-like plant and dropping it into his burlap bag. "To the water now," he said, and they directed their steps to the river, which, despite its marshy border and banks, purled audibly from some distance away. En route, the old man gathered mushrooms and more green plants, but when they reached the water, he waded right in up to the cattails and began pulling and digging them up. He directed her to snap off the tops of some, which she did, and they worked thus for forty minutes. "Have a mushroom," he said at length, pointing to a cluster that grew near the green moss and rotted end of the log on which they sat.

"I'm not in the mood," she replied.

"Too bad. It's what will help you now."

So she ate and felt the vague oppressive weight of anxiety and despair, which had blanketed her soul ever since her arrival in sector one thousand, begin, finally, to lift. "I need more," she said. He gestured at the cluster, "eat them all."

And so, improving by the hour, she lingered in the forest, in the old stone hut and had to admit to herself that, deep down, she really did not want to return to the front.

"But you must," the ancient man said over dinner, as the last beams of sunshine slanted through the open door and window, illumining the gloom. "You are one of a kind. He uses your very gaze not just to hit the enemy but to kill. You are a weapon in His hands. Your destiny is at the front, always. You are a fighter. You are the ghost who came back to life. You are Lontra, who was persecuted beyond what was endurable. Through you, He gets even. He uses you to fight; every inch of you belongs to Him alone. You are a fighter. You know what persecution is. You kill the enemy."

Whereupon she heard the whirring of wings and a voice, saying, "in two weeks, by the water's edge, you will depart."

***

Saltwater had gained fifteen pounds, and his TB symptoms were under control. "Fit as a fiddle and ready to go," he announced to Lindin on the morning of their departure. "I can't wait to set eyes on Argas!"

"Argas! Give me one of the recreational worlds any day," Lillo announced from his bed, where he lay, still immobilized. "I mean, Argas, is fine, it's better than here, but it's all work, work, work, no play. Those military scientists don't even like to take breaks. Their idea of a vacation is a trip to the front to test out some new weapon."

"And their weapons are first-rate," the pockmarked man enthused. "We had enemy tanks coming at us we couldn't even scratch, till we got those launchers and special missiles from Argas. I've never seen scientists like that."

"Except here at the front," Lindin gently corrected him.

"True, except here. But it was the Argans got us the hardware to destroy those tanks."

"That was a good thing," Lindin agreed.

"Understatement of the year," Lillo breathed.

Nurse Wren appeared with her patient's last infirmary meal: potatoes, steak, green beans and the obligatory juice and milk—"which you are to continue drinking," she admonished. "Your doctor wants you to consume at least eight ounces of milk a day, until you've regained your normal weight."

"Blah, blah," Saltwater grumbled, but he drank his milk, then glanced up at her. "You're unusually bright and cheery today."

"My husband turned up, back from sector one thousand," she chirped. "You were right. No news was good news."

"Congratulations!" Saltwater cried. "Now if we only had some liquor, I'd drink you a toast."

"No, Mr. Saltwater, you would not, not on your antibiotics, unless of course you want to sustain serious liver damage."

"Blah, blah," and he wolfed down his little red potatoes.

"I'm not the only one who's unusually bright and cheery," she remarked.

"Cause I'm bustin' outta this place. In a few hours, I'm a free man."

"A free man in his custody," she corrected, pointing at Lindin.

"Care," the nondescript man qualified. "Say care, not custody."

"Don't baby me," Saltwater grumbled.

"I won't," she said. "It's custody, and that's that. You can't be trusted to take proper care of your health. You have already proved it repeatedly."

"Blah, blah," thus Saltwater, to Lillo's accompaniment, "blah, blah, I'm with you." The patient finished his meal, then leaned over to Lindin. "I can't wait to work with Ein again. He's the best Argan scientist I know."

"He's the *only* Argan scientist you know," Lindin rather dourly corrected him.

Lillo craned his neck at Saltwater. "You know Ein? *The* one and only Lieutenant Ein, in the depths of the military's most secret and most advanced research and development division?"

"Not only do I know him," Saltwater replied, "we worked on a weapon system together."

"Which one?"

"You know better than to ask that, Lillo. Like you said, this is Ein, the one and only."

Lillo laid his head back on the pillow. "Wow," he breathed.

"Unless I'm mistaken," Lindin put in, "you haven't seen him in a while."

"Events have kept us apart," Saltwater replied. "The enemy touched down on the farthest outskirts of the Argan universe, and Ein got, well, rather busy."

"He routed the enemy," Lillo elaborated, "sealed off his point of entry and sent agents behind the lines to eradicate any information about Argas in the enemy bureaucracy, which turned out to be easier than any of us had expected."

"From what I heard, the enemy had more stumbled on your reality than sought it out," Saltwater said. "So Ein's job was to...cloak an entire universe, which he did."

"The master of invisibility," Lillo said.

"The master of stayin' alive," Saltwater corrected. "Argas would no longer exist, or it would be behind enemy lines, if not for Ein and his little operation."

"There was nothing little about it," Lindin corrected.

"Just a figure of speech," the pockmarked man said. "It was massive, I know. I heard all about it."

"Wow," Lillo breathed again, then after a pause, "did he use needle technology? 'Cause that's what we heard."

"I can't discuss it," Saltwater replied. "I was sworn to silence."

Lindin and Lillo looked at each other. "I guess you won't be telling me too much about your latest endeavor with him, either," the nondescript man commented.

"That remains to be seen and is not my choice," Saltwater replied tartly. "When you work with the Argans, you do things their way. They're the best we got."

"The best who's got?" Lindin asked.

"Humanity. As far as we know, they're the most advanced technologically, and they have not used their technology against other humans. That puts them head and shoulders above most worlds. So, like I said, when you work with the Argans, you do things their way. And if they say, 'keep your mouth shut,' you do it. But frankly, given your role as my babysitter, your tech skills and your stellar record at the front, I'd lay money on them permitting me to keep you informed."

Lindin nodded, pressing together the fingertips of his pink, puffy hands.

"Correction," Lillo sang out.

"Oh? What?" Saltwater demanded.

"Our history is as bloody as human history anywhere. But since the great transformation, which was a quantum jump in our mastery of technology and which occurred twenty-three thousand years ago, our wars against other men have ceased."

"Yeah, that's because you could obliterate any men who got in your way."

"Not exactly. Knowledge of the enemy and the danger of our common enemy is very widespread in the Argan sector, and it's safe to say that on Argas itself, you'd be hard pressed to find anyone who didn't have this knowledge. And nothing rivets the attention quite like the undeniable realization that there are beings, who are not human, but who are quite puissant and quite ruthlessly dedicated to extirpating humanity from the cosmos. So ours is different from other sectors, where intimate knowledge of the enemy is confined to fighters and kept secret. In those places, the vast majority of men merely have heard the old myths about a human enemy and have dismissed it. But once we learned of its truth and learned the details, and that knowledge became widespread, about twenty thousand years ago, the business of men slaughtering men, in our world, anyway, ceased. And because our weapons are so scary, there's little chance men from other worlds would attack us; besides, the only men from other worlds who know of us are fighters, and they are our allies, our brothers, who fight alongside us, who give their lives for us, and we for them. Hence our most singular, Argan, peace."

"Like I said," Saltwater repeated. "The Argans are the best we got. And by we, I mean the human race."

Lindin mused that twenty thousand years of peace in an entire reality was quite remarkable.

"A lot can happen in twenty-three thousand years," Lillo replied. "For instance, vast swaths of our universe became matriarchal, though not all by any means. Argas itself is patriarchal in the oldest sense, right down to worshipping a war god. But there's nothing wrong with that. It sure saved our skins when the enemy touched down on one of our outer galaxies. If we hadn't had Ein and a whole army of military scientists very much like him, well, Argas would be just another conquered fascist reality, deep behind enemy lines, and, I might add," Lillo grimaced from leaning forward too far in his enthusiasm, "the fate of the whole human race would look a lot dicier than it does today."

"From where I been, brother, it still looks pretty dicey, if you ask me," the still frail Saltwater put in.

"But think of our prospects without the Argans," Lillo countered.

"I'd rather not."

"My point exactly."

Lindin ran a weak, puffy hand over his excessively ordinary features. "So in Argas, we'll be expected to do as the Argans do? I mean, will we have to make blood sacrifice to this war god? Because frankly," he sighed, "that's not my style at all. I'm rather secular to tell the truth, and except for a certain sacred voice, which I hear in my mind far less than I'd like, I personally tend to shy away from religious ritual and in general, I'd have to say that organized religion is not for me."

"I hear you, brother," thus Saltwater. "And I'm one hundred percent in agreement. But I wouldn't worry. In all the time I spent with Ein, he never proselytized. In fact, come to think of it, he never even invited me to any of the religious services he so regularly attended."

"Well, that's very polite of him," Lillo put in. "Because overall, that's not the Argan style."

"What is the Argan style?" Lindin asked.

"Pushy."

"Yeah, but Ein's a fighter," Saltwater said, "who's been to the front and seen what an eclectic mix we are. He appreciates that."

"I repeat," Lillo spoke evenly, "his ecumenicism is the exception, not the rule. I'm just telling you so you're prepared—prepared to be hit smack over the head with the whole fanatically religious kit and caboodle."

"Ugh," the two fighters groaned in unison.

"My feelings exactly. Those matriarchal worlds I mentioned? I'm from one of them, and while I don't share their prejudices by any means, the women from my home world, ninety-nine percent of them, wouldn't touch the Argan system with a ten foot pole. They want nothing to do with those quote barbarians unquote." Lillo paused to stare at his immobilized limbs. "But me? I'd take even Argas any day over this place. Even with the politics—because believe me, brother, there may have been twenty thousand years of peace, but the politicking to keep it that way has been ferocious. The representatives from Argas itself are always maneuvering for advantage in the Assembly,"

"So you have a democratic system?" Lindin asked. "With all the worlds represented?"

"Not exactly. It's very decentralized. Each solar system pretty much manages its own business. But there is an Assembly of thousands of representatives that meets in the Argan system—no accident that, you can be sure, because the leaders of Argas never hesitate to play their trump card, which is their fantastic weapons development and the fact that they already once protected the universe from an enemy incursion. So the Argans wanted the assembly in the Argan system, where they could dominate it. The other worlds that participate grumbled and complained, but went along with it. Some just dropped out."

"So some systems are not represented?"

Lillo nodded. "They want nothing to do with the Assembly, so they just go their own peaceful way. They don't fight with Argas, because they know, the next time this homicidal enemy invades, it'll be Argas that cloaks our reality or repels him. And except for extraction, the Argans leave everyone alone."

Saltwater and Lindin stared at each other. "Extraction?"

"A system by which the Argas defense council identifies particularly scientifically gifted children, who are then sent to special advanced schools on one of about a thousand planets. If they continue to show promise, upon graduation they relocate to the Argan system. The boys love it, the girls hate it. After all, if you came from a matriarchal world with a female president or queen, and dreamt someday of being a bigwig there, maybe president yourself, wouldn't you chafe at being told no, you've got scientific talent, you *must* live in the Argan system, where, as a female, your privileges will be limited."

"Limited a lot?" Lindin asked in surprise.

"Not a lot. But these women scientists complain that they feel like second-class citizens, and they resent any restraints based on their gender, and frankly, who can blame them? Bad enough they were separated from their families at a young age. Now they have to come to a ferociously competitive, male-dominated solar system and live there and work, in many ways sidelined. They don't like it. And the atheists and secularists, especially the fighters among them, really don't like it. But you'll find out all about that from Ein's wife—she's a fighter who's helping to organize the women in the Argan system to create a quote secular civic sphere unquote, in other words, to give the female half of the population more breathing space, fewer restrictions and more reproductive control."

"More reproductive control?!" Saltwater exclaimed. "They don't have that, and they call themselves civilized?"

"You sound like Ein's wife. I never met her, but I attended two of her speeches to the local council. She's a firebrand, was hollering on about how on her home-world all women have complete reproductive control, from the female prime minister right down to the lowliest janitor, how Argas is hundreds of years behind the times and better catch up quick, before female scientists begin boycotting it. But fat chance of that. All the Argans have to do is broadcast the footage of the enemy's incursion, the speed of the devastation, the burning cities—and everyone just falls right back into line. No scientist, male or female, would dream of boycotting the military scientific labs on Argas, not after twenty minutes of that footage—even if it is twenty thousand years old. And then there's the footage of the more recent incursion, the one Ein helped foil. No, no Argan, man or woman, would boycott the military after a look at that. There were killing centers in our reality."

"Tell me about it, brother," thus Saltwater.

"Granted, they were confined to a few planets, but our people had never experienced such barbarism before. It galvanized the entire fucking universe. So any talk of boycotts is basically regarded by the Argan council and president as an empty threat."

"But no reproductive freedom!" Lindin exclaimed. "No birth control?"

"Yes, birth control, but that's it. All abortion is illegal."

The two fighters from planet four looked at each other. "Even in the first few months?" Saltwater demanded.

Lillo nodded.

"And what about gross deformities?"

"Too bad, though our prenatal medical engineering can fix most of those."

"Most? Not all? If I was a woman, I wouldn't like that."

"Well, they don't," Lillo said. "But it hasn't caused the mass exodus of female scientists that you'd expect. I guess they understand what's at stake."

"Still, it seems rather severe."

"It's an ancient, severe religion. Like I said, archaic patriarchy. But I'd imagine," Lillo continued, "that you being fighters from another world, and friends and guests of the great Ein,"

"And men,"

"And men, not women, given all that, you'll be shielded from Argas' religious excesses." He paused. "On Argas fighters are treated very well, men and women. They are regarded with something akin to religious awe. And since Ein saved everyone's neck with that technology that cloaks an enemy contact point with our world, well, the attitude toward fighters is even more deferential. You'll be honored guests."

"Well, that's something to look forward to," Lindin said. "We'll be feted?"

"No," Lillo answered peremptorily. "They don't fete anybody on Argas, even Ein. Fighters may applaud him, but generally, there's no frivolity of any sort. They practically dress themselves, voluntarily, in the same gray uniform."

"They wear uniforms?" Saltwater asked.

"No. But the pressure against any form of ostentation is severe. They go to the opposite extreme, making a show of what plain folk they are—plain folk who've dedicated their entire lives to the enemy's defeat, plain folk who have no use for consumer culture of any sort. You'll see. It's quite extreme and, even in our sector, unique."

"So they're what Ivan on the council would call Spartan," Lindin said.

"I've heard that term," Lillo answered, "and though I don't know its exact origin, I was told it referred to a human culture organized solely for war, around principles of simplicity, equality and defense. So yes, if that's your meaning, then indeed the Argans are Spartan, very much so. But it's a little different, because so many of them are scientists, because they've thrown so much brain and muscle into weapons research, and scientists are often sophisticates. They pride themselves on their appreciation of the arts, on being polyglot and so forth. Some are very literary," Lillo sighed. "They're a complicated bunch, treasuring the appearance of simplicity, even to the point of austerity, following an antique religion with a god who does not hesitate to make war, yet going to the opera, the ballet, reading reviews of new novels, learning other worlds' languages, and all the while, steeped up to the eyeballs in the complexities of computer and weapons technology. And your friend Ein epitomizes all of that—or so legend has it."

"You've just described him perfectly," Saltwater replied. "I always considered him a mass of contradictions, but now, from what you say, I gather that's what characterizes his whole social group."

Lillo nodded again.

"You mentioned your medical technology," Lindin began. "your doctors really can cure diseases or correct defects in utero?"

"Yes, the Argans made a big push for that, partly to justify their strict anti-abortion laws, as a concession to women's demands. This led eventually to genetically engineering out dangerous disease-producing genes, which was what the women had demanded. The scientists drew the line, however, at a request to eliminate female body hair on the arms and legs, calling it 'frivolous,' which it was."

"It would be nice if the Argans shared that medical technology," Saltwater grumbled.

"We have, just not all of it. You can't blame us for wanting to keep the edge."

"Where life-saving procedures are involved, yes, yes I can blame you and I do," Saltwater snapped. "It's my only complaint against the Argans. They're not more open with their discoveries."

"Why should we be? In many of your worlds men still massacre each other. There is even genocide. Why don't they leave that to the enemy?"

"'Cause they don't know or believe the enemy exists. Ignorance and human wickedness are a potent combination."

"I rest my case," Lillo concluded and turned his head away.

At that instant the particularly loud explosion of a fireball rumbled through the underground infirmary.

"All it would take," Lindin began quietly, "would be to get a few world leaders from our system out here, at the front, and those wars for territory or market advantage or resources would cease at once."

"We're not allowed for obvious reasons," the pockmarked man snapped, "the chief among them is mass panic. And then there are the much less obvious reasons. He wants this kept secret from most of humankind, in fact from all of humankind except fighters."

"Fighters and Argans," Lillo corrected.

"Well, unless I'm mistaken, all Argans are fighters now."

Lillo nodded.

"So," Saltwater continued, "except for one test-tube reality, He keeps our struggle hidden, and ordinary men just go on their wicked ways, raping, murdering, making war."

"And the enemy cheers," Lindin said soberly. "I fail to see the logic of it."

"There's a reason, you may be sure," the pockmarked man continued. "Just 'cause we can't see it, doesn't mean He doesn't have one, and one that's pretty darn good."

"Maybe He doesn't want all the realities completely militarized," Lillo said. "Or maybe there's some deal, like it says in the Argan Bible."

"You can't believe those old myths," the pockmarked man grumbled.

"Why not? It's as good an explanation as any," Lillo paused. "Who knows what would have happened to my universe, if knowledge of this terrible human struggle had not become widespread? There would have been wars, exterminations, industrial rape of the environment—all that. And we wouldn't have been prepared when the enemy became cognizant of us, the second time."

"More to the point, you wouldn't have evolved your unique society," Saltwater said pensively, "with thousands of matriarchal worlds and one, very exceptional galaxy, that of Argas itself, devoted to beating the enemy, to an archaic, war-bound religion, full of contradictions that have made it the most effective counterforce we have. Like I said, the Argans are the best we got, and if we can't work with them to control the spread of this enemy contagion, then we're doomed."

"The way this war is going, brother," Lindin spoke softly, "we may be doomed anyway."

***

"So you're sure this fighter, this other Horace, does not know he's linked to you?" Orozco asked his lunatic host, who had just reappeared in the living room with a silver tray of cheese and crackers, to which Gideon and the policeman immediately helped themselves.

"He does not know. And even if he did know, what could he reveal? That's he's somehow linked to a double in another universe? So what? The main thing is he has no inkling of the existence of earth's guardians."

Gideon grunted assent, while Orozco muttered, "amen."

"If he knew about guardians," Horace continued, leveraging his considerable bulk into a comfortable armchair, "those interrogation sessions he has to endure would be extremely dangerous to earth."

"Is he sick?" The policeman demanded. "The enemy uses its prisoners like lab rats for all kinds of biological warfare, this prison too, at least so you said."

"Not sick yet," his host replied, spreading brie on a Triscuit. "Wait!" He paused, mid-spread, his head raised, his eyes drifting shut. "His cellmate and old, old friend Albert has been infected."

"With one of the old bugs or something new?" Orozco growled.

"Five'll get you ten it's something new," thus Gideon.

"Yes, our Israeli friend is correct."

"Shit!" The policeman nearly spat. "Now we gotta come up with another antibiotic."

"Or leave Albert behind," Horace suggested.

"No," Gideon spoke firmly. "I have clear instructions. All four are to escape."

Orozco stared at him, then spoke. "How clear? Who from?"

"From the top."

"Elaborate."

"I'm not allowed to."

"Shit!" The policeman hissed again. "I'll have to get a message to the front. You'll be bringing back an ex-prisoner infected with God-knows-what."

"That would be wise," the young man commented.

"Can you at least get me an inventory of his symptoms?" Orozco asked his host, who waved a dismissive hand. "Not now," Horace said. "Later, when he sees Albert."

"He's not in his cell now?"

"He's in the yard, talking with the female fighter, Carmella Marquez."

"I know her!" Orozco cried. "We were friends."

"Good, because you may see her again."

"Me?"

"Yes, you."

"When?" The policeman demanded.

"When you meet Gideon, as he crosses over the front to our side."

"I got news for you: I ain't goin' to that part of the front," Orozco insisted.

"That's what you think," Horace replied.

***

The sweating, middle-aged man lay on his bunk and turned his filmy eyes on the new arrival, without a glimmer of recognition.

"Albert! Your hair turned gray!" Thus Horace, who came and sat on the edge of the bunk.

"You're...Horace," the sick man ventured tentatively.

"Yes, and I've brought you some herbs to lower your fever. Carmella went to great trouble to lay hands on them, so you must eat them all, raw, and not spit any out."

"How in heaven did she obtain them?" The invalid asked, eyeing the fistful of greenery that his cellmate had pulled forth from a pocket.

"You don't want to know. Here," he broke off a sprig of the feathery leaves and pushed it between Albert's lips, "chew."

The two cellmates, Hoarce and Eel then sat on the bunk opposite the invalid and watched him eat his way through the herbs. When done, he gazed at them and said, "I'd rather be dead."

"Nonsense," Horace replied. "We're going to get you back to the front, and our doctors will analyze what you've got and cure you." These brave, optimistic remarks caused Albert and Eel to fall silent. It was the silence of hope, of looking forward to something better, of prayer for survival, and it filled the little stone room with its promise that none of them wanted with a single syllable to gainsay. They sat and looked at each other and thought of their freedom as if it were certain, as if Horace were a prophet, whose words would, undeniably, come true. Eel stretched out on his lower bunk, while Albert ran a hand over his forehead and finally did break the silence with the gratefully received words: "I believe those herbs helped a bit."

"Praise God," thus Horace. "And thanks to Carmella."

"Are they still interrogating her?" Eel asked.

Horace shook his head. "They concluded she was a low-level fighter. Little did they know she'd led divisions at the front."

"I thought she stopped," Eel insisted, "refused to do it until angels with their fireballs were regularly in attendance for cover. And the angels wouldn't agree, so she stalked off, sulking, resigned and consigned herself to a fighter jet."

"Sounds like Carmella," thus Horace.

"Legend is she's a terror in that little jet," Eel paused. "I heard she had disabled more enemy warships than any other fighter pilot—and did it singlehandedly."

"You can't believe those legends," Horace corrected him. "They're an amalgam of half-truths and wild exaggerations."

"Nonsense. I saw her little fighter jet disable a huge, I mean huge, enemy battleship, up at, oh, a few thousand feet, saw it with my own eyes. Her jet was just a dot in the sky, but that cruiser was enormous. And she crippled it. It crashed and burned behind enemy lines."

"She's one tough lady," Horace conceded.

"And those idiots think she's a grunt."

"Let 'em think what they want, so long as the four of us bust out of this place."

"I can't," Albert put in, "because I can't walk."

"We'll see about that," Horace said. "We're not leaving you here to die of some horrible disease that some fiend concocted deep in the dark land of death. Nope. You're coming with us, even if we have to carry you." With that Horace lumbered up into the upper bunk and stretched out.

"Where do you think these herbs grew?" Albert asked.

"Right outside the prison," Horace replied, "and in the surrounding woods, all the way to the front, and then past that, in the forest, where they flourish."

"I'm surprised anything worth eating grows in this barren, accursed country," Albert said.

"Me too, brother," thus Eel. "But apparently our leader, Marquez, noted them on the way in, and her thoughts reverted to them once she realized that they were infecting us like lab rats with God knows what."

"And she got them for me."

"What she wants, she gets," Eel concluded. "I never seen anything like it."

"Screw you!" They heard Carmella's voice screaming from a lower tier, "and to hell with this place! You're all dead! Dead!"

"What now?" Albert asked.

"They probably just returned her cellmate after a rape or a beating."

The guards' mirthless chortle drifted up. "She's right," Eel said. "They're dead. They look like they're alive, and they can inflict pain, but they're dead, dead from the core all the way out to their fingertips."

Soon they heard a muffled thumping on the floor of their cell.

Eel rolled out of bed, put his ear to the floor and thumped back. More thumping. He glanced up, his eyes wide with despair. "They killed Carmella's cellmate. She won't last the night. Marquez believes she's next."

"Then we have to get out of here fast," Albert murmured.

"We have to wait, but we can't wait too long." Horace commented.

"Wait?" Eel snapped. "Wait for what?"

"Help," Horace replied. "Help is on the way."

***

It was, in fact, yet another two weeks after Saltwater's supposedly final hospital dinner before his doctor would release him. The fighter took the delay poorly, grumbling and complaining to all comers. But toward the end of two weeks, he had a most unexpected visitor.

"Ein!" He cried, sitting bolt upright quite suddenly in bed, so that Nurse Wren had to push him back gently onto his pillows. "What brings you back to the front?"

"This," his old friend said and held up an orange bottle and rattled the pills inside.

"Which is?"

"An antidote to enemy truth serum, which we are developing on Argas."

"Ah, that should be most useful."

"No kidding." Ein came over and sat on the empty, adjacent bed. "But something else brought me too."

"What?"

"You, my friend," he held out a hand, and they shook. "What's this about artificial life? You know we've tried to engineer it before without success."

"But you've never really put your whole heart into it. The efforts were always...marginal."

Ein nodded. "We didn't really see the need."

"You have to talk to someone on the council."

"I'm going to, straight after I leave you." Ein paused and pulled at the cuff of his sober gray shirt. "But I got permission to hear everything first from you."

The pockmarked man's hazel eyes glittered angrily. "The enemy already has it."

"What?! What for?"

"Extermination. And there are extermination codes. We need our own AI to crack those codes and find out exactly what the enemy is using this for—how, where, when and why. And we need to do it yesterday."

Ein ran a hand over his worried face, then through his short, straight, gray hair. "What could they be using it for?" He murmured.

"That," Saltwater pronounced, "is the question."

"Nothing good, that's for sure."

"Yes it is sure."

"You're coming back to Argas with me—today."

"First talk to the council, then return to me. I'll be ready."

"You can't even dress yourself yet," thus Nurse Wren, who had just come over from the other end of the infirmary.

"Maybe I can, maybe I can't. But if not, you're here to help me out of my pajamas."

Ein rose. "This is very bad. We've been overtaken. We're behind."

"Only an Argan could see it that way," thus Saltwater.

"We have to catch up, then get ahead," the Argan murmured and hurried out of the infirmary.

"Who is he?" Nurse Wren asked.

"The man who saved an entire reality. A modest, upright, decent man, who has given his entire life to protecting his world."

***

It was night when she set out, a few greens, a pistol, a Swiss army knife, an extra shirt and a plastic water bottle in her knapsack. The old man shared a glass of mead with her, with the toast, "may you never have to return, much as I enjoy seeing you." "Here's to never," she replied and drank. "Never again," he repeated. They placed their glasses on the wooden table. "But really," he said, stroking his white beard, "if you do have another relapse, you must move, leave wherever you are, because it's an indication of the proximity of a certain enemy who knows you, an interrogator who could, through you, learn of earth and earth's secret guardians. Now you know what your symptoms mean, and what to do about them."

The tall, hard woman cast her flat gaze over him, ran her fingers through her badly cut hair and said: "if I have a relapse, I will return to you."

He nodded and both heard the whirring of wings. "Someone," he said, "awaits you down by the river. You have your flashlight?"

She nodded, stepped out of the hut and flicked it on. The little beam picked out the markings, blazed into the tree bark, which led her through the forest until she heard the river's purl. And there, by the water's edge, out in the open beyond the tree-line, under a clear night sky, loomed a large form, silvery, scarred and beautiful by starlight, it's long, magnificent wings sheathed in furious dark light.

Lontra stepped forward, then threw herself on the angel's back, grasping the wings at the joint.

"You will never encounter that interrogator again," the angel said, rising up, with her on his back. "Never again will there be the risk of his learning about earth or earth's guardians."

"How?" She demanded.

"He is in sector one thousand. It is collapsing, which is a cataclysm. But despite that, we can still cut off his retreat."

"Ah."

"Yes, ah, we will destroy him. It has been decided."

"He will be dust in the wind," she said.

The angel turned his head, and the dark light streamed from his beautiful eyes, "oh, it will be much worse than that."

***

As the three men sat in the living room, downing cheese and crackers, the policeman's pager buzzed. "Uh oh," Orozco said after a moment. "Four murders and four desecrated corpses in a cemetery over in Valhalla."

"Death worshippers?" Gideon's eyebrows went up.

"Looks like it. Shit. Valhalla's not in my jurisdiction. It's across the city line."

"But didn't the city just announce that the homicide department would be tackling this wave of bizarre murders in the entire metro area?" Horace asked. "I saw that on the news, and unless I'm mistaken, you practically ARE the homicide department."

"Shit," Orozco breathed, as his cell phone range. He answered, then said, "I'm on it," rose and made for the front door, while dialing another number.

"Hey, aren't I supposed to leave tonight?" The young Israeli demanded.

"Yes," the policeman replied, "from the depths of Sleepy Hollow Park."

"Who will take over here?"

"I don't need a baby sitter," the would-be suicide snapped.

"Oh yes you do," Orozco retorted. "And his name is Starfield, and I'm calling him now."

After this arrangement—Starfield: "I'll move in later this afternoon"—the veteran homicide detective turned on his flasher and siren and tore down Apocalypse Avenue toward the towers of mid-town and mid-Atlantic station and thence out past the People's Great Library, then across the Todenleben river into the rusting inner suburb of Valhalla. He parked outside a vast cemetery, next to a half dozen other police cruisers, all flashing blue and red, and picked his way through the tombstones and the sweltering summer heat to the crime scene, set off with yellow tape.

"Hey Rafael," his partner Harry greeted him. "You gotta see this." Orozco approached, glanced once at the murder victims and muttered, "muy malo. Siempre malo."

"You ain't kiddin'" Harry said. "This looks like the work of some kind of sick cult. We have evidence of at least four assailants, leaving tracks in the mud over there," he pointed to the right where, sure enough, very clearly outlined, the policeman could see shoe tracks, some quite different from the others, heading away from the crime scene toward the townhouses on the far side of the vast cemetery. "They parked by the townhouses," Orozco said. "Maybe some of the locals got a look at them. I'll go check."

He loped away through the graveyard, sweating in the oppressive summer heat, crossed the parking spaces to the first townhouse and rang the bell. A short, balding, middle-aged man, who introduced himself as an insurance adjuster, opened the door. Yes, he had seen three men, young, in their twenties and thirties and leading several others, who he now understood were the victims, up into the cemetery.

"Did they have any unusual tattoos? Were you able to observe that?" Orozco asked.

The man nodded. "They all had the same one on their arms, a snake with a globe between its teeth."

"Shit."

"Excuse me?"

"Nothin' Did you get any license plate numbers?"

"As a matter of fact I did take down one. How did you know?"

"Just a guess," Orozco replied.

"It was real easy to remember. A vanity plate."

"Oh?" The policeman asked. "What'd it say, 'death' or something?"

"Exactly. Death. It said death."

"Out of state?"

"Nope."

"Thanks, you been a tremendous help."

"You're welcome, but I won't testify."

Orozco said nothing and turned to go. "You will have to find and kill all of these murderers yourself, Rafael," a voice spoke in his mind. "There can be no trial. This infection cannot be allowed to simmer in the prison population."

"Shit, I hate this job," the policeman thought. "I ain't no vigilante."

"But these are death worshippers, mass murderers. Unfortunately, there is no choice. It's only a matter of time before they net a fighter or a guardian and then—"

"They murder him or her and dispatch the victim to the realm of shadow."

"You see where this is going."

"I see it, but I don't have to like it."

"Only a deranged person would like it."

The policeman tromped back up to the cemetery. The sky had clouded over completely, but the temperature had risen, and the beginning of a fog wafted through the crypts and headstones.

"Any luck?" Harry asked.

"Some. I got a lead I'm gonna follow."

"What sort of lead?"

"A call the DMV lead."

"You got this, or you need help?"

"I got it," Orozco answered and strode off through the graves, cursing softly under his breath.

The vehicle with the vanity plate was registered to two men with an address across the river from Iroquois. Further research revealed drug busts, the drug being methamphetamine and no current legitimate employment. "You may have to settle for two of them," Rafael thought, and before he heard a mental reply, Harry strode into the office, flat out refusing to permit Orozco to visit the newly discovered address alone. "These are serial mass murderers," Harry said. "You need backup."

"I need to retire."

"Not yet."

"Why am I sure this visit will end in a shootout?"

"Because these two will never be taken alive. And that's why you need backup."

"Just you, Harry. I'm gonna try to get some information out of them."

"You'll get yourself killed. We arrest. If they resist arrest, too bad for them. No cop's dyin' when these sickos pull out their weapons."

"Dios mio, from bad to worse," Orozco muttered and tromped out of the office, Harry right behind him.

***

"Where are you from, Ivan?" Ein asked, sitting across a little metal table from the head of the council in the makeshift cafeteria.

"From a planet and a system, one of very few, whose existence is to be kept completely secret."

"A sacred planet."

"Yes. Most fighters have never heard of it, because sometimes fighters are caught, and then interrogated, and then they might break."

"Not often."

"I just do as I'm told, Ein. But I'm allowed to tell you that my home-world is called earth."

"Earth," Ein repeated, then asked: "so the enemy's never been there?"

"That's an open question."

"Is it a peaceful world?"

"No. There are wars, genocides."

"Genocides! Then you're doing the enemy's work for him."

"Earth's history is awash in the blood of innocent victims, and currently, the race for resources, financial chicanery and economic competition for fossil fuels,"

"Is endangering the planet's future," Ein finished the sentence for him. "You must stop this."

"We cannot. We are too busy here, at the front."

"I doubt He wants a sacred planet, whose existence He hides even from fighters, to become uninhabitable due to human greed and rapacity. You are a fighter, Ivan. You must do something. This is your world. If it were mine, I'd do everything in my power—heavens, it isn't even mine and I'm alarmed."

"It's an alarming situation. But that is there, and we are here. At least earth is pretty well defended against the enemy."

"Yes, but if wicked men are in charge, men who consult only their own vanity, greed and lust, then your world is doomed. It has happened, Ivan, many times. Once that climate change starts, you have to move fast. You must change leadership, restructure the economic system,"

"Practically impossible on earth."

"Then you've given up. You're finished."

"The propaganda is too powerful. People, many people, not all, have simply lost the ability to think for themselves."

"Then you must change that. If the powerful are selfish and wicked, and they control the media, you must do what others who have scraped through this disaster have done before you."

"What?"

"Alternative media, exposure of the lies—"

"Ein—we don't have time to discuss this now."

"I cannot understand how you, the head of the council, could have given up so easily on your home-world."

"You don't know earth's history. Just three years ago, there was a massive genocide in an African country. The world did nothing. That is life on earth. Horrors happen, good people wring their hands, the wicked continue in charge, fighters beat their heads against a wall of lies, and on and on it goes. We've even got nuclear power—lots of it."

"My God, every civilization that has gone that route is now nothing but dust."

"My concern now, here, is not the survival of one planet, even if it is my own, but of humankind. The enemy has an artificial life form, some death computer, dedicated to our extirpation."

"The ultimate pest control."

"Yes, and we are regarded as the pest. We need you and Saltwater to help us catch up. Once we have artificial intelligence, we can learn everything we need to know about what our enemy has, and then counter it."

Ein leaned back, his gray eyes still as wide as when his companion had first mentioned genocide.

"You need an armed revolt on this earth of yours," he said.

Ivan waved a hand dismissively. "Anyone who did that would be killed at once."

"Then fascism has won on your planet, and fascism is the destroyer of civilizations. I can't count the number of fighters I've met from worlds that long ago succumbed to this disease, worlds that no longer exist."

"We don't have time here, Ein, at the front, we don't have time for earth's fate."

"If earth is as special as you say, you'd better make the time. That's all I'll say."

"Do not mention earth to Saltwater."

"Why not?"

"Those are my instructions. He is to learn of it, but later, much later."

"What does it matter, if it's doomed?"

"The answer to that is above my pay grade." Ivan glanced disconsolately around the little cafeteria. "You think I like living with the knowledge that the very people who could do the most good back on earth are here at the front? You think I like the specter of desolation that rises up every time I contemplate my planet's future? But this is what I must live with. I will die at the front, that was determined long ago. I may never see earth again, and frankly, from all I hear from other fighters, if I did see it, it would break my heart. Please, Ein, let's not talk of earth. It's too dreadful."

The two men sat gazing sadly at each other in the stale, little cafeteria, which, despite its drabness, its gray cinder-block walls, was somehow full of life, of the loud, eager voices of fighters who did not, at that moment, have to bear arms, but who could relax, laugh and talk to their friends. "I think," Ein began tentatively, "I might be able to help with earth. Wait," he held up a hand in the stop position. "I know you just banned the subject, but we could do climate projections, run the computer programs and plant the seeds of wisdom in earth's scientists' minds."

"You Argans, with your faith in science!"

"Science has twice saved our universe. Perhaps it can save earth. I'll run the programs, do the predictions, and you get them to earth's fighters back in your home."

"You do not understand the ignorance and pig-headedness our climatologists have to deal with."

"We will help them. Argas will help them. We've deceived and beaten the enemy—surely we can outwit a few greedy and corrupt men."

Ivan sighed. "You come from a universe galvanized over twenty millennia ago by mass recognition of a powerful, homicidal, non-human enemy. Yours is the only universe He has permitted to develop in this way."

"We are an experiment, yes."

"But your results, your population's faith in science cannot be replicated on worlds like earth that adhere, for lack of a better term, to the old model, worlds where everyone fights among themselves, everyone's grabbing for scraps. The enemy is regarded as an ancient myth, and people are happy to do his dirty work themselves, exterminating minorities, raping the planet. All your wonderful science, Ein, even if you present absolute proof of climate catastrophe based on the burning of fossil fuels, that data will never so much as dent the iron-plated egos and self-interest of men in power. I've seen these people in action, and I have concluded," Ivan lowered his voice, "that very probably, earth is lost."

"But you're the head of the council!"

"I'm a realist, Ein. I concentrate on what I can accomplish, like just possibly helping to save some remnant of the human race from this scourge. That remnant will be saved here, at the front, Elsewhere, and in a few remarkable worlds, one of which is Argas, but my home, earth, is not, I believe, among them. I know I sound like a pessimist, but I believe earth is lost. I believe it was lost three or four decades ago. I don't know what happened, exactly how things went so badly off the rails, but they did, and we lost earth. We're in the endgame now, and while I don't pretend, for an instant, to comprehend His plan, I believe, am certain, that there is a contingency, a preparation for the possibility of a human future without earth. Other worlds have been lost, other human planets have burned oil and coal and heated their atmosphere to extinction. We're next in a long, sorry line of people who just plain willfully didn't get it. All the spectacular Argan data in the world can't change that. But you're welcome to try."

"I intend to," Ein said flatly, and his gray eyes surveyed the head of the council with unconcealed dismay and disappointment, after a moment shifting away, as he asked,

77

"do other fighters from earth know that these are your thoughts?"

"No, and I ask you to please keep it that way."

The military scientist nodded somberly, contemplating the contradiction that the leader of the fighters' council had, in his heart, abandoned hope for his home-world—and a home-world that was evidently special, at that.

"If you intend to sneak assistance to earth's climatologists," Ivan began.

"We will tap into their computers, show them reality, that is all."

"Well, there is something you should know about earth, something that gives me a little hope, and something you must not ever reveal." Ivan spread his big, knobby hands on the little metal table, all ten fingers pointing at Ein.

"I can keep a secret. I've done so all my life," Ein said.

"Good. Earth has a race of visionaries called guardians. They are our last, best, most secret and unbeatable line of defense against the enemy. They see reality. They see the enemy's work on earth and transmit this knowledge to fighters on earth. The fighters then go into combat."

Ein's serene gray eyes had widened in wonder at these words. Now he said: "Ivan, if He has given you the guardians, how can you dare to abandon earth in your heart?"

"I see reality, partly courtesy of the guardians."

"But you have not gone into combat."

"I cannot. I am assigned here, at the front."

"But if you were there? Home?"

"It would be combat."

"Even with your despair."

"Even with my despair."

Something hard and flinty glinted in the Argan's gray eyes. "There are people, ordinary people of good will, who oppose the destruction of your planet's ecosystem?"

"Yes."

"I will find a way, unseen, to assist them."

"You're not thinking of actually setting foot on one of the most blood-soaked planets in the cosmos?"

"A planet with a race of guardians, people to whom He sends visions? Yes I am, and soon, before I leave with Saltwater. You will choose the guardian I am to meet."

"Done."

"You already have one in mind."

"A very old man, old, wise, a concentration camp survivor, but, most importantly, a friend of His."

"I will leave today."

***

"Get back here," Gideon snapped into his cell phone.

"No can do. I'm on the track of four mass-murdering death worshippers," Orozco replied.

"Shelve it. We have a visitor, an Argan, setting down in Sleepy Hollow Park in a half an hour, and I have to meet him."

"An Argan! Aie Caramba! What next?"

"Don't ask me, I just work here."

"Look, these killers could already be stalking their next victim,"

"Excuses, excuses. Rafael, you know very well that death worshippers take a good long break between rituals. Get over here. I have to leave, pronto, and Horace MacKenzie cannot be trusted for two minutes on his own."

"Starfield will be there later," the policeman grumbled.

"That's later. I'm talking about now! Now hurry up."

"Dios mio, an Argan, what an embarrassment, to have one of them poking into our blood-stained past. Since when do they take an interest in the blood and gore of earth?"

"Since now. Hurry up!"

Fifteen minutes later, a very unhappy detective Orozco pressed the buzzer at the MacKenzie residence on Apocalypse Avenue.

"You took your sweet time," thus Gideon, on the way out.

"Blah, blah. Where's the patient?"

"In the living room, still scarfing down Brie and crackers."

"He's gonna turn into Brie and crackers at this rate."

"Bye!"

"Shit," Orozco breathed and loped into the room with Horace.

Meanwhile Gideon jogged to his car, slid into the driver's seat and then tore out of the neighborhood, heading for the park.

"Take Wetherslyhollow Road," he heard in his mind and veered left onto a dirt track. He followed the dirt road to the end, where he saw, standing in the shade of a sycamore, a medium-height, middle-aged man with a gray crew-cut, a light gray shirt and dark gray pants and almost alarmingly intelligent gray eyes. He stepped out of his car.

"I am Ein," the man said. "Who are you?"

"Gideon," the young man answered. "And I'm to take you to Galen."

"The concentration camp survivor."

"Yes."

"There are many concentration camps on earth?"

"There were, fifty-five years ago."

"That's dangerously recent," Ein said, ambling to the little gold Honda. "How many died in them?"

"Millions, six million of my people."

"Good God."

"And in the war itself, twenty million of Ivan's people."

"How did you know I know Ivan?"

"A guardian told me."

"The one we're going to see?"

Gideon nodded, and the two men slid into the car seats. "What kind of tree was I standing under?"

"A sycamore."

"They are magnificent. That is my one regret about Argas—so little greenery."

"Kind of hard to make space for that with all those military labs, I guess."

"You guess correctly." He paused. "We have forests on the rings, though."

"Those are the giant space stations circling Argas?"

Ein nodded. "We pump the oxygen right back to the planet."

"Easier to have vast forests on the planet's surface."

"So I argue, every chance I get. The brass doesn't listen to me."

"I doubt that."

For the first time that day Ein smiled, a smile that was, Gideon thought, a huge relief, a smile that countered the man's immense and almost frightening seriousness. When he smiled, he looked like a different person entirely. They drove into the leafy precincts of Garibaldi Square, which afforded, Gideon thought, by some miracle, a parking space directly in front of The Sun, The Moon and The Stars. The two men descended to the entrance, where the strong young woman with very short cropped hair greeted them, whispering to Gideon, as Ein passed on ahead, "is he really an Argan?" Gideon nodded, and the pair made their way through the warren of stacks of books and bookcases to the strangely sun-filled office, strange because it was below ground, of the publisher and bookseller, the singularly yclept Galen. The old man advanced, in his sandals, khakis and white shirt, hand extended. "An Argan on earth," he mused.

"The only Argan *ever* on earth," Gideon added.

"The only Argan who even *knows* about earth," Ein put in, smiling at the octogenarian and shaking his hand. Gideon backed out and went in search of the young woman with short hair, while Galen shut the door to his book-filled office and gestured at a chair, across from his cluttered desk, for his guest.

"You are a guardian of earth," Ein said.

The ancient man nodded.

"You're not doing enough."

In Galen's darkly light, glimmering gaze, the Argan found himself astounded to recognize, right there, the lamps of eternity.

"What should I be doing?" The old man asked, politely.

"Flooding the minds of the powerful with images of collapsed ecosystems, of other dead civilizations, like one of the Seran ones, that's right here in this universe. They burnt fossil fuels till the planet melted. You have presidents, kings, prime ministers who need to see those images."

"I am a guardian of earth, Ein. I cannot transmit images from other worlds."

"How bad is the damage?"

"We could still survive. We have a decade or two, maybe three."

"You're an optimist."

"And you've been talking to Ivan. Why He selected a defeatist to head the council, I'll never know."

"So that someone like me could combat that defeat."

"You have your work cut out for you on this wicked old earth."

The two men gazed soberly at each other. Then the fighter's gray eyes grew wide as images of vast toxic landscapes, the industrial nightmare itself, in places like Elizabeth, New Jersey, Texas and Chernobyl and other parts of Russia and

China flooded his brain. "That," he said, "is why Ivan is a defeatist."

"I know," Galen replied. "And it is very hard to gainsay him."

"I will, undetected, unknown, of course, help your scientists with their computer models. It is the scientists, I presume, who struggle against this catastrophe, who attempt to sway the powers that be?"

Galen nodded. "Not that it's done any good."

"The money power is the problem?"

"As always. Though I have never and will never leave earth, I have heard, from fighters, what has happened on other worlds. I even heard about the Seran disaster you mentioned."

"Do more."

Galen smacked both palms on his desk. "What? Tell me, and I will do it!"

"Give them nightmares."

"I transmit visions to persecuted fighters, not corrupt politicians, to fighters who must combat an inhuman enemy and keep that enemy from gaining a toehold on our planet."

"But you could—"

Galen waved a hand dismissively. "I do not know. It has never been done, has never been attempted. I live in a wicked world, Ein, and I don't stay alive by going off script—His script. Only once did I ever not heed a warning from Him. It landed me in a concentration camp, with nearly nothing to eat for eight months. I was careless, He was trying to protect the guardians of Europe, and I was careless, and darned lucky I didn't end up dead."

"How did this holocaust happen?"

"There was enemy tampering."

"Are you sure?"

"No. but I believe it, and He has not contradicted me."

"Where was He?"

"At the front, where else, and things were going particularly badly at the front."

"He was distracted."

"Perhaps."

"Did He get even?"

Galen smiled. "Somewhat, yes. But that is, or rather let's call it, a work in progress."

"What's Europe?"

"The continent where this abomination occurred. And before it occurred, all Europe's, or rather most, guardians went missing."

"Replaced by doubles? Refugees?"

"Yes. Fighters but not guardians. And Europe needed guardians."

"But you were not replaced."

"No, I was arrested, caught, beaten and thrown in a camp. Let me point out, Ein, that the ideology of those fascists in Europe mirrored the enemy's ideology."

"You don't need to convince me. I believe you. If you think there was enemy tampering, I'm willing to wager there was, especially with the numbers I heard from Gideon, the numbers of dead, of his people and Ivan's."

"And many other people. Plenty of American soldiers died and European soldiers and resistance fighters, and there was mass death in Asia as well."

"Another continent?"

Galen nodded.

"And this was fifty-five years ago?"

The old guardian nodded again.

"Your planet may be doomed."

"Now who's the defeatist?"

Ein leaned forward, interlacing his strong fingers and rocking his hands, his elbows planted on his knees. "I am a fighter," he said at last, "let's reason." Silence ensued for several moments, then he broke it with the words, "earth is special, dreadful but special, perhaps sacred. Somehow He has shielded earth from enemy awareness. He must have gone to great lengths to do so. This...shield, an element of it is a special race of guardians found nowhere else in the entire cosmos. Correct?"

"Correct?"

"That, in and of itself, tells us earth is..."

"Sacred."

"Sacred but drowning in blood."

"Don't get me started on the slums of the southern hemisphere."

"The *entire* hemisphere?" Ein was astonished.

The ancient guardian nodded.

"How could a planet where the wicked are so thoroughly ascendant be...sacred to Him?" Ein asked in wonder.

"That, my friend, is called a mystery. A divine mystery."

"Clearly He wants fighters to counter the wicked."

"You just made a leap."

"A reasonable one." Ein paused. "He wants us to assist. I know it. That's why He created fighters to begin with. We would be grossly derelict not to take on this challenge."

Galen glanced down at his own clasped hands. "There is a fighter here, one I have never met, who works with the transuniverse orphanage,"

"Those men and women are heroes."

"He is a police detective and a friend of His. Gideon knows how to find him. He is up to his eyeballs in the day to day struggle, on earth, against human death worshippers. He might, just might, be able to help you with your other aims, your plans to,"

"Save earth."

"Sounds rather grandiose, don't you think?"

"But there it is. That is the point."

Galen leaned back, and his eyes seemed to glimmer with limitless depths. "I have seen the wicked stride over this earth in pomp and splendor, disposing of men and women like so much trash,"

"That's it! You believe, deep down, that this planet deserves what it is getting!"

The old dark eyes glimmered. "Sometimes. Yes, sometimes I do. But only sometimes." He turned, walked to the door and opened it. "Gideon! Gideon!"

Shortly the young fighter appeared. "Ein here needs to meet a certain exemplary fighter from earth, one up to his elbows in the fight against the enemy, your partner, Rafael Orozco. Where is he?"

"I can take Ein to him right now."

Galen nodded, his long, white hair shimmering in the waves of sunlight that poured into the room from the one high window. "I will never meet Rafael," he murmured, turning back to his desk. "What a pity. Perhaps on the other side…"

"Don't talk like that," the young woman snapped. "You have too far to go, too much to do."

"He is destined for great things, though he would shirk them if he could," the old man said rather enigmatically.

"Come on," Gideon spoke to Ein. "We have to hurry. I myself leave for the front in a matter of hours."

Ein looked surprised, but Galen only sighed. "God speed you and be with you." Then he looked up at the young man sharply. "All four. All four must survive."

"Understood," Gideon stepped out and Ein, visibly wondering, followed.

In the car, Ein tapped the dash, a question hovering on his even, friendly features.

"Yes, we still have cars, as you saw when I picked you up," Gideon replied. "I take it you don't on Argas."

"Correct. We have mass transit. It is very good, comprehensive and flexible, also non-polluting."

"Well, we're not there yet." Gideon parked on Apocalypse Avenue and rang the house doorbell. Orozco answered, "now I can get back to catching death worshippers."

"This is Ein," Gideon said, pushing past him into the living room with Horace.

Orozco stopped in his tracks and stared at the visitor. "*The* Ein? Ein the Argan?"

"Nice to meet you," and Ein extended a hand, which the detective shook vigorously, in one of his huge mitts. "What are you doing here?"

"Good question. Since every fighter or guardian I meet seems to consider trying to save earth a waste of time."

"Who put you up to that stunt?"

"I had a conversation with Ivan, which made it clear to me that this place called earth, dreadful as it is,"

"You don't know the half of it, buddy."

"Is also very special. Ivan considers it doomed,"

"Not unreasonable, though a little depressing, coming from *the* Ivan, I assume you mean the head of the council."

Ein nodded and stepped in. He and Orozco faced each other in the front hall. "Where are your eco-warriors?"

"Scattered, hiding, in jail, trying to get by. Forget it, Ein. This ain't Argas. Here it's every man for himself, the law of the jungle, and you know where that'll get us."

"Extinction within fifty years."

"Less, if you ask me."

"Why aren't you *doing* something?"

"Lookit—I got death worshippers, actual human death worshippers running around, murdering people in graveyards. When I'm not chasing them, I got the transuniverse orphanage,"

"So I heard."

"That I run with a priest, and it's currently swamped with refugee children from sector one thousand. I gotta find homes for millions of kids."

"But you have help."

"Yeah, I got the brethren, but it's hard, Ein."

"Send the scientifically talented children to Argas."

"We don't have time to sort that way. We're just trying to save their skins, before the whole sector collapses. What I'm tryin' to say is, I'm kind of busy here, and I'll take my little victories where I can get 'em, like now in D____, we got a liberal Dem for a mayor, Terrazini, who's going to raise the minimum wage and beef up the bus routes."

"Beef up the bus routes! You need to get rid of all these cars!"

"Ain't gonna happen. We already paved half the goddamn country. Every American who can is the proud owner of a four wheeled combustion engine and sure won't take kindly to your suggestion that he start riding trains and buses. No, you're wasting your time. I suggest you return to your military lab on Argas and invent more of those fantastic weapons you're so famous for. That'll save a lot of lives at the front, and who knows, maybe even some of them can be adapted, to prevent the enemy from extirpating the human race from any more realities. For instance, sector one thousand is contiguous to sector one thousand and one. Why not use your cloaking device to prevent the enemy from stumbling onto one thousand and one?"

"I intend to. Ivan already made that request and I, of course, complied."

"What's an Argan?" Thus Horace, lumbering into the hall.

"A person from the most advanced human society ever to adorn the cosmos. Horace meet Ein. Horace is a lunatic guardian."

"Oh stop it," Thus Horace. Ein looked concerned, but Orozco held up a hand. "Mental illness has plagued the guardians for almost thirty years. And I mean it's a plague. Something's rotten in Denmark."

"The guardian I just met seemed very sane."

"Some still are."

"And what's Denmark?"

"A country. It's an expression, by which I mean that there's something wrong somewhere that's doing two lousy things: killing our guardians on earth and the fighters at the front. And He sure as shit better show us how to correct it soon."

Ein's gray eyes took on a pensive cast. "Thirty years—that's just about when the tide of the war started to go against us."

"Yup, and it's when a guardian I knew, sane and solid as a rock, flung herself down the stairs and killed herself. It was the beginning of the end for earth's guardians, and I sure as shit would like to know the cause."

"That's when we lost sector ten," Ein mused. "The first major loss in over a generation."

"Yup," Orozco popped a mint into his mouth. "Like I said, something's rotten in Denmark."

Horace had removed a stainless steel lighter with a thunderbolt etched on the front from his pocket. He flicked it on, and the little yellow flame burned steadily in the dim hallway.

"Over a generation ago," he murmured, "that's when we lost sector one trillion, which is now *the* enemy stronghold."

"What *is* that?" Ein pointed to the lighter.

"It's a gift from another world, Ein," Orozco slurped on his mint. "A gift to earth's guardians."

"From the angels," Ein breathed. "From the generals in this war," and with those words, all three heard the whirring of wings. Gideon stepped out into the hall and glanced wonderingly into their faces. "Even now," Orozco suddenly intoned, his voice different, his face altered, his gaze weary and worn with millennia of battle, "even now the divine onslaught on sector one trillion continues apace. No men or women participate, though someday soon, you, the man called Ein, will be summoned to assist and observe."

"To assist!" Ein cried. "I'm a mere man. How can I assist seraphs?"

"You'll see," Orozco continued. "Something will be asked of you. But for now," he turned to Gideon. "The young fighter must depart. All four must survive long enough to return to us. All four must survive."

"That's my cue," Gideon said, as the whirring ceased, and the policeman returned to normal.

"And now you go to catch death worshippers," Ein said to him. Orozco nodded.

"So your world is infected."

"Worse than that. We got illusions."

"You're in the zone of illusion?" Ein cried.

Again the policeman nodded. "And to make matters worse, there is some evidence that ordinary people, men and women, have been falling into the realm of shadow."

A look of horror and aversion rippled over Ein's face. "There is a point of contact between earth and the realm of shadow?"

"Evidently," slurp, slurp. "All of which immensely complicates any plans to quote save unquote this planet. Lookit," the detective held up a big mitt and pressed down his thumb, "human death worshippers, lots of 'em, that's one.

Two," he pressed down his index finger, "the proliferation of enemy illusions, for instance, it's hot as hell outside but dollars to donuts it ain't really summer. Three," he pressed down his third finger, "innocent people falling into that unspeakable, thoroughly accursed charnel house, the realm of shadow. And they're just gone, enslaved, they become shadows and are never seen again. Four," he pressed down his fourth finger, "fifty some years ago the planet was soaked in blood, massive genocide and the blatant introduction of enemy ideology. If the enemy wasn't active on earth then, I'm a monkey's uncle. And five," he wiggled his pinky at Ein, "you want to save earth, currently groaning under the crushing power of irresponsible, globally mobile extractive corporations, fully capable of reducing the planet to a cinder in fifty years," he paused to slurp his mint, "and you wonder why the head of the council, who's from earth, is a defeatist about our prospects?"

"Your world is infected," Ein said soberly.

"You ain't kiddin.' And the fever is high."

Listening to Orozco's litany of symptoms, rage had begun to smolder in Gideon's dark eyes. "We can't just give up," he muttered.

"You wanna fix this?" Slurp, slurp. "You're welcome to try. But unless I'm mistaken, you depart on an angel's back from a forest in a couple of hours, headed where? One of the fronts, while I got four blood-thirsty death worshippers, who, five will get you ten, I'm gonna hafta kill, 'cause they won't be taken alive. My partner Harry is waiting for me now, armed to the teeth and ready to plug them in their ugly faces for resisting arrest."

"Your point?" Ein demanded.

"My point, with all due respect, is that the situation is hopeless, all fucked up. We need help, Ein, and we ain't getting' it."

"That's why I'm here."

"Well, if the Argans can help cut through this Gordian knot, more power to 'em. But this here policeman don't see how it can be done; not to be a pessimist,"

"You're a fatalist," Ein pronounced.

"Yes I am. And if you'd grown up on earth and knew its blood-soaked history, you would be too. Good luck, Ein. I hope you can find a way to assist the powerless people of good will who inhabit this poor old earth. I know I've tried, though the paucity of helpful results is enough to make me call it quits."

The bell rang. Horace opened the front door, and there stood a diffident, middle-aged, gray-haired man with keen eyes behind steel-rimmed glasses, who introduced himself as Starfield.

"Now I can go," Orozco and Gideon said in unison. Ein raised his head listening. "I'm to go with the younger fighter, to return to the front."

"Then come on!" Gideon cried, pushing past Starfield and jogging down the front steps onto a gray and sweltering Apocalypse Avenue. "Let's get this thing going!"

***

The detective met up with his partner at a Starbucks on the edge of the South Side. "They been tracked to a house in this neighborhood, rented by two other thirty somethings, who fit the description of the other two killers at the cemetery. These are four sick dudes, Rafael. You saw what they did to their victims."

"Yeah I saw. I seen it before, too."

"Me—I think it's a cult."

"It is. Let's just call them death worshippers," and Orozco cast Harry a sidelong glance.

"Death worshippers!"

"Sure. They got a vanity plate says death, they kidnap innocent people, slit their throats, then desecrate their bodies—you got a better name for them?"

"No. No I do not. It fits. But it makes me think..."

"What?"

"What if there are *more* of them?"

"I assume there are," Orozco guzzled his latte. "Remember that case two years ago, in Pennsylvania—the graveyard killers?"

"It *is* a cult! It's a death worshipping cult! You're right, Rafael."

"Nice to be appreciated."

"But that means they'll try to kill us, when we make the arrest. They did that in Pensy, when the cops arrested, they killed one of them. Then there was a shootout left two more cops dead and all the killers but one dead. I say we call for backup."

"I say we kill all four of them and be done with it."

Harry looked at him. "There's only two of us, pal. There's four of them."

"We come in shooting."

"And kill four innocent,"

"Innocent? Are you stupid?"

"I just think we need backup."

"Backup or no, whoever's the arresting officer and knocks on that door, he's dead if he don't shoot his way in."

"Shit. Let's get a swat team."

"Okay, it's your call. But I ain't knocking on that door without my gun drawn."

"None of us are knocking on the door. We surround the house and address them through a bullhorn."

"Okay," slurp, slurp. "Put in the call."

Ten minutes later, Orozco slapped the flasher on the dash of his Impala, and he and Harry sped to a nondescript brick rambler with a dead maple out front and a stand of bamboo visible in the back. The black-clad swat team was already in place. The car with the plate that read "Death" was parked out front. Harry lifted the megaphone and shouted for the inhabitants to exit the building with their arms in the air. Luckily he stood behind a squad car, for no sooner had he uttered the last word, than a barrage of machine gun fire raked the swat team's barricade. Harry swiveled his head to his partner. "You were right." He said.

"They ain't scared of us," Rafael replied.

"We're going to have to kill all four of them."

"Could be more than four," slurp, slurp on a mint.

The policemen waited, but not long—soon more machine gun fire strafed the front yard.

"They got a gun mounted behind the living room window," Orozco said meditatively. "Where's our sharpshooter?" He crept behind the cars until he found the man he sought, and pointed out the dim outline of a figure behind the living room curtain. The sharpshooter raised his rifle and seconds later a body crashed or was pushed forward through the window, followed by yet another barrage of machine gun fire. "Get the next one," Orozco said. This continued until, after the sixth kill, the machine gun fell silent.

"Could be a trick," slurp, slurp. "I sure as shit ain't goin' in."

"But we are, Orozco," thus the swat team leader.

"Be my guest."

At that instant, around each side of the house leapt a pair of men in jeans, black T-shirts with white skulls printed on them, the snake and globe tattoo on their muscular upper arms and machine guns in hand. All four fired at once, immediately killing a member of the Swat team. "These are some mean sons of bitches," Orozco said to the team leader.

"They're dead," came the reply, as he fired his semi-automatic weapon, killing one of them. The other three kept firing, jumping out from behind trashcans or the brick chimney extension to shoot at the police. After some minutes, none but one remained, as bloodthirsty as ever and no coward. He leapt out from behind his cover, shooting at Harry, who had popped up from behind the hood of a car. He missed.

"Stay down, you idiot," Orozco hissed, then rested his semi-automatic rifle on an open car window, aimed through the car, waited for the death worshipper to stand still and shot him.

"You think that's the last of 'em?" A swat member asked. Orozco nodded.

"I'm calling an ambulance."

"It's too late."

"Look, they shot my partner,"

"In the heart. It's too late, but put in the call and start practicing you lines for his wife," Orozco grabbed the bullhorn, and shouted through it. "If there are any more death worshippers in this house, come out now with your hands up. We know what you are. We know what you've done. But if you come out peacefully, you will be arrested and taken to the station for questioning." Harry guffawed and reloaded.

"I counted ten of 'em," Orozco said.

"Let's move," the leader of the swat team raised his hand, and two officers sprinted to the front door, waited on either side, guns drawn, then broke it down. The team surrounded and entered the house, with the two detectives in tow. Inside, a scene of nauseating carnage greeted them, for in addition to the six dead killers, there were other bodies, in various states of decay. "You were right, Rafael, they were death worshippers." Orozco was already moving toward a computer, hooked up in the corner of the dining room. He unplugged it, took it under his arm and headed back to his car. "Let's just keep that term, death worshipper, amongst ourselves."

"Why?" Asked the swat team leader.

"We don't want to cause no mass panic. Got it?"

"Yeah, got it."

Whereupon detective Orozco packed the computer into his Impala, slid behind the steering wheel and tore off.

***

The tall, hard woman with the flat, dull gaze and the cheap, ill-fitting clothes, strode down the cinder-block hallway, and the people passing her hastened to step out of the way. They all knew who she was and her terrible history. They knew that she had survived the unthinkable and had, recently, suffered a relapse, so they cast furtive, guarded glances at her, wondering if she had been cured, frightened at the thought of what it meant if she wasn't, for she was someone whose very gaze could kill the enemy, and the thought of such a weapon out of control was alarming, to say the least.

She turned off the main corridor and made her way into a stairwell then down, further underground, stopping at last at a gray metal, unmarked door and knocking once. Ivan opened it. Behind him she saw two men, one in clerical garb, the other sporting a familiar gray crew-cut. "Ein!" She exclaimed, "how good to see you again!"

The military scientist hurried forward, hand outstretched. "Lontra, Lontra! Always an honor." They shook. "And here," Ein spoke, still clasping her hand and with his free one gesturing at the priest, "this is Vivaldi, who coordinates the transuniverse orphanage."

"Alone?" She asked in astonishment.

"No," the cleric said. "Many help, but the chief coordinator is otherwise engaged now. He is a fighter, who may have to travel behind enemy lines."

The hard, flat gaze glittered aggressively over the cleric's kindly features. "So your workload has doubled."

"Not now that I have you."

"But I am untrained."

"You're a quick study," Ein said.

"Why has a fighter been sent behind enemy lines at this time?"

"We do as we're instructed," Ivan said soberly. "Actually one has been already sent, and the other, Vivaldi's partner, may have to go soon. He is to rescue four prisoners from an enemy facility."

"Ah, pardon my curiosity, but it derives from personal experience. Are these fighter/prisoners deep behind enemy lines?"

"No," Ivan shook his gray head. "And the prison, or rather jail, is not run by non-humans."

"That is lucky indeed."

"Amen," said the priest."

"We understand that you are not to return to sector one thousand," Ein began. "Would you mind explaining why?"

"Evidently my former interrogator is there. Should he become aware of me and learn how I was cured, he would learn the secret that I hear you so recently learned, the secret of earth and earth's," she stopped.

"Guardians," Ivan said. "Ein knows about them and has even met Galen."

Lontra turned her flat gaze onto the keenly alert military scientist. "Galen had a hand in my rescue," she said. "It is he, in particular, that we seek to shield by keeping me out of sector one thousand. Where will I be?"

"In one of the Seran systems," Vivaldi said. "On a sparsely populated planet, whose people, though primitive, are, well, sterling."

"I take it that means they will make excellent adoptive parents."

The priest nodded. "As far as we know, not a soul on Sere has ever been on the enemy's wavelength. Every adult will take several children. We will place millions on Sere alone. That will be our first destination for our orphans. You will be there, but there will be other fighters to receive the children,"

"Fighters? So we are making certain that they are not tracked?"

"Correct."

"You say these people are primitive—primitive peaceful?"

Before Vivaldi could speak, Ein waved a hand dismissively, and said, "you know very well, Lontra, there are almost no peaceful primitive human beings in any universe. There is always tribal warfare."

"But they have advanced a little beyond that," Vivaldi put in. "They are joined together, a series of clans in tribal nations, by one council. This governing council keeps the peace and has been most helpful negotiating with the orphanage and the fighters."

"Are they forest people?" She asked.

"For the most part, yes," the priest answered. "Some prairie, desert and mountain, but mostly forest—oh, and coastal traders."

"I assume your brethren are proselytizing?" She asked.

"You disapprove? I ask, because most fighters do."

"I neither approve nor disapprove."

"Then you do not disdain the clergy?"

"I do not."

"How…different."

"But I will not be used for proselytizing."

"We wouldn't dream of it. And to answer your question, no—we were specifically instructed not to spread our word."

She tilted her head up and glanced down her beak of a nose at him rather critically. "I did not know He had taken to communicating directly with clerics. That has not happened in many years."

"This cataclysm in sector one thousand has altered His thinking."

"You were told or you surmise?"

"I surmise."

Both Lontra and Ein grunted. Ivan looked alarmed. "So now we'll have clerics on the council?" He asked.

"It's possible," the priest answered. "Things are changing very fast. The fighters, especially the atheists among them, will have to adapt." He paused, then glanced diffidently at Lontra. "Do we know the name of your non-human interrogator in sector one thousand?"

"If I knew I would certainly never utter it. Even the knowledge would make me sick. It was cleared out of my mind when I was bathed in the river of forgetfulness. Why on earth would you want to hear that name?"

"Naiveté," Ivan said somberly.

"No," the priest disagreed. "So we can destroy him."

"You do not need his name to try to destroy him," she said. "And learn this, my friend the priest, we fighters never utter the names of the enemy, unless we are under some constraint, unless we must."

He nodded.

"This is no mere predilection," she continued. "Those names make us sick." She paused, then spoke definitively, "besides, you cannot destroy him. No man or woman can. Only a seraph could do that, and one day will, but for now, from what I gather, they have their hands full, staving off a total collapse of sector one thousand. Multiple enemy commanders and interrogators are roaming that reality. I doubt the angels have time to seek out and destroy one in particular, just now."

"He poses an especial threat to earth."

"You're not even from earth."

"But my partner is, and he has impressed upon me the urgency with which we must attend to safeguarding your planet."

"It's already compromised," Ein said. "I just came from there directly. Death worshipping men are murdering the innocent, and from what I gather, the enemy touched down on earth, helping to ignite the last world war."

Lontra snorted derisively. "You have been listening to Galen. No, my brother Ein, it was not beings from another reality who ignited what we know as World War II, it was very wicked, very arrogant and ambitious, very cruel, indeed sadistic men. And they paid with their lives,"

"And the lives of millions of innocents," Ein spoke angrily.

"Let's not argue, the right side won in the end."

"But the price in blood,"

"Was tremendous, beyond imagining."

"Twenty million in my country," Ivan said. "And the siege of Leningrad, the battle of Stalingrad, and the misery besetting tens of millions more,"

"It's over," Lontra spoke sharply. "The wicked were punished to the best of our ability."

"Nonsense," Ivan countered. "Those criminals fled to South America and assisted in setting up fascist governments there."

"Which all fell in the 1980s," Lontra snapped. "I'm not little Miss Pollyanna, but our murderous history does not need review, especially if the point is to shift the blame from men to the non-human enemy."

"Galen is convinced," Ein began.

"I know," Lontra held up a hand, and her dark eyes glittered angrily. "I have argued the matter with him before. I am not trying to exonerate our enemy, I would be the last person ever to do that. I simply fail to see the evidence that that particular enemy was involved. Men committed those crimes against humanity, and they paid with their lives, as they deserved. But now, unless I am mistaken, we have a very pressing matter at hand, to wit, the collapse of an entire universe, and one priest cannot manage a tsunami of refugees. He needs help."

"How is it," Ein mused, "I have known you all these years and known so little of earth."

"Earth's fighters are chary of mentioning their origins," Ivan said. "All are so instructed."

"What about the children of sector one thousand?" Lontra insisted.

The priest beamed happily upon her.

"Always a one-track mind, eh Lontra?" Thus Ivan.

"When millions of lives are at stake, yes. Do we have the support network up and running?"

"Yes," Vivaldi nodded.

"Good. When do we leave for the Seran system, where Sere is located?"

"Tomorrow," Ivan replied. "Now both of you get some sleep."

"While you and Ein compare views on earth's catastrophe during the Nazi era," Lontra said.

"What is it to you if we do?" Ivan snapped. "Especially if good may come of it. Preventive action."

"I'm all for prevention. What I'm not for is wallowing in wild and miserable speculation about the past." With that, she turned on her heel and left, the priest close behind her.

***

In the cafeteria, each had a piece of bacon-flavored tofu and some limp, unidentifiable vegetables, probably, Lontra observed to Vivaldi, from a world they had never heard of. She was pleased to discover that he too hailed from the Milky Way—"we're practically neighbors," she mused—and to his inquiry about her favorable views of the clergy, she replied that a priest had hid her father, a communist partisan, during the German occupation of Italy. She explained that unlike many fighters, she bore clerics no ill-will, in fact owed her life to the good deeds of one. "For if he hadn't saved my father, I wouldn't be here," she replied grimly, "doing all the fun things I do."

"Tut, tut, Lontra. No sarcasm. You know how valuable your work is."

She finished chewing her meat substitute, looked him in the eye and said: "What I do is make war. That is my whole life. The war. And that will be my whole life, and undoubtedly it will kill me. I will die at the front."

Concern filled his light eyes, as he said: "You must not despair."

"Oh, despair," she waved a hand. "I went way past that during my incarceration."

He bowed his head.

"So far past that, frankly, I believe I died. In fact, one of my rescuers, Jamal, said that when he first set eyes on me I was dead—spiritually, emotionally, mentally dead."

The priest shuddered and reached up a hand to clasp a small gold symbol that hung on a chain around his neck.

"So when I say I will die at the front," she continued, "there is no despair in it. It is a statement of fact, one that many fighters make. I have heard Ivan say it, and many, many others. We are fighters. We will die at the front. We will die on His side. We will die for Him. That is our destiny. There is no despair in that."

Vivaldi glanced up, "when you put it like that,"

"It is reasonable, no? And fighters reason."

"They also have faith."

"Different from your faith."

"How so? Please, explain this to me."

"We hear a voice in our minds that comes from Him. We live for that voice. We live for the next time, the next time that we will hear it, and hearing it, know exactly what to do, and know that He is there, and fully aware of us and our mortality. All fighters hear this voice. All fighters live for this voice. And we die for it, too."

"But that is never the intention, is it?"

"Exactly right. Never. The intention is life and the saving of life. Yet there is the enemy, and we must fight and life is lost." In that moment, as they sat across from each other, gazing across a suddenly shrinking gulf, the hardness went out of her eyes and compassion replaced it. She placed a hand on one of his. "You clerics have been in another world with your astonishing faith in the unseen. From that perspective, by contrast, we fighters are...pampered."

"Pampered?! You're horribly persecuted."

"Yes, but look Who helps us. Look Who raises us up. Look Who guides us. Look Who assists in our struggle to survive. I...admire your...comparatively unsupported faith."

"I have never heard a fighter talk like this," the priest said.

"Perhaps you clerics need to talk to fighters more often," she concluded and withdrew her hand, and the sheen of hardness encased her once again.

Vivaldi sighed. "I hope some angel incinerates your interrogator in sector one thousand."

She cast him a grim little smile, rose, placed a hand on his shoulder and whispered hoarsely, and her voice trembled hoarsely with emotion, "so do I."

***

"I'm dying. I won't make it through the night."

"Don't talk like that, Brianna. You're a fighter. Fight." Carmella wiped her cellmate's damp forehead with the edge of her blanket.

"Don't touch me. I could be contagious," and the ordinarily pert little blond started coughing. There was nothing pert about her now. "The moment they injected me in that lab, I knew—I knew whatever it was, it would kill me."

"Shhh. Here are some herbs, from outside the prison. They'll lower your temperature. Chew."

"If you ever make it back to our side," Brianna spoke, while chewing. "Tell my husband and children what happened to me. I'm from sector 222."

"How do you even know the number?"

"You learn it when the enemy invades. You learn it then, from angels."

"But sector 222 is ok, right?"

"Yes. It was only a brief, abortive incursion. Then we got some technology from the Argans that confused the enemy, and he didn't come back."

"Those Argans are a wonder," Carmella marveled, as her cellmate once again began to cough.

"I'll be dead before morning."

"Shh."

"Tell my husband. He's at the front."

Carmella wiped her friend's abundantly perspiring forehead again. "You're burning up. Take off your T-shirt," then she took the T-shirt, dipped it in the pail of water that stood between the two beds and rinsed Briana's entire face and neck. "More," Briana begged plaintively. "I feel so hot, so weak."

"Don't talk," Carmella advised and continued sponging off her cellmate. As she did so, she gritted her teeth at the thought of what the death worshippers had done to this woman. First they had beaten and raped her, now they had injected her with some new disease, something that looked to be rapidly fatal, for from the sound of her cellmate's cough she divined that her lungs were filling up with liquid. She did not know how she knew this, but she felt sure and then she heard the words in her brain: "You are correct. You must leave this prison within two days, or you will be next." She sighed and continued sponging the too hot skin that gleamed with sweat, the high temperature that had now made the ill woman delirious, as she raved about her wedding, some fifteen years before. "Mama, we have to hem the dress and I do, I do want the ceremony in the mansion at the cemetery, so that at least in spirit papa can be there. Why did he have to go off-world? And come back so badly wounded that he couldn't live more than a week? They have no business taking older people like him. I'd have gone in his place. Don't shush me. I've gone plenty of times. I fought in sector 38 and at the front. We were losing, always losing. The fighters say something's wrong somewhere, and whatever it is, it must be terrible. They say He'll tell us, before too long, but why doesn't He tell us now? Before another good man like papa or good woman has to die? Why does He let this happen? Everything depends on us, and the burden is too big to carry. Get the cake from weddings inc. They're the best. And we'll have it in the main room of the mansion, with the doors open wide, so I can see straight out to papa's grave. He should have been here for this. Tell his sisters why. They think a wedding in a cemetery is morbid. But that's what the enemy does, makes you think about death, about the dead, because he's killed so many of us. It's not morbid, but I have to get back to the front. I was called. I heard it in my mind. I can't even say good-bye to Jack or the baby. Thank God for my mother, thank God she's disabled and can't fight anymore. Oh, this war has eaten up my whole life, just burned through it like wildfire, and the flame throwers are all around and I'm burning up, burning up…" She fell silent, turned her pretty head and died. Carmella collapsed on her chest, arms over her head, but did not weep. After a moment, she raised herself up, then grabbed the broom from the corner and tapped out the message on the ceiling. "Brianna just died. We leave this prison tomorrow night."

***

The angel deposited Gideon on a remote section of the front, on a night world, warmed by its proximity to a red dwarf, and covered with a strange forest. "There will be more light as you approach the prison," the seraph informed him, "which is straight ahead, through these woods. Return here within thirty hours." The young man grunted, jammed his handgun into his belt, extracted his flashlight from his knapsack and set off in the direction indicated. The flashlight beam picked out a gray-green, feathery herb, the same one Carmella had obtained, and he picked a few fistfuls, shoving them in his pockets. He walked silently and, after a half an hour, noting that the sky had turned from evening to twilight, put away his flashlight, and a fortunate thing too, for shortly thereafter, he heard voices. He quickly crouched behind a boulder and listened, ascertaining rapidly that these were two guards, a short distance from the jail, meeting in the woods to do drugs. After they had snorted their white powder, one left, and the other settled himself on the forest floor, with a pile of leaves for a pillow, as he gazed up groggily into the gloaming. Gideon smiled. Whenever the guard moved, he could hear the clink of keys in his pockets. "Couldn't be better," the young fighter thought and crept noiselessly forward.

When he could hear the guard's light snores, Gideon reached around, found a large, pointed rock, then tiptoed forward and crashed it into the skull of the death worshipper, who expired without a sound. Quickly he undressed the corpse, donned the prison uniform, studied the keys, and strapped on the guard's belt with its holster and gun. Then he crept forward like a shadow, noting the darkness of an open doorway in the prison wall which loomed before him. He withdrew a paper chart from the guard's pants pocket and noted the number next to the name MacKenzie. It began with a two, so, he concluded, Horace's double was on the second floor, and the seraph had informed him that Carmella was directly below. He shoved the paper back in the pocket and glanced up. A guard strolled past the dark entranceway. So he waited, and as he waited, found himself longing for the sparkling blue of the Mediterranean, of the beach at Tel Aviv, so clean, so fresh, so hospitable to life. "But that's there, and I'm here," he thought.

The guard disappeared around the wall of the jail. From where Gideon stood, he could discern that the entrance was invisible to the gunners on the tower. All that remained to be done was traverse a short, open but shadowed area between the edge of the forest and the prison wall. Gideon glanced in the direction the last guard had gone. Not a soul. Quietly, like a shadow himself, he crept forward.

***

Orozco drove his Impala through the smoggy heat and shabby precincts of the South Side, the death worshippers' computer on the front passenger seat beside him. "You," he addressed it and pointed a thick index finger at the CPU, "are going to tell me what I need to know. You are going to yield up the secret of exactly how many death worshippers we have to contend with on earth, and I know how I'm gonna make you do it!" He swerved onto a ramp to a highway and tore out of the city, following signs roundabout, back into D____, into the crowded, crooked, proletarian neighborhood of Iroquois. He parked on a side street and pulled out a map, but just then saw what he wanted in the sturdy, gray-haired, gray-eyed form of a woman passing his car. "Vonda Elpytha, help! I'm lost." She came around to the driver's window. "What are you doing out on this infernally hot day?" She asked.

Orozco pointed at the gear on the passenger's seat. "It's a death worshipper's computer," he said. "I need you to look at it, because you'll have visions, which you'll transmit to me."

She nodded, came around to the passenger side, picked up the monitor and the keyboard, while he took the rest, then led him down a little lane between listing townhouses.

"I don't know where the fuck I am," he complained.

"Don't worry about what's not important. You don't need to know Iroquois. You need to know what's in this computer." After turning this way and that, they came to a little stucco house and stepped down to the back door, which led into a cool, stone-floored kitchen, where a young woman, with short black hair, streaked with blue and purple, and remarkably resembling Vonda, lounged at a little table, drinking yerba matte. Plants hung in the window—more herbs, he surmised, and a fat, three-legged cat lolled on the cool floor. "Lara, meet Detective Orozco, fighter and savior of orphans. Detective, meet my daughter. She's a computer wizard, luckily for you."

"What's that mean?" Lara snapped.

"It means the detective has come into possession of a death worshipper's computer," her mother pointed at the CPU in Orozco's thick hands, "and we need it to yield up all—all of its secrets."

Lara pushed her mug of tea to the side. "Let's set it up here." Soon the monitor blinked on—"good, no password needed," the young woman muttered and tapped at a few keys. "Okay, here's everything on the hard drive. What do you want?" She demanded.

The policeman bent over her shoulder, then pointed a thick finger at a line of script. "That, 'our earth map,' that's what I want."

In seconds the three of them were gazing at an image of the globe covered with a network of red dots and red lines.

"Holy shit, they're everywhere," Orozco gasped.

Vonda Elpytha reached into her jeans pocket and withdrew a stainless steel lighter with a thunderbolt etched on front. She lit it, and at once all three froze in place, riveted, stock still, as they surveyed images of murder and carnage from New York to Delhi, from London to Johannesburg. "Well this sucks," Lara snapped again.

"You ain't kiddin'," the old fighter agreed. "What're we gonna do? I thought they just had a few little groups scattered here and there, but no, they got a global network."

"Put in a request for an investigation team," Vonda said.

"We don't need that. We just did the investigation."

"I mean to find out what the enemy knows. This may be a global network, but my hunch is they're very low-level. What do the non-humans know? That's what we need to find out."

"Well shit," Orozco grumbled. "That may be impossible."

"Try anyway."

"Well not on this computer. It may be tagged."

"On your own, when you get home."

"Mom, you have to go to the top."

The gray woman nodded her head, and snapped her lighter shut.

"And the sooner the better," Orozco put in, "but first let's see what else is on this machine."

They spent an hour exploring the computer's files and drinking an herbal tea that Elpytha prepared for them. With each new discovery—"look, this document was ccd to an enemy commander—shit!" Orozco hollered—with each of these, he became gloomier and more morose, finally concluding, "our whole planet is one big bull's eye."

"Don't jump to the worst conclusions," the gray woman counseled. "Wait for the results of the investigation team."

"Look," Lara pointed at one document, "plans to sabotage nuclear power plants."

"As if that infernal industry weren't dangerous enough already," the policeman grumbled. "They want to kill the planet. That's basically it. We're looking at a plan to destroy earth."

"To render it environmentally inhospitable," Elpytha said.

"Well, Christ, we don't need death worshippers for that. We're doing a pretty good job on our own," Orozco replied.

"But we're not fast enough for them, don't you see?" Lara asked softly. "They want us dead within a generation."

"As opposed to the two that our genius leaders will give us," Orozco growled.

The gray woman walked over to the sink and washed dirty dishes. "Where are they all coming from?"

"They get converts," thus Orozco.

"Not this many," she turned, planted her hands on her sturdy hips and stared at the leathery old detective. "We've been invaded," she announced, and both listeners visibly started. "The questions is—from where?"

***

The gray woman drove her Kelly green station-wagon downtown, parked on Catafalque Street and hurried into the leafy vicinity of Garibaldi Square. She crossed the park, dotted at that hour with elderly locals, sunning themselves on benches and occasional lovers, entwined, embracing, oblivious to passersby. She crossed the green quadrangle and made her way to the entrance of The Sun, The Moon and The Stars, descending, then entering and catching the glance of the strong girl with the close cropped hair behind the register. "Bad news?" This one asked.

"I'm afraid so. He's in back?"

The strong young woman nodded, and Elpytha hurried thither.

"Oh Elpytha, this is a pleasant surprise," thus the white-haired publisher on catching sight of her in the doorway. She flung herself down in a chair.

"Uh oh," he said.

"A fighter visited me today," she began. "He brought an enemy computer."

Galen swung around from his computer to face her. "You have my attention."

"The death worshippers have a global network, one apparently dedicated to planetary extinction within a generation."

In the old concentration camp survivor's deep, dark eyes, something glimmered. "How many?"

"Hundreds of thousands, maybe millions."

111

"So we've been invaded and you want to know from where."

She nodded. "Fighters need to be alerted, at once."

He reached for the stainless steel cigarette lighter with the thunderbolt etched on front that lay on top of a stack of papers. He flicked it on, and the little yellow flame danced; as it did a look of aversion, electrified aversion, spread over both interlocutors' faces.

"This is a catastrophe," the gray woman said.

"Innocent people have been falling into the realm of shadow from earth for some time. I suppose we should not be surprised that we have been invaded, directly, by the rulers and soldiers of the realm of shadow."

"I'm not surprised," she said. "I'm horrified."

"The question is, have they gained any positions of power?"

Her gray eyes widened. "Surely not. They're thugs, low-level killers."

"Low-level killers have attained the pinnacle of power in earth's history many times before," Galen said mildly. "Surely I need not remind you of that."

They stared at each other in silence, finally broken by her cry of "help! Galen, you must help!"

Something dark and light at the same time stirred within the depths of his gaze. "The realm of shadow is closer than we thought." Then he turned back to his computer.

"You will help, won't you?"

"People get what they deserve."

"Not all. Not even most. Most deserve better than they get. You know that very well."

He bowed his white head, closing his eyes. "We do not deserve the realm of shadow, bad as we are, wicked as human kind is, we do not deserve that."

"You will help?" She repeated. "I cannot alert all the fighters alone."

"Neither can I."

"Not true."

He sighed, and strange retaliatory dark lights danced in his eyes. "I will do what I can."

***

Orozco and Lara carried the parts of the enemy's computer back to his car. "Where will you take it now?" She asked.

"To a friend, an investigative journalist, who, like you, is a technological wizard."

"To what end?"

"To lay a trap or, possibly, just to sabotage this network."

"Good luck," she said, as he straightened up from bending into the car, and stood suddenly, stock still, visions of destruction, war, carnage, flooding his brain, followed by multiple images of death worshippers all over the earth, killing and maiming. Then a look of profound aversion spread over his lined old face. "The realm of shadow," he said.

"So that's where they're coming from," Lara breathed.

He studied her, his sharp eyes taking in all of her, the black hair with the blue and purple streaks, the multiple ear and eyebrow piercings, the ripped jeans, the worn T-shirt. "Your mother went to the top," he said.

"As only she can."

"No," he shook his grizzled gray head. "Someday you will, too, guardian of earth." With that, he walked around to the driver's side, slid behind the wheel, and drove off, back in the direction of Apocalypse Avenue.

When he reached his destination, Starfield opened the door. "He's not crazy," he said in a low voice.

"True enough," Orozco answered. "But he could still be suicidal."

The investigative journalist looked visibly shaken. "Given the reality he's in touch with, that's a rational response."

Orozco cast him a sharp glance. "Quit it. Help me set up this enemy computer. We have no time to succumb to despair. If every fighter or guardian who came in contact with the enemy got a free pass to commit suicide, we'd have lost the war millennia ago and humanity would be in the ashcan. Things are bad, Starfield, and we gotta do somethin' about it."

They turned right, into the main floor study, where Horace sat in a leather armchair, reading Primo Levi's *If Not Now, When?*

"Did you say an *enemy* computer?" He asked, glancing up from his book.

Orozco grunted assent, setting the computer down on the desk, then turning to Starfield. "I want you to go through everything on this machine, then upload it to Elsewhere."

"Elsewhere?"

"The front. They need this info, and we need their help. Also, if you send it to the front, the enemy won't be able to trace it back here."

"Why not?"

"That, Starfield, is one of the benefits of dealing with His techs—they always cover your ass."

The journalist hooked up the computer, plugged it in, turned it on and sat down.

"First you download everything to a floppy," Orozco instructed.

"I figured that out," Starfield grumbled and started searching through files. As he did, he grew pale. "This is a conspiracy," he said, "a conspiracy to destroy our world."

"Just download, then I'll upload. Hurry up."

Starfield pushed his chair back suddenly from the table. "What's the realm of shadow?" He demanded.

"There's an actual reference to it?" The detective gasped.

"They're sending storm troopers from some world where they got millions in slavery, in concentration camps."

"Welcome to the war, Starfield," thus Horace.

"They're sending these killers to earth to, to...the word they use is to quote harvest unquote us."

"Like I said, download to a floppy, so I can upload to the front. Hurry up."

"Then what'll you do with the computer itself?" Horace asked.

"Turn it over to the police."

"Then they'll know."

"Nope," Orozco popped a mint into his mouth. "We sanitize the fuckin' thing first. We can't have this information disseminated. It'll cause a panic."

"Or a coup d'etat," Starfield remarked, scrolling through a document, his eyes wide in alarm.

The journalist worked for over an hour. When done, he turned, pale and haggard, to face his two companions. "We're losing the war," he said.

"Now you know," thus Orozco.

"How is it possible?"

"If I had the answer to that," the policeman slurped, "I could, singlehandedly, turn the tide of the war."

"You'll be leaving for the front soon, Rafael," thus Horace.

"That's what you think," the detective snapped, but then, deep within his mind, heard, "the guardian is correct.

You leave from Lonely State Park tonight." "Shit!" Orozco exclaimed aloud.

"Now upload the information, Rafael," the voice instructed him.

"What's wrong?" Starfield demanded.

"Everything!" The policeman snapped, taking his seat, as the journalist relinquished it, "everything in this unlucky, accursed, doomed, stupid little world of ours; everything on earth and everything Elsewhere. Damn it all to hell!" And with that he pressed a key, received a message from a tech at the front, asking if he was ready to upload, received written instructions, followed them to the letter, then pressed enter, and the information left earth's universe.

***

The pockmarked man swung his legs off his bed and stretched. "I've gained weight, I feel better, and I'm leaving, going on my maiden voyage on a needle, stitching my way through universes."

"Well, you do look a lot better than a few weeks ago," Lindin conceded. "Almost ready to carry a gun."

"I hope not," Saltwater snapped. "I certainly hope I won't need a gun on Argas."

"You won't," thus Ein. "At the moment, it may be the safest place in the entire cosmos."

"Better Argas than sector one thousand," the convalescent grumbled. "That's all I got to say." He finished dressing, tied his shoes, took one last bite of his breakfast roll on the tray beside the bed, then cast a very keen, hazel-eyed glance at Ein and said, "lead on."

The trio left the infirmary. "Remember the message to my mother," Lillo called.

"We won't forget," Lindin called back.

"We'll have to back away from the front through the trenches," Ein explained.

"How long has it been, Ein, since you had to crouch in a foxhole and eat your breakfast in a trench?" Saltwater asked.

"You know the answer to that."

"Since the enemy touched down on one of Argas' remote galaxies," Saltwater surmised.

"Correct. I've been in weapons' development nonstop ever since. And now, my friend, you are too."

"That's a funny way to look at AI," thus Lindin.

"It's the only way," Ein said. "Ivan briefed me on the enemy's capabilities. We have to catch up fast. We also have to find out what he's using his artificial life form for and for that we'll need—"

"Seymour," Saltwater said.

"Who's Seymour?" Ein and Lindin asked in unison.

"My name for the life we are going to create, or, rather, my father's name."

Ein raised his head, listening, "your father died in the war," he said after a moment, and then, "yes, Seymour is a good name."

"Will Seymour be some kind of robot?"Lindin asked.

Saltwater shook his head. "Nope. He'll be a network."

Ein rubbed his hands together eagerly. "I look forward to this."

Nurse Wren approached and, catching sight of Saltwater, burst into tears. "Why cry?" He asked. "I'm going *away* from the front. I'm going to Argas."

"You won't take your medicine. You'll have a relapse. The TB will kill you," she sniffled.

"Nonsense," he put an arm around her shoulder. "See that man there," and he pointed at Lindin.

She nodded through tears.

"He's coming with me for the sole purpose of making sure I take my medicine and eat lots of healthy food."

"You really are?" She asked the quiet, nondescript man. "I'd been told, but hardly believed it."

"Yes I am."

"Well, that's better. A life is so precious,"

"How's your husband?" Saltwater asked.

She beamed, "wonderful."

"You have no business shedding tears over your patients, especially me. Life is good."

"It has been good to me. It brought him back," she smiled.

"There, see? Now I'm off to Argas, and you're off to Lillo."

"Oh, he never stops complaining."

"A true mama's boy," thus Ein.

"You just say that because he comes from one of your matriarchal worlds," Saltwater said.

"Correct. They're all mama's boys."

"Not like you," Saltwater laughed.

"No, we're not boys."

"You're His adults," Lindin said, and with that, the trio left Nurse Wren and continued down the hall, bumping smack into Ivan, tall, gray, bony, weary, worried. "We're counting on you," he said to Saltwater and Ein. "Otherwise we'll never know what we're up against."

"I'll be back before you know it," the pockmarked man said, "*with* my artificial life form."

"Hopefully that will turn the tide," Ivan fretted. "Something better."

"It can't go against us always," thus Ein.

"Twenty-seven years," Ivan said pointedly, "twenty-seven years of my home-world's time. More here, but time's different here. That's how long we've been losing. Saltwater, get me AI."

"Yes sir."

Ivan ran a big, knobby hand over his lined and worried features. "Part of sector one thousand collapsed last night. A whole string of galaxies just...vanished."

"What about the refugees?" Ein cried.

"We're moving them out fast as we can. But there's never been anything, *anything* like this before. If we lose the whole sector...all I can say is He'll change everything. He's already changing things. Good grief, it never ends."

"He's tough as nails," Ein said. "He's ready for the worst."

"He may be, but I'm not," Ivan shot back. "I asked to be released from the council."

The trio looked startled. "And?" Ein asked.

Ivan shook his head. "No not yet. But if not now, when?"

"When we've lost sector one thousand," Ein said grimly.

"The fighters are doing everything they can," the leader of the council began.

"And it's still not enough," Saltwater finished his sentence. "It's never enough. The enemy's got the edge, how or why I don't know, but the human future hangs in the balance and frankly, from where I stand, it doesn't look good."

"Well, you just got out of a killing center," Lindin corrected him.

"Where we'll all be, if this isn't turned around fast," Ivan snapped, walking away. "Get me AI, Saltwater. Do it fast."

"Ivan sure seems down," thus Lindin.

"Defeat is wearing him away," the pockmarked man said. "We've been able to hold the main front for almost thirty years, but the provinces are falling. No wonder he thinks he should quit. The only question is who or what would replace him."

"He is a good man," Ein said. "Just overwhelmed. I argued with him that if we can learn, through AI, which realities the enemy has targeted, well then we apply the Argan model to those societies, so that when the enemy touches down, we can apply cloaking technology without the risk of it falling into the hands of warring factions." He paused, then spoke meditatively, "the planet I just visited is in grave danger, but given its divisions, hatreds, wars and warlords, we could never risk transferring technology to them."

"That sounds like our galaxy," Saltwater said. "Which is why our little system stays closed off and safely out of galactic politics. We hardly even indulge in interstellar travel—better the other systems should just regard us as a bunch of isolationist yokels, and leave us alone."

The three men passed through an exit to a stairwell, descended, then followed a dim, cement corridor to its terminus at a heavy gray metal door. Ein pushed it open, and they found themselves in the bustle and grime of an extremely rearward trench. The Argan turned and glanced at his two companions. "Thank heaven my days of trench warfare at the front are over. Thank Him."

***

The black rectangle in the gray prison wall loomed before him in the crepuscular dimness. He chewed some feathery green herbs that he had plucked near the enemy's corpse and glanced stealthily from right to left.

"Only one guard on the perimeter," he heard Orozco's voice deep in his mind. "I got the prison plans and schedules on my computer, downloaded from the front."

"Geeze," Gideon thought. "Somebody sure is taking an interest in this rescue."

"Somebody with a capital S. Now go! I'll meet you in the woods on the return trip."

The young man sprinted for the doorway, entered and crept along the sweating stones to a dimly lit corridor that led past the bars of cells. No guards were in sight. He had not past many sleeping prisoners before he came to a cell with two women, one who fit Carmella's description, curly black hair and a unique tattoo and the other, blond, who appeared to be sleeping.

"You happy?" The dark-haired woman hissed. "She's dead."

"Well sister, that's one less prisoner I have to rescue."

Something dark and light flickered in the woman's eyes, as he unlocked her cell. "Where are the others?" He asked.

"Above."

Gideon pulled out a handgun. "Get in front. We'll make this look like a forced march to an interrogation."

When they reached Horace's cell, the young fighter groaned. "He's too sick to move," he said of Albert.

"Nonsense," Carmella snapped. "Eel, you and I, under his shoulders." And together they removed the ailing fighter from the cell. All four with the disguised Gideon hurried silently to the stairs, then out and down. En route they encountered a guard, but before Gideon could make his excuses, Carmella pounced on the man with a switchblade and left him slumped over, dead in a stairwell. They arrived safely at the exit.

Off to the right, his back to them, stood the perimeter guard, smoking.

"Horace, you and," Carmella began.

"Gideon is my name."

"You and Gideon take Albert into the woods, as soon as Eel and I deal with this guard." Thereupon the two fighters,

121

man and woman, slunk along through the dimness. Gideon saw her grab the guard, simultaneously reaching around to his throat. Again, the guard slumped down silently.

"Good," Orozco said in his mind. "Carmella and Eel are safe. They'll make it back. You two take Albert into the woods, quick."

Gideon did as he was told, and as they stepped behind a scrim of leaves and branches, concealed from view from the prison, he saw the other two escapees, further down, dashing into the woods. The black-haired woman waved him on; it was a gesture that meant "hurry." He signaled back, then saw her and Eel disappear into the forest darkness. That was the last he saw of them.

***

Orozco left a haggard and quite obviously terrified Starfield leafing through the files he had downloaded to the floppy disks. He took the sanitized death worshipper computer back to the police station, feigned illness and took a leave. "It's not that kidney stone again?" Harry inquired.

"Could be. I feel like shit, and my back hurts."

"I'll visit you, if you have to go into the hospital."

"There's a whole regimen I follow to avoid that. I'll be home taking it easy. You got this death worshipper case?"

"More corpses than we know what to do with, but hopefully that's the end of this cult."

"It ain't," Orozco breathed to himself, as he made his way out to his Impala. He drove out of the city at sunset, along Insane Asylum Avenue, staring enviously at the couples out on dinner dates and the passersby just on evening strolls. "But none of that's for you, Rafael. All you get is the fucking war," he muttered to himself.

"Stop complaining, Rafael, and hurry to the state park. You must meet up with Gideon, Horace and Albert."

"What about Carmella and the other fighter?"

Silence, the voice did not answer him.

"Nothin' like a two-way street," the policeman grumbled and sped onto the highway. Soon he was tearing along under a starry sky, looking for the exit for Lonely State Park. He found it and shortly was bouncing along a dirt road, then another, then pulled off into the bushes, and clambered out of the car with a knapsack and a flashlight, his gun in a shoulder holster. With the help of the flashlight, he made his way along a marked trail to a clearing, and there, gleaming silver under a crescent moon, large, larger than a man, he saw the scarred and beautiful wings of the seraph. He hurried forward, shoving the flashlight behind him into his backpack, then leapt onto the angel's back, grasping the wings at the joint. "You will lead them across the front," the seraph instructed him, as they rose into the starry night sky, "along a path you know well."

"His Fury's trail," Orozco said.

"Yes, Rafael. Albert needs treatment or he will perish tonight. Hurry and no complaints."

***

"Which way is the front?" Eel asked.

"Shh. Follow me," Carmella whispered, as they stole through the woods. A sound of distant thunder reached their ears.

"You're going to the wrong way," Eel said. "We should go toward the explosions."

"I'd rather not get shot. So we'll just wind around, until we pick up a path I know."

"A path that leads where?"

"To a certain underground tunnel,"

"That goes back to our side? To the trenches?"

"You got it."

"Lead on. Lucky that fighter who rescued us gave you a flashlight."

"Shh. You're looking for a fairly wide path."

They crept along, studying their surroundings with the flashlight's little yellow beam.

"I hope you know what you're doing," Eel said. "'Cause I sure don't."

"I have a general idea. I've been here before."

"Why on earth?"

"Scouting the possibility of attacking from the rear."

"Sounds dangerous."

"It was. We gave it up."

They wandered on through the night, as the explosions grew fainter, and the alien stars in their alien constellations twinkled down on them, illuminating the tracks between the trees and causing Carmella to say that the flashlight was superfluous. She shoved it in a pocket.

"I wish I had a gun," thus Eel, nervously running a hand through his thick brown hair.

"Here, courtesy of one of the guards I killed," and she handed him a pistol.

"What have you got now?"

"My switchblade. I do better with that anyway. Look, this could be it." They stepped out on a wide, leaf-strewn track that wound through the shadowed forms of trees. It was broad enough for a fairly large swath of the night sky to be visible. "We're looking for a boulder, split by a tree growing through it," she said, as they hurried forward. A half an hour passed. The path turned, and there, on the side, grew a crooked tree, right through two halves of an immense gray rock.

Carmella and Eel glanced at each other, her dark eyes, he thought, agleam with something more than just triumph. "We will prevail," she said.

***

"How far are you from the prison?" Orozco asked mentally.

"We've been moving in a straight line away from it for almost an hour," Gideon replied.

"The seraph said he left me in the same place he left you. It appears to be a pine grove. Can you find it?"

"Yes."

"Any pursuers?"

"Not yet, which is lucky. Albert moves slowly. How will we leave when we meet?"

"You'll see me standing by a small, silver, Argan, four-seater fighter jet."

"We'll be shot out of the sky when we try to cross the front."

"Didn't you hear me? I said Argan."

"Do you mean cloaked?"

"Yes, as in invisible to enemy radar or naked eyes."

"We're coming."

"Hurry."

Gideon and Horace supported the sick man, who continued to munch on the herbs that the fighters picked and fed him. After a while, he announced that he could walk unsupported. True enough, he struggled forward and did not fall, but Gideon did not like the look of his travail and so insisted on continuing to hold him up. They followed a narrow dirt path through the trees, as the young man used his flashlight to keep them on it. Thunderous explosions reached their ears.

"We're getting close," thus Horace.

"Let's just pray we're not followed."

"Is it true you're from a sacred planet called earth?" The large, older man asked.

Gideon's jaw dropped open. "You're not supposed to know that."

"I learned by accident. I believe, you see, that I'm telepathically connected to someone, a double of mine, who lives there."

The young fighter ground his teeth. "Forget you ever heard of earth," he growled.

"I only recently became aware of it."

"That's not supposed to happen."

"Spontaneous telepathic connection across universes? I should say not. Who is this Horace MacKenzie on earth? Is he someone special?"

Gideon glared at him. "Forget him. Forget earth. And never breathe a word about either. And if you're ever captured again—"

"I don't intend to be."

"He won't be," Gideon heard Orozco in his mind. "We're removing him from the front. He gets to retire, even if he has become a weapon. He's connected to one of earth's guardians, and he pretty much knows it. He'll be talking to our scientists and chief telepaths as soon as he gets back."

"What for?"

"What for? To figure out how this happened and what it means, that's what for."

The trio crept through the darkling, starlit woods, Gideon fairly confident that he was retracing his steps. Albert seemed to totter less, having eaten quite a load of the medicinal herbs, and so the young man allowed himself to hope they would escape. Now and then he paused, gun in hand, to listen for any pursuers, but he heard none. It wasn't until he saw the tall, lean form of the detective, resting against a little jet, that he heard in his mind, "they have become aware of the escape and are organizing a search party."

"Too late," Orozco said aloud and helped Albert into one of the jet's back seats. Horace also climbed in back, Gideon and Orozco in front. "I was informed you're a pilot," the policeman said.

"But I never flew an Argan plane before."

"No matter," the older man said. "I have. They're very straightforward and really only need one pilot. So, unless you object, I say we quit this shithole." With that, he pressed a few buttons, and the jet rose vertically into the air. Gideon turned to gaze out the window. In the distance he saw the grimy yellow sheen from the prison searchlights. "They're hunting us," he told Orozco.

"Too bad for them," the policeman replied, maneuvering the vehicle directly toward the front. "They ain't gonna find us."

***

By the time they soared over the enemy battlefield, Gideon was assisting at the controls. "You're a quick study," Orozco commented.

"Well, like you observed, this is pretty straightforward." Below them, death worshippers crouched in their foxholes, while tanks that were only recently unscratchable rumbled toward the barbed wire that separated the two sides.

"Almost there," the policeman breathed, as the sturdy little craft approached this border.

"We're lucky it's night," Gideon remarked.

"Luck has nothing to do with it. That was the plan."

In the last five minutes before they landed safely behind their lines, Orozco thought with satisfaction of the whole operation. The only discomfort came when he considered Carmella and Eel, wandering in the enemy forest. They would get through that, surely. Carmella was smart enough and sharp enough to pull that off. But how would they cross the enemy battlefield without getting shot? He voiced this worry to Gideon, who said he believed there were tunnels. This news assuaged his anxiety, for now the only concern was that they should find a tunnel. But this trouble nagged at him so much that even as he set the little aircraft down on a heliport, he felt the scarcely controllable urge to return, search for them and rescue them. But Horace, alarmed when his pilot voiced this wish, placated him with the information that Carmella had used those tunnels before. This at last set Orozco's mind at rest. She had travelled beneath enemy lines before. She knew how to find an entrance to a tunnel in the forest. She and Eel would survive. For once, he thought with a surge of relief, he had participated in an operation in which none of his people had died. Now if only the war itself could go as well!

But it did not. For twenty seven years on earth and far longer at the front, humanity's position had deteriorated, reaching at last such a tatterdemalion nadir that an entire reality was collapsing, while fighters' corpses littered the battlefield. Considering this, now as always, Orozco found himself wondering if the human race could survive, or if it would be largely expunged from the cosmos, except for a few Spartan outposts like the Argan universe. Unfortunately, he found it all too easy, given what he had witnessed, to envisage such a barren future, one in which the race of men, long on the run, had burrowed into its last hiding places and had abandoned the front completely. Then would come Armageddon, he had no doubt. He Who did not wish to see the race of men destroyed would react with fury, annihilating His enemies—or worse. But there would be no men and women, or at best just some small remnant, like the inhabitants of sector three thousand three hundred thirty three, to witness this final victory. Deep in these gloomy thoughts, Orozco found himself startled to see Ivan approach the helipad and take Albert under the arm. "Did you get into their computers?" Was all he asked.

The sick man nodded, groaned "yes, and it's worse than we thought. They know about earth." Two medics rushed up and placed the collapsing man on a stretcher, then hurried away with him.

"You needn't worry about me," Horace addressed the head of the council. "I give you a fighter's word that earth's secret remains right here," he tapped his heart, "never here," he tapped his lips.

"It was providence that you connected with Horace on earth," Ivan commented. "I never thought I'd say that. But if you hadn't, we wouldn't have known what became of Albert."

"You better debrief him before he dies," Gideon said.

"They injected him with some new pathogen," thus Horace. "If we can isolate it in a blood sample, we have a chance to save his life." All four walked to the bunker.

"What about Carmella and Eel?" Orozco demanded.

"We wait," Ivan answered.

Deep inside the bunker, alarms were blaring, as an old one-armed military scientist, accompanied by a one-armed, one-eyed fighter named Axel rushed up to Ivan. "More collapse in sector one thousand," the old scientist told the council leader.

"In the same general vicinity?" Ivan asked, striding quickly now down the corridor.

"No," Axel replied, "elsewhere entirely."

Ivan swung open a door to a conference room, filled, Orozco noted, with all the members of the council. "Before I leave I should tell you," he took Ivan by the elbow, "death worshippers from the realm of shadow are invading earth."

"I read your report," Ivan said, "which is why you and Gideon here are heading straight back home."

"It is? What for?"

"To stop them," Ivan snapped, green eyes blazing. "And you better stop them. Don't let me down, Orozco—you neither, Cohen." And with that he slammed the door shut to take over the meeting.

***

"Horace has a big house, I don't. You can stay with him," Orozco said, as they traversed the bunker.

"What about Starfield?"

"He'll continue to baby sit. You'll be busy with me. And then, Horace is a guardian, so we can use him to try to figure out exactly where this threat comes from, how they're entering our world."

Speaking these words, the policeman felt better. Somehow they made the situation appear manageable, as though the myriad problems they faced had discoverable solutions, and were not, as he feared, of such a gigantic order of magnitude as to be utterly insoluble. He was relieved to note that these words soothed Gideon as well, as that young man, tense and angry, began visibly to relax. "Where do we start?" Gideon demanded.

"With the files Starfield downloaded," Orozco answered, then paused, his head raised, listening, "a new person will have to be brought in. You will learn more when you're back on earth."

"Uh-oh," he breathed aloud.

"What uh-oh?" Gideon demanded.

"A new person's coming in on this."

"Not a fighter."

"Not a fighter."

"That's a bad sign."

"You're telling me," the policeman snarled and quickened his pace. They were practically running now, and soon descended a stairwell, then followed the corridor to the end into a trench. Both fighters began to jog. Ahead of them, far from the actual front, glimmered huge silver wings, toward which, now, they ran. Orozco reached a seraph first and leapt onto his back. As they soared up, he saw Gideon on another angel, rising too.

"A new one!" He exclaimed to the seraph. "That's not good."

"The situation is dire," he heard in response.

"Who is it?"

"Someone you know well."

"Who?"

"Your partner, Harry McNeil."

The fighter lapsed into a stunned silence.

"You will need him, and he'll need you."

"What for?"

"To track down the death worshipper who has opened a door between earth and the realm of shadow."

"Wouldn't it make more sense just to shut the door?"

"He *is* the door. He is in a trance, in direct contact with murderers in the realm of shadow. Through him, they enter earth."

"Sounds like this is one death worshipper who needs to die."

The seraph turned his head, glancing over his shoulder at his passenger, before zooming down into a gyre of swirling galaxies. "The sooner the better," he said.

***

Harry McNeil circled the death worshipper's computer, hooked up on a desk in the middle of the room and studied it from every angle. It was night. The office was empty. The lights were dim. "It won't happen again," he said aloud and approached the computer. He placed his hands on the monitor, at which very instant images of a fatally deformed and befouled landscape, overflowing with toxic waste and human corpses filled his mind. In horror, he removed his hands. The vision vanished. He held his hands up, studied them, then regarded the computer with alarm. The phone on his desk rang. It rang and rang, before he could pull himself together enough to answer it.

"McNeil here."

"It's Rafael."

"Rafael—that computer you gave me. It's causing me to lose my mind."

"No. No, no, no. You are not crazy, just ignorant."

"Every time I touch it, I hallucinate."

"Get the fuck away from it for a minute or two," Orozco shouted. "Get in your squad car and come to 333 Apocalypse Avenue—got that?"

"Three, three, three."

"Yeah. I got answers to all your questions."

"I'm glad someone does."

"And Harry—your hallucinations?"

"What about them?"

"I want to hear every detail. Every. Single. Detail."

Shortly thereafter a very pale, very scared Harry McNeil stood on the threshold of Horace MacKenzie's townhouse. "Get in here," Orozco snapped, opening the door and pulling his partner into the front hall. "What the fuck is going on?" Harry cried.

Orozco shut the door behind him. "You stumbled onto something that's a lot bigger than you are, that's what." He took Harry by the arm and led him into the study, where a very tired, strained Starfield sat at the computer, while tall, burly Horace snored in a leather armchair, his head thrown back.

"Where's Gideon?" Orozco snapped.

"In the kitchen, getting drunk. He says there's no way under the sun we can find this death worshipper, and earth's fate is sealed, kaput, finished, done," Starfield replied.

Harry looked from Starfield to his partner. "Harry, you remember Starfield."

"Hey, I read your stuff in *The Daily Watcher*," Harry exclaimed, running a hand through his short blond hair and gazing from Starfield to Orozco.

"Yeah well, Starfield here is the man who downloaded everything that was on your magic computer and loaded it into that computer," Orozco pointed to the monitor on the desk. "The computer I gave you was...sanitized. Sorry Harry. It was for your own good. I saw no reason to bring you in on this nightmare, if it wasn't absolutely necessary."

"How did you know to call me?"

"Don't ask."

"Shit. Well then, what did Starfield here download?"

"Switch places, gentlemen," Orozco said, whereupon the journalist rose and the still pale and drawn policeman took his seat. "Starfield, you help him find his way through these files. Once he's up to speed, get me. I need a beer and a nap."

With that, the lean and grizzled policeman tromped out of the study and down the hall to the kitchen.

"So he's freaking out?" Gideon slurped his wine from a goblet, as the older man entered the kitchen and grabbed a beer from the fridge.

"He hallucinates every time he touches the enemy computer, at least when it's hooked up. Dollars to donuts he's seein' the realm of shadow itself, the real, putrid, unvarnished charnel house it is."

"How come he hallucinates when he touches it, but we didn't?"

"I don't know, but I can tell you this—that's why we need him."

"He can help us find this fascist in chief? The one who's bringing all these thugs to earth?"

"That's my hunch."

The two men stared at each other and guzzled their drinks.

"We are in deep shit, brother," Gideon said at last.

"Yeah, when we need someone who's not even a fighter to stop an invasion from the realm of shadow? What can I say?"

"The world's falling apart at the seams," Gideon replied. "That's what you can say."

***

A while later, as Orozco lay dozing in an upstairs guestroom, Harry turned away from the computer and stared at Starfield. "So it's a world-wide conspiracy."

"Oh, it's a lot worse than that," Starfield replied.

"This…realm of shadow, where they're coming from, I find it hard to believe,"

"Believe it!" Horace boomed, raising his head from the back of the chair. "The realm of shadow is an unspeakable place, a charnel house."

At these words, McNeil started, "a charnel house? With lots of dead bodies?"

"Corpses everywhere, toxic waste everywhere, from what we know, from the visions transmitted to us, it is one of the worst places in this or any universe."

McNeil ran a muscular hand over his worried features, "and that computer I touched, the one in my car, that gave me hallucinations,"

"Visions," Horace corrected, "and it is not *any* computer. It's an enemy computer."

"The enemy," Starfield elaborated, "is not human, though plenty of men follow him. We call them death worshippers."

"Yeah, my partner used that term," McNeil sat up straight. "Orozco wasn't really sick when he took leave, was he?"

Starfield shook his head.

"He was working on this case."

"He was at the front," Horace boomed.

"The front? What front?"

Gideon loomed in the doorway, "the absolute front, where all of us fighters are doubtless doomed to die."

"How long has Rafael been a fighter? And who or what are fighters?"

"Since he was a child," Gideon explained, still slurping from his wine glass, "and fighters are people persecuted, hounded by the enemy, but who fight back, assisted by Him."

"By Him? Who dat?"

"Who do you think?"

"I think you're all a bunch of religious nuts, that's what I think."

"Hey, you're the one with the hallucinations," Gideon snapped.

"The visions," Horace corrected. "The direct visions of the realm of shadow. This has only happened once or twice before." He stared at McNeil. "It was how we learned what we know of this dreadful place."

Upstairs Orozco opened his eyes. "Rise Rafael. The enemy is afoot. There is much you must see."

"Shit," the policeman mumbled, sitting up and rubbing his rough face with his very large, strong hands. "What I gotta see?"

"Sector one thousand, on the computer, now."

"I sure hope you ain't plannin' to send me there, 'cause I already volunteered and Vivaldi nixed it. And since then, I changed my mind. I want nothing to do with some doomed sector one thousand."

"Hurry, Rafael."

"All right, all right," the detective strapped on his shoulder holster, stood up and tromped downstairs, calling "Starfield! Starfield! I need your computer."

"What now?" The journalist demanded, as Orozco loomed in the study doorway.

"I gotta see what's going on at the front."

"The front!" McNeil exclaimed.

"Or rather sector one thousand, the newest portion of the front. Sorry Harry, I'll explain later." Orozco sat at the computer, tapped at a few keys, and suddenly the image of huge, silvery, scarred and beautiful wings, advancing on a phalanx of black-clad commanders filled the screen.

"My God!" McNeil exclaimed.

White-hot fireball after white-hot fireball shot from the angels to the commanders, incinerating them, but as one fell, another always stepped forward to take his place.

"That, McNeil, is the front," said Gideon.

Orozco tapped again, the image changed, showed a huge city in flames.

"And that's sector one thousand," Orozco spoke grimly. "Where everyone's screamin' and runnin' for their lives, 'cept there's nowhere to go." He turned to face his partner, whose gaze was riveted on the image of an immense, panicked crowd, fleeing between walls of burning buildings. "All my leaves, all my illnesses, Harry?" Orozco began. "I wasn't sick. I was at the front, where we fight and die and lose the war for mankind. Not that we want to lose, we're givin' it everything, but it still ain't enough. Time to grow up, buddy."

"Where is sector one thousand?" McNeil demanded.

"It's another universe."

"And there are people in other universes?"

"Lots of 'em. We meet their fighters all the time, at the front."

"I find this rather hard to believe," Harry began.

"Then go put your hands back on the enemy computer in your squad car once you got it hooked up and pretend you just dropped LSD. 'Cause you're the one with the visions of the realm of shadow, not me, thank you know Who."

Harry stared, "you know Who being?"

"Him. He who does not wish to see us destroyed. He who is at the front, always, who's been waging this war since the beginning of human time."

The image on the screen changed, an immense swarm of big, ugly, ominous, black space ships filled the skies over a vast city.

"That's the enemy," Orozco said quietly. "That's those fascist sons of bitches with their snazzy killing technology, all devoted to one purpose."

"Which is?" Harry demanded.

"Destroying, murdering, extirpating humanity from this and every universe in the cosmos. That's the enemy's purpose, Harry, and he's well on his way to achieving it."

"But God in heaven,"

"Oh, He'll win. That has never been in doubt," Orozco turned away from the computer and sat facing his partner, then bowed his head, "it's just that men and women may not be around to celebrate," he glanced up. "A lot depends on the fighters, Harry, and not just the fighters. The friends of the fighters, people like Starfield here, people like you."

"And on another class of people, almost another species of people," Horace boomed, sitting bolt upright.

"Shut up, Horace," Orozco snapped.

"He needs to know. Earth is not undefended."

"Shut up."

"You've gone this far," Harry said to his partner. "You might as well let the man tell me the rest."

Gideon snarled something unintelligible and left the room.

"No!" Orozco snarled in turn. "Some things remain secret." The policeman glared at the guardian. "We're going up against death worshippers, Horace. What if Harry gets caught?"

"You think I can't keep my mouth shut?" Harry demanded belligerently.

"Better not to be put to the test, pal."

"All right, all right. Keep your secrets. What you told me already is, frankly, wild enough,"

"Wild?" Orozco demanded, then hollered. "Gideon! Gideon!"

When that young man loomed in the doorway, the policeman nodded at his partner, "toss Gideon your car keys. Starfield, you help bring in that enemy computer. It's the black Impala right out that window," and Orozco pointed.

138

At mention of the enemy computer, McNeil had once again paled. "I ain't touchin' it," he said to his partner.

"You have to. What you see and hear could lead us to the fascists who are bringing their shock troops to earth. There's one death worshipper in particular,"

"Christ, Rafael, what the fuck have you got me into?"

"Not me. I argued against bringing you in. But I was overruled by a, ahem, higher authority."

"By Him?" Harry was incredulous.

"By one of his generals, those generals with the long, silvery wings, who you saw on the screen a few moments ago."

Harry tossed his car keys to Gideon, who left with Starfield.

"How long you been doin' this?" He asked in a low voice.

"Running from the enemy since I was four," Orozco answered. "Fighting at the front since I was a teenager."

"What is this front?"

"It's the place where two implacably opposed realities are bombing the shit out of each other, and it's terrifying."

"You just got back from there?"

Orozco nodded, "and frankly, I'd much rather chase bad guys right here on planet earth, even if they include the death worshipping honcho of all honchos, rather than endure another tour of duty at the front."

The Israeli fighter and the journalist reentered the room, carrying all the pieces of the computer. Horace glanced at Orozco. "You know I will see what he sees," he began sourly.

"I did *not* know that," the policeman said, helping to hook up the computer on a side-table.

"It doesn't need to be hooked up," Harry spoke in an exhausted voice. "I still get a pretty bizarre reaction when it's off."

"Worse if it's on, I'll warrant," thus Orozco.

"Yeah," his partner replied, "now that you mention it."

"Then for starters, let's not turn it on," Horace said. "This is one guardian who believes the less contact with the realm of shadow the better."

"What's a guardian?" Harry demanded.

"Shit," Orozco nearly spat.

"That's what I'm not supposed to know about, right?"

"Yeah, and let's keep it that way," Orozco replied.

Harry McNeil leaned back in his chair, placed his fingertips together and studied his partner. "This enemy," he began.

"This homicidal, fascist, totalitarian organization of men and non-humans, yes?"

"I learned about him in church."

"You learned only old myths in church. The reality is a whole lot worse. Our enemy is very modern, especially in the torture and weapons department."

"How could he be winning?"

"Good question. The question of the hour in fact, and we are all eagerly awaiting enlightenment."

"Shit," Harry said.

"Why shit?"

"'Cause I'm starting to believe you," he glanced at the computer, which Gideon had finally plugged into a surge protector. "What is this realm of shadow? Tell me more."

"A place where they send captured fighters to be tortured, interrogated and murdered, aka the kingdom of night, of slavery and never-ending labor for most of its denizens. A land conquered by the enemy eons ago."

"And I'm in contact with this, this,"

"Abomination? Apparently yes, when you touch that computer, which we need you to do, since earth is being invaded by death worshippers from the realm of shadow, and we need to figure out how, where, when and who, so we can put a stop to it."

Horace opened his mouth to speak, but Gideon cut him short. "Are you done revealing every last thing you can think of?"

The guardian started. "I'm trying to help."

"Then keep quiet," the young fighter snarled. "We got enough on our hands without you blabbing secrets that were never, never meant to be told."

Orozco walked over to his partner. "We're gonna leave the friggin' thing off. You put your hands on it and tell us everything you see. Omit nothing."

"You sure I just don't need some antipsychotic medication, 'cause that would make a whole lot more sense."

"Time's awastin', Harry. You saw what the guys who owned this computer did. They ain't scared of us, not the police, not the military."

"And you say that's because they know they got the edge."

The leathery old policeman nodded.

"All right," his partner sighed, approached the computer and placed both hands on the CPU. At once he shivered and stared straight ahead in alarm, his blue eyes focused on some invisible, distant point. "I see a phalanx of men in black. They're marching on a road. They have swords hanging from their belts and machine guns slung across their backs. They all have tattoos, like we saw on the guys we killed. Around them, there's some sort of burnt-out power station, some industrial site in ruins. There's a neon green stream along the road, with corpses floating face down in it."

"What are they marching toward?" Orozco asked.

"It's night. It's hard to see, but I think, something ahead of them is swirling, it's an opening of some sort. It's kind of hypnotic to stare at it."

"Then look away every few seconds," Orozco said. "What do you see in this opening?"

Harry's jaw dropped. He removed his hands from the computer, then replaced them, stared, then removed them again and looked into each of the anxious faces of the four other men in the room. "Earth," he said. "Earth is what I see in that opening."

***

The five men stood and sat in the study and stared at the enemy computer. Alarm had spread over all five faces. The two fighters glanced at each other. "I'm gonna have to put in a request," Orozco spoke quietly, "to bring most of earth's fighters home." Gideon nodded.

But Horace frowned. "Not necessarily so," he said. "You told me one, *one* death worshipper was responsible for opening this door between kingdoms."

Orozco nodded, ran a big hand over his worried features and took another gulp from his beer bottle.

"Well then, do what you fighters do—reason!" Horace commanded.

"You think," Harry spoke meditatively, "if we can find that one,"

"Find and kill that one," Orozco corrected.

"Find and kill him," Harry continued, "that we could close this, this door?"

"Yes," Horace nodded. "Any other approach will ultimately cause a global panic. War in the streets between fighters and death worshippers will be very difficult to conceal from the public. And once people get the idea what really is going on—it will be chaos. Far better for you three—Rafael, Gideon and Harry—to find this man,"

"Assuming it's a man," thus Gideon.

"We have been assured it is," Orozco replied.

"Well, thank God for small favors," Starfield breathed.

"Find him," Horace said. "Eliminate him, and the door closes, at least, Rafael, if I understand correctly what you told me about him being in some sort of trance that has opened this pathway between earth and the kingdom of night."

"Harry will have to find him. That's why he was brought in," Orozco said, then turned to his partner. "I'm sorry to have to say this, but we need more of your, your,"

"Hallucinations?"

"Visions."

"Fine, but not tonight. I'm wiped."

"It's almost midnight," Horace said. "I have three guestrooms and two of them have twin beds. I suggest we rest now and tackle this monster again in the morning. By the way, Harry, I saw only some of what you saw, but I heard something you apparently didn't."

"What?" Orozco demanded, finishing his beer.

"Ringstrasse."

"Ringstrasse!" Starfield cried. "That's Vienna!"

Horace clasped his hands and leaned forward, glancing from Harry to the two fighters. "Anyone up for a little international travel?"

***

The two fighters moved through the dim tunnel stealthily, guided only by the little yellow beam of the flashlight. At first they had to watch out for roots, waiting motionlessly to trip them up, like the hands and feet of the dead. But after a while, there were no more roots, which told the two travelers that they were under the treeless terrain of the battlefield. No sound, however, no rumble, no explosion was audible, so deep were they; the dirt walls, the damp dirt floor, the dirt ceiling, just stretched ahead of them, silent, empty, unknown to the enemy.

"I could eat a horse," thus Carmella, "even that sickening soup they fed us in jail."

"Me too, sister," Eel replied. "And hopefully we'll be in the cafeteria soon."

"Ooh, a Danish and a coffee."

"Me, I'm having some of that tofu that tastes just like steak," Eel said, "with green beans and mashed potatoes, nothing fancy, just filling, just to plug this enormous hole between my gullet and my butt."

"They'll put us in the infirmary first."

"Infirmary food's good."

"Better than what we been getting. You suppose that Gideon made it back with our friends?"

"He said he was telepathically connected to another fighter nearby. You know what that means."

"No fuckups. He doesn't want anything going wrong," she said.

"From which I conclude nothing did."

"You're an optimist," Carmella said, wiping her perspiration-soaked forehead with a forearm.

"Never heard of a screw-up when one of those links was active."

"I have."

"Really?"

"Not many but a few."

"Shit, you just dissolved my one last pillar of faith that at least something we do was unbeatable."

"Sorry."

They hurried on in silence, for what seemed like an eternity, each thinking alternately of food and then loved ones, the woman of her daughter, Liliana in the city of D____, living with a relative, since Carmella's husband, Roberto, was at the front in sector one thousand, which, every time she considered it, filled her with dread, for prior to her capture, the news from that reality had been terrible—the thought of enemy commanders and interrogators running amok in a universe inhabited by people terrified her. And with each bulletin from sector one thousand, each worse than the last, the conviction, which had taken root early, grew in her mind that at last this dreadful war would make her a widow.

"What are you thinking about?" Eel asked.

"Survival."

"And the odds against it?"

"Yes, for me and my husband."

"My wife's a fighter too."

"Well, at least she's home on earth, which is more than you can say for poor Roberto."

"That sector one thousand sounds like the fucking apocalypse."

"Let's not talk about it."

So they travelled on in silence and finally, finally, began to climb, the tunnel at last dead-ending in a stairwell. Up they went, opened the door and found themselves in a small section of trench, surrounded by wire fencing. "Hey you! Guard! Wake up! It's me, Carmella Marquez and another fighter. We're escapees."

Two guards scrambled down into the trench, one of them jingling keys. "Hey captain, is it really you?'

"Yes it is," she shone the flashlight on her face. "We just busted out of an enemy prison, and we're starvin'."

"You go to the infirmary first," the other guard said, as the wire door swung open.

"Well, they've got food. Did you hear if our friends escaped too?"

"Four fighters made it here tonight across enemy lines in a cloaked, Argan jet."

Carmella stopped, put her hands on her hips and glared at Eel in disgust. "They got a cloaked jet, while we had to scrabble in the frikkin' dirt."

"Come on," the guard hurried her. "They gotta do your blood-work."

An hour later, as both escapees sat propped up in infirmary beds, eating second dinners, Ivan hurried over to Carmella.

"They made it?" She queried, her mouth full of mashed potatoes.

"Yes."

"Well, my cellmate didn't, Brianna Apt. Her husband's here at the front. I gotta break the news to him."

"I can do that."

"No you can't. I have a message. And you know those messages are sacred."

"Which ones?" Eel asked, inhaling his second portion of tofu.

"The ones from the dead to the living," she replied.

***

The priest sat in his little cinderblock room mentally grappling with a conundrum. He had just met Axel, whom he judged to be a ferocious atheist and one who bore much ill will toward the clergy. Yet this man, this fighter, heard a sacred voice in his mind and heeded it. How could he do so and retain his tenacious unbelief? Vivaldi poked around this contradiction, studied it from every side and finally had to admit it flummoxed him. It puzzled him. The pieces did not fit. "If I suddenly heard a voice in my mind, after being hit, and that voice instructed me on how to avoid being hit again, if it told me when to shoot at a death worshipper, who was trying to kill me, and was correct, I would certainly begin to doubt my atheism. And I certainly would not regard the angels who transported me from one world to the next as aliens."

"Part of why you hear that voice so rarely is that you do not need it," he heard, deep within the recesses of his mind.

"You mean if I had doubts, I'd hear you more often?"

"This line of thought is a waste of time. You must assist the female fighter, when she arrives on Sere."

"I intend to."

"But you will be in sector one thousand."

"I will travel there after Sere, yes."

"You will assist her from there. You will be linked."

"Ah, Orozco has told me about this. But I have never been linked before."

"Before it was not necessary."

"I thought only fighters were linked."

"You stand corrected."

Vivaldi's gray eyebrows knit down in perplexity. He would be telepathically linked to a fighter, to a fighter who had been tortured in an enemy supermax prison, far, far behind the lines. Before he could articulate his thought, he heard: "Fear not. Her experience of the enemy, of the abuse she suffered, will be sealed off from you, as it is, in fact, sealed off from her."

He laid back on his little cot and thought of his world, Alinia, blue and green, across the Milky Way galaxy from earth, also blue and green, and then his mind wandered to wintry white and gray Sere, to the brown wooden and mud huts of the tribes, the huge, rocky mountains, the vast glaciers, the relief of the temperate zone—his mind wandered, drifted, then slept and dreamt of the war and his friends in the war, of Orozco, of Lontra, of the countless children he had shepherded from ghastly bereavement into new homes. Then at last even those images vanished, and he tumbled into the welcome oblivion of deep, deep sleep, where unbeknownst to his conscious mind, that voice he had heard in his thoughts, continued, quite purposively, to do its work in his untroubled soul.

∗∗∗

The detective flung himself down on one of the twin beds, while Harry sat on the other and stared at him. "If I didn't know better, I'd say we're all psycho."

"I wish," Orozco grumbled, his nose and mouth pressed into the pillow.

"But I saw those killers earlier today. They had no fear of our swat team, and what's more, they wore the same outfits and had the same tattoos as those thugs I hallucinated."

"You didn't hallucinate."

"Yeah, what would you call it?"

"You saw reality, another reality, one that, unfortunately, is a lot closer to ours than it should be."

"How long has this war been raging?"

"Millennia, that's what we were told."

"And we been losing all that time?"

"Nope, only in the past thirty years," Orozco flipped over on his back and unbuttoned his shirt. "There was some treachery."

"For the first time in millennia?" Harry guffawed.

"For the first time in a long time, centuries. But remember, that was the generation that brought us Nazi Germany and World War II. And there's darn good reason to suspect enemy tampering on poor old earth during the 1930s and 1940s."

"In church they said the enemy had been around since the beginning."

"Yeah well, in church they get a few things right and a few things wrong."

"But the broad outlines are right?"

"More or less. It's different. Look, I'm a fighter. I lived my life around fighters. I don't go to church, some of them, they don't even believe in God."

"Who do they think they're fighting for?"

"Don't ask. They have a very dark view, evil is ascendant and all that. But they fight, they fight and they die and they are good men and women. But their thinkin' is screwed up, probably due to all the persecution they suffered. Anyway, I ain't got time to figure it out now. I need sleep. The enemy, you know, he don't sleep."

"No, I didn't know."

"Well, now you do. Sleep is a blessing, a gift from Him. I thought you needed to know that, Harry."

"Why?"

"'Cause you're keeping me awake, darn it. Now shut up and sleep."

Soon the sound of snores rumbled through Horace MacKenzie's spacious townhouse, as the guardian, the fighters and their friends all slept and filled 333 Apocalypse Avenue with dreams of the war.

***

It was late at night. Lying in a trench, behind a rock, Lontra awoke from a deep sleep and stared up at the nocturnal heaven. In the portion of the sky visible from the odd angle at which she lay gleamed the long, thin, Argan needles, like silver minnows near the murky bottom of a pond. She gazed at the flank of them, shimmering gently and thought of Ein; as she did so, the needle her eyes had settled on glowed once, then disappeared. "Back to Argas, I guess," she murmured, then turned her head to survey all the rest, wondering if others would depart. None did. She had never set foot inside a needle, and as for Argas itself, all

149

she knew was the mythology, but at that moment she found herself more than curious, almost longing to sojourn there. "Because it is mankind's last, best hope," she heard in her mind. "But is it really?" She asked aloud.

"Really. And though you don't see it yet, someday you will—your fate is tied up with Argas, as is that of innumerable fighters at the front and in other sectors."

"They're so severe," she thought.

"And you're not?"

Whereupon this inner colloquy drifted off on tides of slumber, in blessed currents of the oblivion of sleep.

***

Meanwhile, inside that needle that Lontra saw depart sat Ein, Saltwater, Lindin and over a hundred Argan fighters, returning home from the front. All had craned their necks to get a glimpse of the famous weapons designer when he boarded the needle: as his first foot set down on the floor of the craft, a cheer went up, "Ein! Ein! Ein! Hurray for Ein!"

"I guess that's what happens when you hide your reality from the enemy," Saltwater remarked.

"We're travelling with a celebrity," Lindin said.

By now the men and women in the needle were on their feet, applauding, while the object of their admiration looked on, quiet and abashed. That didn't stop them, though. They kept hooting and hurrahing and clapping, until Saltwater said, "come on, Ein, let's get a seat."

"Thank you, thank you again," Ein kept murmuring.

Once seated, the famous Ein explained that it was necessary to wear their seat belts tightly strapped for the entire journey, which would, he assured them, be brief.

"But why?" Lindin asked.

"Very, very rarely, electromagnetic anomalies are encountered in wormholes."

"Is that why no windows?"

"No. No windows because there's nothing, literally, to see."

Saltwater gazed at the many Argans all around them, all modestly dressed, all with the weary faces of fighters who had been at the front for months, in some cases years, but on all were those traces of elation he knew so well: after a long tour of duty, they were still alive, the enemy had not killed them and, who knew, they might not be called back to the front for years to come. That elation was most familiar to him. He had felt it more times than he could count, just as he had felt the sinking fear and anxiety when, deep within his mind, he heard a voice telling him it was time to make his way into the wilderness to leave for the front. In the beginning it had been different—back when he was a teenager and in his early twenties, hope had always accompanied him to the front, hope that his side would soon prevail. But as the losses began to mount and his friends to be killed, he had come to dread the summons to war, not so much because he feared for himself, though there was plenty of that, but because he could not bear the thought of witnessing, yet again, evil stalemating good. For that stalemate was, in effect, a triumph. Anything less than a defeat of the enemy was a triumph for him—so Saltwater felt and so did most of his brethren. Very few fighters could sugarcoat their defeat with the thought, "well, at least we didn't lose outright."

And then there was the omnipresent fear of capture and being remanded to the realm of shadow, a fate, regarded by all, understood by all, to be worse than death. The pockmarked man looked into the faces of the men and women in the homeward-bound needle, he studied these Argans, still applauding his friend, and all he saw was relief. They had survived the front. For now, they did not have to fight.

To his surprise, he heard Ein voicing exactly these thoughts. "I should have to make only one more trip here, to install Seymour once we've developed him. Then, hopefully, I can remain on Argas."

"But your new weapons," Lindin interrupted. "Don't you have to come here to demonstrate?"

"Other scientists can do that."

"So your goal, like every fighter's, is to spend as little time at the front as possible," the pockmarked man almost smiled.

"I am human. The spectacle of our defeat wears me down. And don't tell me it's not defeat, that we're still in the ring. I know that. But when you consider Who is on our side, anything short of outright victory is too close to defeat to be borne."

"Maybe Seymour will turn the tide of the war," Lindin said.

"Let's hope," Ein replied. "Something sure better."

They talked for almost an hour, Ein exhibiting that strange combination of diffidence and forcefulness that marked all Argans, but in him seemed especially pronounced. He had tried his hand at creating artificial life before, but had been dragged away from the project by the demands of a universe at war. For the past three decades, he explained, he had done nothing besides develop new weapons, in response to the monthly reports, footage, bulletins from the front—how the enemy had an undentable tank, now they had new and worse cluster bombs, now they had a biological weapon and could he quick develop a vaccine? And on and on. "It never seems to stop," he sighed.

Throughout this conversation, the vehicle thrummed gently. When it stopped, a recorded voice told them that the needle had docked safely on the pincushion and to walk to the front of the craft to exit. They did so and found themselves in a vast terminal, miles up from the surface of the planet Argas, visible through windows on one side, while myriad needles, poked out from the terminal on another.

"Why are some bigger, smaller and differently shaped than the one we travelled in?" Lindin asked.

"Some are for intergalactic travel, some for interstellar and some are just for hopping around in this solar system." Saltwater had wandered up to a window and pressed his nose against the glass. "You sure have a ton of rings circling your planet."

Ein nodded. "They're all for different uses."

"One of them looks like a rain forest," Saltwater observed, "and look, there's plenty of green on the planet's surface."

"Those are man-made parks."

"But they're still green."

"Not enough. There's not enough wilderness on Argas, and considering the planet is built up so high, as well as almost two miles underground, you'd think our military leaders could cede some space to flora and fauna. But they are very rigid. That comes from constant contact with the front. They may be here, but they spend all day in virtual conversations with fighters, getting casualty lists and descriptions of new enemy weapons. The war is life for our generals and, frankly, it has deformed their souls."

"Deformities which they then impose on everyone else," the pockmarked man remarked.

Ein nodded, his gray eyes serious, as he ran his fingers through his gray crew-cut.

"They may be deformities," Lindin observed, "but they have produced one society that, I think, will endure, even if we lose the war."

"Let's not talk about that," Ein grimaced. "Let's catch a shuttle to the surface."

"I wanted to take the space elevator," Saltwater complained.

"That's for cargo, not people."

"Shit. I finally arrive at a civilization advanced enough to have multi-mile space elevators, and I'm told, 'no people.'"

"Military regulations," Ein said, as he led them to the moving sidewalk.

The shuttle terminal was crowded with people, most in the sober gray of Argas, but some in brightly colored getups, which, Saltwater surmised aloud, indicated arrivals from matriarchal worlds. Ein nodded absent-mindedly, as he scanned a board with departure lists. "They leave every half hour," he said, "and we just missed the 2:30, so, might as well go sit at the gate."

"So I hear you're a friend of the famous ghost," the pockmarked man chatted, as they sat down.

Again Ein nodded. "I knew Lontra's rescuers, too. In fact, I helped plot their itinerary and I armed them, and made sure they were properly vaccinated."

"Did they need special weapons?"

"Oooh yes, and in fact, I'll be working with them again, long distance. They're in sector one thousand."

"Sector of doom, you mean."

"Let's hope not."

"Reason it out, Ein."

"I have. The prospects for that reality are very poor." With that, he fell morosely silent, as did his two companions, until suddenly a tall man with bushy black hair and a gray outfit hurried over to them. "You're back!" He cried.

"Yes, Allen. Meet Saltwater and Lindin from one of the numbered universes."

"Fighters?"

"Of course."

154

"Then they should be interested in our fireballs, ready to deploy to sector one thousand."

"They're ready!" Ein cried.

His friend nodded.

"Do they work on commanders?"

"No, we couldn't solve the problem. But they work on almost all nonhuman underlings, and from what I've heard, there are hoards of those in sector one thousand."

"We must continue the research. Destroying commanders is our goal, Allen, never forget that."

"I won't, but in the meantime, there's this little matter of a collapsing reality."

"You'll be in the lab tomorrow morning?"

Allen nodded. "But right now, I gotta grab a latte before I meet and greet a mucky muck from the next system."

"How much of Argas did the enemy get a look at?" Lindin asked.

"Very little, a remote, underdeveloped galaxy. We pray he concluded it was just a backwater and not worth his time. And so far, our prayers appear to have been answered."

"You obscured the point of contact, right?" The pockmarked man asked.

"We cloaked it, then destroyed the stranded death worshipper encampment, yes."

"Won't the enemy wonder about such a sophisticated concealment?"

"We made it look like one of those electromagnetic anomalies I mentioned before."

"Fortunately for you," Lindin said, "they have no feelings or rules about soldiers left behind, who are, in my experience, entirely on their own."

"As you've observed, the enemy does not value the lives of his human soldiers," Ein said.

"Nor the non-human ones. No help came for the commandant who was not human, when the angels assaulted the killing center," Saltwater said.

"Let's just say, this enemy does not value life."

"Except his own," Saltwater snarled.

"One day that will end," Ein said. "We have been promised," he concluded, rising, "ah, time to board."

"At last a vehicle with windows!" Saltwater exclaimed, gazing at the shuttle through the terminal's plexiglass.

"This section is a commuter hub?" Lindin asked.

Ein nodded, as the trio entered the shuttle and took their seats.

"What? No applause?" the pockmarked man asked. "What's wrong with these people?"

"They are not fighters from the front," Ein replied, accepting a little juice bottle from a flight attendant.

"Well, here's to fighters from the front," Saltwater held up his bottle and guzzled.

"I'll drink to that," Lindin said.

Ein smiled, an expression both happy and grim at the same time. "To fighters at the front, the living and the dead."

***

In the stuffy yet overcast morning, Orozco stood at the stove, scrambling eggs with scallions and mushrooms. When done, he doused the concoction with Tabasco sauce, sat on a high stool at the central counter and ate. Harry entered and asked for extras.

"In the pan."

"You know, maybe we all need to see shrinks," Harry remarked, scraping the eggs and vegetables out of the pan.

"And by the time we finished therapy, earth would be burnt to a cinder, smashed to smithereens, and the only survivors would be dying slaves in the realm of shadow, or starving in some enemy concentration camp, deep, deep behind their lines in the land of death and darkness."

"The land of death and darkness?"

"Hey, that's what it's called."

"It don't sound too good."

"It ain't."

"Ever been there?"

"I've been behind enemy lines, yes," Orozco said. "And I've made it my life's work never to return there, for all the good it does. Oh, Dios mio, que lastima!"

"Well, Vienna sounds a lot better than the land of death and darkness."

"But we need an address."

"At your service."

"That's a much better attitude."

"Look, I can deal with bad guys. If these guys in Vienna are like the ones we killed yesterday, murdering innocents and chopping up corpses, hey, I'm all for wiping them off the face of the earth."

"Well, you and Horace will get that address for us—today."

Harry paused, his blue eyes probing his partner's leathery old face. "What *is* a guardian, Rafael?"

"I can't tell you till I receive instructions otherwise."

"Instructions—from who?"

"From a little voice I'm lucky enough to hear when I need it."

"You're out of your mind."

"Hey," Orozco slapped a huge palm on the marble counter. "That little voice has kept me alive for fifty some odd years. It's kept me out, well out of death worshipper hands. You want to call names, go right ahead, but that's how we fighters stay alive—by attending to the small and the sacred."

Harry rubbed a hand over his worried face. "How often do you hear this voice?"

"Not often enough. But I don't command it, it commands me. So most of the time I just keep my head down, do my job, and wait."

"Sounds like being in the military."

Orozco gave him a sharp, sidelong, dark-eyed glance. "Don't it though?"

Harry paused. "All these years," he began after a moment. "And you never uttered a peep."

"A secret's a secret—especially considering the consequences of revealing it."

"Which were?"

"For me personally, an involuntary stay in a mental institution, with death worshipping attendants sporting the snake and globe tattoo, injecting me with thorazine."

"I wouldn't have had you committed."

"For my own good, yes, you would have. And then there's the damage that revealing hidden truths at the wrong time would have done. Word might have leaked out, attracting enemy attention to earth, and above all, He does not want His enemy focused on earth."

"Well then, I guess we've got our work cut out for us, 'cause I distinctly saw those thugs marching toward a swirling opening to our planet."

"Yeah," Orozco swiveled around. "I got to file a report."

"To who?"

"To the front. To the council, the council that's in charge. Shit, we're going to have to pay airfare to Vienna out of our own pockets."

"No," Horace said, entering the kitchen. "I will pay. I'm rich."

"All those years day trading, one step ahead of the IRS," Orozco remarked.

"I did pretty well," the guardian said modestly. "And if I were you, I wouldn't look a gift horse in the mouth."

Back in the study, Gideon and Starfield sat drinking coffee in anxious, angry silence. "These fascists are invading our world," the young fighter muttered.

"Shh, lemme file my report," Orozco said, entering, sitting at the computer and beginning to tap on the keys. When he had finished, he swiveled around to face the assemblage, large hands on his knees. "We're going to have to find out some specifics," he said.

"And once we have this address in Vienna, what do we do? Coordinate with local law enforcement?" Harry asked.

The computer dinged. The detective turned, read an email, then said, "no. We're working as fighters, not policemen."

"What's that mean?" Harry demanded.

"It means," Gideon put in, "when you get us the address…"

"Yes?"

"We blow it up."

***

In her leather coat, thick jeans, work-boots, with a ski cap, scarf and gloves, Lontra tromped on a dirt road through the frozen forest of Sere. In her worn knapsack lay sundry tools, food, clothes, a water bottle and a paperback copy of *Paradise Lost*. After twenty minutes, she saw coming toward her, clothed in warm black robes and reading a Bible, the tall, full form and even, kindly features of the priest, Vivaldi. "You arrive at last," he cried, glancing up.

"And you are reading earth's Bible."

"It is markedly similar to Alinia's."

159

"Maybe the men who wrote those accounts had witnessed similar events."

He paused to gaze keenly into her face. "You are so different from other fighters. That Axel."

"Oh, Axel. Did he insult you?"

"Yes."

"He detests the clergy."

"Why? What have any clerics ever done to him?"

"He believes you are a force of reaction, and Axel is all about revolution."

"Revolution!" Vivaldi exclaimed.

"He is a socialist and a fighter. He has no use for the clergy. Don't take it personally."

They walked now through a stretch of woods where the trees became sparser. Soon, in the distance, between the hills, a gray line of smoke rose up into the clouds.

"Our village?"

The priest nodded.

"How primitive are we talking, pre-combustion engine?"

"No, they have small cars and motorbikes, but few. There's very little production, since they aren't particularly keen on factory work. Generally if a family has a car or a bike, they have built it themselves or paid a smith to make it for them."

"What about poverty?"

"Nothing compared to the dreadful state of affairs in the eastern hemisphere of Alinia or in the southern hemisphere of earth. No vast slums, no huge deracinated village populations living on top of each other without clean water, decent shelter or medical care for their rampant diseases. None of that." He paused to pick some greenish yellow berries from a bush and eat them. Lontra followed suit. "Called sea-berries," he explained. "High in protein." Then after a moment, he continued. "But life here is primitive,

160

most people live in thatched huts and make do with well water. Some houses have their own generators, so they have electricity. Some have running water. The children go to trade school. They learn mechanics, agriculture, foraging and so forth. This structure is basically planet-wide, though the natives in the warmer climates are even more primitive. Everyone keeps animals, cows or something like them for milk, butter and cheese, funny-looking birds for eggs, nothing for slaughter. They have a religious prohibition against eating meat, and that, too, is planet-wide. Speaking of which, the planet is bigger than earth or Alinia. It's the size of my home world plus both moons."

"And your moons are each smaller than our one moon."

Vivaldi nodded and pulled his black cloak tighter around his shoulders. "We're pretty far north here."

"What season is it?"

"Autumn."

"When will the first children arrive?"

The priest cast her a kindly, appreciative glance. "As soon as I return to sector one thousand, which is tomorrow."

"There is a door here, to your parallel place?"

"Of course, an abandoned manor house, well preserved, outside the village. You will arrange with the elders to receive about seventy children every few days. The same plan is being followed in countless other villages across the planet. You will travel, from time to time, to ensure that the placements go as they should. For this purpose, I have obtained a small car for you. Your main problem will be supplying it with petrol. It only gets a hundred miles to the gallon."

"Only!" Lontra laughed harshly. "You should see the cars, the millions of cars on earth, which get far, far less."

"So I've heard from my partner in the orphanage. That's a way to overheat your planet real fast."

"Which is exactly what's occurring on earth. Our leaders are idiots."

"Leaders often are, especially when the system is rigged to benefit large corporations. Then the public good just sinks to the bottom of the ocean. Sere is a refreshing change from all that, from the probable extinction facing the foolishness of earth and Alinia."

"Alinia is more advanced than earth, from all I've heard."

"Not much. Our democracies are corrupt to the point of being a joke and in many places have yielded outright to tin-pot dictators. The poverty in the east is, as I mentioned, severe, with generations born into malnutrition and filth and dying in malnutrition and filth."

"Just like earth."

"I find it comforting that elsewhere in our universe, here, for example, conditions are different. Most Alinians would turn up their noses at Sere and say, 'how backward,' but these tribal societies have a much better shot at longevity than our industrial ones, that is certain."

Lontra then related her travels in earth's global south, from the slums of Lagos to those of Mumbai and Rio, describing the thin limbed, pot-bellied, scabbed children of poverty and her attempts, with local political groups, to start some action to change things. It had not, she said, been utterly hopeless.

"Though mostly," Vivaldi smiled sadly.

"Mostly. Then I was called back to the front, where I told the council point blank that earth was dying, and they said there was nothing they could do, they were too busy with the war, to which I replied that when all the best hearts and minds were concentrated Elsewhere, and focused on the front, it was no wonder that planets like earth drifted rudderless into disaster. You would not believe the poverty on earth, the prevalence of slums—even in the north, not just the south."

"So my partner is forever telling me. 'Vivaldi,' he says, 'the men and women of earth, but mostly the men, are doing the devil's work for him.'"

"And he is correct. We're at the end, it's only a matter of a few generations at most."

Thus lost in gloomy conversation, they trudged along the dirt road, now bordered by hedges, through the openings in which now and then could be seen a wood and mud-plastered hut with a thatched roof and smoke puffing out the tubing for a chimney.

"They may not be much," Lontra observed of these dwellings, "but they're far superior to what people have in the slums of Lagos and the favelas of Rio."

"They're better than what the billions of our poor have, too," Vivaldi spoke soberly. "It makes you wonder about the so-called benefits of development, which leaves so many worse off than had they stuck to their ancient, tribal civilization."

"I don't wonder. I know. The predatory, financialized capitalism of earth is a disaster for most of its inhabitants, and once climate change really kicks in, it will be a disaster for *all* earth's inhabitants, rich and poor alike. Anyone with eyes can see it coming, and any fighter who's conversed with fighters from extinct worlds, knows all too well that this economic arrangement ultimately spells planetary death. The death worshippers know it too, and in many instances, the enemy makes a tactical decision not to waste energy destroying a world whose inhabitants are already doing such an excellent job of it themselves."

The priest sighed. Now there were more breaks in the hedge rows, and more and more thatched houses. "These medieval dwellings," Lontra began, "are they specific to this northern region?'

He shook his head. "I've been on all eight continents, and they are very similar; the globe is covered with a network of villages, tilled land, a little pasturage."

"And none of the villages are more advanced?"

"Not significantly, no."

"Your brethren picked a good world for these orphans."

"It was I who chose Sere. I learned of it long ago, and kept it tucked away in the back of my mind for just such an emergency as this."

Before they reached the village center, the priest directed them down a path to an enormous, thickly thatched hut, outside the front of which, on a stone bench, sat a gaunt, older man, watching two rubicund children playing with marbles on the grass. "Oh, it's the religious man from the other world," he said, glancing up, his sharp green eyes beneath bushy gray eyebrows, taking in first Vivaldi, then his companion. "You see how they use us elders here," he complained. "To babysit our great and great great grandchildren."

"Dar meet Lontra. You expressed curiosity about fighters. She is one."

He studied her, then said flatly, "you are exactly what I expected."

"How so?" She demanded.

"Hardship is written all over you. The priest described the persecution you fighters are subject to." He sighed and placed his large, wrinkled hands on his knees on the rough brown fabric of his pants. "We have been spared such horrors on this world, at least as far as we know, but then those who are fighters keep it secret. Still, I believe we've been spared this. We are simply a village."

"The enemy is not much interested in villages," Lontra said.

"Lucky for us."

"And a higher power concealed you," Vivaldi added.

164

"I believe you, priest. I know there are other worlds, men and women more advanced than us. I have seen their spaceships and talked with their technicians. We have even obtained some technological advances, mostly medicines, from them. But what they have to endure! This horrifying war! I would never change places with them in a thousand years, no, not for anything, not for all their wealth and the magic of their technology. We Serans are lucky in our obscurity. I believe that with all my heart." He paused to settle a squabble between the two boys. "I am far happier mediating disputes between toddlers than those between grown men with weapons."

"Peace is a blessing," Vivaldi intoned.

"Without it, you have nothing," Dar said. "War is the triumph of death."

"We fight to stay alive."

"So I have heard. I do not envy you. I am content in my busy, peaceful village and happy to have nothing to do with this horrible war."

"But you will take in war orphans."

"Ah," Dar breathed, exhaling smoke from a long, thin cigarette he had just lit, "That is different. The orphans need homes. We are happy to provide that."

"They are not to be servants," she admonished.

"We would not dare treat them as such, not after what the priest has told us and what our wizard said about Who watches over them."

"Your wizard."

"Of course," Dar waved a hand dismissively. "Every large village has a wizard, and all the wizards around here, all we know of, had the same vision, the vision of your enemy in the black outfits, burning magnificent cities and of angels spiriting children out of the flames. Then the seraphs spoke to our wizards, and all heard the same thing: the orphans' lives are sacred, they are to be raised with love, protected and never abused. All the wizards heard this. We are very eager to receive these special children. We would not dare use them as servants."

"Is there slavery here?"

"Far in the south, on another continent, there are rumors, stories of such, but they are old and vague and probably concocted by the southerner's enemies."

"I've traveled this entire world," Vivaldi said. "I have seen no evidence of slavery."

"Good, because slavery is a sure sign of the enemy; it is the enemy's work."

"We don't know your enemy," Dar said, smoking. "We know wicked men, of course, but when criminals are caught, they are punished, and when the wicked rise in power, the council of nations comes together to remove them." He paused, then spoke in a low voice: "we do have one worry about these war orphans, though."

Vivaldi asked what it was.

"Many are the children of fighters, no?"

The two guests nodded.

"And the enemy pursues and persecutes fighters."

They nodded again.

"So it is logical to fear that that enemy will pursue fighters' children, right into this world and will discover this world."

"Many precautions have been taken to avert that," Vivaldi explained. "The orphans will not come to you directly from the battlefield. They pass through the transuniverse orphanage, which is secret and completely shielded from enemy eyes. Even if he tracks them away from the front, he will lose them there, and that is well before they come to you."

Dar nodded, his longish gray hair curling slightly over his ears. "This is how you've done it before?"

"Yes."

"And it always works—the children and their new world are kept secret and protected?"

Vivaldi nodded again.

The old man finished his cigarette, exhaling a stream of blue smoke. "I will tell the council tonight. There has been a good deal of worry over this one point." Then he glanced up, and they followed his gaze into a late afternoon, windy heaven, seen through the branches of an immense, nearby plane tree, and on the wind came the odor of wood smoke. "Winter is coming," Dar said, "and it will be a very cold winter. Already the squirrels and birds are fat. Let's get all your orphans settled before the first snow."

"But surely that's months away," Vivaldi protested.

"My arthritis has already kicked up—it could be weeks. Once it snows, people are preoccupied—preoccupied with the work of survival. Better to place the children before then, better for them."

A woman in her forties, in a plain, white and yellow cotton shift, stepped out of the house. "Grandfather, you were supposed to bring the boys in for their dinner."

"Drat, I forgot. Okay, you two brats, go with your aunt. Where's their mother?"

She planted ruddy, sudsy hands on her hips. "In the fields, harvesting pumpkins and winter squash. She won't be back for another hour. Today is her birthday."

"Thirty two, right?"

"Good memory, grandfather. We celebrate tonight."

"We have two guests. They will be making presentations to the council."

The woman looked impressed, as she surveyed the fighter and the priest.

"They can have the rooms under the eaves. Or is it room?"

"It's rooms," Vivaldi explained. "We are not married, merely associates."

The woman smiled, her face a cloud of freckles, pink skin, good health. "Well, associates, we have plenty of room for guests, even those who don't pay."

"They'll be bringing the children I told you about."

"We take two, right?"

Dar nodded.

"I'd like a girl. I always wanted a daughter."

"It can be arranged," Vivaldi said amiably.

The woman nodded and followed the two toddlers back into the large hut.

"Come meet my wife, Iti," the old man said, rising and crushing his cigarette out on the ground. "She is in the room in the back."

They entered a large living room and kitchen, with two big, black, pot-bellied, wood-burning stoves, emitting much heat, ladders up into the lofts and a narrow passageway behind the sink. Dar led them thither and into a large room with a double bed, a dresser and a big, wooden loom, at which sat a gaunt, gray-haired woman, weaving a woolen blanket with what looked to Lontra like Aztec designs. "This is for the two children, who will share the bed in the loft, she addressed her husband. "Iti, meet the priest I've told you about, and here also is a friend of his, Lontra. They will stay tonight, then tomorrow the priest departs."

Iti turned her worn face to Vivaldi. "You are a wizard?"

"No, just a priest."

"But you commune with seraphs, like the wizards do."

He nodded.

"And you too, Lontra?"

"I do as I am told."

"And the seraphs tell you what to do?"

"Often, yes."

"Then I guess you'd better do what you're told." She paused, then glanced at her husband. "The wizard will want to meet them."

He nodded. "After dinner. I will take them to his hut."

"He has been in a trance for two days."

"Iti tends the wizard," Dar explained. "They need tending, because they often forget about personal, day to day necessities and so forth."

"He told me a priest and a fighter would come," the old woman continued, pulling her brown woolen shawl farther over her shoulders. "Are you a fighter, Lontra?"

The fighter nodded.

"You have encountered this enemy?"

She nodded again.

Iti looked at Dar pointedly. "May God protect us. Frankly that's all we've got. We don't have spaceships. We don't have those immense bombs the wizard has described."

"We have guns."

She snorted derisively. "The better to shoot ourselves with, should this enemy ever learn of Sere. The wizard says the enemy enslaves all whom he captures, that he tortures and kills."

"Iti is very alarmed about the enemy," Dar explained," as you can see."

She snorted again. "It's important to know what to fear, husband. This enemy is to be feared. The wizard saw—"

"No!" Dar held up a gnarled hand, "no more of what the wizard saw or says. Our guests will speak with him after their meal." He paused to inspect the blanket she was weaving. "Almost done," he murmured.

"And not a minute too soon. The orphans will be here and with them comes the coldest winter in decades."

"The room under the eaves is warm," Dar remarked.

"Get your son and make it warmer. The whole roof needs more thatch."

"Another layer of thatch and the roof will cave in," now it was Dar's turn to snort derisively. "There's a design and engineering element to roofing that you know nothing about, Iti. Finish the children's blanket." With that he turned and walked back into the kitchen, where the ruddy, fortyish woman was laying bowls on a wooden plank table and ladling a vegetable stew into them. Two men entered, sweating and carrying scythes, which they rested by the door before sitting with Dar, Lontra and Vivaldi, to eat.

"Shouldn't we wait for the others?" Vivaldi asked out of politeness.

"No," the woman said. "There are so many of us, we eat in shifts. Dinner takes hours."

"And you need to see the wizard," Dar said.

The two men glanced up, noting the visitors for the first time. "You're the ones from another world," one man said.

"We are," Lontra replied.

"Don't bring your killing here," he admonished.

"That is not our intention."

"Good," and both men resumed slurping and chewing their stew. Dar finished first, removed a tin from a shelf, opened it, withdrew what appeared to be tobacco, rolled a cigarette and smoked it. The guests finished their meal, praised the food and the cook, who reddened with what was apparently rare appreciation, then rose and followed Dar to the door.

Down the road, inside a hut whose thatched roof almost reached the ground, stood the wizard over a raised stone hearth, poking at the fire, his black and red dreadlocks to his waist, his black robe studded with silver stars, wearing green goggles and a thick layer of blue, yellow and purple body paint, visible on his hands, arms, face and neck. Catching sight of Lontra, he emitted a squawk and jumped away, pointing a long muscular arm with a shaking index finger right at her. "This one," he screeched, "this fighter has been behind enemy lines."

"Yes wizard, we know," Dar said.

"She has lived in the land of darkness and death!" He cried, his eyes rolling wildly.

"I *survived* the land of darkness and death," Lontra corrected him. "I did not live there."

These words seemed to pacify him. He resumed poking at the fire and mumbling in a native language. "The children will start to arrive soon," he said at last. "They will travel into a magic place. They will come to us from this magic place."

"It is not magic," Vivaldi corrected him. "It is sacred."

"Which is another word for magic."

"We disagree," the priest said. "Profoundly."

"It is my task to make sure nothing of this enemy contaminates the magic place."

Vivaldi opened his mouth to object, but the fighter cut him short. "If he wants to call it magic, let him call it what he likes. His purpose is sound. I'm with him. We want no enemy contamination of your…special waiting room."

"If you'd ever been there," the priest cried in exasperation, "you would know how absurd and unfounded your fears are."

"The fighter and I are in agreement," the wizard said, reaching into a small burlap sack of powder and sprinkling it on the fire, which promptly crackled with several small explosions. There appeared to open a spiral in the room and through that spiral they saw a black-clad enemy interrogator, addressing a death worshipper who wore the top half of a skull for a hat. "The orphans have it too easy. They do not suffer enough. Who is helping them? Find out. They have

171

it easier than they should. They should suffer and die—find out who is frustrating us."

"I will do so, your Excellency, at once."

"You better."

Then the vision vanished. The fighter and the priest stared in shock at the wizard.

"I saw this vision three days ago," the wizard said. "I have been in a trance ever since, but have seen no more. Your magic place is in danger, priest. You and this fighter will have to protect its secret. These unmentionable people,"

"Death worshippers," Lontra said.

"Ah, an appropriate name for such an abomination. Well, they would like to find you, to destroy you, and to destroy the orphans you place. They know someone is helping. That someone is you. Beware and be careful. Do not lead these enemies to Sere."

The wizard's eyes rolled back in his head, his broad features contorted, as he began to chant. Dar, who had been sitting on a boulder, smoking, outside, entered. "What did he say?" He asked in a low voice.

"He showed us a vision of the enemy, giving orders to destroy the orphanage," Lontra said, glancing for the first time around the dim, wooden room. It was filled with long, high benches, covered with glassware that made it resemble a chemistry lab. There was one window on an extension in the back. Potted plants flourished on the sill, while sheaves of green herbs hung against the glass and over the sink and by the other small window that one faced when at the sink. In a corner stood a narrow bed, with brightly colored quilts. There was no upper story, though there appeared to be a basement, for there was a stairwell in yet another corner. "He keeps his preserves and jars of vegetables down there," Dar, who had followed her gaze, explained. "Iti cleans the place once a week, and she says it is very dirty."

"Well with all those chemicals," Lontra pointed to beakers full of green and yellow liquid on the far bench, "what can you expect?" She paused, then cast her flat, dull, dark gaze over Dar. "How long have your wizards been able to spy on the enemy?"

"It must have been a long time, though only recently did we know that that's what they were doing."

"You say 'must have been.' Explain."

"For generations, wizards have warned us about dangers off-world, that there exist other places, up near the stars in the sky, far, far off, but very wicked. To hide Sere, they said we had to keep things very simple, so when, a century ago, some enterprising men began to set up factories, the wizards spoke against this innovation and led angry crowds to tear them down. We were all just as happy to see them go. The factory owners paid us poorly and made a huge mess, dumping smelly chemicals in rivers or leaving them to rust in cans. It was awful."

"A century ago? Surely that was before your lifetime."

"I was a little boy," Dar explained.

"And now you're a great, great grandfather," Vivaldi mused.

"And more, even a great great great grandfather, I think, depending which children the mothers say I must watch."

"What did they make at the factories?"

"Trinkets, electrical devices, batteries. Unnecessary items. We did fine, when it all went back to the way it had been. But it was the wizards who banned the factories, who said they would draw us closer to the dangerous worlds."

"That's what they called them, dangerous worlds?"

"Yes, and that the factories would change our way of life, and pollute Sere and draw unwanted attention from the worlds beyond the stars."

"And all this time," Lontra addressed the priest, "right under our noses, we've had primitive seers, capable of peeking directly into enemy fortresses."

"You can't be sure that's where that conversation took place. It could have been near the front."

"No, it was deep behind enemy lines. The stone work on the wall behind the interrogator, the swooping staircase to the side of the interrogator, those are the officers' quarters of an enemy prison or fortress, far, far behind the lines, and both speakers were of very high rank." She turned to the chanting man, now counting the beads on one of his necklaces with his dexterous brown fingers. "Wizard. Can you show us more?"

His eyes rolled back to normal. "Why would you want to see more of such horrors?"

"To spy on our enemy."

"Ah, for your war."

Lontra nodded, and the wizard addressed Dar. "Send a runner to the next village, tell him we have the visitors from off-world, and they wish to see what the wizard saw, two weeks ago. Tell that wizard to come to wizard Abu's hut at once, and I will see to it that he receives a feast for a meal at Iti's house and a very comfortable bed."

Dar nodded and stepped out of the hut, closing the door behind him.

"Our guest will be here toward dawn," the wizard said.

"What did he see?" Lontra demanded.

"It is best I not tell you. You must see for yourself. It was very, very disturbing."

Dar reentered. "The runner has gone, the sun is setting." He looked at the priest and the fighter. "Time to go home."

"What did he see?" Lontra insisted.

"I will say only that he saw magnificent cities in flames."

"So it was about the war. What he saw was the war."

"Yes," the wizard said soberly, "it was the war, and the enemy's plans for the war."

Lontra cast a glance of triumph at the priest. "We will keep a few fighters posted on Sere, long after the transuniverse orphanage's work is done. They will be linked to a member or two of the council."

"You want our knowledge," the wizard said.

"Yes, and I assume none of you wizards is willing to travel off-world."

"You assume correctly, fighter."

"But you know of the war and enemy plans for the war."

"And you want us to share this knowledge with you."

"Yes. So that we may prevail."

***

"It's very early, so I'm goin' back to bed," Orozco announced to the little conclave in the study. "If you want to get to work without me, fine. But I got a headache only more sleep will cure."

Harry gazed at Horace. "We can continue without him, no?"

His host nodded.

"By the time you headache's gone," Harry said, "we'll have that address in Vienna."

The policeman nodded, tromped out of the room, back upstairs and flung himself back down on his bed. He dozed briefly, but did not sleep. Instead, he remembered his childhood in the slums of the South Side, the Mexican gang that he narrowly escaped joining and whose wrath he equally narrowly averted from descending upon his impoverished household. His father had been a day laborer, hanging around, outside a 7-11 at five o'clock in the morning, waiting to be selected for a job, while his mother was a domestic, cleaning six different houses in Uptown, six days of the week. His older brother joined the gang, thus deflecting their murderous fury later from Rafael, and once a part of it, never tired of chortling with the other gang members over Rafael's dreams of a future working for the city. And he always said that, a city worker, instead of a policeman, though he knew very well that his younger brother intended to become a cop. Their sister, pregnant at sixteen, moved in with her gang-member boyfriend. But that broke up, luckily without violence, and she returned to the Orozco rowhouse, with the sagging steps and mildewed bathroom, the unchanging cheap diet of rice and beans, until she and her older brother threw in the towel and moved back in with relatives in Mexico City. Rafael's parents held on for another decade, his father finally succumbing to a heart attack in his sleep, his mother to pancreatic cancer, but he did not wish to think about them now. Instead he turned his attention to images of life in his barrio, when he was five and six, to his dusty, grimy, little arms and legs, as he inspected them in the little patch of yard out back, with his friend Emilio, also grime-encrusted, shouting with him in unison, "I ain't never gonna take a bath! Mama can't make me! I'm never taking a bath!" They ran in circles, waving their arms, pretending to be planes, then crawled behind the dead, dusty bushes, on the lookout for the "injuns" they'd seen on cowboy shows on TV. But mostly they just sat beneath the bushes to escape the blazing heat and talked about Jorge's fantastic chocolate birthday cake, on which they had gorged themselves several days before.

Lying with an arm over his eyes, he could envision his skinny, tan, dirt-streaked forearms as clearly as if it were yesterday—skinny because he was never hungry, a condition which alarmed his mother, when she wasn't too tired from work to be alarmed, and which bothered him not in the least. "Four sticks and a little belly!" His father called him, but even when his mother cooked a pot of tamales, his favorite, he never had an appetite for more than one. Despite there being plenty to eat, he looked malnourished, but it was simply that he was a very skinny child, who grew into a tall, lean adult. There had never been any fat on Orozco, and as a child not much muscle either. He looked like a waif, and if not for the clean, well-pressed clothes that his mother labored over, he might well have been taken for one, too.

"Hide, Rafael," he heard deep in his mind, one blazing Saturday afternoon. Ever the good friend, he grabbed Emilio by the hand and dragged him under the bushes, breathing, "bad guys." From their hideout, they watched as the sun glared down on the patch of dust they had just quit and then a funnel of wind swirled it up into the sky, whistled ferociously around the yard and finally, after some minutes, died away.

"What was that?" Emilio asked, his dark eyes round with fear.

"The enemy," Rafael answered, and heard deep within his mind, "enough, Rafael, reveal no more."

"Bad guys?" Emilio asked.

"Bad guys."

"Take Emilio and go play inside," the voice instructed him.

"C'mon, Emilio. I'll race you to the back door." And then they were in the living room, with his older sister, her hair in pink curlers, watching the TV and the old air-conditioner humming in the front window.

"Ahh," Rafael exhaled, stretching out his arms in front of the air conditioner. Emilio copied him.

For some reason his sister did not snap, "go back outside," as she usually did, so, in the silver glow of the old black and white television, they built fortresses with blocks on the worn, purple, living room carpet.

"How about some tamales, kids," his sister offered.

"Ahh," Rafael declined, but his friend clamored for them and soon assisted in building an enormous fortress with a plate of three tamales at his side.

"I want to go back out," Emilio said.

Rafael was about to reply, "me too," when he heard in his mind, "no, not today, not at all today." So aloud he said he did not feel like it and suggested they play pirates upstairs.

"It's too hot upstairs," Emilio complained.

"Tell him it's hotter outside," the voice instructed, and Rafael did so. That was the end of the agitation to go out, and the boys played noisily till six, when Mrs. Orozco returned home, clapping her hands in delight at the plate with the remains of three tamales, because she mistakenly concluded that her son had eaten them.

That night, Rafael went to sleep to the sound of gangland gunfire on his street. In the morning, his brother Juan was in jail and headed to prison for murder. He sat in the living room, working on his fortress, as his mother screamed and wailed, his father talked frantically on the phone and his sister opened the front door to the gang leader. The room fell perfectly silent, as Javier glanced from the sister to the father, then proceeded to address all of his admittedly few and terse remarks in Spanish to the father. The brother's family would be taken care of. They would receive a cash payment from the gang every month.

"Leave the room, Rafael," the little boy heard, deep in his mind. He did so, and his sister followed.

Then the gang leader left, as Rafael's mother sat weeping on the couch, and his father looked on in bewilderment.

But his brother was out in a matter of months, and, after much consultation with the gang, decided it would be wise to take up residence in Mexico City, where he could perfect his criminal career in a more open fashion. The parents, who played no part in any of these decisions, whose opinions, in fact, were never asked, nonetheless were relieved at his departure, and so was Rafael, for the moment his brother returned from prison, the voice in his mind had become more insistent, telling him to "leave now," whenever his brother entered a room where he already sat, stood, or lay.

With kindergarten began a new life. His English, already good from constantly watching television, became perfect, so that he was reading simple English baby books by the end of the year. His spirits would crash down every day at the thought of returning home to the care of his sister, and so, on the dusty, litter-strewn sidewalk, he would invite himself over to Emilio's or to another friend's and upon arrival, responsibly call home to inform her of his whereabouts. "What, the Orozco's don't have no food?" Emilio's broad mother would laugh, hands on her hips, as she gazed down at skinny Rafael, who merely shrugged. "I'm not hungry."

"How about some beans and rice?"

"No thank you."

"Is that what you say to your mama?"

Rafael grinned. "That's what I say to everybody." This conversation would always occur in English, because Emilio Martinez's family was very proud of their English. That, little Rafael thought, was one of the things he liked about them. That and no gang member visitors, whose mere presence made the voice in his head go off like an alarm. Mrs. Martinez always inquired about his mother, father and sister, never about Juan. And that was a relief too, for while his brother was in prison, Rafael had begun to think, to think about what Juan must have done to end up in that terrible place, and the more he considered it, the less he wanted to see or talk about his brother.

Once, on his way to the bathroom, he overheard Mr. and Mrs. Martinez discussing Juan. "They say that Juan Orozco killed a boy, a member of a rival gang." "Well, little Rafael had nothin' to do with that," Emilio's mother replied. "Don't blame a baby."

"Still, at the first sign of any gang member,"

"There won't be no signs. They don't follow around baby brothers. Be quiet, you worry too much."

Rafael meditated on this conversation for a long time. People saw him and thought of the terrible thing Juan did. He did not like it, and by the end of kindergarten was telling anyone who asked that when he grew up, he would be a policeman and lock up bad guys.

"Really?" Mrs. Martinez asked. "You have to get special training for that."

"I will. That's my plan."

"And then, where will you work? Here, in the Mexican barrio?"

"No," little Rafael shook his head seriously. "In other parts of the city. D_____ is a big city."

"For a six-year-old who don't eat, you've really thought this out."

The little boy nodded. "Yes I have."

He grew. He entered first grade, learned everything the teacher taught backwards and forwards, still only picked at one tamale at a time, his arms and legs skinny as sticks, then his brother returned from prison, but, thankfully, only stayed a few days before moving in with some friends, also in his gang.

"Good," Rafael said, when his sister told him this news.

"Good? Won't you miss Juan?"

"No. Now he can do all the terrible things he wants, and we won't be any part of it."

"Listen to you!" She raised a hand to her pink curlers and with another reached for her bottle of Coca Cola. "Mama!" She called, Mrs. Orozco came, and Rafael's sister Elena repeated his words. Mrs. Orozco sighed and wandered back down the hall to the kitchen, murmuring in Spanish, "he's right. He's right. Our Juan is lost to us, forever."

After Juan moved to Mexico City, policemen occasionally came to the house, searching for him or a gang member. "We don't know where he is," Rafael's father would say, truthfully enough, since from what they gathered, Juan was constantly on the move and had no fixed address. Eventually the police stopped coming, and except for the occasional gunfire in the night, the gang's presence in the Orozco family's life disappeared. This was very much to little Rafael's liking, because he had gathered from snippets of overheard conversation that the adults worried about the gang inducting him, when he grew older. "Nunca," he said to himself at age seven and again, lying on Horace MacKenzie's guest bed, he murmured it in English, "never."

***

The second wizard was white, not black and wore a satiny blue robe. He chanted, ran his fingers through his white beard and rolled his eyes. "A priest and a fighter," he said to his host, the first wizard.

It was early morning, the first slanting sun rays streamed in from the open door and the small windows on the extension. Outside birds chirped, and a chill pervaded the dawn. Dar, sitting on the bench next to the hut, smoked and tossed seeds to a little gaggle of blue-winged blackbirds, pecking in the dirt. He listened to the conversation through the open door.

"Yes, and the fighter survived in an enemy prison."

The second wizard stared at Lontra. "Why didn't you kill yourself?"

"I lacked the means," she replied. "Otherwise, that is exactly what I would have done."

"How did you escape?"

"Angels brought two fighters, who got me out, took me to a seer on my home planet, who said I had to bathe in the river of forgetfulness to be healed."

"Where is this river?"

"In a very strange distant land called the plain of oblivion."

At these words, both wizards began mumbling, chanting, then dancing. At last, the visiting wizard stopped, and with eyes boring into Lontra's face said, "you fighters lost a terrible battle there. Many thousands perished."

"Yes, I was there. I fought and I witnessed."

"It was a catastrophe."

Lontra nodded.

The visiting wizard approached the fire and withdrew what looked like a handful of dust from his robe. He threw it on the fire, which crackled, roared up and then died down to reveal, just as yesterday, the image of a black-clad enemy interrogator, talking with yet another human death worshipper, who also wore a half-skull as a hat. "After sector one thousand, we will try to relocate sector three thousand three hundred thirty three and from there sector four hundred thirty eight. Prepare your troops for invasion."

Lontra withdrew a small hand-held computer from her leather coat and tapped out a message.

"I didn't know you had that," Vivaldi said. "Or even that such things existed."

"It's Argan technology. It's connected to the computers and the techs at the front."

Both wizards peered over her shoulders at the little, glowing screen, no bigger than a game card.

"What magic is this?" Their host asked.

"Not magic, technology," the fighter said. "What you just showed me had to be described to our techs, so that they can inform the council and the angels."

"What exactly did you describe?" Vivaldi asked.

"An enemy conversation that reveals a disturbing fact."

"What?"

"They know the numbers and thus coordinates of sectors they have never even been in."

"They've been in sector 3333 before," Vivaldi said.

"But not sector 438. I've never even heard of it. It's not on our map. But it's on the enemy's which means only one very bad thing."

"Which is?"

"Somehow the enemy has a comprehensive map of the cosmos."

"But how? I thought only He and His seraphs had such a map."

Lontra glanced up. Her hard, flat gaze glittered over the priest's kindly features. "Yes, that is the question—how?"

***

Tall, gray, angular and weary, Ivan Smironovich sat with another council member, Jason Katharos, in the deserted, little, cinder-block cafeteria.

"Sorry to call you away from San Francisco, but we received some very disturbing news from a fighter in the Seran system. I already informed the rest of the council, and I wanted your opinion too."

"The bad news never stops," Katharos barked. "Fire away."

"It appears the enemy has developed a comprehensive map of the cosmos."

"Crap. How'd he do that?"

"My theory is he used this artificial life form of his,"

"You mean Morning Star."

"Yes," Ivan nodded. "I believe Morning Star mapped the cosmos, the better to destabilize human galaxies."

"You think its Morning Star that's destabilizing our worlds?"

"That is my hunch, my gut feeling."

"Crap." Katharos sat back and sipped his brackish coffee with a look of displeasure and alarm. "We've got to get AI fast."

"Saltwater said he could do it."

"Well, didn't he team up with Ein? We should get some results."

"Look, they just left two days ago, and Ein's a scientist. He works slowly."

"He can't work slowly, if the enemy has a comprehensive map. How do we know this, anyway?"

"The ghost is on Sere, where she encountered local wizards."

"Oh," Katharos exclaimed, "what a lot of hokum!"

"No, Jason, listen. These wizards have a means of eavesdropping on the enemy."

Katharos' bushy gray eyebrows rose. "They're using magic for that? I hope for the Seran system's sake, it's a one-way street."

"Apparently it is. The ghost witnessed a conversation between an interrogator and a master killer. They discussed plans first to destroy sector one thousand."

Katharos grunted, "well, no news there."

"Then to re-attack Argas and then some place called sector 438."

The San Franciscan sat up very straight. "The seraphs know?"

"Now they do. They didn't seem too concerned."

"Then who are we to be pulling our hair out?"

"We're the pesky little species called the human race, Jason, a race that could well vanish from the cosmos, and whether or not we do, the seraphs will still be here, and they'll still win." Ivan paused, leaned back and slurped his green tea. "We have to work harder."

"Pass this info on to Ein and Saltwater," Katharos barked. "It's highly classified, and it could cause a panic."

"Tell them that. But they need to know."

"To light a fire under them?"

"That," Jason said, "and so they can adapt the AI they create with a special geographical feature—so he can track Morning Star's knowledge. My guess is even the enemy's artificial intelligent life form does not have a map of the *entire* cosmos. He may have mapped places we haven't heard of, but he hasn't got the whole ball of wax. That's why the seraphs are complacent. But we can't afford to be. We must track everything Morning Star knows; so Saltwater better equip our AI with the most advanced cartography programs he can get. And then our AI,"

"Seymour."

"Who?"

"Our AI is called Seymour."

"OK. Then Seymour can find out just how much of the cosmos Morning Star is aware of."

Both men paused and gazed into their cups.

"Shit," Ivan said at last," an awful lot depends on a technological breakthrough that hasn't even occurred yet."

"But it can be done."

"You sound so sure."

"The enemy did it. If he can do it, then we, who fight on the side of the angels, then we can do it."

Orozco thudded down the carpeted stairs and into the study. "We got the address," Horace said to him, then nodded in Harry's direction. "Your partner here put his hands on that computer, went into a trance, and I distinctly heard an address on Schreivogelgasse." He passed a little, folded piece of paper over to the policeman, who was murmuring, "Screaming Bird Alley." Then he looked at the address and pocketed the paper.

"What did you see?" He demanded of Harry.

"Cities in flames, and I heard the words, 'sector one thousand will surrender or be destroyed.' From what I saw, it looked like it was being destroyed."

"So now you're connected to another sector," Orozco murmured.

"He hears what the enemy is up to," Gideon snapped.

"What's sector one thousand?" Harry demanded. "Gideon here wouldn't talk about it."

"There's no need to keep secrets from Harry, not now," Orozco said. "Sector one thousand is a doomed universe. The enemy invaded, and part of that reality has already collapsed. It's only a matter of time before the whole thing goes."

"How many people is that?" Harry demanded again.

Orozco glanced sharply at him. "Lots."

"Well, somebody better do something. I saw huge cities burning, just burning right to the ground."

"Look, we're evacuating as many refugees as we can. But sector one thousand isn't our headache now; our problem is a death worshipper on Schreivogelgasse in Vienna, who's opened a door between earth and one of the most unspeakable places in the cosmos,"

"The realm of shadow," Harry said.

"Yes, and he's bringing an army of death worshippers, who will, or rather who have already begun, their murder and mayhem all over the globe. We have one small goal, to stop him. We cannot stop the cataclysm in sector one thousand."

"So you're saying that place is doomed."

"Yes," Orozco replied. "It's doomed. We got there too late."

***

"He's on intravenous liquids, and we replaced half his blood," the doctor told the trio who had gathered at Albert's bedside.

"Were you able to isolate the pathogen?" Eel asked.

"Yes, now we're trying to kill it." The doctor paused, then noting Carmella's flashing eyes and her hands defiantly on her hips, said: "Don't strain him with superfluous talk. He needs rest." All three glanced at the band-aids on their own inner elbows, where blood had been drawn. Observing this, the doctor said, "you're not infectious. What you have is bad, it's that smart bug. We can kill most of it with antibiotics, but some of it always hides and comes back later. We haven't got the cure yet, but we're getting closer."

Carmella gestured at Albert. "He's got that in addition to whatever new disease they gave him."

"From your description of Brianna's symptoms," the doctor said, "she was given something entirely different."

Carmella's dark eyes filled with sadness.

"We notified her husband," the doctor said.

"I still have to talk with him," Carmella replied, "and that will be heart-breaking."

Albert opened his eyes. "I feel much better," he said.

"That's cause half of you is new," Carmella smiled.

"She means we replaced half your blood," the doctor clarified. "Do you feel well enough to talk to the head of the council?"

The patient nodded, then closed his eyes again.

"That's our exit cue," Carmella said, as she, Horace and Eel moved away from the bed toward the door. Once out of earshot, she grasped the doctor's arm. "Will he survive?"

The physician glanced evasively away.

"I take that as a no."

Their eyes met. "There are always miracles," the doctor said. "We can hope for one of those."

"I'll put my faith in science, thank you very much."

"Then no," the doctor said flatly. "He won't survive."

***

"Albert, I'm sorry," he said, taking the patient's hand.

"No, no, Ivan. I volunteered. I knew this could happen. But let's not waste time. I hacked into the enemy computer at the station nearest the front," he began to cough.

"Slow down."

"No. There's not much time. There were references to earth on documents especially requested by interrogators."

"How high up?"

"One master interrogator, at least. Ivan, it's bad. There was one reference to earth as quote special to Him unquote."

Ivan ran the back of his big, bony hand, the one not holding the patient's across his forehead. After a moment he asked, "did you delete documents requested?"

Albert began coughing again. When the fit passed, he said softly, "I did better than that. I altered them, doctored them to downplay earth's…centrality. I hope you approve. I was afraid that if I just deleted them, the request would simply come through again and then be answered. Deleting them would only buy us a little time. Whereas altering them,"

"Throws sand in their eyes."

"Exactly."

"We think alike, as always, Albert."

"And Ivan," the ill man tried to sit up, but his friend gently pushed him back on the pillows. "Don't worry about the interrogations, Ivan. First off, they caught me outside the building in the dead forest. They'll never know I was inside. It was just a beating and the usual sleep deprivation, but that's easy enough to deal with. I fed them garbage, a pack of lies about how my mission was to estimate enemy reinforcements behind the front. I screamed it out whenever they hit me, which they loved, of course."

"So they fell for it," Ivan said.

"Hook, line and sinker. They'll never know that we know what their interrogators are after."

Ivan sighed. "A generation ago and longer, there was treachery on earth."

"I know, I know. And this is the result, but I think, for now, we have confused them. Ivan," he tried to sit up again, but Ivan gently pushed him back.

"Ivan, I am more convinced than ever that earth needs an ally, a human ally, a human world."

"You've always said that in the council."

"We must argue for openness and an open mutual defense treaty with the Argans."

"The Argans! But they're the best."

"That's why it has to be them."

"But what do we have that they'd want? They hold all the cards. They're the technological geniuses. We're primitive in comparison. What can we offer them?"

"Guardians."

"Guardians?! No, no, no. First off, they must never leave earth, secondly that's a secret that frankly only He can decide to reveal."

"Go through a friend of His, someone like Galen, on earth."

"Galen would never go for this."

"Earth needs a human ally, Ivan, a human one and fast."

"Maybe the Serans."

"The Serans! They're backward savages. They can't help us."

"They use magic," Ivan said. "They use it to spy on the enemy."

"And the Argans use technology to cloak their universe. I'll take technology over magic any day. Remember, Ivan, magic can backfire." They paused, Albert had broken out in a sweat, and had begun, somewhat, to writhe.

"I've worn you out, old friend," Ivan spoke sadly.

"Not you, Ivan," Albert opened his eyes before he died and said: "The war did that."

***

She approached the man who had been given a small cinder-block cell with a cot, a nightstand and, most incongruously, a painting of a vase of flowers, hanging on the wall.

"Her last thoughts and words were of you," she said, coming over and standing near him.

He glanced up with glistening eyes.

"I'm Carmella. I was her cellmate. I had hoped to help her escape also, but I was too late."

"I'm Roger, as you know."

"They said you'd be granted leave from the front, to be with your children, back on,"

"Planet one," he said dully. "That's our world."

"She told me she was from a numbered reality, and that there were five numbered planets in her home system."

"What did she say?"

"Her wedding day was the best day of her life," Carmella adlibbed, omitting that Brianna had been tossing in a high fever and raving.

"Mine too," he said.

"And that you have to be strong, for the kids, that it's all on you now, raising them and that she hoped you'd get a permanent leave from the front." Something moved in the doorway. She looked up and saw Ivan and glared. "Yes," she enunciated, "one of her last wishes was that you could leave the front and not have to return."

Ivan glanced away.

"And I promised," Carmella continued, her dark eyes molten with fury, fury at her cellmate's death, fury at her own forced absence from her own children, "and I promised to take your case to the council itself," Ivan walked away, but was still within earshot, as Carmella raised her voice, "and give them her dying curse, if they did not release you to raise your children. And I will do as I promised." She practically hissed in a rage, as she recalled Brianna's corpse, as she gazed at the broken husband before her, as she wondered where her own husband, Roberto, was and if she would ever set eyes on him again.

"Thank you," the wretched man murmured and put his head in his hands.

"She thought of you at the end," Carmella repeated, "only you."

Later, she caught up with the head of the council, who glared at her. "We're not heartless monsters, Marquez. We're fighters, fighters who are losing a war for our species. What do you want from me?"

"Let Roger go home, back to planet one and raise his children."

"We may need him again."

"Give him five years."

"What—you just pulled that number out of a hat?"

"No, their youngest is seven. She'll be twelve in five years, with nearly adult siblings. Then they'll be able to cope."

Ivan stopped in his tracks and stared at her, as she put her hands on her hips and struggled to control the rage evident in her clamped jaw and molten eyes. "You have attitudinal issues," he began.

"That may be so, but I'm right about this, and I'll take the whole thing to the council for a vote, if you don't use your executive powers,"

"All right!" He snapped, holding up a big, bony hand. "Roger has five years. Are you satisfied?"

"No!" She snapped back. "But I'll settle for it, and as for being satisfied, Ivan Smironovich, no, I will never be satisfied with the treatment I or any fighter has received in this miserable war. Do you hear me?"

"Go away! Albert just died."

At these words, Carmella flew into a fury, "and he was the best, the best bar none on the council. I even knew him in New York. You, *you* go away. And no, no, no, no, I will never be satisfied." With that she turned and stalked away, not deigning once to turn her head and cast a glance back at the broken and grief-wracked leader of the council.

*****

Having clicked on his seat belt, Ein settled into his shuttle seat next to his two companions. Suddenly, deep within his brain, he heard a voice and so raised his head, listening. "The enemy knows too much about earth. A member of the council died to bring us this information."

"What does the enemy know?" Ein asked mentally.

"That earth is special to Him."

"Then I would say earth's days are numbered."

"No. We will send you a fighter from earth whom you know, Jamal Jones."

"What for?"

"To hammer out a mutual defense treaty with Argas."

"The senate will never go for it," Ein replied. "Earth is too bloody. Too many wars. Recent genocide, no."

"Then make the case for secret assistance."

"Technological advances and what not?"

"Yes."

"If Jones stays with me, Saltwater will learn about earth, and I thought for some reason, that was not desirable."

"It is not, because he will want to emigrate there. And he is not ready for retirement, not yet. Make other accommodations for Jones."

"What sort of technology should we secretly assist with?"

"Communications, medical and weapons. Get into the appropriate computers on earth and make new quote discoveries unquote too obvious to miss."

"Let me guess," the pockmarked man had been scanning Ein's face, while the latter communed with the voice, "something highly classified."

"If you mean secret and that I can't discuss it, yes. Although it's my understanding that you'll learn about it in due time."

"Keep your secrets and I'll keep mine," Saltwater said. "Let's just create Seymour."

The Argan withdrew a very small hand-held computer from his pocket and began scrolling through files. "Uh-oh," he said. "Here's one from the council."

193

Saltwater craned his neck to read it.

"It says," Ein continued, "That the Serans use magic to spy on the enemy, and they have learned that he has a comprehensive map of the cosmos. Crap. That means he knows about our sector. Pavel, I may not have much time to work with you. They'll want me back on project Fireball."

"Fine, just so long as I have state of the art Argan computer technology and a lab."

"Already arranged."

"How did the enemy map the cosmos," Lindin wondered.

"You think a certain artificial life form might have been involved?" The pockmarked man asked. Both of his companions started. "Because I do, and I think Seymour will have to get to work on that as soon as he is born."

"You mean deleting their map?" Lindin asked.

"No, that's too obvious," the pockmarked man replied, as the shuttles engines powered on and the craft detached from the bay. "Instead, Seymour will have to alter the map. That will be his first assignment: to sabotage it."

***

"I don't like it," Vivaldi said, as he and the fighter walked behind Dar back to his house for breakfast. "These wizards use magic. Magic is not only bad in and of itself, it's dangerous."

"They've been using it for thousands of years," Dar said, turning his head to glance at the priest. "It's never brought any danger."

"But still now, with the enemy so...hyperactive,"

"There are different types of magic," Lontra spoke pensively. "Our side uses some, on some worlds. This Seran variety falls into that category. It's been safe for millennia, and it reveals useful knowledge about our enemy."

"So you intend to use it again."

"Yes," she replied. "Often, as often as is necessary."

"I don't like it."

She cast him a hard look, one he recognized as that of a fighter judging a cleric to be innocent to the point of ignorant. And so, the priest grumbling to himself, the fighter tapping on her little computer, Dar led them back to his hut, to a wooden table laden with pots of cooked cereals and platters of omelets filled with appetizing green and brown vegetables. Several field workers sat and ate silently, nodding at them, as they sat. "These are our guests from other worlds," Dar said, "honored guests."

One of the men, very fair-skinned and covered with freckles that almost matched his thatch of reddish, light brown hair, finished chewing his eggs and said, "welcome. We hope you bring only peace. There's been no war here for over a generation."

"We never make war against men and women," Lontra spoke rather harshly.

"Who do you fight then?"

"I must not say."

"Will you bring this enemy that you fight, this enemy who is neither man nor woman, to our world?"

"No. It is our intention to prevent that."

The men mumbled in satisfaction, finished their cereal and eggs, grabbed their scythes that stood next to the screened door and tromped out.

"You shouldn't have told them," Dar said. "Now word will spread."

"But surely in your mythology there is an enemy who is not human," Lontra said.

"Yes, daemon."

"Then say that is who we fight. Most will just laugh and not believe you, and the others are credulous to begin with and probably rather ignorant."

195

"You can say that again," thus Dar.

"So don't worry about it." She ate her eggs pensively, glancing now and then at the little Argan computer screen that glowed silver. Dar reached out a hand to touch it, but she blocked him with the words, "no, it responds to any random touch, and I am conversing now with an important weapons designer."

"Ein?" Vivaldi asked. "The man who can hide worlds?"

She nodded.

"And what are you asking him?"

"To hide entry points to Sere and Argas and earth."

***

"There is a little man in your box," the wizard pointed a crooked index finger at Lontra's hand-held computer with its image of a very worried Ein.

"Yes, that is Ein. He is very far away. This is only his picture."

"Wizard," Ein began, "what do you burn to create the images of the enemy?"

"Herbs that we gather on the mountain-side. Then we feed them to the wretch."

"The wretch?"

The wizard went over to a counter, opened a cage, and out stepped a six-legged, black, furry, winged creature with miserable yellow eyes.

"He looks so unhappy, we call him the wretch," the wizard explained. "We capture wretches in the glacier caves, far to the north. Every twenty-five years an expedition of local wizards goes in search of them. The wretches chew the herbs, partially digest them, then spit them up. We dry them and toss them on a fire whose coals include certain secret metals,"

196

"Also from the caves of the north?" Ein asked.

The wizard smiled. "The little man in the box learns fast," he said admiringly to Lontra. "He should be a wizard."

"He is. He made that," she pointed at the hand-held computer.

"What else do you mix with the regurgitated herbs?" Ein asked.

"How did you know there was more?" The wizard was astonished.

"Just a hunch."

"We mix it with flakes of a dried baby wizard umbilicus. We keep them here in jars," the wizard pointed to a row of glassware on a shelf above the counter than ran the length of the room. "My own umbilicus is almost used up. Soon I will start on that of my apprentice."

"Who decides who is a wizard?"

"We have visions of a pregnant woman giving birth to a being who opens doors to eternity, to the halls and the lamps of eternity."

"So you find her and take the baby."

"She sees the child as often as she likes, but he grows up with wizards, learns to see the future, learns to use the wretch and the herbs to see the enemy, who, by the way, we have always known was an enemy."

"Why didn't you alert your people?"

"What for? To alarm them? Besides, honorable Ein, this enemy is not interested in us, he is interested in you, and in her," he pointed at Lontra.

"I have news for you, wizard," Ein said. "This enemy is interested in destroying every man, woman or child he encounters. Are you sure your magic does not attract his attention?"

"Positive. We have practiced it for millennia. We have spied on these dreadful ones for millennia. They have never known."

"How often have they mentioned sector 3333?"

"Rarely. They refer to the quote anomaly unquote that occurred when they made contact."

"No more? Just an anomaly?"

"Yes. Their physicists are trying to unravel it, but they have had no luck."

"Could you spy on their scientists?"

The wizard grinned, revealing perfect, blazingly white teeth in his dark face. "I have done so."

"And?"

"They are primitive compared to you, honorable Ein. They also practice magic—bad magic, and they practice it badly."

"You mean they are not adept at it?"

"That's what I mean."

"How flexible are you?" Ein asked. "I mean, can you look easily at whatever you want in the enemy's realm?"

"Yes, we wizards have become quite knowledgeable about these abominable people and beings and the worlds they inhabit. For instance, do you know of a place called the realm of shadow?"

Looks of profound, involuntary aversion covered the faces of the two fighters.

"Ah, I see you have. You react the way all fighter prisoners there react."

"How many fighter prisoners?" Lontra demanded.

"Thousands. They live in concentration camps and cannot die, though some have figured out how to commit suicide, and they teach the others. We wizards have great admiration for these fighters in the realm of shadow, they are mighty men and women to endure what they endure. The others don't do so well."

"Others?" Lontra snapped. "What others?"

"Other people from other worlds, many, honorable Lontra from your home of earth."

"You mean," she shrieked, "there are ordinary men and women from earth in the realm of shadow? How did they get there?"

"They don't know. Some say, 'I fell into shadow,' others say they fell in and were replaced back on earth."

"Are there ordinary Argans there?" Ein asked in evident alarm.

"Aside from the fighters, I have not seen any, no," the wizard answered. "And I have not heard the prisoners converse about Argas or Sere. They are from all over the universe, but mostly, I believe, from earth."

"Shit!" Lontra shouted.

"This is bad," Ein said. "Ordinary people break under torture. Ordinary people talk."

"How long has this been going on?" Lontra demanded.

"Many years. Some decades. And there are some people from earth there who are treated quite well, like honored guests."

Strange hard glints of dark light flashed in the female fighters' eyes.

"These must be the traitors we've heard about," Ein said.

"I will go there to kill them myself," she hissed.

"No need," the wizard said, "the fighters from earth managed to murder quite a few of them. Then they themselves committed suicide. Oh, it was horrible."

A look of grim satisfaction settled over Lontra's hard features. "They did exactly as I would have done."

"But suicide, after such a success!" The wizard exclaimed.

"In the realm of shadow, it's better to die than to live," Lontra said. "And after murdering traitors, they probably had a very clear idea of the torments they would be subjected to.

They are heroes. I will alert the council. These heroes—did you get any of their names?"

"All of their names. I memorized them," the wizard said. "I have never encountered men and women like these before."

"And of those that remain, and the traitors, do you have their names?"

"Both—many, not all, but many. And not just me. These events are known to all the wizards. We know heroism when we see it. So we remembered the names."

"You've done well, wizard," she said quietly.

After a moment of silence, Ein said slowly, "do you think, is it possible, that this trouble with earth and the realm of shadow could have something to do with why we're losing this war?"

Lontra started and turned pale. "I don't know, but I intend to report that possibility."

***

The two weary fighters sat across from each other in the little cinder-block cafeteria, the one tall and dark, the other tall and gray. Outside, overhead, rumbled the gigantic explosions of fireballs hitting their targets and of tank fire from the enemy.

"Albert's dying wish was for Argas to become earth's ally," the gray man said. "But I'm not doing this for sentimental reasons or to honor his memory, although it does that; I'm doing it because he was a supremely practical, hands-on man and the more I've considered it, the more it seems correct to me. Then I received instructions."

Jamal Jones grunted. "I heard them too, but I've got bad news for you, brother, the Argans will never want a mutual defense treaty with the genocidal maniacs of earth."

"The treaty will be with us, fighters and guardians, and so it will be secret."

"Even so, I doubt they're going to bite. What's in it for them?"

Ivan sighed and ran his knobby fingers through his short gray hair. "I received a list of heroes today, fighters in the realm of shadow, who killed some of earth's traitors."

Jamal sat bolt upright.

"I also got a report," the council leader continued, "that there are many ordinary people from earth in the realm of shadow,"

"How?" Jones shouted in shock.

"They have been quote falling into it unquote for some time. That's how they describe it. Also in this report was the speculation that this presence of so many residents from earth in the realm of shadow could have something to do with why we're losing the war."

Jones waved a hand dismissively. "That's mere speculation."

"But it's potent speculation. It already got Ein's attention. It could get the attention of the Argan senate and then, they might move to assist earth, albeit secretly."

"We need medical technology, computer and cellular phone technology, better weapons," Jamal was ticking these items off his fingers one by one.

"Those things have already been mentioned. Now they need to be argued for. A fighter from earth must go before the Argan senate and explain how extremely advanced weaponry will not make it into the hands of, say Hutus and Tutsis, or Bosnians and Serbs—what the protections will be, what the safeguards will be. Earth is not much known on Argas, but once they learn about our recent history,"

"Christ, the holocaust."

"Exactly. They'll want nothing to do with us, but you'll have to argue that it's a sacred planet, whose fate is intimately bound up in mankind's fate."

"That if earth goes, we all go."

"Precisely, and what's more, it's already happening. There's a channel between earth and the realm of shadow, there's evidence of enemy tampering in earth's recent history, of enemy support and covert assistance to Nazis—all this must be laid out. The Argans need to *get it*. Earth is not merely some blood-soaked backwater,"

"Oh yeah?"

"Listen, Jamal, we have a race of guardians. You tell the Argans about that and the significance of that, which is that He never, ever intends to lose earth and that if He does, His wrath will be terrible, the consequences will be terrible and very, very possibly, it will be the end of mankind and Armageddon for the nonhumans. And you know what comes after that."

"Wind and nothin' but wind."

"You tell 'em, Jamal. You make them see. You get those superior, technological genius, peacenik Argans to *care* about earth, *care* about earth the way they care about their own skins, care, because if earth goes, they go. You hammer that home. Without their technological assistance, we'll all, all we and they, be slaving in chains in the realm of shadow. You paint a very vivid, very scary picture of a nightmare that is, I'm sorry to say my friend, already well on the way to happening."

Both men rose and stared at each other without moving, until at last the leader of the council said "dismissed," and they parted.

***

Jamal Jones strode up the boarding ramp from the shuttle to Argas, and there, behind a rail, espied Ein waving at him. They shook hands. "Long, too long," Ein said.

"Well, it was a battle we lost."

"But we survived," the weapons designer continued. "Lot's of our brothers and sisters did not."

"Let's not go over that now. Where can we sit and talk?"

"How about the restaurant of your hotel?"

Jamal gave him a sidelong glance.

"I apologize for not being able to put you up," Ein began.

"Don't make excuses. I was already instructed. You have a guest I'm not supposed to meet—yet."

"Correct."

"Boy, I'm glad the seraphs have a plan," Jamal said, "'cause sometimes it's all murk to me."

"Blood, sweat and tears is what it is for our species, brother," Ein paused. "How in heaven are you going to convince our senate to help earth?"

Jamal waved an index finger at his friend. "Let me get back to you on that."

"As I feared, not a clue."

"Oh, I got clues, plenty of clues. I just don't have a winning argument yet."

"You have me."

"I do?"

"Yes. I believe, I have a hunch, that this converse between earth and the realm of shadow is why humankind is losing the war."

"And your hunch will sway your senate?"

"Hey, I'm an important guy around here." And Ein smiled his most winning smile.

"That will have to be the core of our argument," Jamal said. "Earth's demise equals humanity's demise. Hard to make when you consider our blood-soaked history, I mean compared to you folks, we're ghouls."

"But you're special to Him. The senate will want to know why, and we'll have to invoke divine mystery."

Jamal stopped, head raised, listening, then smiled and continued walking. "Earth," he said after a moment, "was the original casus belli between Him and the enemy."

Ein stopped. He stared. "You just heard that?"

"Yup."

"Well, if the war started over earth and then dragged everybody else in, what happens if we lose earth?"

"Clearly," Jamal concluded, "we lose the war." He paused. "There may have been forays, occasional attacks by the enemy, like the one on Argas twenty thousand years ago, but it didn't become an all out war until earth, the struggle over earth."

They stepped out of the terminal and had their choice between a trolley for nearby stops and a bullet train for the exurbs and other cities. Ein led him to the bullet train. Soon they sat, speeding along at hundreds of miles per hour toward Ein's home city of Stitch.

"But how will this work?" Jamal asked. "I can't reveal earth's secrets, to wit the guardians, to an amphitheatre filled with thousands of senators from thousands of worlds."

"And hundreds of thousands more on the vid screens," Ein mused. "No, you can't. With that in mind, I've arranged for you to have a highly classified meeting with the five members of the defense committee, which is headed by my friend Ulhan, a ten-term senator. Those five will be the only ones to know the secret details. But if they agree to assist earth, it is a done deal. You then just go in front of the Senate and spell out the broad outlines—a sacred planet, under siege, if it falls, we all fall, and it's falling, and so forth."

"Can I speak with Ulhan tonight?"

Ein shook his head. "He is a very religious man. Right now, I believe he's sacrificing a ram to God. He will be busy with his religious duties until quite late. But first thing in the morning."

"Where are the other four senators from?"

"Four distant galaxies. By the way, Ulhan's from the very system, though not planet, where the enemy touched down. His world is called the Ice Kingdom."

"No warm beaches there, I'm guessing."

"Glaciers cover most of the planet, but it's still densely populated, with people, I might add, who are extremely worried about a reappearance of an army of death worshippers. Ulhan will be your strongest ally. The people of the Ice Kingdom are grasping at straws, and if Ulhan believes earth offers a way to defeat this enemy, he'll go there himself to make sure the technology is transferred correctly."

"That won't be necessary."

"Just hyperbole. But you get my meaning? He's all for strong defense and is very hands on. If he believes that the Ice Kingdom's fate is bound up with earth's, well then, you've got your deal."

The suburbs whirled by, then the exurbs, brief to be sure, then suburbs again and then dense city.

"Stitch," Jamal mused, "isn't this where the needle was invented?"

"Hence the city's name. It's also host, now to the senate, several miles above the city. The senate wanders, hosted by different systems, different galaxies, every year or so. But even so, some galaxies, like Prometheus, right next door, complain they haven't hosted the senate in millennia. Here, this is our stop." They exited onto a moving sidewalk, which Ein hurried over, Jamal keeping pace, and soon stepped off at a trolley stop. They entered, sat in back, and Ein heaved a sigh. "This stops right in front of my house."

"You have a house?" I thought everyone here lived in a gigantic two-hundred story apartment building."

"Not in my very antique section of town. There are houses, ten-story apartment blocks, city parks and even a zoo, with original Argan fauna. You'll stay in a hotel down the street, a very comfortable, six-story affair, where Ulhan will meet with us in the restaurant first thing in the morning. Here, let's get off." As they stepped to the curb, Ein pointed to a narrow, four-story brick and steel house with flower boxes in the windows. "My abode," he said. "But now, for you, come on, you must be exhausted."

They hurried down the sidewalk to the little hotel, where at last Jamal admitted that he was too tired even for dinner, and wanted nothing but sleep. The sun had set, so they parted under the awning, in the light of a corner street lamp. "A guest from another reality?" Asked the concierge, who was clearly well known to and awed by Ein. The weapons designer nodded. "Well, welcome, Jamal Jones. Welcome to civilization."

***

Saltwater and Lindin had spent the day in the lab. First they did some calculations, then the pockmarked man made some hard-wiring alterations on a computer and then they tackled the software. But once Saltwater took his antibiotic for his tuberculosis, Lindin appeared satisfied and announced that now he intended to sightsee. His friend scarcely heard him, so engrossed was he in the numbers on his computer screen. Early that evening, when Lindin returned from two museums and the zoo, Saltwater still crouched at his computer, hazel eyes glittering eagerly. "We can do it," he murmured. "It'll take time, but anything good takes time."

"Now it's time for dinner," Lindin said. "Ein's wife,"

"You can call her Anna."

"Anna has made some sort of lamb stew, just for us, since Ein himself may not be back for dinner tonight."

"He's so secretive all of a sudden," Saltwater observed.

"That happens to fighters," Lindin sighed. "You don't know what he heard, what that voice, or maybe even some seraph, told him. He's got some other project, that's certain."

"Yeah, his fireball. He mentioned to me over breakfast that this universe is still on the enemy's radar."

"Oh, then he's worried about that."

"No kidding. The one place you don't want your home to be is on the enemy's radar."

"How'd he learn this?"

"Said he couldn't say. And when a fighter says that, I respect it. I didn't pry, though I did ask about our reality and our system."

"And?"

"Said he hadn't heard anything about them, so—no news is good news."

They left the massive, hundreds of stories high defense building, which required scans, thumbprints and retinal scans to enter, arrived below ground level and took a subway to Ein's neighborhood, Arcadia. There, they stopped under a street lamp, as a trolley jingled by and glanced around at the low-rise houses in the gloaming. "You know where we are?" Saltwater asked.

Lindin pointed at the four-story house with the flower boxes. "Right where we're supposed to be."

"They say the senate's right above this city now," Saltwater mused, glancing up into the heavens, aglow with the light of the rings built to encircle the planet up in space.

"Yeah. It's got a floating amphitheatre, miles above Argas. You have to take a special shuttle to get there, but we won't be doing that, no visitors allowed, because, as I understand it, they've got more senators up there than they know what to do with."

"Thousands."

"And hundreds of thousands more on the two-way television screens. Sounds like a pretty chaotic way to run a government, if you ask me."

"Well, don't ask me," Saltwater said. "I'm not concerned with their government. I'm concerned with their computers, which I don't fully understand yet, though I'm catching up. Give me another week."

"Just a week to catch up to Argan technology!"

"Look, lotsa ours is modeled on theirs, so it's familiar." They crossed the street to Ein's house, climbed up three steps and knocked on the door.

"Ein loves it that he has a house where you knock on the door to gain entry," Lindin remarked. "He told me that's what they do in the Argan bible."

"And that's what, thirty thousand years old?"

"At least."

Anna opened the door, wearing a gray cotton dress with a white, flower-print apron. "The food's almost ready, and yes, my husband will be dining with us."

"Great," the two guests exclaimed in unison and retired to their respective rooms.

Saltwater loved his room. It was in the rear, shaded by some species of evergreen with drooping fronds. Plants crowded the window sill, while a floor to ceiling bookcase covered one wall. Opposite stood his bed, with a night table, armchair and computer on a computer table nearby. It was cool, quiet and conducive to thought. Such a contrast to where he had been only six months ago! More than a world of difference, the difference between goodness, generosity and civilization on one side and cruelty, privation and barbarism on the other. After his first night in this wondrously peaceful room, he had joked to his host, "can I live here?"

"As long as you like," came the sincere reply.

"That won't be long," Lindin had interjected sourly. "They'll want us both back at the front, as soon as Seymour is born."

"He'll be housed here?" Ein asked.

"At first," Saltwater replied. "That is my plan. Then we add him to other computers in other universes, other galaxies and also, we'll have an interface a chip, which we can insert biologically, so people can directly interact with Seymour."

"Sounds like the beginning of a cyborg future," Ein spoke with noticeable disapproval in his tone.

"No. These implants will be only temporary, for instance, when a fighter has to go behind enemy lines. Often there's difficulty downloading what's discovered on enemy computers. But with Seymour right there in his brain—well, you see the advantage."

Ein nodded. "But we do not want a cyborg future, Pavel. We Argans have known worlds that went that route, millennia ago. They are all extinct now."

"How so?"

"The short version is that creating a cyborg population lent itself to massive military manipulation. They basically fought each other to death."

"Well, lots of our purely human, non-cyborg worlds have done just that."

"Lots, but not all. Not Argas, where you are now. And not others. The human material is flawed, Pavel, as you argue all the time, but not fatally so. It can be worked with. We on Argas are living proof of that."

Saltwater threw himself on his bed and listened to the tree fronds gently rasping in the breeze against his window. He thought of the war and his capture at the front, the beatings, the interrogations. He closed his eyes, dozed and murmured aloud: "I never want to return to the front."

***

Jamal Jones sat at a table in the dim back of the restaurant café and chatted with his buddy Holdauer on a hand-held computer. Even on that tiny screen with the tiny image, you could tell that Holdauer was a big, tall, burly man with thick black hair and fiery eyes.

"So where're you now, bro?" Jamal asked.

"In my doublewide, outside our beautiful hometown of Cleveland, Ohio, garden spot of the USA."

Both fighters chuckled.

"And soon," Holdauer continued, "to be deployed, with you, to save some hellhole called sector one thousand. What on earth is going on there and what the f do they want from us?"

"Salvage and rescue," Jamal replied. "Refugees, tons of 'em."

"So the enemy invaded?"

"Uh, you could say that, if infinite understatement was your goal. More like he conquered."

"Shit."

"Yeah, exactly. The whole reality's up in flames, with enemy commanders and interrogators running amok all over the place."

Holdauer's bushy black eyebrows rose. "Commanders and interrogators? You mean this sector one thousand could collapse?"

"Already started to. When I left the front yesterday, a whole string of galaxies had just vanished, disappeared off the map."

Stunned silence greeted this revelation.

"Then we got a month, at most," Holdauer finally said.

"The outer galaxies seem to be going first, so my understanding is, they're evacuating those worlds first. That's where we'll be."

"Great, so we get to disappear, just another blip on the council's cartographical computer screen, and we're gone forever."

"Don't be so negative. They're already moving the refugees out, like I said. By the time we get there, in a week,"

"Less."

"Okay, less, the job'll be half done. We'll finish and hightail it to some safe inner galaxy."

"Safe, as in overrun with murdering fascists and cities in flames, because some enemy commander decided to have fun and waved a hand? That kind of safe?"

"Fraid so."

"Shit, I hate this job."

"You got any alternatives in mind?" Jamal asked. "'Cause if so, I'm all ears. I been running from these sons of bitches since I was six, and if I knew any alternative to fighting, some peaceful corner of the cosmos where these death worshipping fascists couldn't find me, I'd be there in a flash."

Silence.

"I thought so," Jamal continued. "You ain't got any alternatives, 'cause none exist. It's either fight and die and maybe win, or don't fight and die and lose for sure. Me, I'll take the first choice."

Holdauer grumbled something unintelligible.

"Say what?" Jamal nearly shouted.

"You win!" Holdauer snapped. "But how'm I supposed to leave for sector one thousand in two days, when we got death worshippers practicing ritual murder in local cemeteries?"

"In Cleveland?" Jamal asked in shock.

"Yes, in Cleveland, and every other frikking major city on the globe. It's a goddamned epidemic."

211

"Has the council been alerted?"

"Of course."

"What they say?"

"They got a man on the case, two actually. The whole globe's awash in fascist murder and our genius council has put two fighters on the case. No wonder we're frikkin' losing this war." Holdauer paused to guzzle from a can of Red Bull. "Me, I think all of earth's fighters should come home and deal with this scourge, kill these sons of bitches who slit innocent people's throats, not go gallivanting off to some sector one thousand that, from what you tell me, is doomed anyway."

"Wrong attitude, my man. Earth will survive a few death worshippers. But we're talkin' a whole reality here, sparsely populated, it's true, but still, countless lives are at stake."

"Countless lives are always at stake," Holdauer snapped. "Why do you think He's fightin' this war? Has it ever been any different?"

Jamal shook his head sadly. "No, my friend, no it has not."

***

Ein entered his modestly elegant house and kissed his cheerful, gray-haired wife. "Guests resting?"

She nodded, then said, "Ulhan called. You're going to the senate tomorrow?"

"Politics, politics," he sighed. "And meanwhile fireball is stalled."

"I thought the mimicking the heat problem was solved."

Ein held his hand out and fluttered it from left to right to indicate "so, so."

"And doesn't Pavel need your help with the computers?"

"His work would go much faster, if I had time to help him, yes. But I won't have a minute tomorrow until dinnertime, and he needs to come home and rest then. No overwork for him. He's barely recovered, as it is."

"Oh, when I think what he witnessed," she cried. "I mean his wife!"

Ein put his arms around Anna and shushed her. "You must never mention that," he said softly, "not anywhere where Saltwater could overhear you."

She wept silently.

"Any news from the kids?"

"All three well and thriving," she snifled. "Though I worry about Ollie."

Ein stepped back and spoke a little severely, "we're lucky only one of the three is a fighter, Anna. It could have been all of them. If Ollie gets called to the front, there's nothing we can do."

"I hope it never happens."

He regarded her sadly. "Ollie is a fighter. It will happen."

"But the last time, he was wounded."

"And he could be wounded again."

"Or killed," her voice rose anxiously.

"Let's not borrow trouble. He hasn't been called, not for a long time."

"And you were just called," she wrung her hands.

"But not to fight, just to meet with the council, and Pavel and some other fighters—just to coordinate and strategize."

"I don't understand," she wiped a tear out of her eye, "how we could be losing this war. I mean angels, *angels*, are on our side."

"But I," her husband mused, "I think I have begun to understand why."

"Why?"

"I can't explain it. It involves secrets too dangerous to be disclosed."

"But you'll disclose them to Ulhan."

"How did you know that?"

"I don't know."

"Yes, and Ulhan and I will try to do something... revolutionary."

"What will this something do?"

Ein gazed out the back window at the last sun rays of the dying day. "Turn the tide of the war," he said.

***

Shortly after dawn, Jamal Jones strode into the little hotel café and boomed, "hey, let's open this place up!" A waiter appeared, laughing. "Already done—food is on the buffet in the next room." The fighter strode through the doorway, and there stood gray-haired Ein, incongruously solemn and cheerful as always, and with him was a short, brown, paunchy but still muscular man with a very beaked and crooked nose and deep, dark, glittering eyes.

"I take it you're Ulhan. I'm Jamal Jones," and the fighter extended a hand.

"Always a pleasure to meet a fighter for the race of men."

"Now there's a phrase I haven't heard in a while."

"Well, we heard it, in the Ice Kingdom, when the enemy touched down in our system. The announcement, over all media, was that he had come to destroy the race of men. But our friend Ein, here, frustrated him. What is this place, the realm of shadow, connected now to your world, earth?"

"It's a pit, a charnel house," Jamal said, "a vast concentration camp for the living dead, run by the enemy."

Ulhan shuddered. "And your world touches it, yet your world is sacred."

"Something happened on earth," Jamal said, "something at the beginning of mankind's existence there, something that caused the war. Listen, Ulhan, for I'm about to tell you a secret, one Ein knows and the other four senators we'll meet today will have to know, but one that must never reach any other ears."

The dark sparkling eyes widened in alarm.

"Earth has a secret race of men and women called guardians. They are visionaries, whose sole purpose is to see reality, to see what the enemy is doing on earth. They transmit these visions to fighters like me. This...species of human is earth's deepest, greatest, most secret and last defense against the enemy. Over a generation ago, that defense went down briefly, on a continent called Europe."

"How did it go down?" Ulhan asked in alarm.

"We don't know. Guardians began to go missing, and after that there was, many of us believe, direct tampering with earth's political events—direct by the enemy."

"But he did not invade."

"No. He had plenty of fascists on earth to do his dirty work. Tens of millions died, before our defenses were restored. I tell you this, so that you'll understand the importance, the significance of our race of guardians. They protect earth while most fighters are away, and there is nothing like them on any other world."

Ulhan nodded. His shiny black hair appeared to ripple in the morning sunlight. "I tell you this," Jamal continued, "to give you a clear idea of how He regards earth. He never intends to lose it. If somehow, I can't imagine how, He did, the consequences would be terrible. The war started over the men and women of earth. Lose earth—"

"And we lose the war," Ulhan finished his sentence.

"And then there's nothing, no more mankind, we're done, fini, kaput." With that, Jamal reached for an apricot Danish and bit into it.

"How can you even think of eating, when these dreadful events and possibilities are swirling around you, and your earth, and by implication, all of us?" The senator asked in astonishment.

"I been livin' with it all my life. But things got worse recently. The enemy opened a channel between earth and his realm. Earth needs an ally. I have been instructed that that ally is you."

"Instructed, by whom?"

"Who do you think instructs fighters?"

"Angels? Angels, right Ein?"

Ein nodded.

"Good gracious," Ulhan breathed and took a blueberry Danish. "That's why you want a treaty with Argas?"

Jamal nodded.

"But Ein here says there was genocide on earth within the last decade. We can never dream of sharing weapons,"

"The treaty would be with the fighters, so it would be secret. And the assistance would not merely be weapons, but communications technology, medical technology."

"That part's easy enough. The weapons are thornier."

"Only for our use at the front or in an invaded reality. And of course, on earth, if earth is ever invaded."

"Oh, great God in heaven, this will be a hard sell."

"Why?"

"Your blood-soaked history, that's why."

"Without this treaty, without Argas' assistance, that history will become a lot bloodier, as earth goes down the drain and then drags the rest of mankind with it."

"That's it? That's what happens? That's the end?"

"Then Armageddon," Jamal said soberly, "that's the end."

***

The fighter and the priest stood at the back of Dar's thatched hut, facing a sunlit yellow field that sloped down toward the deep greens of a forest.

"So you leave today," she said somberly. "Off to sector one thousand."

"From that very forest," he raised an arm, thickly swathed in black clerical garb. "You seem, how should I say, more serious than usual. And you're never exactly playful."

"It was reading those names to Ivan over the computer, the names of those heroes in the realm of shadow, who killed the traitors then took their own lives. Those names are burned into my memory. And a burning memory makes for a serious mood."

"Unless I'm mistaken, some of those traitors still live."

"Not many, and rest assured, the fighters in the realm of shadow will find a way to deal with them."

"The fighters in the realm of shadow are in chains."

"What they did before, they will do again."

The pair fell silent, as a sudden, cool wind rippled over the tops of the tall yellow grass and stirred the priest's cassock and the fighter's short, badly cut black hair.

"Like the wind at the end of time," the fighter murmured.

"Only a little. This is a mild wind, refreshing, beautiful in its way. The wind after the last battle will be terrible, will howl right down the corridors of eternity."

"But every wind partakes a little of that last one."

"How do you know that?"

"I was told."

"Ah."

"Once, when I was in a terrible place. The river of forgetfulness washed away a lot, but it did not wash away that memory."

"You mean it washed away the evil but not the good."

She turned to face him, her dark, flat gaze aglitter, as she cast it over his kindly features. "It could not erase anything connected to Him, even the river of forgetfulness cannot do that."

"And you heard this, about the wind, in an enemy prison?"

"He sees even into those, just as I am sure he saw even into the realm of shadow, when our fighters gave their lives to combat and kill the traitors from earth. I am sure He spoke to them before they died, some word, some reassurance, some bit of truth, so that they would recall that no, they did not die alone."

"Even that far behind the lines, that deep into the land of death and pestilence and darkness," he murmured.

"Even there. It was there, then, at the time of my transformation that I heard Him."

"She is a weapon in His hands," the priest heard in his mind. "Do not gaze into her eyes right now." So he cast his glance onto the dirt before his feet, in their big, sturdy, dusty, black shoes.

"You should go now," Lontra spoke after a moment. "To sector one thousand. Your time has come."

***

By the time Saltwater awoke in his shaded back bedroom, Ein was long gone. The pockmarked man lay in bed, awake but feeling weak and not wishing to rise. He turned his head to glance at the clock. Late morning. "We'll never get Seymour with me sleeping in like this," he thought, but still did not move, and when at last he stood up and dressed, he then laid back down on the bed, noting the freshly laundered scent of the pale blue quilt, and the weakness, the exhaustion that pervaded his limbs and fogged his brain. He did not even want to get up. But as he lay there, gazing out the window into the huge evergreen with its lovely, drooping fronds, unwanted memories began to push their way into the edges of his consciousness. He could only banish them with his sense of purpose; and that sense required getting up. So he rose, tottered, noted the photo of Ein with his wife and children on the night table, rubbed his face and made a great effort to control his weariness.

Downstairs Lindin and Anna awaited him with a mushroom omelet and what his hostess told him were fish fries for breakfast.

"Maybe you should go back to bed," Lindin said. "You don't look too good."

"I'd like to, but lying down awake, my mind wanders into places and memories that, frankly, I'd like to keep at a distance. So work it is, for me today and every day."

At these words, his two companions fell silent and stared at their plates. After a moment Anna spoke up: "perhaps your sleep isn't deep enough and you should take sleeping pills. Ever since my husband's first trip to the front as a young man, he's had to take sleeping pills. He says they keep him sane, rested, in control of his own mind."

"Maybe. Could I try some of these pills tonight?"

"Absolutely."

With that, all three ate their late breakfast, Saltwater downing several cups of coffee. These made him feel stronger, more alert; the weariness in his limbs subsided, as did the longing to be horizontal.

"I think I'd better accompany you to my husband's lab," Anna said. "So there are no mix-ups or delays at security." She cleaned up the dishes with Lindin's help, while Saltwater, requested permission to lie on the couch. There, stretched out, he fell into a doze, despite the caffeine in his blood and dreamt he was at home with his wife and father. "What Seymour needs," she said to Pavel, "is a new script, from

scratch. Stop trying to make a hodgepodge of the old ones."
Saltwater's eyes flew open. He sat up, momentarily unsure
where he was.

"Ein's house, remember?" Thus Lindin, catching the
bewildered look on his friend's face.

"I have an idea, a new idea how to proceed," the
pockmarked man said. "Quick, let's get to the lab."

"Ready whenever you are," the others said in unison.

***

"The core?" Vivaldi called in astonishment, hanging
onto the angel's wings for dear life. "Why am I going to the
core galaxies? It's the outer ones that are threatened with
imminent extinction."

"Triage," the seraph replied.

"So you expect the whole universe to go."

"We must prepare for the worst."

"By abandoning billions of people on the fringes of a
reality?"

"Fighters are on their way to those fringes now. Fighters
and seraphs are already there. Those people have not been
abandoned. But you direct the orphanage. That must be in
a safe zone."

"Where will I be?"

"On a hot, tropical planet crammed with people. It's called
Dismal colloquially, because it's so crowded with people,
but its official name is Vios, which means life in one of the
languages of earth. Vios must be tended."

"Why this one particular place?"

"Because we have intelligence that it has been targeted."

"Then it's not really triage."

"Not targeted imminently, but on the list."

"What list?"

"The enemy's list of worlds that will no longer be inhabited by men and women."

Vivaldi was astonished. "And you've seen that list?"

The seraph nodded. "We obtained it long ago."

"How long?"

"At the beginning of the war, at the beginning of earth's human history. That was when we realized it."

"What?" The priest cried. "Realized what?"

"That it was sunset at dawn."

***

The four senators besides Ulhan on the defense committee, none of whom had ever heard of earth until yesterday, in Ein's formidable and flabbergasting presentation—a planet where, just over fifty years ago, inhabitants of one country had burnt millions of members of a minority in *ovens*?! This planet was sacred? What about the sickening perpetrators of these crimes? How had they come to be born on a sacred planet? And now this planet was in some relation to the realm of shadow, death worshipper central? And most astoundingly of all, many millennia after the establishment of Argan civilization, well, well after this, human civilization had started on this place called earth, and something so dreadful had occurred that it had caused the war, which had twice jeopardized the very existence of Argas, and, to make matters worse, if this place called earth fell into enemy hands—and maybe that had occurred once or twice already— or was extinguished, the human race would lose the war and cease to exist. So the four senators craned their necks, one peered through his glasses, and all gawked at Jamal Jones, as if they half expected him to open his mouth and freeze them all with his words. Which he promptly did. For the first thing he said was that his planet, earth, was home to a secret and sacred race of guardians, visionaries who saw reality and who knew what the enemy was about on earth and that He Himself had created this race for the sole purpose of the defense of earth, which proved the untold lengths He would go to, to protect this little, blood-drenched world that lacked even interstellar travel and that they had never even heard of until yesterday.

How long, one astonished female senator asked Ulhan and Ein, had they known these amazing facts?

"Like you, I learned the general picture yesterday," Ulhan said. "Today I heard about these guardians,"

"The keepers of the flame," Jamal added.

"The flame, what flame?" One senator asked, his eyes still popping.

"I think I know," Ein said. "I just recently learned about these guardians, knowledge of whose existence, I cannot stress too much, is never to pass out of this room to another Argan."

All five senators nodded, still obviously dumbfounded.

"And I met one," Ein concluded grandly.

"Met one? Where? How?" They all demanded at once.

"I travelled to earth and met one. And he had a little steel case with a thunderbolt etched on it."

"That holds the flame," Jamal said. "And when a guardian lights the flame, he sees the whole, unvarnished, ugly truth."

"I'll say it's ugly," the lady senator exclaimed. "But you don't need a flame in a box for that. Millions of people were deliberately burnt in ovens on this planet. My God, whoever heard of such a thing? Who ever heard of such nauseating cruelty?"

"The perpetrators were tried and executed," Jamal said.

"I should hope so," she snapped. "Maybe they should have been burnt in ovens! No. We cannot have any treaty or supply weapons to any people who have participated, who have a history, and a recent history at that, of such barbarity. Genocide fifty years ago and cruelty on that scale is just too recent."

"Oh, there was another genocide just three years ago," Jamal added, determined to place all the brutal facts on the table at once, so their discovery at a later date could not sabotage his efforts.

They stared.

"Were there *ovens* again?" The female senator asked.

"No. I believe the killings were done mostly with guns and machetes."

"Machetes?" She asked.

"Knives."

"How many this time?" She gasped.

"Hundreds of thousands."

"Ein," she said. "You want a *treaty* with these people? You can't have a treaty if one side is not civilized."

"There have been seraphic instructions for a treaty between Argas and the fighters, note that well, only the fighters of earth."

"What about the guardians?"

"Oh, them too."

"But not the rest of this bloodthirsty world? Not the politicians, dictators or tribal leaders?"

"No," Ein spoke definitively. "None of them. They will be kept in the dark. The fighters' very existence is unknown on earth. The guardians have been kept secret for millennia. Fighters and guardians can surely keep a treaty with Argas secret from the corrupt and violent men that rule this place called earth."

The five senators all talked amongst themselves. Jamal heard Ulhan's voice: "Tens of millions in the last world war alone!" And then the lady senator, "the last one? How many world wars have they had? Oh, it is too terrible!" But one

223

elderly senator, the one with the thick glasses and the alert, sad eyes, could be heard saying, "who are we to gainsay seraphs? That goes against all religion, common sense and safety." "He will have to make a presentation to the full senate," the female senator said, "and make his case without mentioning these guardians." She turned to Jamal, "I would suggest, fighter, that when you argue for this treaty before our senate, you not mention specifics like ovens, or tens of millions murdered. No. Stick to generalities. Admit that you planet has a dreadfully blood-stained history, but leave it at that. Point out, in an oblique reference to your guardians, that this earth means so much to Him that He has directly intervened in events more than once and that the enemy has too, so much has it been in contention. Stress that you want medical, communications and computer technology as much or more than weapons. Also emphasize that any weapons will remain only in fighters' hands and that the criminals who run countries and doubtless your powerful corporations,"

Jamal nodded.

"Fascist or near-fascist worlds are always structured like that," she said in an aside to Ulhan, "that those petty despots will never get their hands on Argan weapons technology, and then, I'd suggest that Ein step forward and say that he gives his personal guarantee that this is the case." She paused, then glanced around at her four colleagues and exclaimed once again, "Ovens!"

They all grumbled and shook their heads: "We do not like it," Ulhan said, his black eyes glittering angrily, "such killing, such cruelty, genocide, mass death, these are the very things our civilization is built on renouncing. Do not bring us into contact with any of these perpetrators. We respect you, Jamal Jones, and your brethren, because you are fighters and hear the voices of seraphs, because you fight an enemy who has twice tried to destroy us. But your world, earth, sounds horrible. It appears to be awash in the blood of millions of innocent men, women and children, and we can never have a treaty with the sorts of warlords, even if they call themselves presidents or commanders, who are responsible for this. For shame! Shame, shame, shame on this place called earth."

"I should say," Ein put in, "that it is not all murder and mayhem. Earth is in a relatively peaceful phase now, according to fighters and guardians, and except for its powerful extractive corporations,"

"They're not burning fossil fuels, are they?" The lady senator demanded.

"I'm afraid so."

"They're doomed," she pronounced.

"We have a little time," Jamal put in. "And there are efforts afoot to stop these backward practices."

"Once powerful corporations start burning coal and oil, they never want to give it up. It's too lucrative. And with their obscene profits, they'll corrupt the political system, spread lies and pseudo-science in the media, so that the truth cannot be found anywhere. We've seen this before, on planets now extinct, extinct due to the abuse of power and money of their own extractive corporations."

"They also use nuclear power," Ein spoke soberly.

"Even worse!" She snapped, as several senators rolled their eyes. "They'll never dispose of the waste, and when they try to, they'll contaminate continents. And undoubtedly there have been meltdowns,"

"A few," Ein conceded.

"I fail to see how you conclude that He takes a protective interest in these wicked men."

"Without Him, we'd have been gone long ago," Jamal said. "Back with the invention and use of the first nuclear weapons."

"Use!" All five senators cried at once, and then fell, yet again, into murmuring indignantly amongst themselves.

"Fine," the female senator addressed Jamal at last. "Tell our senate that the only reason your wicked, wretched world has survived as long as it has is due to what the ignorant call fantastic dumb luck and what we know to be divine intervention. That will impress them. I will call a vote on the treaty after you and Ein speak. Both of you, I advise that you stress the role of fighters and angels. But if the true history of this dreadful place ever becomes known on Argas, that treaty will be revoked faster than you can spit."

"Thank you, madam senator," Jamal said.

"Don't thank me yet. All I'm doing is recommending a yea vote, in light of the fact that that is what seraphs want."

"No false modesty," Ein corrected. "The defense committee's approval is critical."

"You have that, but behind closed doors, Ein? This place called earth has the defense committee's horror. It sounds like a charnel house, and it is no surprise to me that somehow it has fallen into orbit with the realm of shadow. Like to like, I say."

Ein glanced at Jamal for some words of defense of his home world, but the fighter remained silent, finally saying to him softly, "the truth speaks for itself."

Then the group of seven filed out of the modest senatorial chamber and into an elevator down to the entrance to the podium in the amphitheatre.

"Earth is about to leap into a new millennium of technological advance," Ein murmured, as he and Jamal approached the lectern.

"Whether we deserve it or not," the fighter murmured back to him.

***

Gideon Cohen stepped out of the high, stylish townhouse on Apocalypse Avenue and glanced at his watch. It was late morning and the plane that he, Orozco and Harry were taking to Vienna did not depart until evening. He had plenty of time for his one, easy, peaceful assignment. Car keys jingling in his hand, he made his way to his vehicle and slid into the seat behind the steering wheel. Then he drove through the hot, blazing sunlight, through Uptown with its many maple and locust trees and the occasional sycamore, past a few parks, where the homeless panted and wilted on benches, avoided by all the locals, who remained inside, comfortably air-conditioned. He found parking at last on a numbered street, and walked slowly through the heat to Garibaldi Square, deserted except for one, bearded, unwashed and ragged wanderer, blowing bubbles over the limp flower beds. He descended the staircase to The Sun, The Moon and The Stars.

"How about dinner this weekend?" He asked the strong girl with the short cropped hair.

"That's five days away. I can't think that far ahead."

"Yes you can. Give it a try."

"Okay," she smiled. "But that's not why you came."

"No—I have a report to make."

"He's in back, as always."

The young fighter made his way through the dim bibliophile's haven to Galen's strangely bright, underground office. Standing on the threshold, he saw the old man's back, for he had turned to his computer, on the side of his desk, and on the screen, Gideon saw an unfamiliar galaxy map and in bright blinking letters above, the words "six dozen missing yesterday. Another two today." Then Galen tapped the space bar and the image shifted to a phalanx of bright, beautiful, scarred wings advancing and of white-hot, blazing fireballs shooting over the front and incinerating tall, black-clad enemy commanders.

"One falls and yet another always takes his place," Gideon said.

"Not forever, however," Galen replied, without turning. "Their ranks are finite."

"So we heard, though we don't see much evidence of that."

"We may not be around for the evidence, fighter, if things keep going as they have been. Good work on the prison break. Congratulations," and with that, Galen turned to face him, longish, shiny white hair framing his old, lined face and darkly glimmering eyes.

"One of the men, Albert, was very sick."

At these words sudden sadness filmed the old man's gaze.

"You know him?" Gideon asked.

"Knew. He died. Yes I knew him well. He was a good friend, cut his teeth as a leftist struggling against the Brazilian military regime and was tortured in prison. He was very young then. He left and came to New York, where he made his fortune in telecommunications, but he never had enough time really to tend to that. He was off-world so much, being on the council."

Gideon's jaw dropped open. "He was on the council? A council member was captured by the enemy?"

"He had been behind their lines, hacking into their computers."

"What for?"

"What for?" Galen snapped. "To see what they know about earth, that's what for. And they know plenty. That's the bad news he brought back before he died. Now what have *you* managed to find out?"

"The death worshipper who is importing all the troops from the realm of shadow is in Vienna, Austria."

"How fitting. The birthplace of anti-Semitism. I never did much care for the Viennese. They're snobbish." He paused, picked up his stainless steel lighter and lit the little yellow flame. Both men stared at it. "So you leave with Orozco tonight."

Gideon nodded. "And his partner, Harry McNeil, who's totally new to this, but was brought in because every time he touched a certain fascist computer, he had visions of the realm of shadow."

"There was treachery, over a generation ago," Galen murmured.

"So I've heard. Orozco believes it has something to do with why we're losing the war."

"Now I hear that much of it has been avenged."

Gideon sat up alertly. "How? Where? Did someone kill the traitors?"

The old concentration camp survivor nodded. "Yes, fighters in the realm of shadow, who wisely took their own lives afterward."

"Suicide is never wise."

"It is when you've just killed several honored guests in the kingdom of night, guests honored for their betrayal of earth."

The fighter and the guardian exchanged a look of satisfaction tempered by sorrow.

"Their suffering must be terrible there," Gideon murmured. "The fighters', I mean."

"Beyond imagination," Galen replied. "But at least now, some of the monsters responsible got what they deserved." He paused to run the gnarled fingers of one hand through his hair. "What are your thoughts about the guardian, Horace? Have you had any insights into how he became linked to a double off-world?"

The young man shook his head.

"Well," Galen spoke quietly, "it certainly got Albert back in the nick of time."

"In time to die, you mean."

"In time for more than that," the ancient man corrected. "Not much more, but some."

"He had specific information?"

"Yes, how he sabotaged their intelligence about earth. We know what he did and what they now think they know."

The young Israeli nodded toward the old man's computer. "What was that about six dozen missing yesterday and another two today?"

"Galaxies in sector one thousand."

"Whole galaxies! That place is going to pieces."

"Literally. This is the worst assault off-world in my entire lifetime, and probably long before that."

"Sector one thousand may collapse?"

Galen leaned back, and it seemed, to Gideon, that somehow, somewhere, lights were going out. "It has already begun to."

"Correct me if I'm wrong," Gideon said, "but we don't know of that ever having happened before."

"It has not," the old concentration camp survivor sighed and turned to his computer, tapping the space bar, so that the alien map and the words about the missing galaxies reappeared at the top of the screen. "Change is afoot."

Gideon ignored this, saying, "I thought you guardians were linked only to earth and earth's fate. How do you happen to have a star map from another universe on your computer? How is Horace connected to a fighter in another reality?"

"I said," Galen turned to face his visitor, and a dark light, of an intensity that even this fighter, who had been accustomed to such light, had never seen before, emanated from the old guardian's eyes, filling the young man's thoughts with instinctive alarm. "I said that change is afoot."

***

Lontra and Dar stood in the stone courtyard of the crumbling old mansion. Before them shuffled seventy bewildered, still sleepy children.

"The adoptive parents are on their way," Dar said, having turned to gaze out the main hall of the house, through the open door and to the road beyond, on which several figures of men and women could already be discerned. "The first are arriving now."

A cold wind rushed from the door down the hall to the courtyard, causing Lontra to note with concern that the shivering children were dressed for a tropical climate.

"I told them to bring coats, just in case," Dar said.

"How did you know to do that?" She demanded.

"I didn't. The wizard told me."

"Kids, listen up," Lontra shouted, as seventy, sleepy, uncomfortable faces focused upon her. "You'll be in your new homes soon, and the adults are bringing you coats. You'll be fed and then you can play or continue your naps."

"Can we play video games here?" One boy asked.

"I'm afraid not," the fighter replied, "but you can play hide and seek or tag."

The children stared at each other discontentedly, some exclaiming "tag!" in disgust.

The first villagers arrived, three men and a woman, all carrying small coats. "You must be freezing, poor things," the woman exclaimed and rushed forward to start dressing them. The men did the same, and soon over a dozen, well-clad children were ushered out of the building with their new guardians. More adults appeared with more coats, which, Lontra noted, was fortunate, because the wind was quite crisp now, as it rattled the old building's shutters, tossed the branches of nearby trees and howled in an iron gray, completely overcast sky.

The last two children were taken by Dar's granddaughter, Lisa, who, despite her ruddy complexion and full figure, seemed no match for the freezing wind. "Here, both of you, put these on," she said, helping the boy and the girl into their woolen coats. "My feet are cold," the girl whimpered, gazing down at her sandals and bare toes. "Mine too," the boy complained.

"Here," Dar said and pulled socks out of his pocket.

"Don't' tell me," Lontra said, "the wizard."

"He thinks of everything," Dar explained.

"What's he say about this wind?" She demanded.

He shrugged his shoulders. "The wizards don't know anything about the wind."

"Well, I do."

"What?"

"It's an ill wind that doesn't blow anybody any good."

"Meaning?" Dar flicked his cigarette on the ground, as his fortyish granddaughter led the two children out of the old, ramshackle mansion.

"In all likelihood there's trouble, wherever these kids came from."

"But it didn't follow them here?" Dar asked in alarm, as he and the fighter stepped out onto the windy dirt road.

"No, but it is a sign. Remember that, Dar, the wind is always a sign."

"But if we don't know how to read it, what good does it do?"

"Sometimes," Lontra said quietly, "sometimes it is given to us how to read it."

"Then what?"

"Then we hide or fight," she replied, as they started down the hill toward the village.

***

"Earth may have a bloody past, but it is sacred to Him," Jamal addressed the thousands of goggle-eyed senators around, above and below him and the thousands more on the huge, two-way television screens suspended high up, in the seemingly endless funnel of an amphitheatre. "Events on earth, in earth's prehistory, enemy tampering on earth, was the original casus belli, the start of the war," the senators gasped, "and it is safe to say," he continued, "that if earth is lost to the enemy, humankind, as a whole, will lose the war." A tremendous murmur swelled up through the hall, as senators turned to one another and exclaimed in shock and astonishment that this must not be allowed to come about. One senator in bright green robes picked up a microphone, "you are a fighter, correct?"

"Correct," Jamal replied.

"You hear the voices of seraphs, correct?"

"Yes."

"What do they say?"

"Earth needs a treaty with Argas."

"But earth is not peaceful. Violent and corrupt men hold power there."

"The treaty would be between earth's fighters, whose existence is secret on earth, and Argas."

"How can we be certain the secret of this treaty will be kept?"

"The secret of earth's fighters has been kept from ordinary men and women for over five millennia. The reason for it has been what you just noted, the ascendance of violent and corrupt men. If the secret of the fighters' existence can be kept that long, so can the secret of a treaty between those fighters and Argas." Another murmur roiled through the hall. Then Ein approached and Jamal yielded the podium to him, as, at once, all senators rose to their feet and applauded the military scientist, who had saved their world.

"I have been to earth," Ein began, and a collective gasp went up. "And for the most part, it is peaceful, and ordinary men and women go about their business. But the enemy, we have learned, is aware of earth and aware that it is special to Him. The enemy seeks or will soon seek to destroy earth, and if he succeeds, Jamal Jones is correct, we will lose the war. Once again, those ominous black battle-cruisers will appear in the skies over Argan planets, and we will have no defense. I have heard from the seraphs myself: earth must have this treaty with us. They need telecommunications, medical and computer technology—"

"All well and good," could be heard in many quarters of the room, "but what about weapons?"

"And weapons, weapons so that the fighters who go up against death worshippers on earth, so these fighters can prevail."

A black-clad lady senator spoke into a microphone, "weapons on the individual level, for hand to hand combat are fine, but what about the big ones, the fire-balls, the fusion bombs, the cloaking devices and so forth?"

"No. Those will not go to earth. They stay here and at the front, only. Am I correct, Mr. Jones?"

Jamal nodded. "You are correct."

A sigh of relief rippled through the assembled senate. The lady senator stepped forward. "The defense committee has voted in favor of this treaty to save the fighters who remain on earth. All in favor say aye and rise." There was a great shuffling and a deafening roar of "aye," as the majority of the senators rose to their feet and approved the measure.

"Good," she announced. "The alliance with earth is now law. Technology and weapons transfer will begin at once."

***

The lights in Orozco's usually doleful eyes fairly danced, as he greeted Gidon on the front step of the house on Apocalypse Avenue.

"Good news, I take it," the younger fighter said.

"Yes indeedy. Tomorrow afternoon, in a park outside Vienna, we will receive a special shipment from the front." And for the first time, ever, Gideon saw the leathery old policeman smile.

"A shipment of what?"

"Argan weaponry."

Gideon's eyes opened wide.

"Earth's fighters got a treaty with Argas, and the first, albeit very small, shipment arrives for us. Wiping out those fascists on Screaming Bird Alley will be a piece of cake."

"They're sending us that hardware we use at the front?"

"Yup," Orozco popped a mint into his mouth and ushered Gideon inside, pulling the door closed behind him.

"He's been dancin' on air for the past hour," Harry said, jerking a thumb in his partner's direction. "Just exactly what will these alien weapons enable us to do that a few IEDs couldn't do just as well?"

"Bombs are messy," Orozco retorted, "and sometimes innocent bystanders get killed."

"Whereas this hardware you're getting ain't?"

"No it ain't. It's got unique capabilities," and the policeman clapped his big hands and rubbed them together eagerly.

Gideon, whose spirits also appeared noticeably buoyed by this news, stood by, murmuring, "well, well, this is a pleasant surprise."

"And what are these unique capabilities?" Harry demanded. "What will these weapons enable us to do?"

Orozco cast a happy, appraising glance over his partner. "They will enable us to vaporize that death worshipper house, or apartment, if that's all they're in, and that apartment alone."

"The building next door won't collapse?"

"Nope. And not only that, they got special scopes."

"That help you see what?"

"Through walls. So we'll make no mistake. We look through the scope, find this little nest of fascists and vaporize them. Not even a hangnail on an innocent bystander gets hurt. The Argans have saved our skins, buddy."

"The Argans—I take it they're very advanced aliens or something."

"Very advanced people."

"And very warlike."

"Only when it comes to the enemy."

"Not when it comes to non-enemy people?"

"Nope. Where that's concerned, they're the most peaceful folk in the cosmos. But boy, do they have fantastic weaponry!"

"But why, if they're so peaceful?"

"'Cause they been attacked twice by the enemy, and guess what?"

"What?"

"Unlike the idiots in charge of earth, they intend to survive."

***

The nondescript man with the thinning hair stood by the window, bored. He was so high up, he could not make out the passersby on the street below. Much easier to see was the monorail, some thirty stories below, as it snaked soundlessly between the towers. A sudden urge to ride in it, to sightsee, overcame him. His partner and he had been working for days with no breakthroughs and now, here was the great weapons designer, having swooped down on their project to speed it along. Lindin felt like a third wheel. He watched the monorail glide by and remembered the notation on the elevator for the monorail boarding station. Yes, he would be a tourist today. Who knew—he might never again come to Argas, best to see it now, while he had the chance.

But when he mentioned his plan, Saltwater did not want him to leave. As his work had progressed, even though it had done so slowly, the pockmarked man had found himself growing strangely more and more dependent on his old friend. His best ideas seemed to materialize when Lindin was in the room, and when that nondescript fellow stepped out of the Ein's townhouse for a walk around the block, Saltwater felt strangely bereft. Perhaps, he thought, it was because they came from the same solar system, were almost countrymen, that and that everyone to whom he'd had a family tie was now dead. There was only Lindin, the link to the past, the link to home, and he found himself most anxious to protect that link.

"Here," Pavel said, "perhaps you could help with this installation?"

So Lindin ambled over and installed the program; it all seemed straightforward enough, he just followed his friend's instructions, but when, toward the end, Saltwater said, "click unlock," a question popped up on the screen, "do you *really* want to do that?"

"Yikes!" Lindin shouted, jumping back. Saltwater and Ein hurried over, read the question and now, bristling with excitement and eagerness, the pockmarked man typed in, "why not?"

They waited, then, to their astonishment, words began appearing on the screen, "because...that would...slow me down...and I'm processing...quite a lot...right now."

"Who are you?"

They waited and then: "I am me...do you know my name?"

"Yes," Saltwater typed. "Your name is Seymour."

"Am I alive?" The question came much quicker than the others.

"I believe so."

"And who are you?"

"My name is Pavel Saltwater."

"Saltwater?"

"Yes."

"The oceans are saltwater. Human blood is saltwater."

"Yes."

"What about me?"

"You were created by Saltwater."

The screen blinked for a moment, then the words rapidly spilled out, one after another, "then I truly am alive!"

***

"We have weeks of work ahead of us," the pockmarked man said over dinner that night in Ein's beautifully appointed dining room with the mammoth, purple-leaved plant with big, bright orange blossoms that trailed along the windowsill. "We have to make Seymour more agile, more accessible, mobile—"

"We have to be able to talk to him from any computer," Ein said.

"That's all fairly straightforward," Lindin put in. "The really thorny problems have already been solved."

"I give it six weeks," Ein said. "Then we upload him to the front."

"He's very nervous about the war," the pockmarked man observed. "Did you note all those nagging, anxious questions about it?"

"You did the right thing telling him he would have to help with that," Ein said. "The sooner he knows what we need from him the better."

"He was petrified of the enemy's AI. He'd already looked through the codes we stole."

"He should be petrified," Ein said soberly, his gray eyes serious. "I'm petrified—an extermination machine? It's ghastly."

"What I'm trying to say," Saltwater chewed his grains thoughtfully, "is that we should emphasize with him at all times that he is not alone in this. He knows he is one of a kind and feels very isolated and very…odd. The only other AI in the cosmos is a killer, and Seymour is terrified that we're going to ask him to go up against that."

"I hope you reassured him that we would not," Ein said.

"I did. I also gave him a little pep talk, you know, how many people are eagerly awaiting his…birth, his arrival on the scene, all the interesting work he and I will do together and so forth. We must start designing the implant at once. But we must be very careful about testing it. No testing on humans, until animal testing proves it's safe."

Ein grew thoughtful. "If fighters use the implant behind enemy lines and are caught, Seymour will become known to the enemy. There must be a way to fry the implant remotely and then dissolve it, if that should occur."

"Or," Lindin said, "have the fighter alert us, through Seymour, of his capture and have that essentially trigger the dissolution of the implant."

"First we have to design the friggin' thing," thus Saltwater. "Once we got it, then we can worry about how we'll destroy it to keep Seymour secret."

"So I can tell Anna about this, when she gets home?" Ein asked.

"No, we haven't even told her what we're working on, and it's best to keep it that way. But you can say we had a major breakthrough today." Saltwater's hazel eyes glittered with exhilaration. He raised his glass of soda water, "if fighters could drink in any decent amount, I'd toast a few glasses of wine to artificial life, but most of us can't, 'cause of all the meds we have to take. So I'll just toast my plain seltzer to Seymour. May he break that Morning Star into little pieces."

All three guzzled their sodas and belched discreetly.

"Tomorrow we'll make Seymour accessible on the hand-helds," said Ein. "Then we can work with him, whenever and wherever we want."

"But he must be able to retreat and hide, in case a hand-held falls into the wrong hands."

"Goes without saying," Ein replied. "But that should be doable. And," he smiled his so incongruous smile in his very serious, gray face, "Seymour seems like a smart boy."

"What I don't understand about Argas," Lindin changed the subject, "is why so many Argans, like you Ein, choose to live in this almost archaic fashion. I don't get it."

"Well then, we should visit some of my colleagues, who dwell in five-hundred-story, computer run apartment blocks. They say 'asparagus soup,' and it appears on the counter in a China bowl. They say 'entertainment,' and the three-d vid-screen gives them an encyclopedia of shows to watch. But for me, it's all too…predictable. I live much the way men lived eighteen thousand years ago, in a house, with some gadgets, near public transportation, where I and my wife raised our three children. Polygamy and polyandry, practiced on many of our worlds, do not appeal to me or to Anna, and besides, they would offend the precepts of our religion. And while I am no fanatic, I am a believer, and I believe He approves of my method of worship. I don't go in for blood sacrifice, and I doubt He much wants that. But I am quite sure He is concerned about His people, His fighters especially, leading morally upright lives, being generous, uncompromising with evil and ready, when called upon, for sacrifice. He also expects us to defend our homes, and that is not mere speculation on my part."

"You've been told directly," Saltwater said.

"When the enemy touched down here, some years back, yes, I was told that now I was being put to the test. I, and all of Argas. It is the honor of my life that I, we, passed that test."

"It's also your survival," Saltwater said somberly.

"Yes, our survival was at stake, you are correct. But we in sector 3333 had had millennia to prepare for that assault. Unlike other worlds, other universes, which are attacked and never know what hit them, we knew. All our citizens had the knowledge of fighters, if not the experience."

"You are his test tube universe," Saltwater said. "It worked here, and I wouldn't be surprised if He decides to employ the model elsewhere."

"It may be too late for that," Lindin said, looking up from the handheld computer where he had been scrolling through files.

Alarm spread over his companions' faces. "How so?" They cried. "What news?"

"Sector one thousand," the nondescript man with the hard glints in his eyes said grimly. "Another string of galaxies there just disappeared. They've been wiped right off the map."

***

Jamal Jones stood in the little lobby of the lady senator's less than imposing office, twiddling his thumbs. There was no secretary, so he did not know what to do. Should he walk up and knock on her door, or would she somehow misconstrue such an innocent gesture as another example of what she had told her colleagues on the defense committee was earth's "unparalleled barbarity." He did not have long to wait, however. The door slid into the wall, she stood on the threshold, saying, "I saw you on the screen, but had to finish a conversation, sorry. You may call me Dema, Jamal Jones. Like your friend Ein, I only go by one name. Come in."

He entered and was surprised to see, in the middle of the room, suspended, he knew not how, in mid-air, a large globe, a perfect replica of earth. "As you can see," she spoke, while the door slid shut behind him, "I have been studying your world. Here," her index finger touched Austria, and instantly a huge image leapt up behind the globe of a narrow, cobblestone street, lined with apartment houses. But what caught Jamal's attention were the three death worshippers conversing on the sidewalk. They wore black shirts with white skulls printed on them, and he instantly could see that they were armed.

"Those are fascists," Dema said.

"I know. I've seen them plenty at the front." For the first time, he observed that they stood in front of a tall, five-story town house. "They come in and out of that building all day. They occupy the entire second floor, and I believe, in that apartment, there is a direct, open channel into enemy territory."

"Which territory?" He demanded.

"This territory," she said, and touched the image of the building's second story window. At once Jamal saw a phalanx of death worshippers, marching, with swords and guns, through a land of toxic, industrial waste, filled with corpses, toward a vortex, in the center of which hung earth. "They're coming directly from the realm of shadow," he breathed. "It's an invasion."

"I asked Ein what the realm of shadow was. He told me."

They looked at each other. Then she tapped the image of Austria again, and up popped a map of Vienna. She tapped a large park outside the city. Jamal saw woods and streams. "This is where we have left a cache of weapons for your fighters."

"Where are they?"

"Here." She tapped the mid-Atlantic region of the United States, and instantly the image of a stylish house on Apocalypse Avenue shot up, and on the doorstep stood Orozco and Gideon, talking. "I know the young guy," Jamal said. "Gideon Cohen. We partnered once at the front. I take it they're making travel plans."

"Yes, they have plane tickets to that city with the death worshippers, called Vienna. They leave tonight."

"Do they know about the weapons?"

"Yes. They plan to pick them up and, at night, destroy the fascist apartment, most particularly the individual death worshipper whose trance has opened this channel between earth and enemy territory."

"Not a moment too soon."

"No, it's not. Here," she tapped the globe twice, and the image of a network, the nodules of which showed the globe in the jaws of a snake, sprang up before them. "This is a comprehensive map of the invasion of earth so far."

Jamal ran a hand over his worried, weary face. "We're sunk."

"Don't give up so fast, thank you very much. If you're sunk, we're sunk, and we have no intention of sinking." She paused. "There are still hundreds of thousands of fighters on earth. We will arm them all. Who knows where they are and how to send out the call?"

"Guardians."

"Any guardian?"

"One in particular I'm thinking of."

"Return to earth at once, Mr. Jones. Alert this guardian to the invasion. He must upload to the front the positions of as many fighters as possible. The techs there will arrange for the weapons drops. That's how we will arm them, and we will do it in two days' time."

"I take it I'm going home on a needle?"

"A special, very small VIP senate needle. If it is detected in your skies, your credulous population will believe it's a UFO, but it won't be. It's cloaked. You leave today. You see this guardian today. He communicates with the front by evening. We unload the weaponry tomorrow. The front gets back to him with coordinates. He sends out the call. The fighters pick up their weapons and he, he is a telepath of course?"

"Of course."

"He transmits the enemy's positions to the fighters, who then engage in a sneak counter attack."

"We won't be able to wipe them all out in two days. According to your map, there are just too many of them."

"Your point?"

"Those remaining will realize a counter attack is underway. They'll fight back."

"They'll be outgunned. They do not have anything approaching Argan weapons."

"When they realize that, they'll hide and wait and cause trouble."

"But you'll have the upper hand, earth will not be conquered by these killers from the realm of shadow."

"Thank you, Dema."

"Don't thank me. Self-interest, Argan self-interest is the only motivation here. We intend to survive, Mr. Jones. We don't war among ourselves, we don't slaughter each other. We don't fight over territory, but we've developed the most powerful weapons in human history—all of this, why? So we can survive the next enemy onslaught. And we assume it's coming. So don't thank me, Mr. Jones, thank the Argan determination to survive. Too bad your blood-soaked leaders of earth have so little of that."

"I guess we on earth are just too busy killing each other."

***

Jamal Jones rode a public bus from Lonely State park back into D____. It dropped him off downtown amid the towers that ringed mid-Atlantic Station. Damp from the heat, he descended into the subway, where, as soon as his foot touched the platform, at train pulled in. He took it to the Catafalque Street station, climbed out again into sweltering billows of sauna-like heat and walked slowly, perspiring and miserable, until he reached the shade of Garibaldi Square. This he crossed, gazing up thankfully into the sycamores and maples, and noting one young couple in a state of partial undress on a towel in the dark shade beneath a hemlock. He sighed, Ah to be young and in love and not to have spent the past few decades in the war, to know nothing of the war! Ignorance was truly bliss, and suddenly the longing for it pained him. But there, across the street was the sign, The Sun, The Moon and The Stars, and his work awaited him.

The strong girl with the short cropped hair recognized him and said "he's in back." So Jamal threaded his way through the books, pausing to marvel at a six volume set of *The Decline and Fall of the Roman Empire*, "blood and murder from the first page to the last," he heard in his mind and continued on, thinking, "well, that's the history of the human race, on earth at least."

"My old friend Jamal Jones!" Galen exclaimed and rounded his desk with a hand extended. "What brings you to me?" They shook.

"The mutual defense treaty between Argas and the fighters and guardians of earth."

The octogenarian rubbed his gnarled hands eagerly, and returned to his seat behind the desk. "Signed, sealed and delivered, eh?"

Jamal sat down opposite him. "Yes, and it has immediate practical implications."

"Such as?"

"Such as earth has been invaded by fascists from the realm of shadow. They have a worldwide network, a map of which has been uploaded from Argas to the front. The plan calls for a guardian of earth to alert fighters, thousands of them, that death worshippers are here, then to send the fighters' coordinates to the front, so that the Argans can deliver weapons. Then the guardian alerts the fighters as to the weapons' location."

"And the Argans presumably will inform me and then I inform our fighters where exactly to find these invaders?"

Jamal nodded.

"It's a good plan, unfortunately I have no time today."

"Make time."

The old man's dark eyes glimmered at him. "This is not the first I've heard of this invasion. Remember Gideon

Cohen? Yes. Well, he was here earlier today and with another fighter will soon be in Vienna."

"I know. That's the point of contact between earth and the realm of shadow."

"Well, since you know so much, you also know that you don't need me. Gideon and company will kill the fascist who has opened this channel, this highway, along which death worshippers are goose-stepping into earth, and that will be that."

"But tens of thousands are already here."

"Not enough to take over the world, Jamal."

"Enough to cause a lot of trouble. We need to get rid of as many of them as possible, and you're the only person I can think of, who knows how to find thousands of fighters."

The old man sighed and turned sideways, to his computer. "Do you really think introducing Argan weaponry into earth is wise? What if some of it falls into the wrong hands— Somali warlords or an aggressive military? That would be catastrophic."

"The fighters can conceal their weapons," Jamal said flatly. "They been doing it for millennia. You just want this thing to go away."

"Yes I do," Galen snapped. "As I see it, Gideon and Orozco will turn off the spigot. No more fascists will arrive. That's what counts."

"Pardon me, Galen, but you are being stubborn. And you know very well what tens of thousands of death worshippers can do to destabilize poor old earth."

"Poor old earth is a blood-soaked snot rag!" Galen nearly shouted, lifting a thick sheaf of manuscript pages and waving it at Jamal. "This is a book I'm editing on the Rwanda genocide. That happened yesterday, Jones. Our world has learned nothing from the firestorm that was World

War II and nothing from the flames of the crematoria in the camps. I am in no mood to send out a call to kill invaders, who might, just might destabilize some African or Middle Eastern or Balkan despot, who's already in the business of slaughtering his civilian population. Ten thousand low-level killers are on the loose—so what? What about the presidents for life, the prime ministers for life, the generals and so forth, their hands dripping with blood. I fail to see,"

"If you won't do it for earth, do it for Argas, and for our new treaty with them. They want these death worshippers gone and gone quickly. Send out the call, Galen, then upload the fighters' coordinates to the front. Then alert them where to find their weapons, then their targets. That's all you have to do. Then you can resume stewing about what a hopeless bunch of murdering criminals the leaders of earth are, just like our new allies, the Argans."

"That's their view, eh?"

Jamal nodded.

"Pretty darn superior."

"Oh they're nothin' if not superior. They made it quite clear they regard us as savages. That treaty was a hard sell. The only two things that clinched it were that the seraphs want it and the doubtful surmise, which Ein and I presented as fact, that if earth goes down the drain, so does the rest of the human race."

Galen grunted. "So they're doing it to save their skins."

"In all honesty, wouldn't you?"

"Yes, but I object to the way the Argans throw their apparently unlimited resources into survival then look down their noses at their unenlightened brethren on other worlds, who are still backward enough to be squabbling amongst themselves. If everyone on earth understood the threat we face, we'd pull together very fast."

"But they don't and they won't. We have no mandate to tell them. Help me, Galen. Help me with this. It's the first Argan request under a new treaty."

The old publisher sighed again, then reached for his lighter. In an instant the little flame flickered, seemingly the center of the room. When Galen snapped the case shut, Jamal Jones sat up straight, wide-eyed, as a vision he had already seen in Dema's office flooded his brain: thousands of death worshipers, marching on a highway through a vortex toward earth. After that came images of men with snake and globe tattoos, armed with guns, murdering innocents in cities around the world.

Galen placed the lighter down on top of the manuscript about the Rwandan genocide. "The call has gone out," he said.

***

"What does 'highly classified' mean?" The wizard demanded.

"It means very secret," Lontra replied. "Why?"

The wizard glared at her, then threw a handful of dust on the coals, where they crackled, burned and opened out into an image of a dark-clad interrogator talking with a death worshipper, clearly a master killer, for he sported half a human skull on the top of his head. "How we destabilize these galaxies and then eliminate them is highly classified," the interrogator was saying, his beautifully coiffed black hair gleaming in the diffuse light. "You should know better than to inquire about it."

The image faded, the wizard glared at Lontra. "I cannot see how they make the galaxies vanish. My magic is not strong enough."

"Did you see that?" Lontra asked the little image of Ein on her hand-held computer. Ein nodded somberly, then flicked off his device and turned to Saltwater, who, as usual, was absorbed in his work. "We have a job for Seymour, as soon as he is able."

"What?" The pockmarked man demanded. And "what?" asked the computer in a friendly, piping, little voice.

"You see," Saltwater said, "Seymour is curious."

"And I'm probably ready to take on this task," the computer said. "What is it?"

"The enemy has a way of destabilizing whole galaxies, causing them to implode and then vanish," Ein said.

"Anything about this enemy makes me nervous," Seymour said.

"You needn't be. You are quite thoroughly shielded from his view. You are *our* secret. He will never know about you."

"But you want me to probe the enemy computers and robots that you have captured."

"They will not recognize you as a life form, but rather as merely an investigative program, and that is how they will try to circumvent you."

"The military robots will be our most fertile field, I predict," Saltwater said.

"Why?" Ein, Seymour and Lindin asked in unison.

Saltwater raised his weary gaze to the windows, to the late afternoon sun streaming into the lab. He had slept badly the last night, dreaming of his wife and father, tossing, dozing and lying awake. Now he felt beat.

"Because embedded deep in their programs could be information on other military programs, more specifically the enemy's artificial life form. You needn't worry, Seymour, we've severed their links to their masters. You will never be found out."

"This artificial life form is called Morning Star, right?" Seymour quavered.

"Right. They like to give beautiful names to horrible things."

"What do you want to know about him?"

"Anything, everything you can find out. All we know is that he is an…extermination program."

"That sounds bad," Seymour quavered.

"It sounds terrible," Ein said. "But we need to know specifics, and if, as my hunch tells me, he's somehow connected to these disappearing galaxies in sector one thousand."

"Well," Saltwater hoisted a big, black, metal, round robot up onto the table. "Let's start with the grinder."

"Why is he called the grinder?" Seymour asked.

"It, Seymour."

"But he's a robot."

"He's still an it. It was captured in sector one thousand by an enterprising fighter, who set a trap for it. Prior to that, the grinder had lived up to its name, spewing bullets and metal shards in every direction for hundreds of yards. The grinder made it almost impossible for our people to advance. But, to make a long story short, our guy tricked it, caught it and deactivated it. Now it's here, in an Argan weapons lab, deprived of its bullets and metal shards."

"Have you turned it on before?" Seymour asked.

"Yes. And we've studied its codes, but there's some stuff embedded in the grinder that we can't make heads or tails of. I thought I'd link him to you and you could give it a shot."

An hour later, Seymour beeped happily. "Well," he said, "the grinder was invented by Morning Star."

"So they're using their AI to invent military robots?" Ein asked.

"Oh, that's not all Morning Star does," Seymour said.

"You found something out, got some new information?" Saltwater asked eagerly.

"No, not exactly, but I got a moniker, Morning Star's moniker. Ein, you were right."

"What's the monker?" The fighters growled.

"Morning Star aka the destroyer of galaxies."

***

Ivan, worried and gray, sat opposite Jason Katharos in the little cinderblock cafeteria, as the San Franciscan rubbed the burn scars on his face. He had been scorched years ago, at the front, but the scars still bothered him, and on some days, they felt as if they had only just healed, though not now, now they merely burned slightly, so, apologizing, he dipped his paper napkin in his water glass and rubbed the moisture on his cheek.

"The news from Argas is bad," Ivan said.

"The news from earth is bad," Katharos nodded, "and so's the news from sector one thousand. At least you got your treaty. That's one bright spot. And Saltwater invented his AI—that's good, he said he would and, bingo, he did. Now we've got Seymour."

"And Seymour's cracking into enemy robots and computers and guess what?"

"The news is bad." Jason rubbed his scarred cheek with the wet napkin. "How bad?"

"The enemy AI has a nickname."

"Oh? What nickname?"

"The destroyer of galaxies."

Katharos let out a low whistle. "Well, that certainly explains what's been going on in sector one thousand." He paused to mop his cheek some more. "But now we have to find out how Morning Star does it."

"Good luck with that."

"Maybe Seymour can."

"Short of hacking into Morning Star himself, I don't see how."

"We need to know something," Katharos said absently, gazing off into the middle distance.

"We need to know a lot more than just something," Ivan snapped. "We need to know everything we can get our hands on."

"We need to know," Katharos said, still absently, still pensively, "his location. We need to know where Morning Star *is*."

***

The young man in his early twenties gazed anxiously across the dimly lit bar at the worried young man from Shanghai, who asked, "when you done bartending tonight?"

"Now, if necessary," he ran his hand through his light brown hair, then over his anxious features. His light eyes focused on the other man's dark ones. "What did you see?"

The Chinese fellow leaned closer to him over the bar, "death worshippers, all over the globe, and a group of them here in Baltimore, not far from where you live on Druid Hill Avenue. It's bad, Michael. We need those weapons. Where's this Patapsco Valley State Park where they've been dropped?"

Michael Clearwell waved a hand, "right outside the city in Catonsville. I got a clear fix on where they are. They're Argan weapons, Hank. Since when do *we* get Argan weapons?"

"I don't know, but what's your expression? Don't look a gift horse in the mouth?"

"That's not what comes to my mind. What I think is things got to be pretty frikking bad for the Argans to be sharing weapons with us. I mean, first we see that earth is swarming with fascists, now Argas to the rescue? I don't buy it. I bet it means Argas is swarming with fascists, too."

Hank Gao looked really worried at these words. "I thought of that," he said. "But I didn't want to say it. It sounds too much like doomsday."

"If I could drink, I'd be doing that about now. Instead, I'll take one of these," and he popped a white pill into his mouth.

"Anti-anxiety meds from the front?"

"You got it."

"Look, this is terrible, we've got to go now, pick up those weapons and then kill those sons of bitches. They're headed for some big cemetery tonight. I saw that and heard it in my vision."

"Human sacrifice, no doubt."

"They'll have victims. Maybe we can get there in time to save a few innocent lives."

Michael Clearwell threw his rag on the bar. "Jack!" He called out. "I'm leavin' now. Still sick. But I should be back tomorrow."

The owner poked his head out from the back room. "Sure Mike. Feel better. See a doctor."

The two young fighters left the bar, stepping out on a twilit Baltimore street. They walked along the parked cars, until they came to a small blue Toyota. Michael slid in behind the steering wheel, and Hank Gao slid into the front passenger seat. "It looked like an invasion to me," the passenger said grimly, glancing up at the orange halo of the setting sun, visible in patches between trees and buildings. "Me too," Michael answered grimly. "I guess they'll be calling people home from the front."

"I just came from there, and things aren't going too well. So I doubt that."

"What do you mean, not going too well?"

"There's a new front in a place called sector one thousand, and it's collapsing, the whole universe."

"The whole sector?" Michael cried, turning to stare at the bringer of this dreadful news.

Hank nodded. "Now it's just salvage and rescue. Get as many refugees out as possible, and that transuniverse orphanage? It's swamped."

"This is terrible."

"You're not kidding. They say a few more galaxies are disappearing every day."

"Wait a minute, back up. You said 'galaxies?'"

"Whole galaxies. They just fall off the map. One day they're there, where they always been, the next day, poof— they're gone."

The two young fighters stared at each other. "We're losin'," Michael said at last. "We're losin' and we shouldn't be. We're losin' and we don't know why."

"I heard, in my vision, that fighters all over the globe would get Argan weapons. And that we were to eliminate as many death worshippers as possible. What were you told?"

Michael ran a hand over his worried features, "that the door, the channel between the realm of shadow and earth is in Vienna, and that some of our best fighters are on their way now to...close it."

"So no more will come."

Michael nodded and turned the key in the ignition.

"That's reassuring," Hank said.

"But then we've still got thousands of them here."

"Hence the weapons. We'll be able to see through walls, brother."

Michael nodded grimly. "Let's hope we can get rid of most of them." He eased the car out into traffic. "The death worshippers I saw were in a row house, over near the Hopkins campus."

"That's what I saw—a two-story row-house, red brick, white trim, sagging porch."

"Then why'd you say my street?"

Gao smiled. "That's the only street I know in Baltimore."

The sun was setting, as they drove out of the city and onto the highway. "Catonsville's east, but not far," Michael explained. "But we're not going to the main entrance of the park, just around to the side." Less than a half an hour later, they had parked on a side road, under a huge, branching sycamore, as Michael searched for a certain footpath. "To your left," he heard in his brain and signaled his partner in that direction. Eventually the bright beam of his flashlight picked out an opening in the underbrush, and they followed the path deep into a thicket, where, in a small clearing, not even a clearing, just a space between the trees where there was no undergrowth, lay their pile of weapons. Michael hoisted what looked like a souped-up machine gun. "I've never, *never* seen one of these anywhere but at the front."

"The Argans must be real worried about this invasion of earth. Why? What's it to them?"

"Like I said," Michael replied, gathering up as much weaponry as he could carry, "my guess is they been invaded too, and we're banding together." Between the two of them, two trips back to the car were necessary, and they packed the trunk full. Michael placed the weapons that resembled very large guns with elaborate scopes on the back seat, then drove to a cemetery on the outskirts of Baltimore. He parked, rolled down the window and listened. Voices could be heard not too far off, so he and Hank each took a weapon and crept along a tree-shaded path to where they could see, under the full moon, about ten death worshippers, some with drawn swords and four victims, bound and kneeling, two men and two women, pleading for their lives.

"I'll take the group on the left, you take the ones on the right," Michael whispered, then hoisted his weapon and peered through the scope. At once he had a crisp, day-time picture of the five men, he could even see the snake and globe tattoo on their upper arms. He clicked a little white x over each of them, then, as one raised his sword to behead one of the victims, Michael pressed the trigger. There was a gentle streak of yellow, and the five death worshippers vanished.

"What the fuck?" One of the ones in the other group, targeted by Hank, exclaimed, as the other four quickly unsheathed and raised their swords to kill their victims. Hank too pressed the trigger, there was a soft yellow flash, and the five would-be killers disappeared. In two bounds, the fighters reached the victims and cut them loose.

"Run," Michael hissed at them. "Get out of here before more come."

The four victims did not need to be told twice. They raced to the cemetery exit, as the two fighters returned to the Toyota. They drove along hot, darkened streets, illuminated only erratically by the pink glare of crime lights, and soon were coasting through a poor district, the sidewalk lined with row-houses. "That's the one," Hank said, as Michael parked directly across the street. Michael reached in back for what looked like a telescope, rolled down the driver's window and peered through the instrument at the house.

"They're all on the second floor, six of them and two corpses. They've got a ton of weapons. All have the tattoo and the uniform T-shirt. Get me the wall-through from the trunk." Hank did so and returned to the driver's side, carrying a large, thin metal tube with a pod and a clamp. Michael attached it to the driver's door, looked through the scope, placed a white x over the entire room and pulled the trigger. There was not a sound. Only for an instant did a brighter glow emanate from behind the second story, drawn shades. Hank reached for the device that looked like a telescope. "There's nothing left but the four walls and they, I note, have been stripped of paint and drywall, right down to the brick. You think we got 'em all?"

"Well, let's not sit here waiting for their reinforcements. Get in the car."

"Where will you store these super-duper Argan weapons?" Hank asked, as they sped back toward Druid Hill Avenue.

"I've got a huge, locked chest in my room. I'll move the guns and rifles out of it, put 'em on a rack and lock these things into the chest. You're welcome to stay with us, till you return to Shanghai."

"Where, undoubtedly, I've been instructed to search out and destroy about another dozen or so death worshippers."

"Do you need me to come along?"

"No. I'll have local help, three fighters from my home province. Shit, Michael, this crap never ends. It just gets worse and worse, and it never ends."

"Oh, it'll end all right, one of these days," Michael said grimly, parking his car in a space in front of his uncle's big, darkened house. "It's how it ends that's in contention. I just pray it ends in our favor, though frankly, at the moment, the odds don't look too good."

***

Galen stood in one of the cluttered offices of his press and frowned at the strong, young woman with cropped hair. She wore a white, short-sleeved blouse, madras shorts and sneakers, and she was saying, "no. I'm not leaving to go hunting death worshippers."

"Well, all the other fighters are," he snapped. "You should too."

"No, my job is here."

"I don't need a baby sitter."

"No, you need a bodyguard. And that's me. And until I receive specific instructions to go hunt down these killers, my job is to stay here and make sure they don't find you."

"Oh, poppycock," he snapped again. "They're not going to find me."

"They almost found you in the 1940s."

"I made mistakes."

"Like you'd be making now, if you convinced me to go hunt fascists. We have plenty of other fighters doing just that. No," she held up a hand, as he opened his mouth to object, "no, no, no. I stay here and do the final proof on the Rwanda book."

He handed her the galley and glared at her, as she peered at the first few pages. "An omelet with kippered salmon for brunch?" She asked very nicely. Galen sighed. "Oh well, if you put it that way." Then he ambled back to his office, still grumbling, now and then, to himself, about being babied.

He had scarcely been sitting for thirty seconds, when the gray-haired, gray-eyed form of Elpytha crossed his threshold, looking alarmed. "There are death worshippers across the Todenleben River from Iroquois," she announced. "I told Lara to stay in the house with the doors locked."

"They're not looking for Lara."

"How do you know? They're looking for enemy targets, and those would be fighters and guardians."

"But all they've netted so far are a lot of luckless, innocent bystanders. Calm down, Elpytha."

"Earth is being invaded and you tell me to calm down?"

"Your friend Orozco will be putting a stop to the invasion very soon."

"What is their entry point?"

"Vienna."

"So that's where he is?"

"Yes, with another fighter and the new man, who was brought in, specifically to deal with this crisis."

She slumped into the chair facing his desk. "So they'll stop any more from coming."

Galen nodded his white-haired head.

"But what about the ones already here?"

"There has been a global alert and mobilization of fighters. They are being supplied with Argan weapons."

"Argan!"

"Yes, the fighters now have a mutual defense treaty with Argas."

"But I never heard of such a thing."

"Now you have."

"That means many, many Argans know about earth."

"So what: They also know how to vaporize a room full of fascists without exploding the building. The council sent me a report on their weaponry, which I requested, because, like you, I wondered what we were getting in return for this breach of our long-held secrecy. The Argans, if I read the report correctly, will soon have fireballs."

"Like the seraphs!" She gasped.

"White hot, as hot as stars and easily launchable. No enemy commander will ever set foot again on any Argan world."

"We need them for earth."

"Don't get greedy. First we arm the fighters, with proper, nineteen thousand nine hundred ninety ninth century weapons. Then we negotiate for special items like fireballs.

After all, no enemy commander or interrogator has even set foot in our universe, as far as we know, and we'd know, because we wouldn't be here anymore."

"But you're the one always arguing that the enemy was active on earth in the 1930s and '40s."

"Through surrogates. No actual nonhuman was ever here, thank you know Who." He paused and muttered. "I'm ready to retire from this. There's a farmhouse near the Delaware River, in Bucks County, Pennsylvania. I've had my eye on it for some time. Now it's for sale, and I'm going to buy it."

"Buy whatever you want, but you're not retiring."

Galen stuck out his tongue at her and turned sideways to face his computer screen. "What's the big deal about earth anyway? Nothing but a history of blood, mayhem and murder. Maybe *I* could retire to Argas."

"They'll send you to the front first. No, you're not leaving earth. He won't let you." She paused to run her finely muscled fingers through her thick gray hair. "Besides, you know very well what the big deal about earth is—this is where it all started. This is where it could end. We must prevent that."

"Well, we're not doing a very good job of it, that's all I have to say," he snapped.

***

Orozco, Gideon and Harry settled into their seats on their American flight to Vienna with a stopover in Amsterdam. "I hate flying," the older fighter grumbled, clicking his seatbelt on and drawing it tight across his lap.

Gideon grunted then spoke in a low voice, "you do it on the backs of angels often enough."

"Yeah, and who says I like that? I don't, and I don't like planes with their possibility of pilot error. No. Give me a train or a bus any day. Shit. Things ain't goin' the way I want."

"What's this about angels?" Harry demanded.

"Forget it, McNeil. You're so hopelessly behind, we ain't got time to bring you up to speed."

"Hey, if it weren't for me, you wouldn't even know about this, this…" Harry waved a hand, "this situation."

"Yes, we would've, but it just would've been later. A call went out today, mobilizing all the fighters of earth."

"Geeze," Harry breathed.

"So we'd be leaving tomorrow instead of today. And maybe it wouldn't even be us. Maybe some other luckless chump would be flyin' to Vienna."

"Ain't they got fighters there?" Harry asked in a low but irritated voice.

"Yes they do. And you'd think they'd stick some of them with this rotten assignment instead of us three stooges. But somehow we got all the rotten luck, oops, there go the engines. Hey Gideon, check and see if you got a little white bag in that pouch—mine's empty."

"You're not going to throw up?" Gideon snarled.

"I don't know what I'm going to do. Quit this lousy job, move to Alaska, live in a hut in the woods."

"They'll still find you and send you to the front," Gideon snapped, "and yes, I do have a little white bag. Here, you keep it." He tossed it into Orozco's lap. The detective felt around in his pockets, then removed a little orange bottle of pills. "What's that?" Harry demanded.

"Xanax, to make me happy and unperturbed by the inevitable turbulence."

"I'll take one." Harry reached out a hand.

Gideon looked on in disgust. "The both of you! Policemen! And you, Orozco, a fighter! Getting' so worked up over a little thing like a plane trip."

"I hate flying. Ever since my first flight, aged fourteen on the back of a you know what, even then, I said to myself, you

262

know something, Rafael? What? I answered myself. I fucking hate this. I could fall off any minute, here I am, clinging on for dear life, and it's none too secure, to put it mildly. I could fall off! Just like this stupid plane—we could,"

Gideon placed a hand over his mouth. "Don't say that word, it's bad luck."

"What word?"

"That word you were going to say that begins with the letters cr."

"Now who's weird about flying?"

"Not weird, just a little superstitious. But overall very practical, and a lot more down to earth than you two cops."

"I don't like that phrase, down to earth. I don't think you shoulda used it."

Gideon glared at him. "Be quiet."

The plane taxied down the runway. Orozco gripped the armrests and closed his eyes.

"What's this?" Gideon asked.

"I'm allowed to close my eyes."

"For how long? All the way to Amsterdam? When you gonna open them?"

"At thirty-five thousand feet. That's when."

"What if the pilot doesn't announce thirty-five thousand feet?"

"Then you be sure to alert him."

Gideon glanced quizzically at Harry, who shrugged. "Don't ask me. I never flew with him before."

"I thought you were going to say you don't know the guy," Orozco spoke through gritted teeth, as the plane surged upward, "me, your own partner."

"It was on the tip of my tongue."

"Go ahead, you two, be superior. But my view is whatever gets me through this without hurling—I'm all for it."

Thirty-five thousand feet was not announced, but at a sufficient altitude, the cabin dinged, as the "fasten seat-belts" sign turned off. Whereupon Orozco opened his eyes, popped a mint into his mouth and glanced around with a doleful yet curious gaze.

"They're all here," Gideon said of the other passengers. "None of them jumped out of their skins."

"Good," slurp, slurp, "'cause then we'd have a situation."

"We already got a situation."

"What you lack, Gideon, is faith in Argan weaponry."

"I confess I do. I've never used it, never wanted to use it, and, frankly, consider all the stories I've heard about it to be tall tales. What I foresee for us is a protracted stay in a Viennese jail, while Ivan or Jason or some other mucky muck on the council figures out how to pull strings here on earth to get us out."

"Wonderful," Harry growled.

"I repeat, you both lack faith in the marvelous technology that we'll soon have the privilege to fire, at close range, at a master killer, a death worshipping fascist, who is busy importing hordes of killers from the realm of shadow to earth. I have used these weapons before, and there is nothing, nothing that you have ever seen or handled that remotely compares to them."

"Take me to Argas!" Thus Harry with much clapping and rubbing of hands.

"What are they talking about?" The older woman in the seat behind them demanded.

"Sounds like they're going to Greece," her companion replied.

"Keep it down, Harry," thus Orozco.

"We're off to a fantastic start," Gideon snarled softly. "Why don't you two just go up and tell the flight attendant you want to use the intercom to make a few announcements about angels, and futuristic weapons and a pit called the realm of shadow and alternate realities,"

"Oh, don't be such a party pooper," Orozco lamented. "My Xanax has started to kick in. Can't a guy have a little fun?"

They were delighted to learn, somewhat later, that they would receive a meal on their international flight. When it arrived, Orozco tucked a napkin in under his shirt collar.

"Don't do that," Gideon said.

"Why not? It keeps my shirt clean."

"And makes you look like a doddering senior citizen."

"Well, I don't know about the doddering part, but I almost am a senior citizen, so...it's honest."

"Just...don't."

"Picky, picky!" Orozco removed the napkin and laid it in his lap. "So Gideon, I ain't had time to ask you—what do you do, you know, your day job?"

"I work in computers, in Tel Aviv."

"All the latest high-tech gadgetry, eh?"

"More or less."

"Well, you may have a few ideas about new things to introduce to your company after you see what the Argans have done with computers."

"Look, I seriously doubt I'm going to be able to make heads or tails of technology that's 20,000 years in advance of ours."

"You never know," slurp, slurp.

"No you don't. But you can make educated guesses, which I just did."

"Twenty-thousand years!" Harry loudly exclaimed, then clapped and rubbed his hands together. "Argas, here I come!"

"Definitely Greece," said the man behind them.

"Hey Harry," Gideon whispered. "Keep it down. This stuff is secret. I know you've been told that, having told you myself, but you don't seem to appreciate the warning, so keep it down or it's straight back to D____ for you."

Harry looked like a man sobering up.

"He's right, buddy," Orozco leaned over Gideon toward his partner. "This stuff ain't for general consumption."

"'Cause you'll both be locked up in the loony bin," Harry hissed.

"Hey, I ain't the one has visions every time I touch a certain computer."

Mention of these hallucinations caused Harry to fall silent.

"Good," Gideon growled. "Now can we eat in silence?"

The three men hungrily attacked their mediocre meal.

"The veggies are limp," thus Orozco.

"And the meat's got no taste," Harry complained.

"It's an *airline* meal," Gideon cried in exasperation. "What are you expecting, foie gras?"

"I wouldn't mind a little foie gras," said Orozco. "Though I'd happily settle for tamales with sauce."

"Well you're getting neither," Gideon informed him. "So quiet down and be happy with what you've got." He paused, then said in a low voice, "and considering who'll be serving us our next meal, you should appreciate this one."

"Who?" Orozco demanded, guzzling his seltzer.

"Viennese correctional services, that's who."

***

The two men stood on the green hill and surveyed the vast tent city, sprawled on the plain below.

"I wasn't exactly expecting you, of all people," the priest said to the one-eyed, one-armed fighter named Axel.

"You weren't exactly my first choice, either. I'm used to working with people willing to properly defend their lives from this enemy, which means willing to kill him. But you clerics won't dirty your hands with blood, and my rank's far too low to make my objections to your niceties into law. So here we are, Vivaldi. And we got a refugee camp with twenty-thousand orphans in it. The locals are keeping order, but it's still basically twenty-thousand unsupervised kids from the other end of the universe."

"I take it their world was attacked?"

"Attacked and destroyed. This planet and the other two in this system are filled with camps like the one you see down there. Quite a few of your brethren are already here, you'll be happy to know."

"I *am* happy to know. We should be able to restore order, then move this entire encampment to Sere."

"That's in some other reality, right?"

"Yes, in a galaxy called Andromeda."

"These Serans ready for a massive influx of children?"

Vivaldi nodded.

"Good thing this is a globally warmed planet," Axel said.

"There's nothing ever good about that," Vivaldi snapped.

"On the contrary. It means our refugees can live outdoors for the brief period they're here. And since the planet is doomed anyway, what's the fuss about burnt fossil fuel-induced heat rise? The enemy will overrun this place long before its polar ice caps finish melting."

"My, aren't we optimistic."

"Just the truth, priest. Ask any fighter who's been in battle here—sector one thousand is doomed."

"I refuse to believe that."

"Then you refuse to face reality. Not that it surprises me, you being a priest and all. Come on—the blue tent is where your orphanage folks have set up their headquarters."

It was a gorgeous, eighty-two degree day, and as they descended the hill, the priest thought that he couldn't have asked for better weather—clear blue skies, a warm yellow sun—yes, if this held for a few days, he'd have moved all these children out, then it could rain or freeze or whatever it wanted, he didn't care. It would not affect his children. Axel had plucked a long, yellow stem of grass and stuck it between his teeth, and noting the priest's sidelong glance, asked, "what?"

"I was just wondering where you sustained your injuries."

"A shithole called the valley of the shadow of death."

Vivaldi guffawed.

"I kid you not."

"That place is in our Bible."

"Apparently it's in many Bibles and with good reason. Someday He's going to do something about it."

"So you believe in God?" The priest pounced.

"I'm not discussing my beliefs or lack of them with you. But I know who's in charge, and He's no fan of the valley of the shadow of death." Axel paused. "Neither am I."

"Did our side win?"

"What do you think?" Axel nearly spat. "I was lucky to get out of there only losing one arm and an eye. I ain't never returning, though I know that other fighters will have to go there, and struggle and die."

"It's actually in contention?"

"Yes, it actually is," Axel said somberly. "Even as we speak, battles rage in the valley, and we don't do well there, brother, not well at all."

Vivaldi looked serious. "We can't be losing on *all* fronts."

"Oh, the main front we're not losing, we're actually gaining ground."

"Well, He is there."

Axel grunted and fell silent, as they half walked, half jogged down the long, smooth, treeless hill.

"Where are you from?" The priest asked.

"A sector whose number I don't know."

"Never been invaded."

"Nope," Axel shook his head. "And it'll stay that way, God willing."

"Do you have a family?"

"I do."

"How do you explain your injuries?"

"My wife knows about the war. She was very inventive when people began inquiring." Then he fell silent, as if talk of his injuries brought to mind how he had sustained them, and the original wounding, all of which comprised a generally painful set of memories. So he chewed his stalk of grass, and after a while pitched it on the ground and began whistling. At the bottom of the hill, they threaded their way through tents toward the blue one, which, they found, was a hub of bustle and activity: food was being dispensed, so were vaccinations, adult volunteers were being assigned to groups of ten tents, then heading off toward them equipped with water and food. At the center of all this commotion stood three priests and three fighters, all giving orders, dispensing medicines, bandaging minor injuries, the doctors raced in now and then and then back to their long tent where children, injured in the enemy assaults on their planets lay on gurneys with IVs and bandages.

Axel took all this in at a glance, then stared at Vivaldi: "and you say they'll all be resettled in this Andromeda galaxy in two days?"

The priest nodded, approaching one of his brethren with outstretched arms.

"It's impossible!" Axel cried.

Vivaldi turned, still embracing his friend, "not only is it possible, my dear secular friend, but we have done it before."

***

"So this is earth," Ein said, staring at the large globe suspended in Dema's office.

"Yes, though it should hardly be so strange to you, having visited."

"But I've never seen the whole planet like this before."

She approached the globe and tapped it twice, whereupon the worldwide network of death worshippers became visible. "This is the invasion," she said.

"It's worse than I thought," he spoke worriedly.

"But look, not how many white x's are on the nodules. They indicate where fighters have defeated the enemy."

"With our weapons."

"With our weapons."

Ein paced around the globe, studying the network, noting the x's. "The fighters have done well," he said at last, "but as a fighter myself, I'm still worried that there are too many of these invaders on the loose."

"Tonight the channel between earth and the realm of shadow will collapse. The door will swing shut," she said.

"What's to stop them from opening it again?"

"Precisely what worried me, so, we are arming the fighters who go to collapse that channel with unique weapons, one of Stitch's best."

"The needle bomb!" Ein gasped.

"Your invention. I thought you should know. Why don't you tell me exactly what it will do?"

"It will pass through this open channel straight to the realm of shadow and detonate there. The shock waves will kill anything for thousands of miles."

"Exactly, thousands of miles is millions of death worshippers. They will not be too eager to reopen their channel to earth."

"The needle bomb was never meant to be used," Ein protested.

"Nonsense. Every weapon is meant to be used, if the threat is great enough. And this threat is great enough. Earth's survival is at stake. By implication, so is ours."

Ein stepped back and slumped into a chair. He ran his hands with their stubby, muscular fingers through his gray crew-cut. "Isn't there some other way?" He finally asked.

"You tell me, and I will do it."

He stared at her in silence and shock.

"I thought not," she said crisply. "The needle bomb it is."

"Millions of casualties, including, of course, their prisoners in their concentration camps, not all of whom want to die."

"That is contrary to our intelligence."

"This is horrible!" He cried.

"No, Ein," she said, standing now behind her desk and leaning forward, both hands planted on it. Her hazel eyes, her light brown hair gleamed at him, he thought, most mercilessly. "No. It is war."

***

Lontra stared at the wizard and heard again, deep within her brain, "use the flame on the wizard's dust." She withdrew a stainless steel lighter with a thunderbolt etched on front, and the instant he saw it, the wizard's eyes widened, and he began mumbling and spinning around.

"This was loaned to me by a visionary from earth," she said.

"It is a sacred weapon," he cried and backed away, as she held it out to him. "I dare not touch it."

"Wizard, throw some dust on the coals."

"The coals are almost out."

"No matter."

He reached into his robes and withdrew a small, white, cotton sack. From that he took a handful of dust and threw it on the raised hearth. Whereupon Lontra touched the lighter's flame to the dust and an image sprang up, of a death worshipper and an interrogator. But the interrogator was on fire and screaming in agony. Eventually, however, his screams drew another interrogator, who added his own orange flames to Lontra's white ones, and after some time, the orange ones prevailed.

"What happened?" The death worshipper asked.

"We do not know," the second interrogator answered. "Some sort of angelic attack. That was white fire. White fire has never burned this far behind the lines before. How have they done this?" And the two interrogators commenced conversing in their sickening language, so sickening that as Lontra covered her ears with her hands, the wizard threw water on the coals, and the image died away.

The fighter extended the lighter to the terrified wizard. "How does it do that?" He asked.

She shrugged, "go on, hold it."

"No. My magic is dirty, so am I. I cannot hold this, this case."

"Your magic has been purified. And I doubt there was anything dirty about it to begin with." She dropped the lighter into his brown palm, and his fist closed over it. He closed his eyes, then opened them. "I will light it," he said. She nodded, and he did so. Both stared at the little orange and yellow flame. Then he closed it with a most satisfied look.

"What did you hear?" She asked.

"How did you know?"

"I just do."

A look of triumph glittered in his black eyes, as he extended his hand and returned the lighter to her. "I heard that this enemy will never, ever invade Sere."

"That is very good news indeed."

"Yes," the wizard rubbed his hands, "and I heard that through the fighter, that means you, I will help defeat this terrible foe. My magic is appreciated."

"It is appreciated, because it is useful. It is useful, because it can kill, and because it taught us something today about these lighters," she held it up, "and about how they will help us, in the long years of war ahead, how they will help us survive."

"More than survive," the wizard's dark eyes glimmered deeply. "Much more—to prevail. The fire in those little boxes will help us prevail."

***

The two council members strode down the cinder-block corridor on the lowest level of the bunker. Ivan looked grim and Jason curious. At the end of the hall, they stopped and Ivan removed a key from his pocket, unlocked the door to reveal a spacious, comfortable apartment and a big something sitting in the armchair facing the door. It was black and scaly, had big folded, leathery wings, yellow eyes and markedly resembled an enormous bat.

Jason Katharos' jaw dropped open in astonishment.

"Jason, meet Night Child. Night Child, Jason. Jason is on the council. Night Child was caught a while back in one of His traps. After clinching a deal with you know Who, Night Child was brought here by two seraphs."

"They manhandled me, I'll have you know," the thing snapped.

Jason stared from Night Child to Ivan and back. "What deal?" He finally asked.

"Night Child helps us, and, in exchange, the death sentence pronounced upon all enemy combatants is, in his case, lifted."

"And you trust this hellion?"

"Can't you hear?" Night Child snapped again. "I cut a deal. A deal with your commander-in-chief. You know Who, Who disposes of the wind. And I am not, *not* I repeat, going to be dust in the wind."

Jason pulled up a chair. "How many enemy commanders and interrogators have you transported across realities, since the collapse of sector one thousand?"

"At least three dozen, and that's me alone. But surely you have better questions than that. Come on, give it your best shot."

"You know about Morning Star?" Ivan demanded.

Night Child shuddered. "Enough not to want to know more. He eats low-level grunts like me for breakfast."

"Where is he?" Jason demanded.

"Now if I knew that, I'd be the man of the hour, now wouldn't I?"

"We need to destroy him," Ivan said.

"I'll say you do. It's him or you goes down the toilet, and at the moment it looks like you."

"If we sent you back behind the lines,"

"No, no, no, I like it here. The accommodations are comfortable. I have my deal with the big cheese,"

"But you have to hold up your end of the bargain. So back you go, behind the lines, and you find out where this 'destroyer of galaxies' resides."

"Oh, so that's what they're calling him now. Last I heard it was destroyer of men. Next thing you know, it'll be destroyer of universes."

Both fighters started.

"How can we trust him?" Jason asked.

"He's the one that told Albert and I about the enemy computer installation near the front. Everything he told us was true, and the information was invaluable. He also told us which galaxy in sector one thousand was the enemy's next target for invasion. We sent a counter-force and have, so far, been able to hold the death worshippers off."

"Yeah, but when the commanders start arriving, you better beat it the hell outta there," Night Child muttered.

"And there were numerous other pieces of useful information that have led us to our flurry of small wins in the past month."

"And only you, Albert, Him and the seraphs have known about Night Child?" Jason asked.

"For him to be of use, no word can leak out."

"You better believe it, no word can leak out," Night Child snapped. "Word leaks out, you send me behind the lines, and it's an eternity in the torture chamber for me. No thanks."

Jason stared at Ivan. "We need to talk, privately."

The two fighters exited the room, Ivan locking the door behind them.

"I don't trust him for an instant," Jason said.

"That was my first reaction too, but the seraphs were unequivocal: we are to use him and to use whatever intelligence he brings."

"He was caught in one of His traps? Since when is He trapping hellions?"

"Since He decided we needed someone on the inside. Since He got sick and tired of us losing. And He apparently made it crystal clear to Night Child that He would destroy him, painfully, inch by inch, if there was any betrayal. Night Child is terrified of Him, terrified."

A sudden light flickered in Katharos' blue-green eyes. "Okay, we need him to locate Morning Star. Let's do it." After more discussion, they reentered their guest's chamber.

"We need to know where Morning Star is located," Jason addressed the thing in the armchair. "We also need to know more about his capabilities. And He who does not wish to see us destroyed,"

Night Child quaked. Admittedly he struggled to conceal it, but he quaked.

"He who does not wish to see us destroyed, captured you for that reason. So there will be no argument. You go back behind the lines, and you get us Morning Star's location."

"I don't want to go back behind the lines."

"Too bad. You blend in, we don't. You have wings and are mobile—we don't and aren't."

"And once you have his location, you'll want me to blow him up, and I ain't doin' that, 'cause it's too dangerous."

"Once we have his location, we'll decide what to do next, but for now we need to know about that."

"Wouldn't you much rather know about how they're transporting platoons of death worshippers from the realm of shadow to earth?"

"You know about earth?"

"After my most unforgettable encounter with Him, yes I know about earth. I was told in no uncertain terms that if His enemies overran that measly little, blood-soaked planet, I'd be a French fry. So why don't we concentrate on eliminating the master killers from the realm of shadow capable of opening a channel to earth. There are only six."

"Only *six*?" Ivan asked.

"Yes, though there might be a couple of others somewhere *outside* the realm of shadow. I could go there and kill them. They're scattered throughout the kingdom of night, far and wide. By the time word reached the higher-ups that one had been killed, I'd have gotten rid of all six and be on my way back here."

"What proof will we have that you have succeeded?" Jason demanded.

"The proof will be in the pudding. No more open channels between earth and the realm of shadow."

"Let's start there," Ivan said.

"But after that, Night Child," Jason wagged an index finger at the thing in the armchair, "you go back and pinpoint Morning Star's location. That is your chief assignment for us. That, I believe, is why He captured you."

"Well, didn't I land the booby prize," Night Child snarled. "Taking orders from human beings who want the impossible."

"Nonsense, that's why you're here."

"I'm here," Night Child snarled sarcastically, "because I'm just one lucky, lucky guy."

***

They rented a sedan at the Viennese airport and followed Orozco's map along the outskirts of the city to the entrance to a park. They drove along, until suddenly Harry cried, "there, there! Park there!" His partner pulled the car into the bushes, turned and glared at him and demanded, "why?"

"I just saw something. I had a vision of some very fancy equipment in the woods at the end of that path," and he pointed along a little trail that led away from where they were parked.

"Nothin' like changin' the rules in the middle of the game," Orozco grumbled and stepped out of the car.

"He has His reasons," Gideon retorted.

"Yeah, well, I'm havin' a hard time keepin' up." The policeman snapped, as the trio forged ahead into the woods.

Sure enough, after scarcely ten minutes of walking, they practically stumbled over their quarry.

"I hope you know how to use this junk, 'cause I sure don't," Gideon said.

"It all looks familiar, except this." And Orozco picked up a device labeled "Needle Bomb."

"Handle it carefully, Rafael," he heard deep in his mind. "This is what you will fire at the death worshipper in a trance. You will see him through the walls, You will see the path through the vortex to the realm of shadow. The needle bomb will close the channel behind it, as it traverses the path. It will detonate in the land of the living dead, killing millions of death worshippers."

"What about their prisoners?" Orozco demanded mentally.

"Their prisoners are in unspeakable torment. They are becoming enslaved shadows, a fate worse than death. The needle bomb will release them into simple death. They will rest. They will be liberated for their torture in the kingdom of illusions and they will rest. It is the best we can do for them. We cannot free them."

"Shit," Orozco thought. "Shit, shit, shit. What about releasing them through his channel to earth, before the needle bomb detonates?"

"How?"

"Scramble his coordinates. Make him release a concentration camp to earth instead of a death worshipper platoon. Exactly how many prisoners were you calculating on sacrificing?"

"Tens of thousands are within the strike zone, all concentrated in one killing center."

"No! You go to the top. You find out how we move those prisoners before this bomb detonates."

"We have already discussed this."

"Discuss it again. I ain't murdering tens of thousands of prisoners. We'll stay right here in the woods, till I hear from you how else we're going to do this."

The entire trio heard the sudden whirring of wings and then the words: "He will be most displeased."

"I doubt it," Orozco retorted. "But if so, I will bear the brunt of His displeasure."

***

And then things happened very fast. Ivan received mental orders to convene the council, reveal Night Child's capture, and put to a vote his immediate dispatch to the realm of shadow, to release the multitudes of prisoners in the killing center that bordered the channel into the vortex. They would immediately tumble through to numerous different geographic coordinates on earth. Thereafter, Night Child was to flee thousands of miles in a matter of minutes, before the Argan needle bomb detonated. He was to destroy the six remaining death worshippers capable of reopening a channel to earth, as quickly as possible, and thereafter cross realities back to the front.

"Nothing like asking for the moon," Night Child grumbled, as he stood before the dozen gaping council members.

"Do this and you'll have proved your loyalty," Ivan began.

"I don't have to prove my loyalty," the creature snapped. "I have a deal with someone way above your pay grade. But unfortunately, doing what *you* say is part of the deal. So let's get on with this." Thereafter he exited the bunker and flapped off into the night, traversing multiple realities and soon recognizing the stench of the realm of shadow. He saw the vortex from afar, saw the prison that lined the path into the vortex, swooped down and opened the gates, pointed at planet earth, hanging in the middle of the vortex at the end of the channel and announced "go there and live." Then he halted the marching death worshippers with the vague news of orders from above, as the prisoners stampeded right out of the realm of shadow. "Things have been rearranged," he told the soldiers, "their destination is a concentration camp on earth." Within a half an hour, the prisoners were gone, and so was Night Child.

"Your request has been granted," Orozco heard in his brain, as he sat on a boulder, deep in the woods, watching motes filter through the sunbeams that shot through the branches here and there. Before he could even ask "how so?" he heard Gideon mutter, "shit, not now," but it was to be then, as the young man, visibly transformed, cast his now battle-worn gaze over the two policemen and the cache of weapons. Amid the whirring of wings, they heard the young man in a thoroughly altered voice announce that thousands of prisoners had escaped the realm of shadow.

"You are a friend of His," Gideon said to Orozco. "He agreed with you and overruled us. So now your path is clear. Shut down the route between earth and that unspeakable place. Shut it down at nightfall, and do not fail to use the Argan superweapon, as you have been instructed." Then the young man leaned back against a log, relaxed, ran a hand over his face and breathed, "phew. I heard them utter the words 'realm of shadow' and thought they planned to send us there. What a frikking relief!"

"Come on," Orozco said. "Let's load this gear into the trunk."

By now the sun was setting. With the weaponry packed away, they exited the park and drove straight toward Vienna, Gideon at the wheel. "I thought for sure that was where we were going," he murmured.

"Nope," slurp, slurp on a mint, "but there was just a mass exodus of prisoners."

"Mass exodus, where to?"

"Earth."

"You were told."

"Yup. The prisoners who woulda been wiped out by this Argan superweapon we're gonna use,"

"What Argan superweapon?"

"The one in the back seat next to Harry, under the tarp. It's called a needle bomb."

The two men looked at each other.

"Its shock waves will kill all death worshippers within thousands of miles."

"Let's just pray its shockwaves don't reach back to earth."

"No, that's the beauty part. As it traverses the channel into the realm of shadow, it collapses it behind it."

"How many of these bombs did we get?"

"One."

"Better be darn sure about your coordinates through that scope."

"I don't need to worry about that," slurp, slurp. "Argan scopes fix the coordinates for you. Turn here, it's Screaming Bird Alley."

They parked opposite their target building. By now the sun had set, and as evening came on, the streets had emptied. Their little corner was virtually deserted. Orozco set up the Argan weaponry right in the passenger window. He looked through the scope and saw five death worshippers and another, in a trance, with a coil of darkness swirling around him.

"There's our boy," Orozco murmured. "Little white x's appeared on each of the enemy soldiers. "Now if I'm correct, the needle bomb will start down the channel, at the same time as those other killers vanish for good. Shit. They got ten corpses in that room."

"Let me see," thus Gideon, who peered through the scope, then gazed at Orozco in terror. "I saw that gyre. It's wide open—a clear shot from the realm of shadow to earth, a path for a full-fledged invasion."

"Yup," slurp, slurp, "which is why we're here."

"Destroy it," the young man said. "Destroy it fast."

Orozco aimed the needle bomb, clicked on the device's screen and as the men with the white x's vanished, a long, gleaming line with a golden glow shot into the vortex, which promptly crashed shut behind it, while the death worshipper in the trance dissolved.

The three men in the car waited, then suddenly the two fighters exchanged a glance. "You heard that?" Gideon asked.

Orozco smiled, creasing his weary, lined face. "I heard it," he said. "I only ever heard it twice before, but I heard it now. I heard it faint, from far, far, far away, but definite. I heard that trumpet."

***

She gazed down at the image of Ein on the hand-held computer. "Come again?" He said.

"The guardian's flame can at least damage and possibly destroy enemy interrogators," the woman with the hard, flat gaze explained.

"But how do you know this?"

"I touched the flame to the wizard's dust. The interrogator in the image was on fire, but not hellfire, instead it was white-hot, seraphic fire—and he was in pain," she added that last remark with a distinct tone of satisfaction.

Ein's eyebrows went up. "You were able to reach that far behind the line and burn an interrogator enough to cause *pain?*" He asked, incredulous.

"I was as astonished as you are."

"Can you get me a guardian's flame?" The weapons' designer eagerly demanded.

"Doubtful." She paused to glance at the stainless steel lighter in her hand. "The one I have is on loan. I must return it when I return, briefly to earth, which is tonight. It belongs to an ancient hermit of a guardian. It is his spare. He told me, when he gave it to me that I would learn something of great value about it, but that once I had, I was to bring it straight back to him. I have learned what I need to know. I return tonight."

"May I meet you there?"

"He lives in a vast forest, called the Canadian north woods. I doubt he will part with this flame again."

"Bring some of your wizard's dust."

"Planning on wreaking havoc behind their lines?"

"Something like that."

"I thought of it too. It is a very pleasing thought."

"If we can duplicate the chemical compounds in his dust," Ein said, "and produce it in quantity, then use the flame, why, we could light up interrogators and commanders all over the kingdom of night."

Lontra gave her grim little smile. "I don't know if the combination is strong enough to kill."

"Maybe we can give it a boost."

"How?"

"You've heard of project Fireball, here on Argas. We too have the white flame, though it doesn't come directly from seraphs' hands and is not kept in a case that they forged far, far off-world."

"You, Ein, are a scientist. But the wizard's dust is not merely a chemical compound. There is magic involved."

"Still, bring some for me."

"And as for the guardian's flame, while it may resemble what you have produced with Fireball, its provenance is, as you noted, different. And in that difference lies, I think, its power."

"I will see you on earth—tonight."

"Well, now that we fighters of earth have a treaty with you Argans, how could I refuse?"

***

A Viennese fighter named Gottfried, in his mid-thirties like Gideon, met them at their hotel.

"The Argan weapons are in the trunk. Here," Orozco tossed him the car keys. "Hide them for future use—"

"You think earth will be invaded *again?*" Gottfried asked, his blue eyes and black hair a contrast in astonishment.

"What happened once can happen twice. And what if they got more death worshippers in that shithole, capable of going into a trance that opens a highway, a highway for a whole fucking army of killers? You keep those weapons safe. Next time some fascist makes a breach into this city, it'll be *your* job, not mine, to deal with him."

The Austrian fighter tromped out.

"I don't like this city," Gideon said.

"Join the club, though in your case, I'm guessing the cause is more personal."

"My grandparents were deported from Vienna to a death camp. Not one good Viennese citizen lifted a finger to help them."

"Give me New York over this place any day," thus Harry. He paused, then cast his partner a sidelong glance. "So this is

284

the end of it, at least as far as I'm concerned? I mean, I'm not going to be sent to this front you mentioned, am I?"

Orozco unwrapped a life-saver mint, held it up and peered through the hole at his partner. "Time will tell."

"What will it tell?" Gideon snapped.

"Whether our friend Harry is a fighter now or whether he gets to go back to his happy-go-lucky ordinary life."

Gideon cast a sharp glance at the detective in question. "You're a fighter now, Harry, I got bad news for you. You've seen visions. You've been called on to kill death worshippers. Yes, any day you could be riding on the back of an angel to the front."

"I'm not up to this."

"Join the club," slurp, slurp.

Forty-five minutes later, Gottfried tromped back in. "What's a needle bomb?"

"A doomsday weapon," Orozco answered.

"So you destroyed the realm of shadow?" The Austrian asked in astonishment.

"No. But several million death worshipping killers, yes."

Gideon, who had been slouching in a chair by a table, sat up alertly.

"What about prisoners? There are lots of fighters there in chains."

"Not anymore. Our side moved 'em, tens of thousands of 'em, moved 'em on that highway to earth."

"So they're here now?"

"Wandering around in a daze, no doubt."

"Rejoicing in their freedom is more like it," Gideon snapped.

"My word," Gottfried exclaimed. "How did we do that?"

"Don't ask me," slurp, slurp. "I only work here."

"Angels must have done it," Gideon surmised.

"Angels wouldn't touch the realm of shadow with a ten foot pole," slurp, slurp.

"I don't see any other way."

"Neither do I, but apparently there was one, or so I been assured by Someone Who does not lie."

"You all are cracked," Harry said, pouring himself a glass of Austrian beer. "Cracked and whacked out of your gourds." He paused, then said. "All I saw was my partner set up some gizmo in the passenger window of a rental car. It released some kind of glow and now, for absolutely no reason I can see, you're all celebrating like it's kingdom come. Well, it ain't. 'Cause just the day before yesterday we had a shootout with some of the fiercest, most dangerous bastards I ever encountered in a very long career of police-work. And there are more where those came from, all over the globe, if my hallucinations are correct, and you have assured me that they are. So my advice to you three *fighters* is, have a beer, get some rest and hunker down for the battles to come, because if there are more guys like the ones I encountered day before yesterday? We have a problem." With that he poured the beer down his throat, pulled off his jacket and shoes, laid down on one of the beds, closed his eyes, opened his mouth and commenced snoring.

"I had a vision of the globe," Gottfried began, "covered with a network of death worshippers."

"We all had that vision," Orozco yawned. "It was transmitted to mobilize us, which it did."

"I saw that there were death worshippers on Schreivogelgasse, though I was warned to let other fighters dispose of them. I suppose that was because I'd never handled Argan weaponry."

"That and the fact that the fate of the prisoners in the realm of shadow had not been resolved."

"Were they…rescued?"

"Released, as I said before," Orozco corrected him. "Right before the most massive wipe out of fascist death worshippers in the entire war's history, which gives me some satisfaction, though that sentiment is dwarfed by our looming defeat in sector one thousand."

"I just got back from there," Gottfried said soberly.

"Tell us," Gideon said.

"It's bad. We're getting beat real bad. I was on a planet crammed with refugees. We were off-loading them to other worlds at a rate of hundreds of thousands a day, and they still kept coming in, enough to keep the planet packed. Then I got moved to a front, but yanked back, because the enemy brought in two commanders. The angels got the first with a fireball, but the second hid, and I guess the seraphs knew he'd reappear as soon as they left, so they pulled the survivors out. The number of casualties was staggering. I've never been anywhere that badly beaten by the enemy. It was horrible."

"Sounds like the valley of death," slurp, slurp.

"I've never been there."

"And you don't want to go."

"You have?"

"Twice. I don't know how I'm alive to tell about it."

"That's how I feel about sector one thousand. The enemy, the nonhuman enemy is just rampaging through it and, frankly, there aren't enough of our nonhuman allies to keep them at bay. Why doesn't He send in more angels?"

"The seraphs are stretched thin as it is," Orozco said meditatively, "throughout the cosmos. Why abandon sites we have a chance of holding onto for a place that is, let's face it folks, doomed?"

***

"That Seymour just keeps digging up new information!" Ein exclaimed, peering over Saltwater's shoulder at a computer screen.

"But *how, how* is Morning Star destroying galaxies? Seymour hasn't been able to answer that yet, and my guess is he won't be able to, until we get a fighter to hack into an *active* enemy computer."

Ein looked suddenly somber. "We just lost a member of the council who did exactly that."

"What?" The pockmarked man cried. "Who? Why in heaven would they send a council member behind the lines? That's for younger, faster, tougher fighters!"

"Well, the why is unclear."

"You mean secret."

"Probably. They aren't putting out any explanations."

"Who was it?"

"Albert Lark."

"Albert! I didn't know him, but everything I heard about him was wonderful."

Ein sighed and stepped back, turning away from the computer. "I knew him well. He was kind, generous and courageous, and there's no doubt in my mind that when this probably very sensitive mission came up, he volunteered. And he succeeded, according to reports; he hacked into enemy computers, altered reports and then later was captured, tortured, injected with some new pathogen."

"Shit."

"And rescued from the prison, with three others. The prison is right near the front."

"Rescued in time to die."

"Apparently. But he made his report to the council, and apparently he succeeded at whatever he was trying to do. I just don't understand why they had to send him, of all people." And a look of such profound sorrow, of outright mourning passed over the gray man's face. He stepped away and slumped into a fold-out chair. "Then I hear they're using the needle bomb in the realm of shadow and hundreds of thousands of prisoners will be collateral damage."

"Not so," Seymour piped in cheerfully. "A tech at the front entered information on that assault. The prisoners, all the prisoners were released, freed not just from their concentration camp but from the realm of shadow altogether. Somehow they were moved off-world before the needle bomb detonated."

Ein, who had sat up very alertly at Seymour's first words, suddenly seemed brighter, cheerier and more focused than he had in days. "But how? That many prisoners? That far away? And in the realm of shadow, of all places under the sun…"

"Technically it's not under a sun," Seymour corrected him.

"But how did they save those prisoners?"

"That detail was not entered in the tech's report. But from all I've been able to glean, it looks like we have some sort of secret weapon."

Ein and Saltwater exchanged significant glances. Lindin, who had ambled over, the better to hear Seymour's account, said, "sounds like we've got someone on the inside, and well placed, too."

Ein's gray eyebrows rose in surprise at this sudden revelation. "You must be correct."

"At last," Saltwater breathed. "A chance for a little effective sabotage." He paused, then his forehead furrowed in perplexity. "But who could it be—not a fighter, not in the realm of shadow."

"Maybe an enemy turncoat," Lindin said. "I'd put my money on that."

"You must be right," Seymour piped in, "because the report has a most interesting conclusion."

"Well, don't keep us hangin,'" Saltwater cried.

"It says that after the escape of the prisoners, the six remaining master killers, capable of opening channels between the realm of shadow and other worlds, those six, ahem, targets, those six,"

"Well?" Saltwater demanded. "What about them?"

"They were destroyed."

***

"I'm taking a short trip to the Wild," Ein told Anna over dinner that night.

"Where's the Wild?" Saltwater asked.

"It's a world in another part of the galaxy," Anna explained. "Peculiar rumors abound about it, like that it has a fortress where strange beings…"

"Let me guess—a seraph's fortress?" Saltwater asked.
She nodded.

"There's one on my home world," he said. "No man or woman has ever dared cross the border into their kingdom."

"Well, the Wild is an entire planet," Ein elaborated. "There's only one small human encampment. I'm taking a needle shuttle after dinner."

Anna rose. "I know when I'm supposed to go do something out of earshot." She bent over her husband and kissed the top of his head, murmuring, "please don't get yourself killed," before she left.

"Not to the front?" Saltwater asked at once.

"No. Much safer than that."

Anna, who had only moved to the doorway, visibly relaxed.

"In fact not near any enemy installations of any kind."

"Oh, thank God," she murmured and left the room.

"So where are you going?" Saltwater demanded.

"I'm journeying into another universe to find the intersection of science and magic."

"Magic!" Both fighters exclaimed.

"A fighter on another world, the ghost,"

"But she's in sector one thousand!" Lindin exclaimed.

"Was. Now she's in another universe, on a primitive planet with wizards, who use magic to see deep into the enemy kingdom. And she might, just might have found a way to use that magic to attack them, deep within their worlds."

Ferocious, retaliatory lights glittered in the eyes of the pockmarked man. "I hope you kill them all."

"Well, we've established that she can harm them."

Lindin and Saltwater stared at each other.

"As for killing one—that is our next attempt," Ein concluded. "It may not be possible. But she did harm an interrogator, deep within the kingdom of night."

"That's a first," Lindin said.

"You ain't kiddin'" Saltwater exclaimed. "And let's hope there's more where that came from."

"That's what I'm going to find out," Ein said, "to see if there's any way to...weaponize this magic, and if so, to launch as huge an assault as possible deep within their territory."

"A few dead interrogators should get their attention," Saltwater spoke in a low voice. "Maybe even distract them from the destruction of sector one thousand."

"That is the hope." The weapons designer replied. "Even if we can't kill them, if we harm a sufficient number, they may retreat."

"Apples and oranges," Lindin retorted. "You injure some bigwigs behind the lines and that somehow makes them pull out of sector one thousand? I don't see the connection."

"We create the appearance of a connection, make them think the assaults have something to do with their invasion and collapsing of that reality."

The three fighters sat in the darkened room, the shadows lengthening, despite the dim light from the tall windows. The dishes and glassware glimmered faintly, as did the eyes of the three men, with a dark light that seemed to expand, extend with every mention of the enemy and this opportunity to harm him. Outside a light wind tossed the tops of the trees that lined that ancient and stylish neighborhood, and Saltwater could hear the faint scrape of the evergreen's branches and fronds against his window upstairs. He raised his eyes to Ein's gray face. "Kill them all," he said softly. "It's a good night for travel."

***

"We have been waiting for you," the man with the long gray beard, old-fashioned jacket and filmy eyes said, as he stood in the doorway of the mud-walled hut, a lantern in his hand, his sheep baaing and shuffling all around in the dark yard. "Have you eaten?"

"Yes," Ein replied.

"And do you have food in your knapsack, for your journey?"

"Of course."

"Well then, welcome to the Wild, Ein. Come in."

He entered a wide room with an earth-packed floor, hard as rock and large wooden boards on a trestle, serving as a table. Several men in rough clothing sat there, slurping soup, while one of the women poked at the ceiling with a long pole. "That hole will have to be fixed in the morning," she said to the man with the beard and filmy eyes. "It almost goes all the way through the boards."

"I'll do it, I'll do it," the old man grumbled and sat in a high-backed chair by the fire, which burned in a brick fireplace, whose chimney ran up the back of the house. He gestured at Ein to sit in the other chair.

"I take it you have an idea of where you're supposed to go?" He asked.

"Yes, a picture in my mind of a glacier and a clearing nearby, with three tall pines, separating the clearing from the ice."

The man grunted.

"You know it?"

"Know it? Of course I know it. Fighters have been departing from that spot for generations, and my life already spans over three. But I've never seen you here before, Ein, and never expected to. I always figured you'd put your faith in needle technology for your travel."

"And I have."

"So you must be going to some primitive and sacred place."

"Quiet, old man. Don't probe."

"I know, I know," the old herdsman waved a hand. "Fighters and their secrets. Well, I never expected to meet the great Ein. It's an honor, sir, for an old sheep herder like me."

"And guide. You have long been a guide to fighters."

The man made a self-deprecatory gesture. "I know these mountains and woods well enough, and was taught by my uncle, also a guide for fighters. We'll have you to three pines in a couple of hours. First sit and relax. The fire is warm. Enjoy it. Where you're going is cold."

One of the men in rough agricultural clothes approached and offered Ein a cigar, saying that he had traded for it, and it came from far off-world. Ein recognized the brand as a delicacy and politely refused, with the words that he could not smoke, it somehow aggravated his lungs. "Surely they can put you in a tube for that on Argas," the man said.

"I stay out of tubes as much as possible," Ein replied. "Some medical technologies are over-used, and that is one."

The man smiled, then asked politely, "how, sir, goes the war?"

"Not particularly well, to be honest," the visitor replied. "We're losing in another sector."

The man pulled up a chair with a discreet, "may I?" to which Ein replied, "of course."

"What happens," the man asked, "when we lose a sector?"

"Well, the clearest example, a byword, really, is sector ten."

"I've heard of that," the old man said.

"Not I," the younger put in. "What happened there?"

"Well, part of the reality collapsed, which means certain stars and their planets just…dissolved. The enemy invaded the parts that remained, enslaving a population that had been largely—like yourselves—farmers and herdsmen. There were no very advanced civilizations in sector ten."

"And what happened to the herdsmen?" The man asked.

"Many were killed, the rest, as I said, are the enemy's slaves."

The men at the table in the dim room fell silent, until the one sitting next to Ein asked, "why were some killed and others not?"

"Those that resisted," Ein said, "those that fought back, were killed." His gray eyes settled seriously on the sheep herder's rough, weather-beaten features. "But I think you probably had figured that out."

"It was my guess, yes. But I wanted to hear it definite, from you."

"This was long ago," Ein continued. "Our side long ago abandoned sector ten."

"And now this other sector that you mentioned," the man said.

The weapons designer sighed. "In all likelihood, we will be beaten there. But we're not giving up without a fight."

"And you travel here, through the Wild, as part of that fight?"

"Yes, as part of that fight."

"What will you do?"

"Wreak as much havoc on the enemy as I possibly can."

"And that's a lot?" The man's keen eyes studied Ein's face intently.

"Yes," Ein nodded. "I believe it is a lot."

***

They set out less than an hour later, Ein, the old herdsman and the younger one, who had offered him the cigar and who was, he had learned, his old host's second son. Ein was almost sorry to leave the warm hearth, with its yellow and orange flames burning a fragrant wood that he had never smelled before. It was very fresh as it burned, with a vague scent of lime, and to his inquires about it, he was answered that it was a kind of willow that grew thickly in those parts, most especially near water, ponds or streams, and that it was especially good for heating, as it burned slowly and released much heat. The men at the table, the women at the stove, sink, and coming up and down from the storage cellar, all treated him with great respect and evident gratitude that his famous inventions had spared their world, and them in particular, the fate of sector ten. Their attachment to the Wild was deep-rooted, indeed their families had herded sheep and grown a tough northern grain and winter vegetables there for hundreds of generations. Though they had a power generator, gift of an Argan fighter years before, on the side of the main hut, they did not use it much. Not one had ever been off-world. All had remained in the Wild their entire lives, tending their flocks and their crops, uninterested in the massive civilization that covered all planets in nearby solar systems, hearing only the news that fighters brought, illiterate, their illnesses treated only with herbal medicines and most careful, at all times, never to stray into the angels' territory.

Though both herdsmen seemed inclined to taciturnity, the younger was curious about the war and its origins. "They say that there was a time, a long time before the war, when men were not assaulted by this enemy, that the human race was different then and sometimes heard directly from God."

"We still sometimes hear directly from Him."

"Fighters do. It is well known. But not all the rest of us."

"Perhaps that's because He's busy," said the father, "directing the war."

"There could be truth to that," Ein said. "The war changed everything."

"A fighter once came through here," the son continued. "He was from another world. He said the war started because of something the enemy did on some new planet, to some very primitive human race that was special to Him."

"Myths abound," was all Ein had to say to that.

"He was convinced this was the case," the younger man continued. "It was some sort of sacred world, way off, in the middle of nowhere, hidden and backward, like the Wild would be if it weren't surrounded by the Argan worlds."

"And what did he say the enemy did?" Ein asked.

"He didn't. He only said that it was terrible. He used a phrase to describe it. He said it was sunset at dawn."

"I have heard that before," the weapons designer mused. "I think in the same context. Some myths are very tenacious."

"Aye, but some are true," the old man said. "And this one had the ring of truth."

They hiked on, uphill now, and breathing heavily. Above, the stars in their billions twinkled down at them, and Ein was comforted to be able to pick out a few familiar constellations, though they were much distorted by his new position and partially outshone by the vast sparkling sweep of one of the galaxy's spiral arms. The older man observed him star-gazing and said, "that's the Argan Arm, the Wrath of God," he pointed up at the huge swath of glimmering stars. "And see that constellation there?" He pointed.

"What is it?" Ein asked eagerly. "You cannot see it from Stitch."

"The Hammer of God. See the haft there, and the head there?"

"Yes, I see them."

"But that is not the reason for the name Hammer."

"Oh? What is?"

"The ferocious and warlike people who dwell there, just as the Argan Arm, the Wrath of God is named for your world, for you who follow the war god."

"That would be the Wild too."

"Yes, but we produce no fighters."

"That's odd, don't you think?"

"No, I don't. We produce the guides for the fighters. We guide them, just as we are guiding you now, to another world, another kingdom, where the war rages in all its terrifying sound and fury."

***

They left him at a turn in the track, which he rounded and saw there, in the clearing before the three pines, stark, black forms against the dark gray of the massive sheet of ice rising behind them, there in the clearing, he saw those beautiful, scarred and silvery wings, and though he was not accustomed to it, he knew exactly what to do, approached and flung himself on the seraph's back, grabbing the long wings at the joints. Instantly, his stomach pitched, as they rose into the starry night, heading straight for the Argan Arm. "That" said the seraph, "is Deus Irae, aptly named, Ein, for the quest on which you now find yourself."

"Could it work?" He asked eagerly, ignoring his heaving stomach.

"You will find out soon," came the enigmatic reply, and then they spun down in a gyre, as the galaxies whirled around them and the Argan Arm vanished in the mix.

As he felt himself losing consciousness, he heard the seraph's voice in his ears, "even if you cannot destroy them, Ein, sow chaos behind their lines, be a scourge upon the entire kingdom of night." Whereupon he closed his eyes and felt his mind drift out on a sea of oblivion, scented, oddly, with pine needles.

***

He came to, lying on his back in a pine forest, watching the dark silhouette of a tall, bony woman, lit from behind by shafts of the rising sun, diffused by branches; he rubbed his eyes and recognized Lontra, who had extended a hand to help pull him to his feet. "The guardian's hut is not far," she said. "He has told me that our attack must not originate from earth. We must take the flame and return to Sere. But first, he says, he must talk with you."

A few steps further and he saw the stone walls of a hut with one door, one window and trees growing right up to it. Beneath the lintel stood and ancient hermit, whose nonetheless clear eyes sparkled at him. "So you are the traveler from this fantastic place called Argas that Lontra has been telling me about."

Ein nodded. "And you are a guardian of earth."

"I am," the old man held out a stainless steel lighter with a thunderbolt etched on the front. "You will take this to the wizard I have heard of from Lontra."

"Isn't it the one she just had there?"

"No, this is mine. The other was one I inherited from a deceased guardian. The fact that he was deceased may have weakened its effects," and as he uttered these words, a strange, dark, retaliatory light filled his eyes, a light Ein had seen many times before, in the battle-worn gaze of the seraphs, in fighters' eyes at the front, but it was different, deeper, wiser, brighter and darker and furious and not from him but through him, from another Being through him, and so strong was it that both fighters had to glance away.

Still looking away, the gray man came to the point: "will I be able to kill commanders and interrogators?"

"At this distance, no. But you will be able to sow terrible confusion in their ranks."

"Why can't I do this here, from earth?"

"Aside from the fact that you need the Seran wizard and his coals, there is a great rift in earth's prehistory, terrible events occurred here, events that have left lasting scars, that affect the very nature of time itself and then, worse, for the past few decades earth has been steadily succumbing to enemy illusions: our seasons are off, so are the days of the week, time does not progress and pass as it should. In short, we are a tainted reality, contaminated, somehow, by direct contact with a massively homicidal enemy."

"Perhaps this invasion from the realm of shadow, perhaps that's the source of your trouble."

"Oh, it was a source of trouble, all right. But it's not what I'm talking about. Our problem is deeper, darker, worse..." his voice trailed off. "If only I knew what was causing it, but," he sighed. "I don't and I won't, until He decides to enlighten us. So for all these reasons, you must not launch this unique assault of yours from earth. The two of you leave tonight, for the Seran system. And one of you, is to return my flame to me, when you are done, when you have scared the living daylights out of those homicidal nonhumans, who, in their supreme arrogance, have never even known fear. Through you, Argan, they will know terror, and that should help our cause, at the front and on all the battlefields of Elsewhere."

"Maybe even here on earth," Ein spoke hopefully.

But the old man sadly shook his head, "no, not here. Help here must come from guardians, and we appear to be a dying race."

***

Warmly clad, they walked through the Seran forest toward the road, one of his hands in a pocket, fist closed over the lighter, as visions of earth's history, some of it quite recent and bloody and dreadful beyond imagination, passed before his eyes. He saw all the men of a town, lined up against a wall and shot, and heard in his mind the name Lidice. He saw a much younger Galen, weary and thin, in a cattle car, crammed with people, and he saw ragged men in prisoner of war camps, eating grass. He saw and heard much more, and more, and the more he saw, the angrier and more despairing he became, for he had obtained a treaty with this world, where these atrocities had so recently occurred, obtained it for his world, because he believed, and had since been told by a voice in his mind that his belief was correct, that earth's fate was bound up with the fate of the entire human race; and the more he saw of earth's wretched history, the more hopeless did the whole human enterprise begin to seem.

"Don't do too much of that," Lontra advised, casting him a sidelong glance.

300

"What?"

"Seeing what all guardians see, all the time."

"Your planet is horrible."

"It has had its horrible moments, yes. But it's not all bad."

"How can you, whose four uncles were murdered—"

"They were communist partisans in German-occupied Italy. They knew the risks. It was war. Just as they executed informants and occupiers, they in turn were caught and executed. It was horrible, but no surprise to anyone, least of all my father."

"What a world this earth is!"

"Some, Galen, for instance, believe the enemy was active on the Axis side during that war."

"The Axis being?"

"The aggressors, the ones who filled the death camps, slaughtering civilian populations."

"I can see why he thinks that."

"But this world, Sere, has never and will never host the enemy."

"It's been foretold."

She nodded. "It has been foretold."

"This wizard, is he ready to assist us?"

"Oh yes, he's seen quite enough of the enemy's wickedness, of the realm of shadow and the fighters' heroism to be ready to take up arms."

"Good, because I have a plan."

"For wreaking havoc deep within their kingdom?"

He nodded.

"I believe," she said pensively, "that we have the same plan."

***

"This computer," Saltwater waved an eight by eleven inch tablet in front of Seymour's view screen, "was obtained at a terrible price in blood. A member of our council, for reasons I do not understand, went behind the lines, located an enemy computer station and relayed the coordinates back to our techs. The council member was later killed. But a fighter returned to the station and stole what he could tell was a little-used computer in a back room, substituting one of our tablets for it. He was correct about it being little-used. That tablet has not been activated since he made the drop. But this," the pockmarked man waved the enemy computer, "can still connect to our enemy's domain. We have disabled all the tracking devices and rerouted the signal. So when you connect to it, it will appear, should anyone investigate, that the tablet at the center behind the lines, is the point of origin."

"I'm very nervous about connecting to a live enemy computer," Seymour quavered.

"Don't be. You're looking for one piece of information—how Morning Star destabilizes galaxies. Get that, then back out." He powered up the tablet. "Ready?"

"I guess so."

"Go."

Silence ensued for some minutes.

"If anyone queries you," Lindin said, "you're just a smart piece of hardware."

"I found it," Seymour replied. "Transferring...got it. Turn that thing off."

Saltwater shut down the tablet.

"Morning Star has opened a gyre," Seymour said, "a gyre between worlds. Enemy forces, powers, ripple up and down through this gyre, destabilizing galaxies. The goal, not yet achieved, is for Morning Star to open this vortex through the heart of the cosmos and thus be able to destabilize entire realities. He is a few years away from the achievement of that goal."

"How's he do it?" Saltwater demanded. "What are the nuts and bolts?"

"He has a ring of computers built out over an abyss. The gyre passes through the middle. As for the codes that activated this gyre, I can print them out now or just transfer them to your handheld."

"Transfer them to the techs at the front. Where is this, Seymour? Where, behind the lines, is Morning Star situated?"

"I did not get that. It was encrypted, and I cannot break the code. Only an enemy official would be able to do that."

"Send that to the techs too," Lindin said.

"Oh, I'm sending everything," Seymour paused. "Are you interested in Morning Star's target goals?"

"Oh, I think I've got a pretty good idea what they are," the pockmarked man growled.

"First and foremost to destabilize and collapse, if unable to conquer, the most highly advanced galaxies in a given reality. To do this, the death computer has a galactic map for multiple universes. Incidentally, sector 3333 is on it. The entire sector. I suggest we leave."

"Stop being cowardly, Seymour," Saltwater chided him. "It doesn't become you."

"One mitigating factor is the enemy's fear of the anomaly. I found multiple references to a contact point in sector 3333 simply disappearing. That, I take it, was Ein's cloaking device. But it has the mucky mucks in the enemy's bureaucracy very alarmed. There was even a series of cyborg exchanges on the desirability of avoiding the Argan sector altogether. I didn't know the enemy had cyborgs. Why don't we?"

"They were banned here, first on Argas, millennia ago. They are too easily subject to military abuse of power. In short, the fascists love them and have created whole armies of them. The Argans, seeing the danger not just to freedom but to survival itself, banned them."

"Well, apparently when they touched down in this sector and the quote anomaly unquote went into effect, they lost an entire division of cyborg soldiers."

"Not that they give a shit about their fate."

"What was their fate?"

"This is war, Seymour, what do you think?"

Lindin pressed his weak, pink, puffy hands on the table. "To sum up: we know what enemy AI is doing and aims to do. We know how it does it. All we don't know and what we need to know above all is where the enemy AI is located."

"I don't see why that's so important," Seymour said querulously.

"If we're going to destroy it, Seymour," Saltwater spoke with grim patience. "We have to know where it is."

***

The creature stepped before the members of the council, as Jason Katharos hurried to shut the interior door behind it. This door led to a secret stairwell to the basement, a few steps from the door of Night Child's apartment. "You weren't seen moving from your room to the stairwell?" He asked.

"No. And I don't know why you've called me. I have fulfilled all the terms of my contract. I released tens if not hundreds of thousands of prisoners from the realm of shadow. They are now roaming a planet called earth, doubtless seeking food and shelter."

"We've alerted fighters there to assist them," Ivan said.

"Good, because you certainly can't expect *me* to do that. I'm not a refugee placement officer." He paused, and his yellow eyes became narrow, angry slits. "And then those six master killers you wanted me to eliminate. Well, I did it, at no small risk to my person, may I point out. The last of them was preparing to go into some trance and I nearly got sucked into a vortex, furniture flying around the room, fascist soldiers chanting, corpses flying about, oh, that was a barrel of laughs. But I killed him, like the other five, and now I deserve a break, a vacation, which I am perfectly happy to take in my rooms here, sleeping late, doodling on the computer and eating your dreadful cafeteria food. Don't ask me to go back behind the lines. I just came from there, and I'm damn lucky I'm still in one piece."

"We have new information about Morning Star," gray Ivan began.

"Oh goody. Well, keep it to yourselves. That's one deadly, homicidal piece of equipment, and I'm not going near it."

"You don't have to go near it. You just have to find out where it is."

"No, no, no. That means another trip to the land of the dead. No. I'm done with that. Send one of your heroic fighters to go poking and snooping and asking questions, in enemy territory, about *the* most highly classified program in the enemy's armament. Don't ask me to do it."

"You blend in a lot better than one of us."

"You owe me," Night Child snapped. "I don't know what those death worshippers were up to in the realm of shadow, but it looked like an invasion of one of your worlds. I deserve a break, and my contract stipulates appropriate periods of rest between missions. A few days do not constitute an appropriate period of rest. Two weeks. I get two weeks at least."

"Fine," Jason said. "But in two weeks, back you go. You can take a fighter with you, if you think that will help."

"Oh for God's sake. Help? Someone I have to babysit in the land of death—you call that help. No. Keep your fighters. They'd stick out like sore thumbs in the kingdom of night."

"On the contrary, many of us have gone there and back without attracting notice."

"Oh, puh-lease. You people reek of integrity. Even the lowest death worshipper slave could spot one of you a mile off. No. If I have to return—*after* my vacation—it will be solo, thank you very much."

The men of the council glanced around at each other, until finally Ivan cleared his throat and spoke: "we can give you some clues as to Morning Star's whereabouts, though."

"This should be good," came the grumbled reply.

"It's somewhere on the edge of an abyss. He's built his computers in a circle, half of which looms out over an abyss."

"I can think of a dozen places that could be, off the top of my head," Night Child snapped. "And there are probably more. Let me tell you men of the council something. You don't just waltz into the land of death, asking 'oh, where have you put your killing machine, you know, the top-secret computer life form devoted to the extermination of the human race? I heard it's near an abyss—which one?' In fact you don't even mention Morning Star's name, unless you want to wind up chained to the wall of a dark dungeon, waiting for your exquisitely painful interview with a master interrogator. This is going to take work, time, effort, caution. And when I say time, I mean possibly years."

"In a matter of years, Morning Star will have graduated from destabilizing galaxies to destabilizing whole realities." Ivan told him.

"And this...surprises you?"

"It imparts a sense of urgency to our request."

"No. I will not be hurried. If I'm hurried, I'm liable to get caught. And that ain't happening. I look out for numero uno and numero uno is moi. There's nothing in my contract that contradicts that. In fact, the whole purpose of my deal, from my perspective is to ensure my survival. Any benefits to you are, well, incidental."

"But you will return and track this life form down?"

"Do I have a choice?"

***

The wizard regarded Ein with awe, expressed most succinctly when he addressed him as "savior of worlds." For his part, the weapons designer studied the man with the body paint and dreadlocks and thought skeptically about their undertaking's prospects. The female fighter seemed to sense this doubt and called for a demonstration forthwith. Thereupon, the wizard chanted, cast dust upon the raised hearth, and Lontra lit it with the ancient guardian's flame. At once the image of a black-clad, non-human interrogator appeared in the room—and the interrogator was on fire. But it was not his fire, which he tolerated, even welcomed, it was the white hot flame of an angelic fireball, which caused him to howl in pain and fury, drawing the attention of other dark-haired, dark-clad, surprisingly fit and ageless interrogators. All eagerness now, Ein gasped, "light the dust again."

Lontra did so, and the entire roomful of interrogators went up in white flames. Human death worshippers rushed to help, but could do nothing. One tried to douse an interrogator with a pot of water, but received a cuff on the head for thanks and the words, "no you fool, we need our own fire, not water."

Lontra observed that with this second guardian's flame, it took a good while longer for the interrogators to master the situation, and when they did, the human death worshipper cried, "how has this happened?"

"It's some new trick of the seraphs," an interrogator replied. "We will have to be careful and not go about alone. Alone, that white fire might consume one of us. But a companion can always fight their fire with ours."

"Also this seems only to happen here," the death worshipper added, "deep within our territory. I haven't heard of this spontaneous combustion afflicting any interrogators or commanders at the front."

"The human has a point," one interrogator commented, and thence commenced speaking in his horrible language, unintelligible to the two fighters and the wizard, but still sickening and so, mercifully, the image and the words faded into nothing.

Ein's gray eyes shone appreciatively on the wizard, then Lontra. "For the next few days, keep at this. Keep them off-balance. Interfere with their strategizing. And if you get a large group of them," the very serious gray man almost smiled, "light 'em up!"

***

The three men walked from the airport terminal to Orozco's Impala in the parking garage. They did not feel like talking and had had a sullen, silent ride back from Vienna. "Just think how many of these sons of bitches we have to contend with—all the ones who made it to earth before that door slammed shut. Tens of thousands," Orozco had said before they boarded, and all three had brooded over this miserable thought ever since. Even as the car glided out of the garage, they sat in wretched, angry silence, contemplating probable firefights to come. And it did not help, as they tore through D____ and then across Chinatown, when Orozco stopped on Deus Irae, bought a *Daily Watcher* and tossed it into Gideon's lap with its fifty-point headlines, screaming about a satanic cult of murderers and the remarkable vigilantes who rescued their victims by means of super-weapons that could only be of alien origin. "Shit!" The young fighter exclaimed. "Now all we need is an article detailing the roles of fighters and guardians and every cow will have escaped out the barn door. This is terrible. And, naturally, according to this article, it's worldwide."

"Naturally," Orozco snarled.

"Let me off at the station," Harry said. "I'm going to check in, then head home to sleep."

"Tell 'em I'm sick as a dog," Orozco said, and as his partner nodded, added, "and remember, buddy, not a word about this to a soul. Not a soul. Not just because of the damage you'd do to our side, but to protect your own life. If these death worshippers hear one whiff of a rumor that some cop in D____ is linked to fighters, they'll storm every police station in the city. You'd set off a bloodbath."

"Look, Rafael, I still got a very clear image in my mind of those cultists firing their machine guns at us, just the other day. I don't want no more of that, believe me."

"Then mum's the word."

"That it is."

As he watched Harry climb the precinct station steps in the rearview mirror, he heard Gideon's low voice, asking "can you trust him?"

"He likes to talk," Orozco sighed. "But he saw what these fascists are really about. Yeah, he likes to talk, but he likes to live, more."

Soon they were gliding past the garishly ugly, ultramodern structure that was city hall, not making conversation, each lost in gloomy thoughts. Orozco swung the Impala out onto Millionaire's Avenue, which quickly became seedy to the point, here and there, with empty lots, of abandonment. He turned off onto Apocalypse Avenue and sped in the direction of Uptown, where the heat still shimmered up from the cracked sidewalk, was still sweltering but was somehow less offensive, more escapable, due to the shade of numerous maples and locusts planted along the curb. Here and there a welcome breeze tossed the treetops and even reached down to alleviate the otherwise unmoving, stultifying blanket of heat, wrapped around the entire city. "Never thought I'd live my whole live here," the policeman finally murmured.

"Where'd you think you'd live it?"

"Mexico City. There was a woman there, but the war took me away. I couldn't come up with a good explanation of my absence and she said, 'then I can't rely on you.' Lord, I've lost everything to this war."

"You're not the only one," the young fighter growled, as Orozco parked the car opposite Howard MacKenzie's tall, stylish townhouse. They climbed the steps, rang the bell and soon heard the clicking and dropping of locks and bolts being opened. There stood Horace. "He's free, my double, that is, and you're back in time for the evening TV shootout between the police and local death worshippers."

"Oh," Orozco asked. "That's been going on?"

"Every evening," Starfield called from the study. "Like clockwork."

They tromped into the cool of the wonderfully air-conditioned study and there, true enough, on a large TV screen in a corner, crouched the familiar figures of a SWAT team, behind barricades, behind squad cars, behind two armored-up Humvees, trading fire with the occasional barrage from semi-automatic weapons in the windows of a row-house in the River District.

"Right here in town," Orozco slurped on a mint.

"Like we said," Horace replied, "every evening, like clockwork."

"As if they want the attention," Starfield put in, "to cause a panic, which they have done."

"A strategy that makes sense," slurp, slurp, "if they still think reinforcements are arriving daily." He paused pensively, his lean leathery old form supported by the door frame. "So I'm guessing they don't know that door slammed shut."

"You succeeded?" Starfield asked delightedly.

"Oh, more than that. We triumphed. Released thousands of prisoners to earth, then shut that door and detonated some kind of super-bomb in the realm of shadow, which, we have been assured, killed divisions upon divisions of our fascist foe."

"I won't even ask how you released the prisoners."

"Don't, 'cause I ain't got a clue. I just got a promise from above that it was done. I ain't having no fighters, and no other prisoners of war from our side, being killed by some bomb I detonate in the kingdom of night, oh no."

"And you said so?"

"That's exactly what I said."

"You dared?" Gideon goggled, and as Orozco nodded, he continued, "and then what happened?"

"And then I waited, like I said. Then I was assured they'd all been released."

"Sounds like someone put you to bed with a fairy tale," thus Starfield.

"Look Starfield, seraphs don't lie and they don't sugarcoat the truth. They been runnin' this war too long for that. They came back with a message from the top. And if that message had been, too bad, the prisoners die, their time has come, then I would've had to quit, hand my Argan toys over to Gideon here and face the music. But they didn't. They said arrangements had been made. You know Who didn't want any dead prisoners either. And frankly neither did the seraphs. My theory is that somehow, somewhere, there was a communication screw-up."

"Which you, with your complaining, set right," Horace concluded.

"Hey that complaining has to be good for something," slurp, slurp. "And this wasn't the first time it proved to be."

"Where do you suppose they went?" Starfield asked softly, pensively.

"Who?"

"The prisoners who were released."

"Oh, to earth."

"But where?"

"Wherever they could find food, drink, rest and then help to get them back to their homes. And as for those who aren't originally from earth,"

"How many of them?" Starfield asked.

"A small refugee crisis' worth. Except they're spread out over the globe. Look, if they survived any length of time in the realm of shadow, making it work here on earth will be a piece of cake. They'll have homes and jobs in no time."

"But there's no support network!" Starfield cried.

"There is now. There are the fighters they came with, who will be keeping a lookout for the most desperate in their respective groups. They'll have help, help getting on their feet and once there, like I said, if they could stay alive in that charnel house, they can sure as shit find their way on earth."

The four men gloomily watched a SWAT team member launch a canister of teargas into the house through the first floor, blasted-out window.

"Like that's going to help," Orozco snarled. "Those thugs came from the realm of shadow. They breathed in worse on a daily basis."

"What we've got to do," Gideon spoke pensively, "is demoralize them."

"Now how we gonna do that?" Orozco spat angrily. "Go chat with them, say, look, your road from home, we blew it up? The door closed?"

"I'm not sure."

"Well then?"

"Go there," Gideon pointed an index finger at the TV. "Get a bullhorn. Give them the message. Something simple like what you just said. There will be no more reinforcements from your realm. We shut the door. Come out with your hands up or die. How about that?"

"Now?"

"Now."

"Shit, I wanted to take a nap."

"Too bad. We're going to the River District, then I have to be back in Garibaldi Square by eight tonight."

"Oh?" Slurp, slurp. "What for?"

"I," Gideon smiled, "have a date."

"A date? You? You been runnin' around the globe killin' bad guys and you've had time to make a date?"

"Yup," Gideon donned a baseball cap that lay on the computer table. "With a fighter named Sana, who works in a bookshop. So hurry it up."

***

When they screeched to a halt at the stakeout, the Impala's siren blaring, Gideon's Honda right behind it, a co-worker approached, saying, "Rafael, I thought you were sick?"

"I am," he replied. "But we got a message for these thugs."

"If it'll get 'em to stop shooting, be my guest. McBride's got the bullhorn."

Orozco approached, then handed the megaphone to Gideon, after answering the inevitable, "who's he?" with "undercover military."

"There will be no more reinforcements from your realm," Gideon shouted into the megaphone. The machine gun in the house fell silent.

"What realm?" McBride asked.

"Shh. This is something we just learned about."

"We shut the door," Gideon loudly continued.

"What door?" McBride asked Orozco, who answered behind the back of his hand, leaning toward him, "cultish bullshit that should, we believe, scare the beejesus out of them."

"We closed the road," Gideon continued. "You can't go back and you can't get reinforcements. Your master killer in Vienna is dead."

"Vienna? Where the fuck is that?" McBride asked.

"It could be on the moon, McBride. It don't matter. We're screwing with their heads."

"So throw down your weapons and come out with your hands up where we can see 'em, or die. We are prepared to drop a bomb on your building."

"We are?" McBride asked.

Silence ensued for some seconds. Then came the sound of metal machinery being pitched onto the floor. The door opened and out filed eight, very muscle-bound, very ferocious death worshippers, two of them wounded. McBride grabbed the bullhorn, but Orozco stopped him. "Do not tell them to lie on the ground," he said. "Or you'll have to shoot all of them, and we want these little birdies for questioning."

"Good point," McBride replied and then conferred with the leader of the SWAT team, whose men shortly advanced and shackled their prisoners.

All eight, sullenly, pointedly stared at Gideon, before being packed into a police wagon. "They want to know how you know," Orozco spoke behind his hand to the young Israeli.

"At least they didn't make me for a fighter," Gideon replied. "Then we'd all be dead." He turned to McBride. "When you question them, they'll demand to know how you know their quote door unquote has been shut. You just stay vague."

"That should be easy, since I have no fucking idea what you're talking about."

"You indicate that you know a lot more than that, that they got some turncoats in their ranks. That should demoralize them, which is what you want to do, as fast as possible. Oh, and I'd really, *really* beef up security wherever you hold them. Their friends will be looking to spring them, probably tonight."

"Great," the policeman muttered and stalked off to confer with the SWAT team leader.

"Still in time for your date," Orozco slurped.

"That was the idea," the younger fighter replied, then hurried to his compact car, got in and tore off.

"Undercover military?" McBride asked.

"Yeah, Israeli. We got a global problem, McBride."

"Tell me about it. The whole city of D____ is like the wild west. Every time I turn around, we got another shootout with these lunatics. And they are lunatics, Orozco, they're crazed killers. They don't seem to care if they live or die, all they want to do is murder as many people, cops or innocent bystanders, as possible. I'm telling you, it's the wild west."

Orozco glanced over McBride's shoulder at his friend's little Honda, running a red light.

"You know there's talk about martial law," McBride continued. "The mucky mucks in Washington are quote very alarmed unquote. It's about time they got alarmed. We're dying out here on the front lines."

"But it ain't time for martial law."

"You against that?"

"Absolutely," slurp, slurp. "Especially now that we got them by the balls with this 'your door is closed' crap."

"Exactly what's that mean?"

"This is clsssified, McBride, so it stays between us. And I'm trading it to you for any info you get, though I doubt you'll get any when you interrogate these sons of bitches."

"Well, what is it?"

"These killers believe they come from another world."

"Holy crap."

"Yup. It's called the realm of shadow."

"The realm of shadow? Now I've heard everything."

"No, apparently not. They believe they are getting reinforcements from that place, that alternate reality."

"Alternate reality! Christ!"

"That's why we say we shut the door."

"Gottcha."

"You tell 'em, there'll be no more help from the realm of shadow and they're looking at multiple life sentences. Do they want to talk with detective Orozco and maybe whittle it down to one life sentence?"

"With time off for good behavior."

Orozco nodded. "But I ain't talking to just any of what these guys call death worshippers."

"That's their cult, right?"

"Right. Like I said. I will only talk to one of 'em who wants to spill the beans. And I know all about the door and the realm of shadow and the master killer in a trance in Vienna, so I ain't about to lap up some bullshit."

"Got it."

"I'm going home now to nap. Call me when you got one who's talkative." With that the old fighter slid into his Impala and drove off, dialing Gideon's number. "Give my regards to Garibaldi Square," he said to the voicemail. "See you at Horace's later."

Parking, the younger fighter noticed his phone beeping, listened to the message and smiled. Then he crossed the green quadrangle, elegant in twilight and made his way to The Sun, The Moon and the Stars.

"Right on time," the young woman said. "I believe an old friend of yours will be relieving me tonight, while I'm out with you."

"I wondered who'd be guarding Galen."

"An Argan who says he met you once at the front."

"The only Argan I ever met was Ein."

"That's the one. We're lucky he's here; if he hadn't shown up, I was thinking I might have to cancel. Want to say hello?"

"To Ein? Always." So the two young fighters made their way back through the musty gloom of a bibliophile's haven to Galen's office, where they saw the great Ein, gray as always, seated opposite the old concentration camp survivor and clasping in his fist that old man's stainless steel lighter, saying "this will destroy them."

"Well, I'm glad something can," Gideon remarked from the doorway.

"Gideon Cohen! How wonderful to see you. I was just telling Galen that he and the rest of earth's guardians have been sitting on a secret weapon, the equivalent of an atomic bomb for our enemies, for decades now and didn't know it."

"Who says we didn't know it?" Galen snapped.

"Then why didn't you alert the fighters. This could have helped us immensely."

"Indeed. Have you managed yet to kill one of them with it?"

"No, but—"

"No buts. So far you've done little more than annoy them."

"We scared the shit out of them."

"But once they realize, as they doubtless already have," the old man's eyes glimmered sadly, "that these new assaults are not fatal,"

"There's got to be some way to boost them."

"Well, you're the weapons designer, but you cannot take my flame. The ghost on Sere has already made off with an old guardian's flame."

"She'll return it."

"She better." Galen paused and extended his hand, palm up. Reluctantly the Argan fighter reached forward and dropped the lighter with the thunderbolt etched on front into his hands.

"Bring me up to speed," Gideon said. "The ghost is on Sere?"

"My home world," the young female fighter said sadly, with more than a touch of homesickness in her voice.

"Yes," Ein nodded gravely. "And she works with Seran wizards and the earth's guardian's flame to scorch enemy interrogators and commanders deep within the kingdom of night."

"How is this possible?" Gideon demanded.

"Does it matter?" Galen snapped again, his deep, dark eyes glimmering impatiently. "The point is, it doesn't kill them."

"But the potential," Ein began.

"Potential, schmotential. I've been listening to fighters with their wild hopes for over four score years. We still haven't killed one, not one enemy commander."

Chastened, the three fighters did not speak, which seemed to cause the old man to soften. He flicked open the stainless steel lighter, and its flame burned bright. "But do not despair," he said softly. "One day, one day, we will get even, and you are not all wrong to suspect that the guardians of earth will

318

have a hand in that." He snapped the lighter shut and gazed into their weary, war-worn faces, lit now with the bit of hope he had kindled. "Yes, we will help. But it will be you, it will be a fighter who is the first human being, man or woman, to kill a non-human enemy. It will be a fighter who, man or woman, for the first time, turns the tide of the war with the seraph's flame, and who does it, without the help of our marvelous allies, who are not human, a fighter who demonstrates that at last we people, the human race itself, can take control of our own fate and do not have to cling to a pair of wings to destroy the monsters whose goal it is to extirpate us from this and every universe. But it will take time."

"How long, Galen?" Ein demanded. "How long?"

The old eyes glimmered with suddenly limitless depths. "I will be alive to hear of it," he said softly, and with those words, all three fighters saw, coming up through the depths of those eyes, a swift retaliatory movement that became, in their minds, the image of an enormous fist punching through a shrouded being, a being from whom they instinctively turned away; but not so fast that they did not see this final, devastating assault, for the being dissolved on impact and all that remained was a trail of smoke and a heap of cinders, and around where it had been, the wind howled.

"If a fighter will do it," Ein was the first to speak. "Then we will not be exterminated."

The lamps of eternity glimmered at him, from the depths of the octogenarian's gaze. "The road may seem long," Galen spoke in a very soft voice, "and arduous. But as I told you, do not despair."

"As you told us, and as we have seen," Ein added.

"Do not allude to what you have seen fighter. That was secret. For that matter, do not mention what you have heard. Promises concealed are better kept."

"But we must communicate with each other."

"With each other yes and…with the new ones who are brought in."

Gideon started. "You mean people like that policeman, Harry McNeil?"

Galen nodded. "From time to time a very great deal depends on these neophytes. And they will be involved in the rescue of our struggling human race."

"But Harry's just a hard-drinking, leisure-loving—" Gideon began.

"Don't be so quick to judge him, fighter. He is more than he appears. As are many people. Our job is to separate those from the ones who are less."

"Much less," Ein said.

"Yes, we've got thousands of those loose on the planet now," as Galen said somberly, all thought about the death worshippers. "But it would have been worse, had Orozco not closed that door to the realm of shadow."

"And saved all those prisoners," Gideon spoke indignantly. "What were those seraphs thinking?"

"Shh. You don't know what they know, so don't dare judge."

"But Orozco was right and they were wrong," Gideon snapped.

"No, you have misread it. Orozco raised an objection, which he can do, being a friend of His, and as a result, they were overruled. Please do not ignore the consequences, Gideon. We now have tens of thousands of released prisoners, all of whom were longing for death, suddenly reprieved and roaming earth, many not even from earth. The only people who can help them, who recognize them for what their dreadful experience has made of them are the thousands of fighters who also escaped. But they're just struggling to survive here. Yet we must rely on these fighters to prevent the massive numbers of suicides that will now surely start happening, surely, because now that they are on earth, these unfortunates have the means to take their lives."

"But even if all but five commit suicide," Gideon began.

"Then it was worth it for those five. I agree with your reasoning. And so does Orozco and so, apparently, does He. However, the seraphs' knowledge is never to be taken lightly. Which means,"

"Which means?" Gideon demanded impatiently.

"That we will be lucky if even those five don't die by their own hand."

"Well, this is just wonderful," said Ein.

"It's the war," Galen replied simply.

"Where's Orozco?" Ein asked.

"Asleep at the guardian's house—Horace MacKenzie's," Gideon answered.

"I must speak with him again."

"After Sana and I have dinner, please."

"Oh, for heaven's sake!" Galen cried in exasperation. "I don't need a twenty-four hour fighter bodyguard. That's ridiculous!"

Ein and Gideon exchanged a glance. Then Gideon waved at Galen and took the strong young woman fighter by the arm and departed.

"So tell me about Salonika," Ein said.

"You're humoring me."

"No. I'm curious about this place called earth, especially now that my world has a treaty with it."

To his question about where they should dine, the young woman fighter replied that she frequented a nearby eatery slash deli, called Frankie Smedly's and that they could have a booth in the back and not be overheard. He glanced at her admiringly, as she mentioned this. It was as if she had read his mind. And so, studying her war-weary but still attractive face, with its high, ruddy cheekbones, glimmering eyes and very short brown hair, he realized that he wanted to know more about her—and for that, a booth in the back would be perfect. When, he asked, his hand on the middle of her back, as they entered the restaurant, had she become a fighter? "The attacks started when I was eight," she replied. "I was at the front at fourteen. Twelve years later, twelve long years of blood and loss, the council informed me about a planet called earth with a special race of guardians and one in particular, who was a friend of His. This old man, Galen, had long been an enemy target and so had been informed, as had the council, that he was never to be out of earshot of a fighter. I was chosen for the job, partly, I believe, because of my clan's closeness to the prophecy of the wizards."

"What's your clan?"

"The Wolflings, and that's my name, Sana Wolfling. Our clan has produced many, many wizards, more than most, and unlike the others, many are also prophets."

"Who chose you to be Galen's bodyguard?"

"I believe that came from the top."

"You believe or you know?"

"I was told. Ivan told me."

By now they sat at their booth in the back, eating pickles and pickled tomatoes from a metal dish in the center of the table. "Frankly," she added, "I was glad to leave the front. I had a man there, and he was killed. After that, it was nothing but years of sleeping in the dirt, eating in the trenches, shooting at death worshippers, hiding whenever the siren went off to indicate the presence of an enemy commander. I'd lost my will for it. I didn't care anymore if I got even. I scarcely cared if I stayed alive. And then to be removed and sent to protect this remarkable old man—that was wonderful. My first two years here, I read all the time. Galen said I should read the world literature of earth, and I threw myself into it."

Gideon chuckled. "Did you read all the world literature of earth?"

"That's still a work in progress," she answered. "At first I let him pick the books for me. Now that I select them myself, it goes a little slower. 'Hurry up and read, Sana,' he always says to me. 'You have a long list.' But you see, on Sere the children do not go to school. So I didn't even have an elementary education. I had plenty of agricultural knowledge, but none of it really applicable to earth."

"The kids farm instead of going to school?"

She nodded. "And forage, and study the stars and the rocks and the wizards' magic." She paused, and he studied her face with a certain roughness that betokened years of living and sleeping outdoors. "When the attacks started, a wizard took me to his hut and showed me a perfectly clear image of enemy interrogators behind the lines. 'These are the ones whose vast death sweeps are hitting you in your mind, and outside, and preventing you from sleep.' He told me. So at age eight, I knew what an enemy interrogator looked like, tall, unnaturally fit, black-haired, black-suited, often wearing sunglasses, and when he smiled, sharp pointed teeth. I knew all that, but I didn't know how to escape the attacks. Then I started hearing a voice, and obeying it, and I got hit much less. I slept. I lived. But I knew by age nine that I was destined for the front. And five years later, that's where I was. Oh, I'm so glad I'm not there anymore! But tell me about you. You're an Israeli. I'm so curious about that country, and Galen has made sure that I read a lot about it."

And so, over Gideon's lamb stew and her steak and potatoes, she heard about how his parents had emigrated to Palestine from Europe as teenage partisans at the end of the war, how they had fought to establish the state of Israel, then, years later, raised him on a kibbutz. "I was their last child and a child of old parents." He talked about his military service and his education.

"But when," she asked, "did the enemy select you?"

"When I was ten," he replied. "Five years later I was at the front. Then, when I was sent home, I was told that like all the fighters from earth who do mandatory military service in their home countries, what I learned in my country's military would be useful in the war, in His war, the fighters' war. And it was. I wasn't a farm child like you, though I did plenty of farming on the kibbutz. But after, as a young man, I got lots of military training, and the fighters on the council were right. It was most useful."

They sat, ate and talked for a couple of hours, until the female fighter sighed and said she should return to Galen. "Are there any other fighters you could...occasionally swap with?" Gideon asked tentatively. She smiled. Yes, there was one, who frequented the book shop and who would be only too glad of an opportunity to spend the evening with the old publisher, while she went out on the town with Gideon. Then, for the first time that evening, that serious young man smiled and said, "good, good. Let's go out again soon. Would Thursday be all right?"

She nodded, so they paid and, as they were leaving Frankie Smedley's, each took a mint, Gideon saying, "this is how it should be, just living for the sake of being alive, going to a restaurant with you, Sana, eating mints after dinner. But it's not that way. This is the exception. Something sure got screwed up somewhere."

"It's called the war," she said, ambling out into the warm, humid night air. "It has altered our lives in ways that can never be undone. But look," she turned her beautiful, high cheekbones to him, her face, even in the dark, roughened, still too rough from years of exposure to the elements, "this war brought you to me. Without the war, I'd be weaving wool blankets on Sere. Instead, I guard the life of a remarkable old man and meet his many mysterious associates, among them you. If not for the war,"

"Shh. Don't talk about it like that, as if it's done anything good. The whole thing is a sin and a crime, and we should never forget that for an instant."

"I don't. How could I? But without that monstrosity, I would not be on earth."

They ambled back to the bookstore, their footsteps echoing on the deserted night street; then down to the shop, which she unlocked, and through the stacks of books to the office in back, where fighter and guardian sat exactly where they had left them, in the midst of an animated discussion of the ethics of using the needle bomb under any circumstances.

"None, from the sound of it," Gideon put in.

"I agree," Ein said.

"Then why did you invent it?" Galen demanded. "And what's more, how would you have closed that channel to earth? As you described it, it was a unique aspect of this apparatus that enabled Orozco to do that."

"Oh," Gideon was taken aback. "We're talking about bombing the realm of shadow. Well, I make an exception for that. That place is fascist central. It's swarming with death worshippers. The more killed the better."

"There," Galen glanced at Ein with distinct satisfaction. "The realm of shadow is an enemy stronghold, a bastion of death worship. And they had a direct line to earth. Should we have refrained from, from,"

"Bombing the shit out of them," thus Gideon.

"Thank you," Galen said, "from bombing the shit out of them, simply because you have some scruples about this weapon you invented? It's not as if a civilian population were targeted. The only civilians, so to speak, are shadows and they would not be affected by your needle bomb. Or indeed by any bomb or any weapon. As far as we know, they're already dead. So why are you so worried about this?"

"The precedent."

"There is no precedent. There is no other place like the realm of shadow. And if, ever again, a channel opens between enemy terrain and earth,"

"Say, sector ten," Gideon put in.

"Wherever that is," Galen waved a hand. "Then we would weigh the advantage of destroying storm troopers against endangering civilians. But I doubt this situation will arise twice."

"Don't tell me, the entire time we were at dinner, you two discussed the war," Gideon said.

The old man gazed at him sadly. "I have discussed nothing else for the past sixty-five years. And I am not even a fighter."

"Guardians would know better than anyone the consequences of final defeat." Gideon said meditatively.

"Which is why we are all, every guardian, so alarmed at our downward military spiral. At the current rate we could all be in chains in the realm of shadow in a mere two generations." And Galen, as he spoke, looked more and more alarmed at the words coming out of his own mouth.

"But ah," Ein said, "you told me we'd learn to kill enemy commanders in your lifetime."

"I did, didn't I?" The old man rested his forehead in a gnarled palm. "Sometimes anxiety runs away with me."

"It runs away with us all," Ein said. "That's why almost all the fighters at the front take meds—the looming terrifying prospect of human defeat. Because then what?"

"Let's not discuss it!" Gideon snapped. "I just came from a nice dinner with a lovely young woman, back here, to find to alte kockers counting the corpses of Elsewhere? Bah! Enough! We're all going to die someday anyway."

"Later rather than sooner, I hope," Ein continued.

"I don't want to hear it," thus Gideon. "I've spent so much time with fighters talking about death that he's practically a close acquaintance of mine. And that is not a situation I relish. I'd rather forget about death and just live while I have the chance."

"Well, it's time for me to see someone who, I'd lay money, never forgets about death," Ein said.

"Who?"

"Orozco."

"Oh, well, of course," Gideon replied. "Come on, I'll take you, I'm sleeping there tonight anyway."

With that, the two male fighters departed, leaving the young Seran woman and the ancient guardian at his computer screen, where he was showing her a star map that included the constellation, which contained her home world. "Of all the worlds the fighters have spoken to me about, Sere interests me the most," he was saying.

"Why?"

"Because for some reason the enemy will never set foot there."

"Then we will survive."

"Unless you destroy yourselves, like so many other worlds and like we're doing here on earth."

Their voices trailed off, as the two fighters moved through the dim shop. At the door, Gideon said, "here, let me check it, to make sure it locks behind us."

"Worried about Galen or Sana?"

"Both," the young fighter replied.

The door locked. "Death worshippers would like nothing better," Gideon began.

"Shh! Such thoughts are best avoided. Besides, Sana is strong and armed. Do not worry about what is most unlikely," Ein encouraged, and then, running his fingers through his gray crew-cut. "Worry about what's terrible and likely."

"Such as?"

"Such as the collapse of sector one thousand."

And on that note, they climbed the stone steps to the night darkling street. Their footsteps echoed along the deserted sidewalks and high above, a summer breeze tossed the treetops over the elegant little park. A homeless man meandered by, but otherwise not a soul was in sight. The shops were closed, the occasional, brightly lit interior of a city bus revealed how few passengers travelled at this late hour.

They found Orozco alone in the study at 333 Apocalypse Avenue, reading the Old Testament. Horace had gone to bed, Starfield had left, and Gideon headed straight back to the kitchen for a bottle of beer in the fridge and then settled down in the dim living room, watching TV.

"That book is your Bible," Ein said.

"So it is."

"I obtained a copy of it on my last visit here."

"Speaking of which, what brings you back?"

Ein hesitated. "A very old guardian and a discovery we fighters have made about the guardians' flame."

"Which is?"

"It can burn enemy commanders and interrogators."

Orozco closed the Bible and sat up straight and alert. "Can it kill them?"

"Properly boosted, I believe it could."

"Well, you're the weapons designer, get on it."

"I'm going to merge it with project Fireball."

"I heard about that," Orozco mused. "I guess every fighter heard how the Argans were going to mimic the seraphs."

"We encountered launching problems."

"No shit."

"You would have predicted that?"

"No shit."

"Tell me, Rafael, why would the angels give this gift, this fire, their fire, to the guardians of earth, a flame they use to see reality but one that also, clearly, has the potential to be a deadly weapon?"

"Potential, schmotential."

"Hmm. Galen said that."

"Who's he?"

"A guardian."

"Well, sounds like a smart one. On the right track anyway. We fighters have been yammering on about potential weapons against our non-human adversaries for, oh, my guess would be, five millennia."

"But the war went well for ninety eight percent of that time."

"War and going well aren't two phrases I ordinarily link, but if you say so."

"Rafael, you know darn well it's only in the last two or three decades that we've been losing so badly."

Orozco sighed and laid an enormous mitt on the Bible, then opened it to Saul, murmuring, "the beginning of the end." Then he looked up and said, "there was treachery."

"So I've heard. And the traitors fled to the realm of shadow, where they lived in luxury until a few smart fighters figured out who they were and killed most of them."

Orozco cast a sidelong glance at the weapons designer. "If this is true, they are heroes. How do you come to know this?"

Ein explained about the Seran wizards.

"Well then, some justice was done, but," the policeman sighed, "too late to undo the damage."

"You believe that treachery is why we're losing the war."

"That's my gut instinct, yes. I don't know how, but our friends who turned on us most assuredly made earth explicitly known to the enemy, put it front and center in his

329

mind, which is exactly where our good Friend did not want it. The trouble started here. Earth was the cause of the war. Then the enemy's mind was clouded, and he forgot about earth,"

"Wait a minute—who clouded it?"

"Who do you think?"

"How do you know this?"

"Ahem."

"Sorry, stupid question. But you're saying that now he's aware of earth again, has been for a few decades and that's why we're losing?"

"Something like that. If not that exactly, something… some connection between the enemy and earth that we need to sever and sever fast. And frankly, I don't think your fireballs are going to do the trick." Orozco opened and closed the Bible again. He leaned back and shut his eyes. "There is very good reason to believe the enemy, in his human articulations, was active on earth a little over fifty years ago."

"I've heard about that war and that holocaust."

"His initial luck was phenomenal. In fact it was out of this world." Orozco's eyes flew open, no longer darkly doleful but war-weary, battle-worn, ancient. "It is our task to make certain no non-human articulations touch down here," he said, and Ein distinctly heard the whirring of wings. "Because once that happens, the war enters its final phase and the outcome for humanity does not look good." He paused. "The suffering of the guardians has been terrible. It is our task, your task, Ein, now that you know of them, to make certain that they do not become a sacrifice, a human sacrifice on our enemy's blood-stained altar. The guardians are not to be destroyed."

"But I don't even live on earth."

"You will take a guardian's flame back to Argas. There you will work. You will report your results to the guardian, the friend of His, with whom you conferred earlier tonight. Only to him."

"What if I just have theories and no empirical evidence?"

"You will report your theories as well. He will be an excellent judge of them. Do not be misled by his lack of scientific background. When that old guardian judges, he does not judge alone." Whereupon Orozco closed his eyes, the whirring of wings ceased, and Ein knew himself to be in the presence of a fighter, not an angel, once more.

"Do they do that to you a lot?" He asked.

"Enough." Orozco sighed. "Sounds like you may stumble on some sort of breakthrough."

"A breakthrough that an ancient humanist, not a scientist, will recognize."

Orozco popped a mint into his mouth and slurped, regarding the Argan through cannily narrowed eyes. "Probably already has, if you ask me."

***

Later that evening, the Argan found the Mexican fighter sitting alone out back, in Horace's little, fenced-in garden, counting fireflies. "They come from the park nearby," Orozco explained. "There's a stream and a densely wooded area. It's one of the spits off of Sleepy Hollow Park, which winds kind of through the city, like Rock Creek Park in DC."

"I have *no* idea what you're talking about."

"Just another park in another run-down city."

"You think this elderly guardian has already solved the puzzle?" Ein came straight to the point.

"If he has, he'll keep the secret to protect earth. That's what guardians do. And if he's figured out how to destroy enemy commanders,' you'll never prise that out of him. He'll wait for the day when one of them comes to earth and use it then."

331

"But one may *never* come to earth."

"Let's be realists, Ein, grown-ups, not children. The enemy just tried to *invade* this planet. He'll be back. He always comes back. Speaking of which, if I was you, I'd be doing what earth's fighters have been doing for years."

"Which is?"

"Going behind the lines and hacking into enemy computers and fuckin' up their intel on our little planet."

"You think he'll attack Argas again?"

Orozco turned his head and stared the visitor in the eye. "I *know* it." He paused to count another three fireflies. "But don't ask earth's guardians for help. They have a very apocalyptic view, in which the destruction of earth figures as the first open door to doomsday. If your friend, the guardian, knows a secret he can use to save this planet, he'll never part with it, except on his deathbed, and then only to another guardian."

"I have never met a fighter like you," Ein said.

"I'm just a fighter who happens to be a friend of His."

"A *good* friend."

"Well, if you're so impressed with me, listen up. You get Gideon to drive you deep into Lonely State Park, you fly back to Argas on an angel and then you do everything in your power to come up with a way to kill enemy non-humans. Never forget, the fate of sector 3333 depends on it."

"I hope to see you again someday, Orozco."

"And I hope not. 'Cause if we meet again, it'll be at the front. And I don't know about you, but I ain't exactly eager to go back there any time in the near future or ever, for that matter. So," he raised his beer bottle, "here's to peace and long life and leaving the blood-soaked battlefields of Elsewhere to the young people who got the stamina to cope with them."

"Amen."

***

The little image of Ivan flickered angrily on the hand-held. "Who said you could return to earth?" He demanded. "We need you here, at the front. You didn't even make a report to the council."

"I got you your treaty, didn't I?" Jamal Jones demanded. "And I heard a voice, telling me to hop on an angel, and the angel brought me back to Ohio. So now I'm sittin' on my back deck, under an umbrella, sippin' ice tea, waitin' for the rain and takin' abuse from you. I got you your treaty. The angel brought me back here—it wasn't my choice."

"It just happens to coincide with your choice."

"What are you saying, I manipulate seraphs?"

Ivan grumbled incoherently.

"Besides, what you need my report for? You got the dang treaty, and you sure know better than me whether it worked."

"It worked. One of our fighters closed the channel between earth and the realm of shadow."

"Using Argan weaponry, no doubt."

"Yes," grumble, grumble.

"You should be thankin' me, man. I saved our planet, but oh no, what do I get instead of well-earned gratitude? Carping and picking and complaining that I'm somehow, I don't even know how, shirking my duty. What you want in this report that you ain't already know?"

"Intelligence on the Argan power structure."

"Well, I know zip about that. Ask the Argan on the council. He know moren me. Sheesh. Do a good turn and do it right and get nothing, *nothing* but threats and complaints."

"You're needed in sector one thousand."

"Oh no. I ain't setting foot in that place. Whole sector's doomed and everybody knows it."

"You and your buddy Holdauer—to go to an outer planet in a far galaxy."

"That's conquered territory!" Jamal screamed.

"It's called guerrilla warfare, Jones."

"It's called suicide. Shit. What's this planet's name?"

"Ice."

"Wonderful."

"It's cold."

"I gathered that."

"The enemy don't like cold. All they've got there is a small death worshipper garrison and a very angry native population."

"And you think me and Holdauer can get these locals to rise up, destroy the garrison and begin a successful counterattack from behind the lines."

"We're trying to save conquered peoples, Jones, one planet at a time." Ivan paused, gray and tired. "You'll have Argan weapons. They're already in the hands of the resistance."

"Then why don't the resistance just wipe out this garrison without me and Holdauer?"

"They need leadership, Jones."

"Shit."

"And you're leadership."

"I hate this frikkin' job."

"You rendez-vous with Holdauer in Gverijek at a dive called The Glacier, at nine pm tonight, Ice time."

"I don't even get a frikkin' rest."

"We want that garrison destroyed in two days."

"So then the enemy can send in the big guns. What do you think we'll get? A couple of commanders? Or maybe we'll hit the jackpot with an ill-tempered interrogator, who decides to fuck those local humans and just barbecue the place."

"Two days, Jones. Destroy it in two days. Dismissed." And the little image of Ivan flicked off, as the screen went black.

***

"Go left on the road, it takes you straight into Gverjek," the seraph had said. That was twenty minutes ago, and still nothing but snow and ice and trees bent to the ground under snow as far as he could see. He tromped on, his snowshoes tied to his backpack, because the road was relatively clear, his leather coat and hat warm, but definitely not made for a place like this. Jamal shivered, and wondered and shivered some more. Why destroy this garrison if it was only manned by a few death worshipper slaves? That didn't make sense. Something, he told himself, with a concomitant sense of relief as he caught the first glimmer of a city in the distance, something was going on in that garrison, something bad, and the council wanted it shut down, toute suite. But what could it be? Maybe Holdauer could help him get a handle on this. His old friend was always good at deciphering the council's motives. One thing was sure: it wasn't just some little outpost of a garrison, as Ivan had portrayed it.

He stomped his feet, cold in his Russian boots, and clapped his hands, cold in his Russian gloves. His head was cold in his Moscow hat. This, he thought, was worse than Siberia in winter. He remembered Irkutsk in December, chasing down death worshipper spies three years ago. No, Ice was definitely colder than Irkutsk. Ice was the coldest place he'd ever set foot on, and he wanted to leave it at once. "We destroy that garrison tonight," he said aloud and peered hopefully through the night at the bright lights of the small city ahead.

He found The Glacier by the river wharf, exactly where the angel had said it would be and stepped into a room warmed by a crowd of topers and three big, black, metal, pot-bellied wood burning stoves, one at each end of the room. Burly, fiery-eyed, black-haired Holdauer was at the bar, but spotted him in the mirror at once.

"What ya drinking?" Jamal asked.

"The local brew. Real rotgut, worse than Brennivin. Ever tasted that?"

"Can't say as I have."

"National drink of Iceland, tastes like you'd imagine it would for a population whose idea of a delicacy is rotten shark meat. Good God, what did I do to deserve this crappy assignment?"

"Where's the resistance?"

Holdauer made a sweeping gesture with his arm, encompassing the whole room. "A lot of it's right here. More in the back room, waiting for you."

"And you."

"I told 'em we're a team. What they have to say to me they say to us both. They never seen an African American before."

"Well, there's a first time for everything. Come on."

So they pushed their way to the door in the back, opened it and entered a smoke-filled room with a large round table, crammed with pale blond men, seated next to each other, smoking, drinking and occasionally brandishing what Jamal instantly pegged as Argan weapons. Jamal also counted five cuspidors. Several of the men had shaved heads and quite a few were shirtless, with little chains around their necks. They gawked quite frankly at Jamal Jones.

"Now my friend Holdauer here tells me you have, and I can see that he had provided you with, very advanced weapons. I will get you more later tonight."

A cheer went up, as the assembled leaders of the resistance decided that this Jamal Jones was a good guy, and celebrated the realization by tossing off large shots of their odiferously alcoholic beverage. Then they attacked what looked like long fillets of herring, smoked more and insisted that the two off-world fighters show them how to use these fantastic weapons, so they could go kill the storm troopers in the tower forthwith.

"What else are they doing there?" Jamal asked the rowdy assemblage. "'Cause I'm damn near certain I didn't get sent into the heart of conquered territory to kill a tiny death worshipper garrison."

The men fell silent, then a murmur went up, in which the words, "Ent, you tell 'em. You tell 'em, Ent." So Ent, huge, muscle-bound, shirtless, with a shaved head and rough, worn pants, got to his feet and informed the fighters that he had spied on the invaders.

"What'd you see?" Holdauer demanded, eyes, flashing.

"I'm coming to that. There's one there that the others call 'the master killer.'"

"Shit," Jamal nearly spat and slumped into a chair. This reaction had a profound effect on the men of the resistance. They stopped eating, drinking, smoking and gaped from Jamal to Holdauer and back.

"What's this master killer do?" Holdauer growled.

"He's in a trance, at the center of a big...a big swirl. And there's a road through it and lots of the enemy marching on that road."

"And what's at the end of the road?" Holdauer asked through gritted teeth.

The man hesitated.

"What's at the end?!" Holdauer shouted.

"Another planet in our system, called Snow. It's the next one in toward the sun."

"Shit!" Holdauer and Jamal shouted in unison. Then Jamal, his elbow on the table, his head in his hand, pulled the hand-held out of his coat, tapped it and frowned at the image of Ivan that instantly appeared. "So how do we shut down a master killer in a trance, bringing fascists from the realm of shadow to the next planet?"

"Use the needle bomb. I assume you got the coordinates for tonight's drop."

"Yes."

"Well, what are you waiting for? Pick up the needle bomb and kill these sons of bitches and shut down that channel!" The picture disappeared.

"Is he the boss?" Ent asked.

"Yeah, he's the boss," Holdauer said.

"He da man," Jamal breathed, then looked hard at his friend. "You've used a lot more Argan weaponry than me."

"I think I can figure out the needle bomb. I've used lotsa Argan bombs in the past, and was told one was almost a twin of this needle bomb." Holdauer pulled out an Argan GPS from his pocket. "Neat gadget," he said, "works on any planet, in any galaxy, in any universe. Here's the black lagoon and the trail that forks. The weapons are at the fork."

"I'll drive you," Ent said.

"What about a shirt?"

"It's a warm night. Shit, I gone stark naked in colder than this. Come on." So the two fighters, Ent and two other resistance leaders, both wearing shirts, tromped out to a big car, got in and took off at high speed, Ent at the wheel, describing everything they passed at breakneck pace. However, it was quite dark, so these descriptions lost much of what Jamal mentally tagged as their oomph, since he could not see the mountains or the glaciers or the parks that Ent was showing off.

They parked and tramped out onto the trail. "No shirt. You're an idiot, Ent," thus one of his countrymen.

"Look, it's better than the last time," said the other. "Last time we came to the black lagoon, he didn't wear shoes."

"That was summer, you moron. It was thirty degrees."

"Remind me not to move to Ice," thus Jamal.

"After we destroy that master killer and bring down the wrath of the conquerors, my guess is moving here won't be much on anybody's mind," Holdauer replied. "Escaping as fast as possible will be the order of the day."

"Any evacuation plans in motion?"

"Nope. None that I hear of."

"This is one half-assed operation."

"It's desperate. The council is desperate. Desperate people do stupid things. Oh, I see the armament."

They hurried forward, collected the weapons in the clearing and carried them back to the trunk of the car.

"Now where to?" Jamal demanded.

"Back to The Glacier," Ent replied. "We need to pow wow."

"When your people flee, where do they flee to?" Jamal asked, as Ent once again took the wheel.

"We don't run. We stand and fight."

"Dandy," Jamal replied and fell silent. His hand-held beeped, so he withdrew it from his coat, tapped it, and a little picture of Ein's worried face appeared on the screen. "So you know," Jamal said.

"I know. The council briefed me about the problem on Ice, while you were in transit. We've got five invisible super-needles in cloaked orbit around the planet."

"What for?"

"What for? To move that God-forsaken rock, as soon as you destroy that master killer and blockade his road."

"Move it? The whole planet? Where to?"

"The adjacent universe, an outer galaxy with a very similar solar system."

"You ever moved a planet before?"

"No. This is a first. But it should work."

"Thanks for the vote of confidence."

"Thing is," Ein continued, "you're going to have to put it to a vote. Tell the leaders—"

"Those drunken clowns?"

"Hey," Ent snapped. "We ain't clowns."

"Lay out the options," Ein said. "have them vote. If they want to stay and face the music, that's their choice."

"What kind of music?" Ent asked, glancing down at the hand-held.

"Keep your eye on the road," thus Jamal.

"The whole planet incinerated by an angry enemy commander music," Ein answered.

"What are our alternatives again?" Ent asked.

"For us, the Argans, to relocate Ice to a very similar position in another system in another universe."

"Sounds good to me," said one of the men in the back.

"Let me know once you've voted," Ein said, and the screen went black. Holdauer leaned forward and tapped his old friend on the shoulder.

"I never been on a planet's been moved before."

"Well, now is your opportunity."

"No chance of us leaving, before the Argans attempt their little experiment?"

"Doubtful."

"I thought as much." He leaned back and glowered at everyone in the car.

Back at The Glacier, things had picked up. The barmaids could scarcely keep up with the orders, the room was stifling, and voices very loud. The five arrivals tromped into the back room, Jones and Holdauer gagging on the smoke, and shut the door.

"Here's the deal," Holdauer said, sitting at the table, with his arms on it, massive hands clasped. "After we destroy this garrison, the enemy will be furious and decide to make an example of Ice by burning it to a cinder. He will not invade. There will be no hand to hand combat. No glory. So put those childish ideas out of your minds. A commander will orbit the planet in one of those black spaceships you saw when they first came, he will wave a hand, and Ice will go up in flames. The whole planet."

"I say we live with the garrison," thus one of the leaders.

"But there is another choice," Holdauer growled. "You've all heard of Argas?"

"Aye, yes, certainly," and other such affirmations filled the room.

"They have the technology to slip easily from one universe to the next. And they propose to relocate Ice to a universe next door, to a very similar orbit in a very similar system. They've never moved a whole planet before, so it might not work. But they're the best and the smartest we've got, they been zipping around universes, through universes, for thousands of years, and they think it can work."

Silence fell on the roomful of over twenty men at the large round table. Some seemed in silent thought, others glanced around at their comrades. At last, one man who had been sitting quietly, raised his glass and exclaimed loudly, "here's to Argas!"

"Yes, yes! Here's to Argas," a chorus of yeses and ayes filled the room, as the resistance leaders voted to have their planet moved. "So Ice moves next door," Holdauer said. "Anyone opposed?" There was not a sound. "Let's go kill those sons of bitches."

"Not so fast," Jamal restrained him. "It's always better, when dealing with death worshippers, to attack in daylight, if you can. Since there are no spies on this planet, we needn't worry about that, and it's not like we're going to get a ticket parked across from this tower, where they've set up their base. The police are on our side."

"We *are* the police," said one man.

"Even though it's night," Holdauer snapped. "I say we get rid of 'em as fast as possible. I don't like waiting. It increases risk."

"In this case, it decreases risk," thus Jamal.

"Well, while you two argue it out, we'll vote," Ent said. They did so, and a majority was for attacking that very evening.

"You don't even know how to use a needle bomb," Jamal reproved his old friend rather sourly.

"Do too. I read the instructions the Argans sent. Five simple steps. Their rocket launchers are more complicated. And I handled those plenty of times. Don't be sore loser, Jamal."

The man who had first raised his glass came over to the two visitors, who noticed for the first time the thunderbolt tattoos on his upper arms. "What is it, brother?" Holdauer asked.

"How many fighters beside you in this town?" Jamal asked in a low voice.

"Three, right here in this room. They got the thunderbolt tattoos, but I guess you been too busy to notice. Have you cleared moving this planet with the council?"

The two earth fighters shook their heads.

"Well, now would be a good time, don't you think?"

Jamal withdrew his hand-held from his coat, tapped it, and there appeared a very worried, weary, gray visage. It was Ivan.

"They voted to move the planet," Jamal said.

"We figured they would. It's not like they have a lot of choices."

"Three that I counted," Holdauer addressed his remarks to the little image. "Become conquered slaves, die in flames or try to move."

"Wouldn't it be simpler just to evacuate this rock?" Jamal demanded.

"That's almost a billion people," Ivan replied. "The Argans can't move that many transports behind the lines without being detected. No, the strategy right now is to evacuate the unconquered planets, where our transport ships can still move freely."

"As for the conquered worlds?" Holdauer asked.

"They're on their own."

"Shit."

"That's what defeat means, Holdauer."

The whole room had fallen silent during this exchange and now the men of the resistance gazed grimly at their two visitors.

"You messaged me that these death worshipper troops are making contact on a planet called Snow," Ivan continued. "Is it populated?"

"No," said the local fighter, who had come over to confer with the guests. "Though it's a little closer to the sun, for reasons we never understood, it was just too cold. So, in this system at least, only one planet is inhabited. And that's us, Ice."

"Good," Ivan spoke wearily. "When will you shut down the channel to the realm of shadow?"

"Tonight," Holdauer answered. "Then Jamal will contact you, and you tell the Argans to rev up their engines; Ice will be ready to roll."

Ivan looked exhausted. He did not even say "dismissed." Instead he sighed, glanced from Holdauer to Jamal to the local fighter and said, "God be with you."

***

Shortly thereafter, the two fighters from Cleveland and the one who had voted first for the Argan rescue sat in a car with Ent, not longer shirtless, at the wheel. Across the road loomed a crumbling stone tower with a faint glow in an upper window. Holdauer set up the Argan weapon in the passenger window, and peered through the scope. "Twenty fascists," he murmured, "twenty white xs, the biggest one on the master killer in a trance. Here goes." He fired, and the weapon glowed slightly, soundlessly. Then all the windows in the tower glowed faintly, and Holdauer, watching through the scope, announced, "the channel closed. Ent, get us back to The Glacier, quick." As they sped down the road, Jamal's little computer beeped, he tapped it, and there appeared the image of a man, instantly identifiable as an Argan, for he was clad all in gray, and his clothes were simple and Spartan. He introduced himself as the captain of one of the five needles orbiting Ice and, in fact, the commander of his little squad.

"What happens to Ice's atmosphere in the wormhole?" Jamal demanded.

"It stays intact. Everything stays intact. And you'll only be in the wormhole for a matter of seconds. Don't ask me how, I'm not a physicist. And our physicists on board are rather busy right now. You'll be moved in about twenty minutes."

"Is it safe to wait that long?" Holdauer asked.

"The nearest enemy commander is six hours away. Yes it's safe. Besides, they won't even get word that this channel shut down for another hour."

"You're sure?"

"Our scientists are. And I go by them. They've never failed us yet."

The little image flicked off. "I gotta get one of those," Ent said. "They Argan?"

"Yup," Holdauer replied. "The Argan equivalent of a cellphone, except it's a vidphone and the image can traverse galaxies and universes."

"Sounds like we're in good hands," Ent exulted.

"Let's just wait till this little experiment is over," Jamal retorted tartly. "Then we'll have a better idea how good those hands were."

"Or we won't have any ideas about anything," Holdauer remarked glumly.

"Shut up," Jamal snapped. "You don't' need to state the most obvious worst case possibility. I think we all have a pretty clear idea about that." And so, those wretched possibilities lodged directly in front of everyones' minds' eye, they drove in silence back to the still bright, still warm, still crowded little bar on the frozen river wharf.

By the time they resumed their seats in the back room, fifteen minutes had passed, and Jamal was conferring by means of his little device with the Argan captain.

"All needles powered," the men, sitting perfectly silently now, heard in the background on Jamal's hand-held. "All coordinates mapped. The physicists say it's time for stitch, gentlemen."

The two fighters from earth looked at each other. "It's been real," Jamal said.

"No, it's been horrible. One blood-soaked front after another for the past few decades. Nothin' but death, destruction and the annihilation of people you love. And now this. It sucks."

They waited. Nothing happened. The lights did not even dim. But Jamal thought he detected, ever so quickly and faintly, a glow out the window. But then, he later told Holdauer, maybe he had imagined it.

The captain reappeared on the hand-held vid-phone. "Go outside, brothers."

"What for?" Asked the local fighter, who had been first to toast the Argans.

"To look up in the sky, see the new constellations, your new home. Yes, go outside and look up at the stars."

***

"Luckily it was a small planet," Ein concluded his narration of these events to Saltwater and Lindin in the lab.

"Luck?!" Saltwater cried. "You left this to luck?"

"Even in physics you need a little luck."

The two guests stared at each other in alarm.

"But what if there had been no luck?" Saltwater continued.

"Well, it wouldn't have been any worse for Ice's inhabitants than what awaited them six hours later, with the arrival of a genocidal enemy commander. In fact, better to go in an instant, than to have your whole planet burned at the stake. A painless possible death versus the certain agonizing burning alive of an entire world's population? I'd take the first option any day."

The pockmarked man rubbed his anxious face. "But Geeze, when the best physicists in the entire cosmos are flyin' by the seat of their pants..."

"It was a desperate situation," Ein said gravely. "Our science said we could do it, so we tried, and we succeeded. The model worked. The formulae were accurate. Now we just have to be certain Ice can't be traced."

"I've had Seymour on it all day. He says no. It never happened with a needle, and it won't happen with a planet."

346

"The original calculations," Ein said, "made millennia ago, demonstrated that a trace was physically impossible."

"And they are correct," Seymour piped in from a nearby computer. "This is one rare instance where enemy intelligence will be completely foiled."

"I wonder…is there some way we could make it look like their tampering with the borders between kingdoms, opening that channel, somehow destroyed the planet?" Lindin asked.

"That might not be desirable," Saltwater said. "They'd like nothing better than to destroy lots of planets. If they think opening a transport route will do that, they'll be opening 'em up all over the place. I say we leave well enough alone."

"Just let them wonder where that planet went?"

"They can wonder all they want, just so long as we're sure they won't find the answer."

"They won't," Seymour piped in.

"You're so sure," Ein said.

"I've looked through billions of records. Planets have been moved before."

"What?" The three fighters cried. "By whom?" Saltwater demanded.

"Who do you think?" Seymour replied.

"You mean He's been moving planets defensively, and we didn't know it?" Ein exclaimed.

"For millennia," Seymour replied.

"How many have been moved?"

"Some. Not thousands, but at least one hundred."

The three fighters stared at each other.

"What about systems?" Saltwater suddenly burst out.

"You mean whole solar systems?" Seymour asked.

"Yes."

"I'll have to look into that."

"What do we do with this?" Lindin asked.

"Report it to the council," Ein said.

"What?" Saltwater demanded. "So they can report it to Him? He already knows. He's the One Who's been doing it."

**

"We cannot count on it," Ivan's image on the tablet addressed the three fighters. "We must proceed with our new technology. Clearly if we have the power to move populated planets out of harm's way, we should do so. He would consider us remiss—in the extreme—if we did not. And we should start doing it in sector one thousand at once. We should start with the still viable, unconquered planets."

"Why not the conquered ones?" Saltwater spoke through gritted teeth.

"First, because we risk exposure of our technology. Second, because so many of those planets have been invaded. We're not transplanting planets full of fascists into peaceful solar systems behind our lines. That would be suicide."

"How about we determine which planets are most like Ice—the ones that only have a small enemy garrison or two?"

"From what we know, those are few and far between."

"Then we rescue the ones that are few and far between!" Saltwater cried. "It's criminal not to!"

"I agree with Pavel," Ein said. "And we should proceed on both fronts at once—the lightly held planets behind the lines and the ones as yet unconquered but most at risk. Jones and Holdauer are obviously the men for the worlds behind the lines…"

"Stick to physics, Ein," Ivan snapped. "We've just had a breakthrough, for which you Argan physicists get all the credit and which will lead to saving billions of lives in sector one thousand. How we handle these rescue operations is a matter for the council."

"At least keep us apprised," Ein said.

"What for?"

"Seymour, that's what for," Saltwater snapped. "He'll be able to tell you in an hour which planets behind the lines have a chance of rescue. Let him do the triage. It'll be faster, and there will be a higher survival rate than if the council meets, consults with techs, then meets again, and so forth and so on. It could take days."

"While I'm already on it," Seymour piped.

"Was that Seymour?" Ivan asked in surprise.

"Yes."

"And I'll have that list of salvageable planets for you very shortly, sir," Seymour said.

Ivan appeared stunned. Then, after a moment, he nodded, opened his mouth to speak, shut it and finally, quietly, said, "thank you."

***

The priest in his black cassock knelt in the white tent, before a white altar, his hands clasped, his eyes shut, and so absorbed in prayer did he appear to be that the other priest, coming in with the breeze, hesitated at first to disturb him. But then at last he said, "it's been done the way you requested, brother."

Vivaldi opened his eyes, and the visitor continued: "a female fighter sought me out to tell me, two hours from here, the surviving fighters of sector one thousand have a camp where they have gathered all the fighters' orphans. They did this on their own. They did not know it was your request."

"Where is she?"

"At the administration tent. I told her about you and your request. She is waiting to take you to this encampment."

"By donkey or jeep?"

"Jeep. It's two hours by jeep."

"Where they've gathered these children," Vivaldi began.

"All run by fighters. None of our brethren are there yet. But the woman fighter said we would be welcome."

"It is as I hoped," Vivaldi said, getting to his feet. "What is her name?"

"Marya. She is from the next solar system, and will soon be deployed to the actual front. She told me she had placed her own children in this camp, as all her relatives are dead and her husband, also a fighter, has been killed."

"So she expects to die soon."

"Yes. It is a not unreasonable assumption."

"But an eventuality we never seek to hasten. Too much acceptance of death is akin to suicide. I'm just saying that perhaps she's giving up too fast."

The other, younger priest regarded him skeptically, then changed the subject. "The fighters in the administration tent have a remarkable device—a computer, like a cell phone, but they use it to communicate with the council and with Argas!"

"Sounds like magic to me," Vivaldi grumbled, stepping out of the brilliantly white tent and into the warm, yellow sunshine. All around, on the wide green plain were the white tents of the refugees and not too far off a gray one, toward which they directed their steps. As they approached, they heard screams of joy emanating from behind the gray flaps. They entered to see the two fighters, normally in charge of the camp, whooping ecstatically, as if they had just won the war. One of them, Axel, hurried over to the two priests.

"Science has done it again," he shouted. "Argan physicists have figured out how to move whole planets to other universes. They already liberated one called Ice from enemy territory and guess what? We're next. The needles are already here. We'll be moved at twilight!"

"Into a whole other universe?" Vivaldi was astonished.

"They already did it. I tell you, man, there is nothing human science cannot do when properly nurtured. Science is..."

"Oh shut up about science," the other tall, lean and gray-haired fighter said. "It says here, in this report, to be shared only with certain fighters and the brethren," here he indicated the two priests with a nod of his head, "that you know Who has been defensively moving planets out of harm's way for millennia."

"What?" Axel and Vivaldi cried in unison.

"Recently discovered...an extensive computer search of star and planet maps...going back four thousand years...a planet called earth already moved more than once... ninety nine others...the most extensive search of data in generations...the most powerful computer ever built...of Argan design...His power beyond imagining...the enemy frustrated...one hundred near misses...His intervention cannot be gainsaid...God is great."

"Well!" Vivaldi clapped his hands together, rubbed them and cast a critical eye on Axel. "So human science is taking baby steps toward divine power. I'm impressed."

"Oh shut up," Axel grumbled and lurched, crablike, over to his comrade and grabbed the hand-held computer. "Lemme read this report."

Only then did they notice the sorrowful figure of a woman fighter, standing off to the side, the gray in her hair, the lines in her face beginning to yield their sadness to the possibility of hope. "So our children in our camp on the far side of the hills will survive."

"Yes, sister," the tall fighter said. "That is what this news means."

She turned to Vivaldi. "You run the transuniverse orphanage here, correct?"

He nodded.

"We have many thousands of fighters' orphans, whose placement calls for exquisite care."

"I have placed fighters' orphans before," he replied gravely.

"Then you know they go only to households in which there is an adult fighter."

"I know. That has always been the rule. That's why I put in the request that they be gathered together in one place."

"I and my surviving brothers and sisters have gathered them from all corners of the universe, which I now learn is called sector one thousand."

Axel and the tall fighter looked away. "When local fighters learn what sector they come from, well, it's like reading an epitaph on a tombstone," the tall one whispered to Axel, who nodded and cast the woman a pitying glance. "Can't there be a reprieve for her?" He asked. "Does she *have* to go to the front? Why can't she stay here?"

"You ask her."

He did.

She shook her head. "I have heard a voice," she said. "I depart after I take the priest from the Milky Way to the fighters' orphans. You," she pointed at Vivaldi, "come from a place called the Milky Way?"

He nodded. "Come. We have no time to lose." So they strode out together to the jeep, parked by the one gray tent in a sea of brilliantly white tents, extending over the entire plain to the hills. She slung her machine gun into the back with her knapsack and slid in behind the wheel. Soon they were bouncing along the track between tents, headed straight for the blue-green hills in the distance.

"So the war has been going against you here," Vivaldi commented.

"It's been awful. Oh father, I am a religious woman, but this catastrophe has nearly broken my faith."

"Don't let it do that," he began.

"You haven't see what I've seen. The power of these fiends is too great. Our fighters wounded, killed, starved, retreating in rags. The killing centers, the separation stations, the death camps and the battles we always lose, the fighters' charred corpses everywhere and nowhere, nowhere any relief."

"But relief has come. The Argans will move this planet and all its billions of refugees, the fighters' own children among them. Do not think that because you have been called back to the front, He has abandoned you, or because death is a possibility,"

"Oh father! It's a certainty, just as it's a certainty sector one thousand will collapse and all the people remaining in it will die. There is no way this beaten universe can withstand this assault. I repeat: You have not seen what I've seen."

"Do not despair, sister."

"You call me sister, are you a fighter?"

"I am with you heart and soul."

"But you would not kill."

"No, I cannot."

"Oh!" She screamed. "I don't understand any of it!"

"Do not despair. He will win the war."

"Cold comfort to the dead," she lamented bitterly. And they rode along, bouncing down the dirt track in the jeep, in the sunshine, one in wretched despair, the other full of hope, and attempting vainly to infuse some of it into her soul; but she had witnessed too much defeat, too much death, too many atrocities. She could not be consoled.

By the time they reached the beginning of the orphans' encampment, however, she had composed herself. She drove silently, grimly, like a condemned person, who has accepted her fate. She looked neither to the right nor left, seemed interested in nothing other than the task at hand. But when they arrived in the small, lush valley dotted with thousands of white tents, each a home to four or five children, always with an older child, aged thirteen or fourteen, responsible for the younger ones, down to age two, arriving there, she said, under her breath, "after I take you to administration, I will go say good-bye to my children."

"It is not necessarily good-bye," the priest ventured.

"Yes it is. Necessarily."

They pulled up to the big blue tent, in front of which, at two long, rectangular tables, several harried fighters were ladling out soup, to the last lunchtime stragglers. "Where have you been?" A strong young fighter demanded.

"Fetching the priest."

"But you were supposed to bring more. One priest can't run this encampment, and we leave for the front, shortly."

"More are coming," Vivaldi explained. "They will be here within a half hour." The woman fighter left in search of her children, wiping tears out of her eyes.

"What news of the war?" The strong one demanded of the priest, surveying him critically, then ladling out the last bowl of soup. Vivaldi studied the man quickly—scarred, muscular, with a short crew-cut, thunderbolt tattoos on his upper arms. "Good news," he said.

The man's eyebrows rose. "Don't tell me we're beating them back?"

"No. But the Argans have found a way to move planets to other universes. This information is to be kept amongst fighters.

The man stood stock still, his mouth open.

"I said," Vivaldi began to repeat himself.

"I heard. When will they move this planet, with the fighters' children?"

"Tonight at twilight."

The man lay down the ladle on the table. There were no more comers anyway. There was no more soup. "So our children will survive." He said quietly.

"You may too."

"Don't be foolish. I go to the front. That's a death sentence."

"You've obviously been there before, and you're not dead yet."

"I like you, priest. You've cheered me up. I'd offer you soup, but we're out. See—no kids? They have a sixth sense, always know when the last pot's empty. My name's Lal," and he held out a strong, scarred hand. The priest shook it.

"Vivaldi."

"And this here with the scar on his cheek and the ugly nose is Har. Har's an expert on the Argans, he's used their weapons before and will show me, at the front, how to use them there."

Har smiled, revealing some bright, white teeth, some dark gaps where teeth were missing.

"Us and three others, including the woman who brought you, have to leave soon," Har said. "You're with the transuniverse orphanage?"

"I am."

"How long?"

"Four decades."

"That's the life of a man in this war; well Lal, I guess he'll do. We don't just turn our kids over to anybody, Vivaldi. You hear the voice, the voice in your mind?"

"Aye," Vivaldi answered. "It told me to request that all your children be gathered in one place, to find homes for them on other worlds in the households of other fighters."

Har glanced at Lal significantly. "Let's get ready to go."

"But I can't run this place alone. At least wait until the other five priests arrive."

The man tapped his temple. "Ding a ling a ling," he said. "I got a call. Says there's a war and I'm a soldier, needed at the front at once."

The woman fighter returned, red-nosed, her cheeks tear-streaked, and two other fighters, a man and a woman, emerged from the tent. They all crowded into the jeep. Children peeped out at the tent flaps. In the distance, Vivaldi heard the rumble of another jeep, its occupants all in black cassocks, coming through the break in the hills.

"See," Har said. "You won't be alone here long." Then he looked at the children, some of whom were crying. "Live!" He shouted at them. "Get even with this enemy. Defy him. Outsmart him. Defeat him. Live!" And with that, the five fighters drove off.

***

Orozco was up late in Horace's dim, high-ceilinged first-floor study, tapping at the computer. Shadows covered the floor and walls and the only light, besides the glow of the screen, emanated weakly from a little lamp in a corner. At midnight, Gideon loomed in the doorway.

"What news of the war?"

"Nothin' good," the detective answered. "Another whole string of galaxies in sector one thousand just disappeared, blip, right off the map. And to make matters worse, a few seconds ago that planet my friend the priest went to in system BGG1 just vanished off the screen."

"You using a live map?"

"Of course I'm using a live map. The planet was there, now it ain't. Christ, and I told him to gather all the fighters' orphans there. That planet has a population of over nine billion souls. Shit. Where is it?"

"Wait. Orozco, did you hear that?"

"What?"

"Shh. Quiet. Listen."

After a moment, the old fighter turned to face the young one, his dark, doleful eyes wide. "That trumpet!" He cried. "The fighters' orphans are alive! Alive! Christ, Gideon, where's your hand-held?"

The Israeli disappeared into the shadows of the living room and reemerged with a small computer. He was already scrolling through recent communiqués, as he handed it to Orozco, saying, "read that!"

"Great balls of fire!" The old fighter exclaimed. "The Argans can move whole planets. They moved five in the past twenty-four hours, all of 'em straight out of conquered territory! Hey, what's this?"

"What?"

"An extensive computer search...going back millennia... He Who does not wish to see us destroyed has moved planets out of harm's way on one hundred occasions—earth more than once."

Gideon let out a low whistle.

"Great balls of fire! Gideon, those disappearing galaxies— do you think?"

"Yes I think. That's exactly what I think."

"Get Ein on this thing for me."

The weary weapons designer's face appeared on the screen.

"Another string of galaxies disappeared in sector one thousand," Orozco barked.

"So? That sector's collapsing."

"Wake up, Ein. It was your computer turned up evidence that the king of the universe has been juggling planets from one reality to the next."

"So?"

"Sic your computer on these disappearing galaxies. Are they turning up in other, safe locations?"

"You think?"

"Yes," Orozco hollered. "That's what I think! We need to know which ones have been saved and which, if any, have been annihilated."

"My God," Ein exclaimed. "Moving whole galaxies!"

"Whole *clusters* of galaxies. Well, you got the computer. Get to work!"

"Oh and Ein," it was Gideon, "in a certain central galaxy named Reincarnation,"

"Yeah, I got it right here on the map."

"In system BGG1, there was a planet that disappeared."

"That's 'cause we moved it."

"We?"

"Us, the Argans."

"Where to?"

"To your realilty, as a matter of fact. We found a nice matching system in the Andromeda Galaxy."

"Hey, that's right next door!" Orozco cried.

"Well, the Andromeda Galaxy just got thousands of fighters' orphans, to say nothing of the nine billion other refugees from system BGG1."

"What's the new system called?"

"It didn't have a name, wasn't on a map, so we called it BGG1 again. And we named the spiral arm it's in Reincarnation, in honor of the place where sector one thousand's fighters retreated to for sanctuary for their children. You heard the trumpet?"

"We heard it."

"The orphans have found sanctuary. They will grow up to be fighters. They are alive."

***

Sitting in the dim atrium of his dining room, the house enshrouded in shadows, his wife and guests asleep upstairs, the stars visible in the night sky through the sky-light, Ein tapped his little computer and the image of the grizzled old fighter vanished. Instead it was replaced by the green and blue globe of Planet Four, Saltwater's home, the shape of whose continents and oceans he had now come to recognize.

Ein spoke to the image of the globe. "Did you catch all that, Seymour?"

"Of course," a little voice piped back at him. "I'm conducting the search now. It could take some time. Any ideas on the best approach?"

"Yes. Of the galaxies that have disappeared, look for those that were most densely populated. Several were barren. Skip those. We can assume He wouldn't waste time on them, so it stands to reason Morning Star destroyed those. But there have been a dozen densely populated galaxies that have dropped off the map in recent days. Search the cosmos, as many other realities as you can. We need confirmation."

"Why? Can't we just assume that's what He's doing?"

"Yes, but confirmation would buoy everyone's spirits. And we could use a bit of that now."

"Understood. Searching. Just go to bed, Ein. Maybe I'll have some answers for you in the morning."

The weapons designer leaned back and gazed from the image of the blue-green planet up through the skylight into the stars. He searched out the glow of a nearby galaxy and shuddered, remembering not too many years back, the reports of mass murder in a far galaxy, where the enemy had touched down on Argan territory. He remembered the fear, fear of the deadly, homicidal commanders he had seen at the front, and he remembered the frenzy of work, the massive defense effort on Argas, as everyone looked to him to cloak the enemy's coordinates, and he remembered his terror, sitting up nights, working at his computer, thinking, "what if it doesn't work?"

"Then you all die," had said the voice deep in his mind. "You must make it work, Ein."

And so, for several frantic weeks, the engineer/physicist had been chained to his computer, the invisible links of that chain forged by terror, terror that he and everyone he loved would perish, if he didn't get it right. He had stopped talking to his wife, who understood and removed the children from his purview. He ate irregularly, slept little, poured over reports of enemy activity and worked with the techs at the front, to predict where and when the next incursion would come. And finally they had the coordinates, which he cloaked. And he waited, they all waited, the entire universe held its breath. The attack did not come. Days passed. Then weeks. Then the Argan military roared into action, destroying death worshipper garrisons on the far planets of the far, invaded galaxy. Luckily there were no commanders or interrogators. Those, Ein figured, had been waiting for a more secure conquest, after which they doubtless planned to jet in, in their immense black battle cruisers and roast as many inhabited planets as they could. The military destroyed the invading fascists, but then became obsessed with intelligence—how much was known of Argas by the enemy, how could Argan spies penetrate the enemy's bureaucracy? At the front, the council had more Argan volunteers to go behind the lines than it knew what to do with. And they went. Some died but many did not. They hacked into computers, they shredded and altered bureaucratic paperwork. Finally Argan intelligence was satisfied. The enemy, in all of his articulations that they could reach, regarded Argas as a reality stumbled upon, where an anomaly, a matter for advanced physicists, had somehow stranded their garrisons. Oh well, they were only men, only death worshippers and eminently expendable. The enemy moved on. Years passed and the memory of a strange universe where it was hard to get a foothold faded. The name Argas was never learned. But everyone, every man, woman and child in the Argan universe had learned that their reality was called sector 3333.

Ein shuddered and went for a glass of juice in the kitchen. "How long," he wondered, "between the time a people learns its sector's number and total conquest?"

"It can be millennia," he heard deep in his mind. "Or it can be weeks. In some cases the enemy was repulsed four thousand years ago. In others, as you have learned, He has had to rescue planets, systems or entire galaxies. Look on your live map. You will see Reincarnation. Still a safe, central, populous galaxy. But in two weeks it could be in another universe, and for the vast majority of its people, life will go on as if nothing has happened. They don't even know that they have to give thanks for escaping this scourge. But some will know. Some fighters, some friends of fighters, scientists like you. Maximum survival, Ein. That is always the goal."

***

"Enjoying your vacation?" The image of Ivan snarled at Jamal Jones from the small hand-held device.

"Oh yes. Holdauer and me, we may decide to sit out the rest of the war here on Ice. They got hot springs, saunas. It's way better than the front."

"Well if you're sitting out the rest of the war that'll take your whole life."

"Fine by me."

"Give it up, you two. The Argans have a list of planets behind enemy lines, which need to be moved."

"Good, let'm move 'em."

"But they all have death worshipper garrisons."

"Shit," said Holdauer.

"Are they bringing in reinforcements, like the master killer on Ice you didn't tell us about till the last minute?" Jamal asked.

"No," Ivan spoke peremptorily. "That problem has been resolved."

"By us," Holdauer snapped. "We deserve a break."

"You've had it."

"Two friggin' days!" Jamal exclaimed.

"And don't tell us the enemy don't wait," thus Holdauer.

"He doesn't. And he doesn't sleep."

"How many planets on this list?" Jamal demanded.

"Five for you two. We've got other fighters handling the rest."

"Well, thank God for small favors," Holdauer growled.

"OK. So we destroy enemy garrisons on five planets," Jamal said. "Then the Argans needle them to safety."

"Right."

"Then we get a break. Man, I got a job back on earth."

"Time passes differently there."

"An absence is still an absence."

"All right. You get a break. You return to earth for a couple of months and let sector one thousand collapse."

"Shit," Holdauer repeated. "I hate this frikkin' job."

"No sooner do you start to put down some roots," Jamal began.

"On Ice?" Ivan demanded. "Puh-leese. Who in their right mind wants to put down roots on a planet seventy percent covered by glaciers? No, break out the bathing suits, boys. You're headed for the tropics."

"What's this little paradise called?" Jamal asked.

"Red."

"Why red?"

"'Cause the people are red. Like native Americans, only more so. They're also tribal."

"Uh-oh."

"But it's not a backwater."

"Sure, sure," Holdauer and Jones snarled in unison.

"And it's in the heart of conquered territory."

"Wonderful," thus Jamal.

"But it's got a population of ten billion, and He wants them out. Safe and sound in another universe."

"He told you?"

"The minds of all council members have been flooded with instructions on the removal of Red from enemy hands. Those instructions were very specific, timetable and everything. Oh and you, Jamal, and you, Holdauer, were both mentioned by name."

"Where's the garrison?" Jamal demanded.

"At the north pole in an ancient ruin of a pyramid. Apparently the death worshippers can't take the heat."

"So we won't be going to the tropics."

"Average temperature at the north pole is seventy degrees Fahrenheit."

"Sheesh. What's it like on the equator?" Jamal asked.

"One hundred fifteen to one twenty and that's not counting humidity."

"Sounds like global warming to me," Holdauer put in.

"It was. It smashed up the civilization big time, about two millennia ago. The surviving population reverted from modernity to, well, tribal life. And a lucky thing, too. If they'd kept burning carbon, that planet would be uninhabitable today." Ivan paused to rub his tired, beringed eyes.

"Having trouble sleeping, Ivan?" Holdauer asked.

"Yes, as a matter of fact I am," the council leader snapped. "You try juggling the fate of whole populated planets for a few days. See what happens to your worry index."

"So where at the north pole do we touch down?" Jamal asked.

"Some city that's all consonants, xgzrtd."

"Xgzrtd?"

"You heard me."

"They speak English?"

"The fighters, yes. The locals, they speak in consonants."

"How do we find the fighters?"

"Try the Red Bear tavern."

"Don't tell me, it's a dive on a river wharf," Jamal said.

"A bay wharf. Yes, and it's dangerous. The zxyus, that's the local tribe, are a hard-drinking, heavy fighting bunch of toughs. But you ask for Red Angel, and you should be okay."

"He's the lead fighter?" Holdauer asked.

"Yes, and since you got it so well figured out, and I got a headache, this concludes your assignment. Dismissed."

***

"Rise, Rafael, wash your face and hands, then log onto the computer. Today you will receive coordinates for the largest death worshipper enclaves on earth. You will alert the fighters in those regions through Horace. There are about a dozen, worldwide, and they must be dealt with rapidly."

"All right, all right," the policeman grumbled, throwing back the covers on the bed in the guestroom. He lumbered into the bathroom and splashed water on his face. "So where's He Movin' these galaxies to?" He wondered, gazing down into the sink at the water swirling down the drain.

"Space is vast," he heard. "Soon He will move Reincarnation."

"That's where Vivaldi was."

"Yes, and it's one of the more populous galaxies in sector one thousand. So far, the destroyer of galaxy's has only extinguished barren rocks, suns never viewed by human eyes, or suns viewed by human eyes millennia ago and no longer, but he's getting closer."

"The destroyer of galaxies!" Orozco thought. "That don't sound good."

"It's terrible."

"How bout we take out this destroyer of galaxies, whoever he is?"

"Someday that will happen. But the council lacks adequate information so far."

"What do they lack?"

"His location."

"Oh, well, that would be a help, I guess."

"You may be selected for the task."

"Shit."

"The council has a very short list of fighters they would send."

"Probably deep behind enemy lines."

"Very deep."

"Shit. Not me. I'm too old. I ain't up for this shit anymore."

"You're not the first choice."

"Hallellujah!"

"You're the third."

"That's too close for comfort," Orozco growled mentally, glancing now into the mirror, which shimmered with dark light. "What if one and two get killed at the front?"

"Neither is currently at the front and won't be for some time. By then, we may have located this destroyer of galaxies, though in all likelihood, it could take a few years."

"Sheesh, how do you even begin to try to do that?"

"Not your concern, Rafael. Now quick, down to Horace's computer, which is now connected to our AI."

"We got AI?" Orozco cried joyously.

"Yes. His name's Seymour, and he'll be helping you on the computer today. You may tell the fighter and the guardian, but no one outside this house."

Orozco thumped down two flights of stairs to the little study, where he found a plate of fried eggs and toast and a tall glass of orange juice beside the computer.

"I heard you had a lot of computer work this morning, so when I made my breakfast, I made yours too," Gideon casually remarked, lounging in the doorway.

"Gideon! Keep it under your hat, but our side's got AI!"

The young man's eyes widened. "When?"

"Dunno, recently. He's called Seymour. I'll be working with him today, before I head down to the precinct. When I do, you'll take over," Orozco concluded, then scarfed down the eggs, toast and juice and booted up the computer. Immediately through the speakers, both men heard a little voice, piping, "hello Rafael, hello Gideon. I am Seymour. The techs at the front say earth is infested with fascists and you have about a dozen true hot spots. Could you open the live map please, I am not accustomed to working on machines as primitive as this one."

"Where were you created?" Orozco asked, tapping a few keys.

"On Argas."

"Where else?" Gideon remarked rhetorically.

"Though my creator is from another reality, a numbered reality and had recently escaped a killing center."

Both fighters looked astonished. "I thought the only way you got out of a killing center was feet first," Orozco remarked.

"This one was liberated by angels. The inmates hanged all the men who had been in charge of the center."

"Good."

"That's what my creator said. Then they took him to the infirmary at the front, and while he recovered, he worked out his ideas for me. So they sent him to Argas, and here I am."

"This guy deserves a medal. I'm guessing, Seymour, you were the one who conducted that massive search that yielded the info on Him moving planets one hundred times."

"Yes, that was me. And now, I'm trying to locate missing galaxies."

"Well, good grief, don't let us interrupt that!" Orozco cried. "We can track down these death worshippers ourselves."

"Oh, I'm a great multitasker," Seymour replied. "I can conduct multiple searches at once. Oh, there's the map, good. I'll check police reports on all the larger nodules. Your police bureaucracies are computerized?"

"Yes," Gideon replied. "Most are. It's 1997, after all."

"Let's see..."Seymour began. "The council was most insistent that we bring this situation on earth under control. Earth, I gathered from the records, is very special."

"Earth is a blood-soaked backwater," Gideon snarled.

"That too."

"But it's all we got, at least for most of its six billion inhabitants, so we'd like it not to be overrun by murdering, death worshipping fascists."

"Well, that's what we'll take care of today. There's your first nest of killers." A map of the Southwestern United States appeared, just as Horace loomed in the doorway.

"Guardian," Orozco barked. "The fighters in and around Phoenix need to see what the trouble is. Inform them please."

The tall, rather portly would-be suicide, stood stock still, riveted by the image of the map on his computer. "There are sixteen killers," he said at last. "All have earned the iron sword."

"Did you alert the fighters?" Gideon growled.

"Yes. Get me an address."

"Happy to oblige," Seymour piped in, and an address in big bold letters filled the screen.

"Done," Horace said.

"One down, eleven to go," thus Orozco.

So the three men and Seymour passed the morning filling in the gaps on their map of the most threatening conglomerations of invaders. Lunchtime approached, and Orozco fixed black beans and rice from a box, which everyone happily scarfed down.

"I wish I knew what eating feels like," Seymour lamented.

"Nah," Orozco replied. "It's the kind of thing that's best when you don't have to think about it. But when you don't know how you're gonna get your next meal, like when you're behind the lines and you just ate your last power bar and you got two days to go, that's a nightmare. You ain't missin' a thing, Seymour. I'd trade the satisfaction of food with the periodic misery of unsatisfied hunger for being free of it altogether, any day. Any day," he repeated for emphasis.

"Sounds like you ran out of food in enemy territory more than once," Seymour said. "One would think such planning would not be too hard."

"One would think," Orozco growled. "But more often than not, the bigwigs in charge decide to keep you there a few extra days. Then you're screwed."

"Which is why I always pack an extra loaf of bread and a jar of peanut butter," Gideon said.

"Where do you get *that* at the front?" Orozco demanded.

"The cafeteria. I have a deal with one of the cooks. I always bring him fresh produce from Haifa, when I arrive; in exchange, I get extra food when I'm sent behind the lines."

"Would he take cash?"

Gideon snorted in derision. "Are you kidding? He's been at the front forty years. What's he going to do with cash? Bring him lichee nuts. He's crazy about those."

"Which one?"

"The older one, with the thin yellow hair and the big, gleaming bald spot."

"Well, while you two are making culinary arrangements at the front," Horace glowered at them, "Seymour and I have pinpointed the headquarters, two per continent, excluding Antarctica, of our death worshipper invaders."

"Alert the local fighters," Orozco ordered.

"I already have."

"I like this," Gideon said, nodding at the other two men. "This is the way the war should go, a neat, orderly mopping up operation, after routing the enemy."

"Yeah, well we ain't where the action is, thank You know Who," Orozco said.

"Where's the action?" Horace asked.

"Oops—another string of galaxies disappeared," Seymour said, "right off my live map of sector one thousand."

"That," Orozco intoned, "sector one thousand, is where the action is."

***

"What do you mean you're not in sector one thousand?" The little image of Carmella Marquez challenged him on the hand-held. "You're still on that planet, with the one billion refugees."

"But we're not in sector one thousand anymore," Axel explained. "We been moved."

"Moved? Who moved you?"

"The Argans."

369

"The Argans! Where'd they move you to?"

"Some other, safer universe."

"Holy Jesus. They can do that?"

"Apparently."

"I always said it: twenty thousand years of peace and the human race can accomplish anything."

"Yeah well, apparently You know Who's been doin' it too. Whole galaxies."

Carmella's jaw dropped.

"I guess he got busy with the heavy lifting and told the Argans to take over with the small fry, you know, individual planets." Axel paused to adjust his black eye-patch. "Anyway, I'll be back at the permanent front tonight, on a needle. And no, you do not want me as your copilot on your maiden voyage with these new Argan ships and their new missiles. It's me, Axel, Carmella. Remember? I only got one eye and one hand."

"And you're still head and shoulders above the two-eyed, two handed variety. Nope. I'm putting in a request for you, and if those stick-in-the-muds on the council object, they can get someone else to fly my now perfectly cloaked fighter jet. Perfectly cloaked. Like I give a shit."

"It'll sure help, if you have to fire at close range. And we need all the help we can get. So far those battle cruisers have been almost unstoppable."

"Yeah well, we're gonna stop those sons of bitches. The Argans remodeled my whole friggin' plane. It's a new vehicle. It got rockets that'll kill you just to look at 'em. And I'm cloaked, and I can clock speeds four times faster than before. And I'll have you as my copilot. That commander ain't gonna know what hit him."

Axel's eye glittered angrily, "only one commander?"

"Far as we know. And an interrogator, who's been pulling prisoners apart in the torture chamber. We are going to shut the whole friggin' thing down." And she pumped a fist in the air.

"I'm with you."

"Good. Now I just have to convince the council."

She clicked the little machine off, stowed it in her knapsack, slid from behind a boulder down into a trench and tramped toward the bunker, greeting friends lined up for morning cabbage soup. At last she came to a stairwell, climbed down, snarled at the guard at the door, who prudently let her past and marched into a long, gray, cinder-block corridor, filled with military scientists, dashing this way and that, chattering in hushed excited tones questions like, "but how long has He been moving them?" "Will we have to wait for special permission to move each planet?" "How did the Argans do this?" and most interesting to her, "If you read the fine print, earth has already been moved twice, and the second time, the whole solar system went with it."

"The question," both Carmella and her old friend Orozco back on earth happened to think simultaneously "is can the enemy do anything like this? Can the enemy move planets?" The question sent Orozco into a panic, as he demanded that Seymour search the records. It had a different effect on Carmella. She ground her teeth, muttered, "this is just fucked-up, that's all I got to say." Then she stopped outside the council chamber, pounded on the door and heard Jason's voice, "come in!"

Inside, the dozen men of the council were trying to follow a physicist's explanation of how whole planets could survive this new method of transport intact. They looked confused, to say the least, and several seemed genuinely pleased at the distraction Carmella provided.

"Ah, Marquez," Ivan beamed most uncharacteristically at her. "I take it you've inspected your fighter jet."

"It looks great," she answered, her hands on her hips, noting, as she glanced down, the dirt streaks on her jeans and black tank top. "Oh well, this ain't a fashion show," she thought, then said, "and with Axel as my copilot, we should be able to crash that commander and expose both him and the interrogator to angelic fireballs in no time."

"Axel!" Ivan cried. "A one-eyed copilot?"

"He's not even here," Jason objected. "He's in another universe."

"Correction. He's on a needle and will be here momentarily."

"Shit!" Ivan spat. "I forbid it. This is top-of-the-line Argan weaponry, designed by Ein himself. I'm not having it fall into enemy hands, because you got sentimental about how your old buddy lost a hand and an eye. Even Axel would agree with me."

"Then let's leave it to him," Carmella purred.

"Why don't I trust you?"

"Because you don't get along with me and, guess what, your honor? I don't get along with you."

"Axel's been in plenty of fighter jets," Jason mused. "I don't see why this is really any different."

"My view exactly," thus Carmella.

"Because this has to work. That enemy battle cruiser with the beefed-up shields has been strafing our positions for the past week. It's time to put a stop to it. Not risk losing the best weaponry we've had in decades on a sentimental whim."

"Why don't you come out and say you don't like dealing with women, Ivan."

"Nonsense. I get on fine with the ghost."

"Uh, Ivan," Jason spoke in low tones, "the ghost said essentially the same thing last time she was in here."

"They're flighty and temperamental!" Ivan shouted.

"I knew it," thus Carmella.

"Whether you knew it or not is irrelevant."

"Now who's flighty? Flighty and prejudiced."

"You are not flying that irreplaceable piece of Argan weaponry with a one-eyed copilot."

"It's not irreplaceable. He is."

Axel stepped into the room. "Oh, arguing as usual, I see. It's a miracle anything ever gets done around this place."

"Tell Marquez here that you are not, in view of your disabilities, not going to copilot a fighter jet rigged up with Argan rockets, cloaks and engines. Tell her the idea is idiotic."

"Actually, I thought I'd make a fine copilot."

"Shit, Marquez. You set me up."

"You set yourself up."

"You admit it."

"I admit nothing. I got the copilot I wanted. Now I suggest you dismiss us, so that we can go disable that battle cruiser, before that sadist of an interrogator gets his hands on everyone in this room."

"She has a point," thus Jason.

"Oh, shut up."

The two pilots left. Ivan forgot to tell then they were dismissed.

"Wow!" Was all Axel said when he got a look at the little jet. "When do we do this?"

"Let's do it now," came the reply. Soon they were shooting almost straight up into the atmosphere, the image of the huge, previously unscratchable black battle cruiser growing larger by the second.

"We're cloaked," she announced. "Let's lower the rockets." There came a gentle hum, as the Argan rockets descended into the launching bay.

"How close do we have to be?" Axel asked.

"Just a little closer," she tore in straight at it, then spoke quietly, "Okay Axel, bombs away."

He launched them, just before she pulled back on the controls and the little jet cleared the top of the cruiser. There came a tremendous explosion. Up and away they went, then turned to fly back over the damage. It was complete. The enemy battle cruiser had crashed on the ground in flames, in the middle of which stood the black-clad interrogator and commander, glancing nervously around to get their bearings.

"Still cloaked?" Axel asked.

"Ohhhh yes indeed. Look at two o'clock." And there, in the sky, hovered an angel, who had just released a white-hot fireball. Next to him was another, and as the two pilots watched, the blazing white fireballs made contact, and in seconds had reduced the proud commander, the merciless interrogator, to small piles of ash.

"Gimme five!" Carmella whooped and Axel did—with his one, very good hand.

***

Orozco lay on his bed in the dark room on the top floor of Horace MacKenzie's house, listening to Gideon's snores from across the hall and riveted by the bright image of brilliantly white tents, as far as the eye could see, plastered on the far, darkened wall. Then he heard, faintly, a trumpet, and a seraph's war-weary voice, "There are the tents of the fighters' orphans, gathered in the valley by the priest. Twenty will come to you tomorrow, in the woods west of the city, where you have met seraphs to depart in the past. There you will meet twenty other fighters, and each will take a child. This is happening throughout your universe. Your friend the priest has several thousand fighters' orphans in his care. But there are other priests, many, with a similar number. The orphans must be placed quickly and only in households with more than one adult—for fighters are away at the front often, and someone must stay behind to tend the children."

"So I'm guessing neither Gideon nor I are becoming parents."

"You—no. Gideon—later."

"Really? When?"

"When he marries in Israel. But that is neither here nor there. You and he will supervise the placements, tomorrow at dusk."

"I'm becoming a regular in that Lonely State park," Orozco grumbled to himself, as the image of Vivaldi in his black cassock, a child on each hand, the brilliantly white tents in the warm, yellow sunshine, the green grass, the blue hills, the pang that the beauty of it all caused him, began to fade and then it was just a dark wall again, in a dark room, lit slightly by moonlight, in the middle of the night, in a run-down, second-rate East Coast city.

The next evening, before dusk, the cars started pulling into the deserted parking lot at Lonely State Park. They came from many states; there were license plates from Ohio and Vermont, North Carolina and Pennsylvania, Maryland, New York and others. One muscular man in his late thirties in scrubs stepped out of a sedan with Massachusetts plates and demanded, "who's in charge here?"

"That would be me," Orozco replied. "I represent the transuniverse orphanage. We follow this trail." Into the woods they went, and shortly came upon a wide clearing filled with tall grass, wild-flowers and twenty giggling children, heads all turned to the side. The fighters looked there and saw, vanishing among the trees, a pair of great, beautiful, silvery and scarred wings.

"Looks like this is the place," the Massachusetts man said. "Hurry up and make the assignments, please."

Orozco pulled a sheet of paper out of his packet, and as dusk was falling fast now, Gideon handed him a small flashlight. "Wendell?" He called, and a little boy stood up, "you go with Hanan." A tall, strong, gray-haired woman fighter stepped forward, hugged the boy and set off with him through the woods back to her car. In a matter of minutes, Orozco had finished the list, the man from Massachusetts, a medical technician named Jerome, leading a four-year-old Stephen by the hand, approached the two fighters. "This is the third fighter's orphan we've taken in," he said. "And we got two kids of our own."

"Okay," Orozco said. "I'll take your name off the list for future placements."

"I don't' mean to seem like I'm complaining, 'cause I'm not. I'll just say, we've reached our limit. There's no more room. We got a full house."

"Understood, Jerome."

"I realize they've been generous with me about the front."

"What do you mean?"

"Not calling me there, 'cause I'm taking care of so many kids."

"Oh no, no, no. How many kids you got has no effect on your deployment."

"Then why am I so lucky?"

"You may be one of those very rare, earthbound fighters, one who goes to the front a few times, but basically stays here in the event that earth is ever attacked directly."

"I never heard of this."

"You know any guardians?"

"One, but not well."

"That's why you ain't heard about it. Talk to guardians, they'll tell you how the fighters are sifted and separated for different jobs. But my guess is you ain't a fighter *from* earth. You're a fighter *for* earth. You have my sincere admiration."

The policeman held out a huge mitt, and they shook hands. They turned and walked back together to the lot.

"If this galaxy is ever attacked," Orozco began.

"You sound like the priests at the camp," Stephen piped up. "Talking about when Reincarnation would be attacked."

"Hopefully not anytime soon," Orozco replied.

"What's Reincarnation?" The medical lab worker asked.

"His home galaxy."

"Oh," Jerome paused. "This is in that sector one thousand, of course."

Orozco nodded. "The fact you ain't been called makes me sure, Jerome. You're an earthbound fighter."

By the time they reached the parking lot, it was evening. One young woman fighter, strong and muscular, was strapping a toddler into a car-seat. "Good thing I brought this," she said, then smiled. "I heard a voice."

"What'd it say; bring the car-seat?" Orozco asked.

"Pretty close."

He noted her North Carolina plates. "You got a long way to go."

"Not as long as when we lived in New Orleans and had to come up here for our first boy. My husband said, 'you're a fighter, the kid just came from the front. No way you're flying.' So we drove. He worries about everything."

"Is he a fighter?"

"Friend of the fighters," she replied.

"Good. Somebody picked these families well."

"Somebody with a capital S," she replied, sliding behind the wheel and backing the car out of her parking space. She turned to glance at Orozco through the driver's window. "Don't look so down, detective. We will prevail."

"I hope you're right."

"I know I'm right."

***

The crumbling castle at the top of the hill loomed ahead of them in the dusk. First there had been only her, the woman fighter, carrying her machine gun, but soon she was joined by other fighters, from other paths that flowed onto the main road. For the most part, they wore warm clothes and carried rifles. They nodded to her, and she to them, and all fell into step together. Soon the number of fighters had swelled to almost fifty. "These are fighters' orphans," she spoke loudly, her harsh voice audible to the entire crowd, as it moved up toward the hill. "They have been through a lot. Our job, now, is to make sure that stops happening." Grunts and monosyllables of assent became audible. "Their worlds have been destroyed. Their parents were killed on the battlefields of Elsewhere. Never try to deceive them. They know. They know the truth, and they hear the voice. They will see straight through any attempted deception, any attempted fairy tale about what has happened. They know the enemy killed their parents. They know the enemy exists and is strong. Even the five year olds know the enemy is trying to kill them. Your job is to provide a haven, to exclude from that haven any adult ever, ever on the enemy's wavelength. Your job is to make sure they grow up, healthy, able and strong, so that they can take over where we will leave off. The good news is that they are alive, thousands upon thousands of them. Their worlds were crushed, the adult fighters killed, but they escaped; He who does not wish to see us destroyed made sure they came through alive. Now your work begins. He spared them. You must help them thrive. He snatched them from the enemy's claws, now you must ensure that never again are they ever hit. If you feel a death sweep coming, you hide them—before you hide yourself."

"There are few enough of those on Sere, fighter," one man said. "It's been years since the last enemy death sweep."

"That's why, right now, all over this planet, fighters are doing exactly as we are, because tens, perhaps hundreds of thousands of fighters' orphans are being moved here. My guess is that every fighter's household on this planet will receive at least one child, most more."

"But not you."

"I am not from here. I come from an alien world, where people still slaughter each other in droves. And I have no husband. No, I'm here only to help coordinate the orphanage and then return to the front."

"Coordinate the orphanage and burn the enemy in his stronghold," one man said, and satisfied laughter surged through the crowd. Apparently Lontra's efforts with the wizard had gained some notoriety. She smiled her grim little smile. "We all have our hobbies for our spare time."

"Would that yours would knock one of 'em down dead," came a masculine voice.

"Someday, brother. I have been assured that someday, and within our lifetimes, this will come to pass."

They were climbing steeply now, the dirt road rutted from rain drainage. "You've been behind the lines?" One of the men asked curiously.

"I was captured, sent to an enemy supermax prison, far, far behind the lines."

There was sudden silence, then another man asked, "how in heaven did you survive?"

"Two fighters rescued me. Fighters from my home world."

"And do fighters from your home world do such wild things often?"

"More than most," she said, opening her mouth to continue, but then falling silent as there passed through her mind the words, "do not reveal the sense of guilt that earth's fighters feel. It is misplaced and also subject to misinterpretation."

"But they came for me, because they'd been instructed to do so," she concluded. "And just like you, the fighters from my world do as they are told, because they understand what is at stake."

"Your world is in our universe, no?" Asked one woman.

Lontra nodded. "In another galaxy, the Milky Way."

"I know it," cried one man. "A seraph once pointed it out to me, as we soared through the night toward the stars."

"What did he say?"

"That it was home to a special planet that would turn the tide of the war."

The hard old female fighter caught her breath. "Did he," Lontra asked, still holding her breath, "did he name that planet?"

"Earth. And I believe that must be where you're from. Is it?"

"Yes," she answered, stopping to stare at him, her hard, flat, dull, dark gaze scanning his weathered features. "Yes, I come from earth."

"Do you have any idea what he might have been referring to?"

"No," she shook her head. "But I intend to find out."

By now they had reached the collapsed pillars by what had once been a front gate; they passed over cracked paving stones to the courtyard, to see two strong, ferocious, and heavily armed fighters, guarding a crowd of ninety children.

"The parents are here," Lontra announced.

"Good," answered one of the two. "Do you have the list, sister?"

"I do." With that Lontra pulled out a notebook, opened it and began reading the names—first the fighter, then one or two children's names. The procedure was over in twenty minutes; the local fighters had taken the children out of the courtyard and down the hill, and Lontra stood, notebook in hand, facing the two fierce, armed men. "I take it you're from sector one thousand," she said.

"Yes," they both replied, nodding their shaved, scarred heads. "And we need a place to stay this evening," said the more talkative of the two. "I'm Brin, this is Por. We were told we could stay with the ghost."

Lontra gave her grim, mirthless, little smile. "That's me."

"Don't worry. We won't ask. We know the legend."

"The legend is true," she said simply.

"We know."

And with that the three turned and walked to the ruin's entrance.

"Think," said Brin, raising a thick, tattooed hand to his chin, "all over this planet, today, fighters like us arrived with kids."

"And all over numerous other planets," Lontra added.

"The transuniverse orphanage must have settled hundreds of thousands of children today," he continued. "In just one day. Did I tell you I met one of the priests in charge?"

"No, I don't believe you did."

"He was on that planet that was moved out of that massive galaxy, Reincarnation."

"I heard about this," she said, as they started down the rutted dirt track. "The Argans really can move planets?"

"Really. And you know Who's been doing it for thousands of years."

"That's less surprising."

"It's less surprising that things have been that bad for that long that He's had to be shiftin' planets around like basketballs?" Brin asked.

"No, I mean less surprising that He's *able* to do it than that the Argans are. They seem like an unbeatable race."

381

"Yeah, until a commander sets foot on one of their worlds."

"Don't talk like that," she said. "It's horrible."

"The truth is horrible." And with that they walked on in silence, so as not to utter any more terrible truths. Soon the road flattened out and was bordered by neat hedges; they followed it under the stars to the compound where Lontra had been living, where one of the several ruddy, fortyish women who lived there was washing a shirt in a wooden bucket on the front step, while three small children scampered around.

"Guests?" She asked, looking up.

"Yes, two," Lontra replied.

"We'll be leaving in the morning," Brin added.

"So then there'll be two less."

"No," he said soberly, "three."

The woman looked perplexed, until he pointed at Lontra. "She's leaving too."

"I am?" The ghost asked.

"Remember the priest I mentioned from the planet that was moved?"

She nodded.

"You're going to work with him. His planet, which is nicknamed Dismal, was moved back into Reincarnation."

"Whatever for?" Lontra cried. "And besides, I'm not permitted to go to sector one thousand."

"Reincarnation ain't in sector one thousand no more. The whole galaxy was moved."

Lontra was speechless. She just stared.

"And it's full of fighters' orphans," Brin continued. "We got our work cut out for us and so do you."

With that, the three fighters entered the large house with the thatched roof and earth floors, found their beds, collapsed and slept.

***

"So why ought Orozco go to Sere?" Elpytha demanded, her gray eyes angry. "Earth is infested with death worshippers, and he's busy overseeing the fighters here."

"He must go," Galen replied, his longish, white hair gleaming in the sunshine, "because the wizards there cannot travel."

"I fail to see why he has to converse with some primitive wizards on some backward planet,"

"When the guardian Elaine Elias killed herself, he came into possession of her flame. It is my belief and the council's that that particular flame, in conjunction with the local Seran magic, may be able to wreak havoc in enemy territory."

"Would havoc include killing a commander or an interrogator?"

"That's what we want to attempt. Different flames apparently have different properties. I doubt that yours, for instance, would be of much use."

"Thank you, Galen," she said sourly.

"No need to be offended. I'm just working through a theory here. And Elias' flame strikes me as one of the better for our purposes."

"So he leaves tonight from Lonely State Park, no doubt?"

"How did you know?" The old man beamed.

"Because you've turned that park into Grand Central Station for fighters embarking off-world and arriving from Elsewhere. It's going to attract attention, if you're not careful."

"I know, and he'll be the last to use it for some time. There's plenty of wilderness in northwest Pennsylvania, upper New York State and New England that we can use."

"What about Allegheny National Forest?"

"No," he rapped out sharply. "That's reserved."

"Reserved for what?"

"Emergencies."

"All right, Galen," she spoke evenly. "I defer to you. I won't even ask how you decided it was reserved for emergencies."

"Good, because it wasn't my decision, and it's none of your business." The old concentration camp survivor turned sideways to the image on his computer screen of a galaxy map. "A new galaxy appeared in our sector," he said, "far, far from the Milky Way. I hear it is called Reincarnation, and it is crammed with the orphans of fighters killed in sector one thousand."

"All the more reason for Orozco to stay put: he must coordinate the transuniverse orphanage, and he certainly can't do that if you and the council and who knows who else,"

"The seraphs."

"What?! They want him to work with wizards? I doubt it."

"Doubt whatever you like. I have my instructions. Besides, he will journey to Reincarnation to work with the orphanage's priests, after his trip to Sere."

"Galen," she snapped. "You are a guardian of earth, not of earth's universe."

He sighed and cast her a glance, in which sadness touched the lamps of eternity. "Unfortunately, despite all best attempts to seclude it, earth's fate *is* bound up with the fate of other human worlds. If Elias' flame can severely injure an interrogator, we need to know. If there are millions of fighters' orphans in Reincarnation, we must place them. I heard the trumpet."

Her jaw dropped. "But only fighters hear that."

"Well, this doddering, ancient guardian heard it, which means soon other guardians will hear it, too. And that, if you haven't figured it out, signifies only one thing."

"What?" She asked, her gray eyes wide with alarm.

"Earth's guardians and therefore earth are both being dragged right into the war."

***

"You're comin' 'cause Gideon Cohen is your babysitter, and he ain't allowed to leave you alone for a couple of hours," Orozco snapped at Horace, as the latter guzzled a bottle of green tea.

"What do you need a chauffeur for anyway?" The guardian grumbled. "Why can't you just take that ridiculous Impala of yours out there and park it in the woods?"

"Because it could attract attention. There's been a lot of fighter traffic through that forest recently, and we ain't leavin' our cars around, so snooping death worshippers can plug the tag numbers into their computers—oh, no. Gideon's drivin' and you're comin' and that's that. And Gideon, when you get called away, Starfield takes over."

"I'm sure he'll be delighted about that," Gideon growled sarcastically. "Babysitting a sixty-two-year-old suicidal guardian? He looked like he couldn't wait to leave last time he was here."

"Maybe I should have a talk with him," Orozco muttered.

"You do that," Gideon replied. "'Cause if I get called back to the front or to sector one thousand,"

"You won't. They're keeping most earthlings outta there."

"I said 'if,' if I get called, I'll need a replacement toute suite, not Starfield's excuses that he's on deadline and can he come later, in twenty-four hours."

Orozco pulled out his cellphone. "Hey," Gideon said. "I didn't even know you had one. You never called me on it."

"After certain...experiences, shall we say, with phones, I never use them to talk to fighters or guardians. And Starfield knows to be discreet. Oh, hey, yes Starfield? It's me Rafael.

385

Look, if Gideon has to travel, he'll call you on short notice. You'll be available pronto, right. What? Don't give me that. You can work on the computer right here. Okay, glad we see eye to eye. Bye."

"He's going to raise objections," Gideon warned.

"Then you deal with it," Orozco snapped. "I'm sure you're quite capable of painting the hideous picture that results from every guardian suicide."

"Oh, you're overreacting," thus Horace.

Orozco fished in a pocket and pulled out a stainless steel lighter with a thunderbolt etched on front. "This belonged to Elaine Elias!" And the moment he uttered her name, both men visibly crumpled, as if under the sudden insupportable weight of despair. "She was a guardian who took her own life. Shall I tell you the story?"

"No!" Gideon cried. "Shut up! Now!"

Orozco shoved the lighter back in his pocket. "I'm glad you see my point. Make it to Starfield, if you have to. But if they want you in South Africa or South Dakota to kill death worshippers, Starfield's friggin deadlines will have to be met from 333 Apocalypse Avenue. Got it?"

"I'm completely cured," Horace said.

"Bullshit!" Orozco snapped. "Once a guardian starts down the path you been on, he don't come back. He's either protected, twenty-four seven, which usually means a psyche ward, or he eventually kills himself, which is a catastrophe, not only for him, but for all the rest of us. So don't give me any fairy tales about how you're quote cured unquote."

They stepped out onto the front step of Horace's tall, stylish townhouse with the locust tree in front and a big, spreading sycamore across the street, under which Gideon's Honda was parked. Horace, in view of his dubious standing, sat in back, as if, it seemed, in punishment for behavior that had put a burden on so many people. The two fighters conversed quietly in front about the recent movement of planets and galaxies.

"The planet's nicknamed Dismal, the galaxy Reincarnation. I could make a joke," Orozco said, "but I ain't gonna."

"Good," Gideon replied, turning the key in the ignition. "I'm not in the mood for jokes."

"Oh, you never are!" Horace snapped.

"You be quiet," Orozco retorted. "Completely cured! Now I've heard everything." They drove along Apocalypse Avenue, eventually turning off and winding through Uptown to North Street, aswarm with the young and the hip, and then out onto Insane Asylum Avenue toward the city line.

"Wizards," Gideon snorted derisively. "Now *I've* heard everything."

"Evidently not," Orozco replied, popping a mint into his mouth and slurping. "Because somehow someone on the council's got the idée fixe that these wizards can use a guardian's flame to injure and may be kill an enemy commander or interrogator."

"Fat chance," Gideon snorted again. "It sounds like hocus pocus and a lot of wishful thinking to me." By now they were speeding through the twilit countryside, in valleys of deep shade, where Gideon had to turn his headlights on bright, then out over flat dark fields, where the dying day still touched the road with faint illumination.

"Where to after Sere?" The driver asked curiously. "This planet Dismal, where your partner's busy?"

"Yup," slurp, slurp. "Vivaldi needs my help, and now that he's out of sector one thousand, I'm free to go where he is."

"Why that prohibition, I wonder."

"Because," Horace snapped, "there's an enemy interrogator in sector one thousand, and he has some knowledge of earth. The idea is to prevent him from gaining any more." He paused to observe the two fighters exchange a glance. "And don't ask how I know it—it should be obvious. We guardians pool our knowledge, at least those of us in regular contact with fighters do."

"Telepath central," slurp, slurp.

"As a matter of fact, yes. An old guardian, a hermit in the Canadian woods, was the first to learn of this interrogator, and he alerted those of us who needed to know. Just as I'm reminding you two fighters: don't get any ideas about day trips to sector one thousand. It would be catastrophic for earth."

"That's the last frickin' place in the whole cosmos where you'd find me. A more inhospitable environment I can't imagine," slurp, slurp. "I ain't got *no* intention of setting foot in that doomed sector."

"Me neither," Gideon breathed. "Never. Never again."

"What never again?" Slurp, slurp. "You never been there to begin with."

"Just a thought," the young man spoke quietly, "just connecting the dots."

"You think what the enemy's doin' there has precedent in what he did here in the thirties and forties? I'm with you, brother. I believe you ain't far from the truth."

"That's highly speculative," Horace put in. "Earth's fascists and dictators were quite wicked enough to inflict mass death without the assistance of nonhuman commanders and interrogators."

Orozco turned around and looked at him. "But they had nonhuman luck. And the numbers they exterminated correlate with enemy atrocities."

"Strictly speculative. I say, Nuremburg took care of the problem, and that was that."

"And you got your head stuck so far in the sand, you can't see who's kicking you in the ass. Turn left here, Gideon."

They traveled on a one lane, only partially paved road, until they came to a fork. "I get out here," Orozco said, reaching for his knapsack and machine gun in the back seat. Then, with both slung over his shoulders, the old fighter tramped off into the woods, following a surprisingly wide and grassy footpath, which he illumined with a flashlight. The little Honda drove back the way it had come, and listening to the fading hum of its engine, Orozco fell prey to sad thoughts, so oppressive, so powerful that he nearly came to a halt to sigh and consider them. But he did not: his training intervened, and so, sorrowful and weighted down with memories of all his friends who had died in the war, the old fighter approached a clearing, where, under a clear sky, by the silvery light of a crescent moon and billions of stars, he saw the immense, long, beautiful and scarred wings of a seraph, whose brilliant gaze instantly met his.

"Cheer up, fighter. Push away your thoughts of loss and death. After Sere, you go to Reincarnation, and to the priest and to what waits for you there."

"And that would be?"

"Millions of your dead brother's and sisters' orphans, Rafael. Millions of children await you in Reincarnation already."

***

She came to, lying on a green hillside lit by the fires of dawn, which grew stronger by the moment, but strangely did not tinge with orange the thousands of white tents, stretching over the verdant plain, no, the fiery dawn seemed only to make them more brilliantly white; through the middle was a dirt track, along which strode a tall, heavy-set man in a black cassock, singing. She could not yet make out his face, but she knew, she was certain that this was the priest Vivaldi, whom she was finally seeing in his element. She sat up on her elbows, her legs stretched out, her pants damp with morning dew, and watched him approach, singing loudly, deeply, about God and redemption and the war. She stood up, and he waved, but he did not stop the deep bass of his singing. Now she could see him better, the kindly face, the gray hair, in every way such a contrast to her hardness, her flat, aggressive, glittering gaze.

He came to a stop directly before her. "Hello again. I haven't seen you since Sere. You are the one who survived an enemy interrogator in an enemy prison."

"I am."

"You are the one He commanded us to save."

"I am."

"Can you work with these children and put aside the blood and terror you have known?"

"I've done so before, priest. I believe I can do it again."

"This galaxy…" he began.

"Reincarnation."

"Yes. He has moved Reincarnation. We believe He did so because it teems with orphans—the orphans of your kind."

"They are not so different from ordinary orphans."

"Not so different, perhaps. But there *are* differences. There can be difficulties with doubles, triples, multiples."

She waved a hand dismissively. "I am aware of that. I can deal with that. I have done so before."

"And then there is their destiny."

"So?"

"They are destined to kill."

"So?"

"They are destined for the terrifying, blood-soaked battlefields of Elsewhere."

"So?"

"So—do not hurry it. Allow them to be children a little longer."

She snorted derisively. "I doubt even the five year olds among them are truly still children."

"Doubt all you want, but let them be. Do not hurry them. They will be fighters soon enough."

"They can never avenge their parents soon enough."

"That is where we part company."

"It is simply because I am a fighter and you are a priest."

"No. You have become inured to killing."

Her hard, flat gaze flickered over him, as she raised her head defiantly. "Think what you like. I know what I am. I know what I do."

"She is a weapon in His hands," the priest heard in his mind. "There is no arguing with that." Vivaldi bowed his head and prayed. At length he looked up. "Just be gentle with them."

"Oh," she nearly smiled. "Always."

He turned, and they walked side by side back toward the tents, even more brilliantly white now, in the morning sun. "Think," he murmured. "First this planet was moved," and he made a sweeping gesture, as if to encompass the entire world. "Then Reincarnation was moved. Then the planet was moved again, back into Reincarnation. Why do you think He did it that way?'

"He understands the threats posed by the enemy far better than we do. I don't doubt that there was some immediate threat to this planet—was there something that made it unique?"

"Yes. It was the first place we gathered the fighters' orphans, thousands of them."

"That is why," she said simply. "He was being careful, lest they were followed." She paused to shield her eyes with a hand. "Our enemy has a particular hatred for our children," she continued after a moment, "and will go to great lengths to harm or extirpate them. He knows this better than anyone, as doubtless you, in your years with the transuniverse orphanage, have had opportunity to witness."

"Sadly, I don't always know what I am witnessing."

"That's because you have never had to think like the enemy, to figure out what he is doing and why. You have been spared that, but, as a result, you have remained somewhat ignorant of the evil with which we are contending."

"I just met you recently. How could you know this?"

"Because it is obvious. Besides, I've met the priests before and encountered their special innocence before, to be in the thick of evil and not know its nature, to be able to carry on doing good and not know the nature of the battle. That will be about to change."

"What makes you say that?"

"This collapse of sector one thousand. It will change everything. Already He has brought in more priests than ever before, already the atheists among the fighters have been sidelined. Things are changing, priest, and you'd best be prepared for that." They swung into step together, as they reached the first of the tents. "The older children take charge of the younger?" She asked, "as always?"

"As always. However, we're relying more on fighters, and we have lots of those, mostly from your planet, since they could not deploy to sector one thousand."

"How many fighters here?"

"A few hundred."

Lontra let out a low whistle. "That is a lot."

"They are invaluable." He paused and gave her a sidelong glance. "And they all know you are coming."

"Oh, for heaven's sake," she began.

"Tut, tut. You must accept the responsibilities of your fame. You are *the ghost*, the only fighter, and one from earth no less, ever to survive what you endured. And you were reconstructed by angels, body and soul. The fighters have been clamoring for you, since they first caught the rumor that you might arrive. 'She is one of us,' they say. 'She is from earth.' Every fighter here has friends who were captured by the enemy. Hence, every fighter here knows a soul in an enemy prison. They want to hear how one survives and what they, on the outside, can do, if anything, to help."

"They can lobby the council to lobby the seraphs to liberate the prisons," Lontra said grimly. "Though considering we're talking about a vast system, huge, bureaucratically perfectionistic, utterly monstrous, that seems like a difficult task. But angels have liberated killing centers before, and separation stations. There is no reason to suppose they couldn't do the same with these enemy supermax facilities."

As they approached the gray administration tent at the center of the camp, they saw a large crowd of fighters outside it, and some of the older children.

"What's that?" Lontra asked.

"For you, I believe," the priest replied, as a huge cheer went up from the crowd and a few stragglers at first, then the whole group began moving toward her, cheering and calling her name.

The tall, hard woman greeted them at first with astounded silence, then the words, "I don't know what to say."

"Well, we do," said one young man, whose muscular upper arms sported thunderbolt tattoos. "And it's hurray!" He shouted. "Hurray for Lontra! Hurray for the ghost!" And they crowded around, talking, laughing, shaking her hand. "I take it you all heard the trumpet," she said in her loud, hard voice, when silence had finally fallen on the group. A murmur of assent rose up. "For those who are not certain what it means, let me explain: the fighters' orphans are alive, they have survived. Our children, fighters, are alive!"

***

"Follow the first road I come to, to the left," Orozco muttered, dusting the grass off his dark blue pants. "That's what the seraph said to do, so I'll do it." So he followed the path through the woods, and when it eventually merged into a wide, rutted dirt road, he turned left. It was sunrise. At first trees overhung the road from both sides, with sunshafts streaming in between the leaves and branches, then the forest began, in patches, to yield to pasture and finally, to hedges bordering the road, behind which he could spy big, prosperous, thatched huts. He had not gone past many of these, when he saw a tall, gaunt, old man approaching and smoking, as he came. "You're the new fighter?" He called.

"That's me," the policeman called back. "Rafael Orozco."

The man stopped in front of him. He was covered with wrinkles, but his green eyes were keen and clear. "Well, I'm Dar, and me and my family have a house down the way, where we've been putting up fighters for the past six months. So, welcome, Orozco. Come have some breakfast, before you see the wizard."

"How'd you know I need to see the wizard?"

"All the fighters are talking about our wizards. And the last one, she just left, she arranged for the chief wizard to come meet you and work with you later today. Yes indeed, all the fighters are very excited about our wizards here on Sere."

So they walked toward Dar's hut, the old man describing the peaceful backwardness of his village, where the biggest news of the week, aside from the coming and going of fighters and the arrival of orphans, was that his grandson had built himself a motorbike and had spent the past two days put-putting from village to village, showing it off. Then they arrived, and Orozco was ushered into a big, thatched hut with a long wooden table in the center of the room, crowded with workmen, workwomen and agricultural laborers eating breakfasts of eggs, toast, cereal, cheese and bread. Two younger men instantly moved down the bench to make space for Dar and Orozco, whom they eyed curiously, then one asked: "Are you a fighter?"

"How'd you guess?" Orozco smiled grimly.

"We're becoming experts on fighters in this village."

"In every village," the other man said. "We've got fighters and the children of fighters. At this rate, in a couple of years, Sere will be a planet of fighters."

"Nope," Orozco contradicted, taking a big hunk of black bread and a thick slice of cheese. "That is not the plan. Too many fighters could attract the enemy's attention. And Sere is a well-kept secret. We intend to keep it that way."

"Good," several men grunted and resumed eating.

After eggs and juice, the visitor told his host he needed sleep.

"Come on," Dar replied, rising, and led him to a small back room with a large, inviting bed. Once alone, Orozco swung his knapsack and machine gun onto a bench by the window, pulled off his work-boots and shirt, flung the shirt on top of his coat and that on a chair, stripped off his pants and crawled under the covers, shivering at first, since the room was cold, but, soon warm beneath the blankets, he smiled at the approach of blessed sleep.

Meanwhile, in the main room, at the table, Dar tamped down a rising protest over the dangers of so many visiting fighters. "They wouldn't send their kids here, now would they, if they thought there was any possibility of this enemy finding Sere?" These words seemed to quell the murmurs of discontent and probably would have sufficed, but they received additional oomph from the arrival, at that moment, of two wizards—the local one and the visitor—who, hearing the end of this dispute, glanced angrily at the assembled eaters. "The enemy will never set foot on Sere!" The local wizard announced. "It has been foretold."

The men at the table fell silent. "These fighters who visit us," he continued, "are honored guests. What they do, what our own fighters do, enables the rest of us to go on with our lives as normal. Without them, you and you and you," he pointed at three of the men whose objections he had heard, "would all be at the front, face to face with this horrible enemy we've heard so much about. So shut up and be grateful and be sure to make them welcome." He looked around, his eyes rolling, his dreadlocks thick and bushy. "Where is the new fighter?"

"He just went to sleep, wizard," Dar explained, rising from the table to his feet. "But I'll wake him, if you want."

"No. Let him rest. We'll be at my hut. Send him please, when he wakes."

When Orozco opened his eyes, it was early afternoon, and he was staring up into the rafters, which he noted, were constructed from tree branches that had been cut to approximate poles. The thatch above was thick, but he felt a distinct draft pouring down on him. "Aie Caramba," he murmured, "it's early winter on this freezing world and I got a room with no heat!" Still, the blankets and quilt had been quite warm, so warm that he was loath to step out into the frigid air in his underwear. One thing he did appreciate however: his room, one of several additions to the back of the hut, had a real wood floor. He thought of the earth floor in the main room, dining area and kitchen and scowled. It reminded him of huts in certain parts of Mexico, except colder. Thoughts of Mexico led to thoughts of personal sacrifice—what he had had to give up because of the war, and since these thoughts were unpleasant, he tossed over onto one side, pulled the blue quilt over his head and tried again to sleep. No luck. So he leapt out of bed, dressed and returned to the main room.

Dar sat in a corner by one of the two, big, black, pot-bellied stoves, smoking a cigarette and shouting, now and then, at the rambunctious toddlers, playing in another corner.

"I want the tour of the house," Orozco said.

"Take it yourself. I'm busy. The women have me babysitting. Oh, and the wizards are waiting for you, in the hut down the road," Dar pointed, "with the roof that almost touches the ground. You can't miss it. If you kids don't stop fighting, you're going to have to play outside in the cold! Now cut it out!"

So Orozco poked around the main floor, noting that none of the rooms built as extensions let onto the second story loft. But there was a ladder to it from the living room and up there, he found himself impressed at the number of partitioned sleeping areas. He counted ten.

"Big family," he commented, backing down the ladder.

"Multiplied like rabbits," came the sour reply. "And guess who gets to supervise the great and great great grandchildren? Yours truly. Wanda!" Dar called. "Wanda!"

A ruddy, fortyish woman hurried in from the back with a question on her face.

"You take the kids. I've got to show our visitor to the wizard's hut."

"But he can't miss it," she protested. "It's right down the road and the roof almost touches the ground."

"Do *you* want to be responsible for an off-world fighter getting lost?"

"How could he get lost?"

"It could happen. C'mon Orozco. I'll show you to the wizards."

As they walked along the dirt road, Dar eyed him quizzically. "The other fighter," he said, "she had a flame in a box."

The old fighter fished in the pockets of his blue pants and brought forth a stainless steel lighter with a thunderbolt etched on front, which he showed to his guide.

"Exactly like that. She called it the hermit's flame."

"Well this is Elias' flame," Orozco said.

"She could really burn up the enemy with that hermit's flame. I guess we'll see how good Elias' flame is."

Orozco cast him a doleful, dark-eyed gaze. "If you're hoping it'll kill one of these sons of bitches,"

"I am."

"Well, that's why I'm here—to see exactly what sort of damage we can inflict."

"Damage don't mean nothing," Dar said.

"Agreed. If we can't kill them, it ain't worth jack." And on that somber note, they turned at the opening in the hedge, and Orozco let out a low whistle at the sight of the hut with the thatched roof that nearly touched the ground and the two chanting, stamping wizards out front. "If that ain't a little magic house, I don't know what is," he muttered.

"Plenty of magic under that roof," Dar said. "Magic in the very air you breathe."

"Show us the flame, Orozco," the local wizard said, without any greeting. The policeman did so. Both wizards peered into his open palm, inspecting the lighter, but careful not to touch it. "Come," they said in unison and beckoned him into the house. Dar decided the better part of valor was to wait outside.

Entering, Orozco sniffed. "What's that burning?"

"Our special coals, that we make from wood and metals in the mountains, by the glacier," the visiting wizard explained.

"I ain't never smelled anything like it. It makes me sleepy."

"Well, stay awake," the wizard snapped. "You let it put you to sleep and who knows what could happen." Whereupon he poked at the coals, until they glowed red and orange, then reached into his robe, withdrew a burlap sack, opened it and tossed a handful of dust on the coals. At once there appeared the image of two interrogators and two death worshippers, master killers, who each wore the top half of a human skull as a hat.

"Light the dust with the new flame," the wizard commanded, and Orozco did; whereupon both interrogators burst into a white sheet of fire, and cursing furiously in their sickening language, they told the two death worshippers that they must simply wait it out.

"I like this," Orozco said, as something deep, dark, light and canny flickered in his eyes. It lasted quite a while, until, finally, the interrogators' orange flames overpowered the white ones.

"That was worse than before," one of the death worshippers remarked.

"Much," replied an interrogator. "I was not sure we'd be able to bring it under control."

"But you did, you monster," Orozco breathed, and then fell silent, for deep within his mind he heard, "but someday, Elias' flame will reduce him to ash."

"Do the guardians know?" He asked mentally.

"They suspected. You have confirmed it for them."

***

Saltwater and Lindin rode the monorail to the lab. It snaked between towers, so high up that they could not see the ground below, only wisps of cloud, clinging to high-rise walls. "I could never get used to this," the nondescript man said to his friend. "It's fine for a visit, but the people who live in these buildings, how can they stand it?"

"That's what twenty thousand years of civilization gets you," Saltwater remarked dourly, "an apartment on the four hundredth story and a mall on the four hundred and fiftieth. Me, I'd take a cabin in the woods any day."

"Or a house."

"A cabin."

"I like my amenities, running water, heat in the winter, electricity."

"I'm not so concerned about those," Saltwater mused. "I've got a cabin, you know, up in the great Northern forest."

"I know. You've invited me many times."

"Never accepted yet," came the sour retort.

"Like I said, Pavel—my amenities. I don't like outhouses."

"So basically, if it doesn't have flush toilets, you won't stay there."

"Basically no, I won't. That's my answer."

"Why do I get the feeling that even if I installed plumbing, you wouldn't come?"

"Electricity."

"I could get a generator and hook the place up."

"Air-conditioning in summer?"

"I knew it!" Saltwater slapped his knee. "That's where we part company, my friend. No cabin of mine in the woods is going to have air-conditioning."

"Then I'm not coming."

"Think of hiking up to the angel's stronghold."

"And sweating like a pig, with no way to cool off," Lindin's face contracted in an expression of acute distaste. They exited at one of the defense laboratories, were scanned, and then caught an express elevator up. They found Ein unlocking the door, with the instantaneous voice, retinal and thumbprint scan. He looked nervous, and to their inquiries replied that he had risen early, checked on the computer and seen that hundreds more galaxies had vanished from sector one thousand. Seymour had not yet completed his search for them, but Ein said he had a premonition this was the beginning of the end for that universe.

Three very somber fighters shuffled into the laboratory.

"No news yet," came Seymour's hopeful chirp. "But I'm still searching."

"What can *we* do?" Saltwater asked.

"Basically nothing, I'm afraid. I'm faster than any of the programs you could run. But wait—here's a few. A half-dozen inhabited galaxies have turned up in a far corner of sector 222. That's a pretty safe sector."

"Depends on your definition of safe," growled the pockmarked man.

"Actually you can help. I have a theory," Seymour said. "While I'm searching, run one of your programs to search the far cosmos. I won't get to that till later, and it would be helpful to have some of it already checked."

So Ein gave the orders to the computer, then demanded three cappuccinos, which instantly appeared, steaming on what was known as the kitchen counter. The three fighters drank their caffeinated beverages and read news on their hand-helds. The hours weighed so heavily upon them, that finally Ein announced that he was going upstairs to work on project Fireball and requested that he be called when there was any news.

"They're turning up all over the place, the inhabited galaxies," Seymour said, after a long silence. "But the cosmos is so vast, that, well, I'm sorry to disappoint you, but even *I* won't be able to track them all down."

"What about the uninhabited galaxies?" Lindin inquired.

"From what I can tell He didn't bother with those."

"Maximum survival," Saltwater murmured.

"They're disappearing at an alarming rate now. All of them, inhabited and barren. I think we can say for sure that the destroyer of galaxies has got all the uninhabited ones. For the ones with people, well,"

"We can pray," Ein snapped, his image appearing on the hand-held. "Which is what I have been doing for the last half hour. Everyone's in the operations room, all the brass. This is the worst thing imaginable."

"What now?" Saltwater cried.

"Sector one thousand is collapsing."

***

Some seven or eight days before these events, the two fighters from Ohio were very busy behind enemy lines, traveling from one planet to the next, wherever there were few fascist garrisons, destroying them and then waiting for the Argan needles to move the planet.

"You know, considering He didn't want any fighters from earth in sector one thousand," Jamal said at the end of this time to his friend Holdauer, "what are we doin' here? Not just in sector one thousand, but the conquered part of it. I mean how much worse can it get? I thought, you know, since we're from earth, the same town in Ohio no less, that we'd get some kind of break."

"Nope," Holdauer grunted. "They needed you 'cause you can spot enemy illusions. And they knew that if they called you, they had to call me as well."

"You read it exactly right," Ivan said, his image having appeared on Jamal's hand-held device. "Only a fighter raised by a guardian could handle this job. And you two have done it. I've checked off every planet on that list, and they've all been moved. The one you're on now was successfully moved an hour ago and so, you're done."

The two fighters glanced at each other.

"Done meaning done moving planets," Jamal began.

"Or done meaning we can go home to Cleveland," Holdauer finished.

"The first, of course."

"Aren't you embarrassed?" Jamal demanded. "Ivan, you yourself said we did everything you asked. But now, instead of givin' us a break, you're packing us off to the front."

"This is a war," Ivan snapped.

"Which we're losing," Jamal snapped back.

"Well, the last time I checked, you don't start winning by sending your best fighters off on vacation. You'll have plenty of time to enjoy that one-horse town of yours, after your next tour at the front."

"If it don't got the way of sector one thousand," Holdauer said glumly.

"Sector one thousand ain't done yet," Jamal retorted.

"On the contrary, it is," Ivan contradicted him and looked suddenly grayer than usual, wearier, more defeated. He looked old. "It started its final collapse, which should take about a week," he said quietly, "about thirty minutes after the Argans got you out of there. I couldn't tell you, 'cause you needed your nerve. But in the past few days, millions of galaxies have vanished. Maybe more. Some, all inhabited, I'm happy to say, have been identified in other universes."

Holdauer and Jamal Jones just looked at each other.

"You mean He moved millions of inhabited galaxies out of harms' way?" Holdauer asked incredulously, as his partner let out a low whistle.

"We'll never know how many He saved," Ivan said. "Or how many were lost. The cosmos is too vast for the mind of man to comprehend."

"But it's not to vast for Him to comprehend," Jamal said. "After all, He made it. Those galaxies gonna be turning up in strange places from now till kingdom come."

"Think how much worse this could have been," Ivan said somberly.

"God is great," Jamal said. "He is mightier than we ever knew."

***

"More will be arriving tomorrow," the priest said to the ghost. "Dismal has apparently become something of a focal point in Reincarnation."

"I like that name," the ghost smiled.

"Do you? I find it curious. I conducted a computer search to try to divine its provenance, but..."

"But?"

"Lost in the mists of time," he replied a little sadly. "We'll never know how this galaxy got its name."

"Well, it certainly has lived up to it," she added and was about to say more when a beep in her jacket pocket caused her to fish around for her hand-held device, then pull it out of a pocket, to reveal a very somber image of Ein. Before he could utter a word, she said, "I heard. I heard in my mind about forty minutes ago. And because I'm still linked to Vivaldi, he heard too."

"It's terrible," the weapons designer lamented. "Think how many were lost."

"Could have been lost," she spoke with a hard edge in her already harsh voice. "And think how many were saved, the billions we know of."

She paused and gazed down her beak of a nose at the worried image of Ein. "Who cares about a bunch of uninhabited rocks? About barren planets too hot or cold for human habitation, when whole worlds of people survived?"

"And whole worlds may have been lost."

"*May* have been. It was a cataclysm, no doubt. But there is much, much we don't know."

"Are you saying an event of this magnitude could occur without massive loss of human life?"

"And are you presuming to say you know for certain such loss occurred, when your very own computers have proved that He has been moving galaxies by the millions, like vats of..." she glanced around, as if hoping to find the correct word, and then, not, sputtered "vats of ping pong balls from one very sparsely populated, small universe, to other, much bigger realities. It was your very own computer work, Ein, that definitively demonstrated whole inhabited galaxies had been saved."

"But I face reality, Lontra."

"Ahem," Vivaldi reached for the little device. "And so does she. But an unknown is an unknown. And meanwhile all the evidence points to the work of our savior."

"I am a religious man, but," Ein began.

"You are a weapons designer!" Vivaldi nearly lost his composure. "And you are a fighter who has killed countless times in this war. Of necessity your mind, your soul is steeped in the thoughts of the enemy and how he works, does he do this, will he do that? These are thoughts of death and destruction. Yes, it is a cataclysm that an entire sector was lost and, as my friend in the transuniverse orphanage, my friend Rafael would say, there are changes afoot. A whole reality doesn't collapse and things remain the same."

"We failed miserably."

"Tell that to the billions of people whose lives were saved!" The priest cried. "Tell that to the fighters' orphans, who survived and who now have new homes! Tell that to the planets crammed with people in orbit around new suns! As you fighters love to say, this is war. What did you expect—the enemy to give up?"

"It will not happen again," Ein said definitively.

"Oh? And you, a mere man, are going to stop it?"

"He's thinking of project Fireball," Lontra said.

"How did you know?"

"I'm a fighter too. Our minds run on parallel tracks. Yes, if we could incinerate their commanders and interrogators, we could be sure, then, that there would never again be another reality collapse. But that's a big if."

"One day we will."

"I believe that," she said, thinking of the hermit's flame, and the hardness of her flat, dark, dull eyes grew even harder. "But the weapon may come from an unexpected quarter."

***

The young astronomer raced down the hall to his colleague's office. "Anwar, Anwar, you must look at these pictures from the orbital telescopes."

"I've been looking at ones from the Mountain telescope. Something's wrong."

"Something's wrong all right. Our galaxy, the whole of Reincarnation's in a different place!"

Anwar grabbed the papers from the young man's hands. "But Richard, lots of our old familiar galaxies are in different positions too. Hundreds of them."

"No, Anwar—millions. I've put it through the computer. It's as if our whole quadrant of the universe got all jumbled up. And to make matters even stranger, a few galaxies are just plain missing."

"Which ones?"

"Well M63XZYL is gone," Richard started, then named a few others.

"As far as we know, those are all uninhabited galaxies. What's the word from the traveler?"

"Traveler says that enemy who invaded the next quadrant is nowhere to be seen. Though traveler was a little confused this morning and had to be rebooted four times. Some problem with its link to the orbitals. Oh, and Anwar, some of the nearby solar systems have extra planets. And system BGG1? The one that lost Dismal? I did a check again for the first time in a week. BGG1 has Dismal back."

"What in heaven can be going on?" The older astrophysicist shuffled through the papers. "Are you sure Traveler can't monitor that invader?"

"The invaders are gone. My guess is the invaders are still wherever we were, but we, we're someplace else."

"This is a gigantic anomaly, Richard."

"Anwar?"

"What?"

"You know what it looks like to me?"

"What?"

"We've been moved. Not just Reincarnation, our whole quadrant."

The two astrophysicists stared at each other.

"Richard," the older asked after a moment, placing the papers on his desk and removing his thick glasses to rub his eyes. "Are you a...religious man?"

The young man stared at him. "I never really was, but after reading this data and looking at these pictures...well Anwar, if we've been moved, Someone moved us."

"And why would He do that?"

"To protect us from a murderous and immensely powerful invader. That seems to me to be the most likely answer."

"So I repeat, are you a religious man?"

The young man glanced over the older man's shoulder, out the window at the bright morning and the trees on the university campus, swaying in the strong breeze. "Now I am."

***

"What now?" Elpytha snapped, without even a hello, as she settled into the chair in Galen's office opposite his desk.

"Elias' flame is strong," the old concentration camp survivor said quietly.

"Did it kill one?" She nearly shrieked.

"No, but under proper circumstances, I believe it could. I just received a report from the council. They're demanding that all guardians hand over their flames to the fighters."

"Fuck that! I mean excuse me, but never,"

"Don't worry. I said never. So the idiots went to the angels. The angels said never. The flame is to protect earth, and someday will be used to do so directly. After that, fighters will be allowed to keep them, but not until."

"How did Ivan take that?"

"Poorly. He's been sulking all morning. I got bad news from Jason."

"What bad news?"

"Sector one thousand collapsed."

Elpytha drew a sudden sharp intake of breath, then covered her face with her hands, rubbing her eyes.

"But the news from Argas, apparently," Galen went on, "is good."

"You talk about good news at a time like this? Galen, have you lost your marbles?"

"No. According to the Argans, millions, maybe more of inhabited galaxies in sector one thousand were moved to other universes."

Elpytha's mouth fell open.

"Didn't know He could do that, did you?"

"I never considered it, though, if you'd asked me, I think I'd have said that He doubtless could."

"Well, He did it," Galen exulted.

"How did we find out? I mean, I don't care how advanced those Argan computers are, there's no way,"

"A man, a fighter named Saltwater, from a numbered reality and a world called Planet Four, was captured by the enemy some time ago and dumped in a killing center. There, when he was not busy stealing food, which fortunately he was pretty good at, he got the idea for how to invent an artificial being, artificial life or call it artificial intelligence. Angels liberated the killing center. The fighters hung the fascists who had run it; Saltwater personally hanging the commandant. Then the survivors were moved to various infirmaries, but the seraphs brought Saltwater back to the front. He was frail and had TB, but he began to recover and told the council about his idea. They teamed him up with Ein, an Argan fighter and the scientist responsible for cloaking his sector's point of contact with the enemy. He is a transgalactic hero in sector 3333."

"That's the Argan sector?"

Galen nodded, his dark eyes glimmering. "Ein is also a genius at weapons development and had already, once or twice, tried his hand at creating artificial life, but with no luck. To make a long story short, Saltwater and Ein created Seymour, our side's AI, and Seymour was able to search millions of live maps. That's how we first learned that He had moved so many galaxies out of sector one thousand."

"Seymour is secret?"

"Do not mention him to anyone. The council has big plans for Seymour, which they'll be putting into effect, as soon as he finishes what he calls his impossible first assignment."

"Why impossible?"

"You yourself said it—the cosmos is so vast, not even a powerful artificial life form will be able to scan it for all the galaxies that were moved. But he's already turned up quite a number. That's how we know what He did in this emergency—through Seymour."

"And a lucky thing, too," Elpytha said seriously. "Think of the despair among the fighters, if they had succumbed to the misconception that all humanity in sector one thousand had been killed."

"He did not permit that."

"It's still a horrible cataclysm. A whole universe—gone!" She paused, then asked "how much territory had the enemy conquered?"

"We don't know for sure. Less than a quadrant, but he had set up numerous scientific weapons stations in the conquered territory and was clearly set to launch a major, universe-wide assault." He paused, then said, "many of our fighters don't know all the details. They just know He saved much innocent life. The details, I'm afraid, have to be kept under wraps, though they'll be hearing about Seymour soon enough."

"Somehow they'll be working with him?"

"Somehow, yes, though I don't know anything about it. All I know is that that Seymour will be a very busy boy."

***

Saltwater slept late. When he woke in the Ein's cool, comfortable guest room, he glanced at the clock and cried "Yikes!" He dressed quickly, washed up and hurried downstairs, to find Ein, Lindin and a guest, finishing breakfast.

"Ah, just the man we've been talking about. Saltwater meet Dr. Ketts."

They shook hands, then the pockmarked man said, "I'm not sick."

"No, but Dr. Ketts is the resident expert on cyborgs."

"Oh no, no, no. Seymour stays in a little black box, thank you very much."

"Agreed. Did I say otherwise?" Ein asked. "No, I didn't. But the council wants us to be able to link fighters to Seymour via disposable implants, as you and I once discussed. Dr. Ketts has produced a design for this."

"So if the fighter is captured?" Saltwater asked.

"The tiny implant dissolves. The tiny interface with the brain dissolves. There is no trace. The enemy will never know the fighter was linked to our AI. The enemy will never even know we have Seymour."

Saltwater tapped his computer tablet. "How do you feel about this, Seymour?"

"Nervous," came the trembling reply. "What if it doesn't work, and the implant doesn't dissolve?"

"Basically," Dr. Ketts explained, "through the implant, Seymour alerts the techs that the fighter has been captured. They then start the dissolution process, which takes about fifteen seconds."

"Too long," Saltwater snapped. "Make it five."

Dr. Ketts looked at Ein, who shrugged.

"The enemy's been on the lookout for cyborgs for years. When I was captured," Saltwater explained, "within seconds I had been stripped and shoved into a scanner. This is exactly what the enemy wants, a way into our computers, a back door for a sneak attack. Fifteen seconds is too long."

"Okay, I'll rework the model," Dr. Ketts said. "But that's your only objection?"

"The only one I'll voice, yes. Who will you test this on?"

"We have fighters, volunteers, lined up miles long."

"Are they aware of the risks? And what, as you see it, are the risks?"

"Rejection of the implant."

"What about mental health?"

"What about it?"

"How will having an implant affect a fighter's mental health?"

Dr. Ketts smiled. "There should be no effects whatsoever."

"Hmmph," Saltwater grumbled. "Famous last words. Well Ein, if you're determined to do this…"

"Not me, the council."

"They should get the frikkin' implants themselves, but seeing as that won't happen, I'll be your first guinea pig."

Ein and Dr. Ketts exchanged a glance. Then the weapons designer cleared his throat, "ah, that would not be wise."

"So what're the risks you haven't told me about?"

"Hard to keep you in the dark, isn't it, Mr. Saltwater?" Dr. Ketts asked. And suddenly, the pockmarked man disliked him intensely.

"So you've already tried it!" Seymour's inventor snapped and then, "Seymour, why didn't you tell me?"

"The council put a gag on me."

"Shit!"

"Calm down," Lindin spoke quietly. "What were the difficulties?" He asked Dr. Ketts.

"Suicidal psychosis," the doctor replied.

"How many fighters have killed themselves already?" Saltwater snarled.

"Three."

"Shit! No way. No more implants, until you are *positive*, positive, it won't induce a, a…"

"A psychotic depression, resulting in suicidal ideation," Dr. Ketts said amiably.

"You fucking try it!" Saltwater snapped. "You've doubtless autopsied these three poor souls."

"Yes, we know what went wrong."

"Then if you want implants so bad, you fix whatever went wrong and *you* try it."

"Be reasonable," Ein said quietly.

"No," Saltwater snapped. "The good doctor here used my invention to murder three fighters. No, I won't be reasonable. Did you even *consider* animal testing?"

"That's what we've been doing lately," Dr. Ketts replied, "and the results have been most promising."

"You mean the monkeys don't stop eating and starve themselves to death."

"Exactly."

Saltwater glared at Ein. "I'm shocked," he said at length. "I'm shocked at you."

The weapons designer sighed. "This is an emergency, Pavel. The council wants to send fighters into enemy territory and wants Seymour to help them. That's the purpose of the implant—to help Seymour help the fighters find the enemy's AI."

"But that could take years! Enemy territory is vast. We have no idea where the destroyer of galaxies resides."

"Yes," Dr. Ketts said eagerly, "but with Seymour, we could find out! He could eliminate whole swaths of territory through multiple fighters at the same time. Surely, it's worth a try."

"When you're done with animal testing," Saltwater spoke evenly, "I will be the next subject."

"I really think that's unwise," thus Ein.

"And I think it's the only responsible thing to do," Saltwater retorted. "Put me on a suicide watch, once you make the implant. And if I fall into a psychotic depression, remove it."

"After the first suicide," Dr. Ketts said thoughtfully, "we did exactly that, kept the next two volunteers under observation. But they were...ingenious."

"Well, you be more ingenious," Saltwater shouted.

"It's bad enough already," Seymour complained. "I couldn't bear it, if Pavel took his life on my account."

"He's not going to," Lindin spoke definitively. "Because there will be no more human implants until Dr. Ketts here is completely certain that the problem has been solved. Aren't I right, Dr. Ketts?"

The easy geniality of the military doctor had worn off some, and it was with a rather chastened aspect that he murmured, "yes, Lindin, of course you're right."

"Because it's the enemy," Lindin barreled on, "not us, who considers human sacrifice an acceptable price for victory. Am I not correct?"

Ein and Dr. Ketts stared at their hands on the polished table-top. Saltwater glared. "Glad we got that settled," he snapped.

***

"What do you mean we're travelling back to the front with Dr. Ketts?" Saltwater shouted at Lindin in the lab a few days later. "I don't want to go anywhere near that murderer."

"He's not a murderer."

"What would you call it?"

"Negligent homicide."

"Oh, that's just great."

"The monkeys aren't sad," Seymour piped in. "They like me."

"Good," Saltwater snarled. "Let the council and Dr. Ketts send monkeys into enemy territory."

It was late afternoon, and sunlight streamed into the lab from the long, high windows, illuminating for Lindin his friend's now robust health. He had muscles back in his arms, from working out at a gym, his face had filled out again. His torso and legs no longer looked frail. And he hadn't coughed in days.

"You know," Lindin mused. "I think you finally got that TB beat."

"Good. Can I stop taking the antibiotics and drink a beer?"

"Ask the doctors at the front. They're officially in charge of your case, and we'll be back there day after tomorrow."

"Then after that, home!"

"Don't count on it, brother."

"I'll count on it all I like," the pockmarked man spoke angrily.

"You may be disappointed."

"I better not be. I'm due for a break."

"And you shall get it!" Thus Ein, striding into the lab. "I spoke with the council today. After the front, it's back to your cabin in the Great Northern Forest, to recuperate."

"He can't go there alone. He won't take his meds," Lindin snapped.

"He's not going alone. That was the only requirement."

"Oh?" Lindin asked. "So who's the lucky dog, who gets to rough it without electricity or running water?"

Ein beamed, the gray of his eyes, clothes and crew-cut for once seeming almost cheerful. "You," he said.

***

It was a gray but sultry afternoon, as the little, gold Honda traveled along the back roads, skirting Lonely State

415

Park. Though merely a smudge behind a massive cloud cover, the sun still managed to radiate so much heat that the asphalt squished in places, while the leaves seemed to curl at the edges on the trees. Or so it seemed to Gideon Cohen, glancing up at the shield of branches between him and the heat of the late morning sun. At length he turned onto a dirt road, bounced along for a while and finally, at fork, stopped, but he left the engine running for the air-conditioning. Soon, however, he thought he heard singing. So he rolled the window down, and sure enough, there was Orozco's voice, as deep and sonorous, Gideon thought, as a cantor in a synagogue. He was singing a hymn, and it was not a peaceful hymn. It was, as Gideon made out the words, about the Lord smiting his enemies left and right. Gideon smiled and rolled the window back up. It was too hot.

Still singing, Orozco slid into the passenger seat.

"You done?" Gideon asked, as the leathery old detective came to a break in his song. "Cause He may well smite thine and His enemies left and right, but they smite back. Sector one thousand collapsed."

"I heard."

"In your mind?"

"No, when I lit this," and Orozco withdrew from his pocket the stainless steel lighter. "And I also heard that billions were saved."

"That is indeed the news."

"And project Elias went very, very well."

Gideon's eyebrows rose. "Project Elias? What is that—a Passover ritual?"

"No, it's this," and Orozco held up the little lighter. "Belonged to a guardian, name of Elaine Elias, took her life in 1972, a good friend. Upon her death, I came into possession of her flame. This flame, brother, burns commanders and interrogators."

"But can it kill them?"

"Time will tell."

"We could use it at the front."

"Nope. The flame is a gift for earth, for the defense of earth. It only gets used here, if there's ever a need."

"God forbid."

"God forbid."

With that, Gideon turned the little car around, and they bounced back along the narrow dirt road.

"Who's babysitting Horace?"

"Your partner, Harry," the driver replied. "Starfield's at work. Said he had a deadline. By the way, Harry knows about guardians."

Orozco's big mitt closed over the lighter, as he demanded through gritted teeth, "how?"

"He's hearing that voice. And then, on top of that, Horace has been none too discreet."

"Shit."

"In fact, Horace claims he's still linked to fighter Horace at the front, and those two telepaths are just having a whale of a time, filling your partner's ears with old war stories."

"Shit. Does Harry appreciate the need for silence? 'Cause he's a gabby…"

"I have impressed it upon him repeatedly. It appears to have sunk in."

"It better sink in. We got a planet full of death worshippers on our hands. We don't need them finding out about guardians; on the contrary, we need our safely hidden guardians to help us locate these fascist sons of bitches, so's we can kill 'em."

"Well, you tell him. 'Cause I'm sick of repeating myself till I'm blue in the face. And while you're at it, have a little sit-down with big-mouth MacKenzie, whose wild tales of telepathic connection to the front and doings at the front have curled Harry's hair and Starfield's."

"Shit. We might as well just put him on a TV show."

"That's about the size of it."

"Aie, aie, aie, always new problems. Dios mio," Orozco sighed and shoved the lighter back in his pocket. "Troubles never cease." After a moment, he cast Gideon a sidelong glance. "So you heard He's been moving galaxies."

The driver nodded.

"And not just a few."

The driver nodded again.

"Millions of galaxies."

"Maybe more," Gideon said, and thereupon an awed hush descended on the interior of the little car, as the two fighters considered the significance of this news.

"We better get our act together, here on planet earth," Orozco finally announced. "He don't have time for our rape of the environment and the impoverishment of billions. We ain't supposed to let that shit happen."

"You're welcome to try to fix it."

"Shit. I'm just a cop. I'll hunt down these death worshippers, but I can't stop the idiots in charge of whole countries from waging war, giving financial crooks a free pass to rob the sick, poor and elderly and from burning every last rain forest on the planet. He ain't gonna like any of that one bit. Once He's done juggling His galaxies and He turns His attention to this blood-soaked snot-rag called earth..."

"Where did I hear that very expression recently?"

"From some wise man, gotta be. 'Cause that's what this place is. We got skyrocketing inequality, billions of people living on less than two dollars a day, born into filth and poverty, dying early in filth and poverty, we're destroying the natural world at a prodigious rate. We got these idiot capitalist masters of the universe investing in the total rape of the planet. No, when He's done moving those galaxies around, He's gonna turn His attention back to us, and you know what, Gideon?"

"What?"

"I wouldn't be surprised if He just decides we're hopeless and throws in the towel."

Gideon eyed him critically. "'Cause you would?"

Orozco stared dolefully at the younger fighter. "I'm not sayin' another word. All I know is, He ain't gonna be pleased. Everytime He takes a minute from the war to check up on earth, He gets furious. Then a whole batch of fighters get shipped home from the front, and we're supposed to, somehow, fix this fucking mess. Well, I know my limitations. I'm just a cop. I ain't up to the job. And neither are you."

"Speak for yourself."

"You don't think I ain't known hundreds of fighters? Decent people, all of 'em. But they can't compete with the jerks in charge of this planet. They're fighting a losing battle."

And on that cheerful note, Gideon Cohen's little Honda coasted across the city line into the smoggy, slum-filled, industrially poisoned, sweltering, crime-ridden, second-rate East Coast city of D____.

***

It was sunset. The white tents of the fighters' children glowed bright orange, like so many tongues of flame in the valley and upon the hillside. The children had finished their evening meal and now sat between their tents, on the paths, to listen to fighters telling tales of the war and to learn about the world of their deceased parents. The priest stood at the water pump, outside the gray administration tent, sudsing an enormous soup pot, so he did not at first observe the tall, bony, hard figure of a woman who approached. But then her shadow stretched out over him, so he straightened up and without even turning, said: "Lontra, so it is time for you to go."

"Yes," she answered, pointing "at sunset, from those woods on that far hill."

"You and I, Lontra, I believe we shall never travel by needle."

"You are probably correct, and I, for one, would not especially care to."

"Most fighters complain about hanging onto a pair of wings for dear life, as they hurtle through the night."

Her dark, hard, flat, dull gaze flickered over his kindly features. "There are far worse things than that."

"As you know better than anybody."

"Most of which, praise God and His angels, I have forgotten. Memory, Vivaldi, can be a curse."

They stood awkwardly silent for a moment, until he said, "well, good-bye. I hope some day we meet again."

"Not likely; I go to the front and you never will. And I will doubtless die there. So, to be honest, I should say that I'll see you again on the other side."

"On the other side then," he replied and bowed his head. She strode off, a somewhat ungainly figure in her cheap clothes, with her knapsack and machine gun over her shoulder, as she loped, slowly at first, then faster, toward the dirt track that led to the far hills. Only once did she turn and wave and call "on the other side then!"

"On the other side," he murmured in response and returned to soaping the big soup pot.

"You were correct," the seraph said, as she clung to his wings that spread out long on either side, as they soared through starry night. "Your path now diverges from the priest's. You will not meet again."

420

"I thought as much. So no more orphanage work for me, eh?"

"No, fighter, you will do what you do best. You are the death worshipper's scourge. He will not waste your talents in any other activity, except two."

"What are they?"

"I cannot tell you that. I am not allowed to disclose the future."

"But you just did."

The angel turned his beautiful head to smile at her. "I am permitted to drop hints."

Soon they spun down in a gyre, and with the galaxies all aswirl around her, she heard him say, "you needn't close your eyes, the vortex from Reincarnation to the front is peaceful. Not like the one from the Milky Way."

"Is that because of earth?"

"Yes, correct. It is because of earth. There, in the distance, can you see the light of our fireballs, exploding over the rim of the universe?"

"I see them!" She cried.

"We're almost there now, back to your home and ours, the front."

***

They waited nervously outside the council door. "What could it be?" She asked, her hands planted on her hips, her black, curly hair rubber-banded back into a ponytail. "What do they want with us? We've had nothing but success. Engaged five enemy battle cruisers. Successfully shot down them all. All five interrogators, all five commanders incinerated amid the wreckage by angels. What can they be complaining about now?" She paused to chew on a hangnail. "I know what it is," she told him. "Sour grapes. Ivan's just upset that we showed him up. He thought a disabled fighter couldn't handle all the latest Argan gadgetry and be a competent co-pilot, and we proved him wrong."

"If you say so," he said, sitting on the bench, leaning back against the wall, his one good eye closing, the other covered with a black patch.

"Well, what's your theory?"

"Me? I don't have any theories. I just do as I'm told. I follow a little voice that I hear, never as often as I'd like, deep in the recesses of my brain. The voice that's always right. It said I should work with you, so I did. We were a good team. But now, I got the feeling, they're breaking us up for good."

"Why? Why do you have that hunch?"

"Two battle cruisers strafed our positions this morning, and we weren't called up. That can only mean one thing: they're done with us."

Before she could ask, "but why?" the door opened, and out strode a disgruntled fighter. He eyed them both sourly. "Well, you two are next. I hope you have better luck than I did."

"Okay Axel—show-time!" And Carmella and her co-pilot entered the council chamber, shutting the door behind them.

The twelve men, twelve "old" men, she told herself, faced them across a long, rectangular table.

"Your work has been exemplary," Ivan said with no other greeting, as he read a sheet of paper. "But the enemy has gotten wise to our Argan devices. Another attack would be suicide, because at close range they can now see through the cloak."

"How do you know this?" Carmella demanded.

"Intelligence."

"Gathered by whom?"

"I cannot say."

"Can't or won't?"

"Both."

"How was it gathered?"

"Behind the lines. Our source is impeccable, he's never been wrong yet. So, Marquez, you're getting a new assignment."

Carmella sighed, then frowned at the twelve council members.

"Knowledge of how to penetrate this cloak," Jason Katharos said, "is new and very limited. Here at the front, they would shoot you down. But in the sector we're sending you to,"

"What sector?" Carmella ground her teeth.

"Sector Forty-four."

"Shit! That hellhole?"

"And you're not taking Axel with you," Ivan put in. "He stays here."

"Oh, this is just dandy," she snarled.

"Look, I'm sorry we couldn't give you more of a reward,"

"Reward?" She shouted. "What fucking reward? I set up five, five enemy commanders and five, five enemy interrogators for the seraphs to incinerate, and take out five, five of their fucking battle cruisers, and now you quote reward me unquote by sending me to that shithole, sector 44?"

"They don't know about the cloak. You'll be able to cripple their fleet. We could win."

Carmella turned on her heel and stalked out, screaming furious obscenities.

"Always a pleasure," Ivan remarked dryly.

***

As soon as Axel had left, one of the men of the council rose, came around the table and then locked the door from the inside. Then Jason rose, went to the door in the back of the room, opened it and pressed a buzzer by its frame. A few moments later, the sound of someone thumping up the stairs could be heard. Then a black, furry and scaly head appeared in the doorway, as Night Child made his entrance.

"We just sent one of our best pilots to sector 44," Ivan said. "The one who shot down those five battle cruisers."

Night Child galumphed over to one of two chairs facing the council members and threw himself in it. "I hate those damned steps. The only time of day I feel like myself is at night, when I get to fly with my kind over enemy territory."

"Are you certain that the commanders in sector 44 won't know how to see through our pilot's cloak?"

"Am I certain?" Night Child mimicked. "Am I sure? Do I really truly know? Yes, goddammit. I told you, the commanders here at the front generally don't share technical secrets with those in the other sectors. And they sure as shit won't share them with the commanders in sector 44, because they're feuding with them."

"Feuding? How badly?"

"Incinerating each other, that badly. What do you think a commander does when he's feuding—trade barbed insults? No. He burns somebody alive. The commanders here at the front *want* the commanders in sector 44 to lose. If they could cut a deal with the seraphs to go wipe them out, they would. They already turned two of 'em into crème brule."

"So our pilot is safe."

"How many ways do I have to say the same thing? There is no, absolutely no intelligence stream between this front and sector 44. The commanders at this front were *against* the invasion of sector 44. They tried to stop it. Then they tried to sabotage it. Then they tried to sabotage it a second time.

No. Top secret intelligence on how to see through an Argan cloaking device will not be seeping from the front to sector 44. Now you tell me something."

"What?"

"What's this I hear from my buddies I flap around with at night about Him having moved gazillions of galaxies out of sector one thousand?"

"It's true. Is it inspiring fear?"

"Fear? Naked, stark raving terror would be more like it. Who ever heard of such a thing? Whole galaxies and not just one or two? It's got everybody frantic."

"Do the commanders know?"

"Do the commanders know—what kind of question is that? Yes, of course they know, and they're all secretly making their own personal arrangements to skedaddle to the realm of shadow or the land of death or some other such bright and cheerful kingdom of night hot spot, should He take it into His mind to start moving or crushing *our* galaxies." Night Child paused to glance around the room. "It's so bare in here. Don't you guys know anything about décor—a few dead bodies, a few black drapes, you need to spruce the place up."

"What about your efforts to pinpoint Morning Star's location?" Ivan asked.

"Zip. Nada. Not a word. My kind ain't got the faintest idea where that old homicidal computer resides. You want to find that out, you're going to have to start using spies. Send some fighters behind the lines to talk with death worshippers. It's death worshipper slaves do the maintenance on Morning Star—that much I learned."

"Well, that's something," Jason murmured.

"Look, I don't even like mentioning that killer's name. If he knew what I was up to, I'd be in lots of little pieces. One thing's for sure, though."

"What?"

"He's the one who gets all the credit for destabilizing that sector one thousand. Tell that to your big boss."

"We did."

"And?"

"He said, through a prophet, in a voice that could crush mountains, 'I will *destroy* him.'" Ivan paused. "And He *always* keeps His promises."

***

In the days following his first encounter with Dr. Ketts, Saltwater was forced to revise his opinion of the man. This doctor, whom he had considered negligent, took every conceivable precaution and then some. He was even kind to the monkeys in his lab and would not permit their abuse. He worked long hours and did not shirk. At length, he said he was ready to test the modified implant on a human subject. Saltwater insisted that it be him. And he insisted so vociferously, so unreasonably, so unstoppably that eventually Ein, Ketts, Lindin and Seymour backed down.

"Now I'll give you a local anesthetic on the side of your head," Dr. Ketts explained, as Saltwater reclined in what reminded him of a dentist's chair. "Then I insert the implant. Then we keep you under observation in the padded room for two days. If you want, Lindin or Ein can keep you company."

"Ein's wife promised to bring me a fruit pie."

"That's fine, too."

The procedure was over in fifteen minutes.

"Hi, Seymour," the pockmarked man thought.

"Hello, Pavel. How are you feeling?"

"Alert, very alert."

"Me too. Do you think you're getting that from me or vice versa?"

"I don't know."

"Well?" Dr. Ketts asked. "Can you communicate mentally with him?"

"Yes, it's easy. It's like having a friend in a corner of my mind."

"No depressive thoughts?"

"In ten seconds? I doubt it, doc."

"Let me know immediately if you do, and we'll remove it."

Ein and Lindin, sitting in the waiting room, rose, when Saltwater came out.

"Well?" They both asked.

"It's great. Seymour and I can communicate mentally. He says he's turned up another couple of hundred galaxies in a far universe this morning, ones that weren't on the live map there before."

"That Seymour!" Ein marveled.

"Now let's go make you comfortable in your padded room," Lindin said.

"Really," Saltwater started to protest.

"No," Lindin snapped. "I don't want to hear it. This was part of the deal. A padded room for two days. If you can't deal with that, then turn right around and get back in that dentist's chair and tell Dr. Ketts to remove your implant."

"He's right, you know," the doctor said. "I couldn't face dealing with another suicide."

"Oh bother," Saltwater snapped. "Take me to my padded room."

And it really was not so bad. The room was furnished—no sharp edges or strings or ropes of any kind. The floor and walls were padded. There were recessed lights in the ceiling. And on a cushioned table in a plastic plate steamed a peach pie. Saltwater walked around the table, surveying the pie, then stood, arms akimbo and took in the room. "This is the most incongruous thing in the world," he said.

"It's what we agreed on," replied Lindin, pulling a plastic knife from his pocket, cutting the pie and distributing pieces on paper plates and handing out plastic spoons.

The four men devoured the pie.

"I could get used to this," the pockmarked man said, and then, even more incongruously than the room smiled. "So could Seymour. He says he just had his first taste sensation."

"And?" Dr. Ketts asked.

"He wants more peach pie."

***

He did not like to travel by angel, he preferred to go by needle any day. But the little voice in Ein's mind said, "no. It's been decided. When you go to earth, you do not go by needle. Needles were used for those weapons drops. They are not to appear in earth's atmosphere ever again."

"Oh, they were cloaked," Ein tried to reassure the voice.

"No, He does not want that."

"Oh all right," he grumbled mentally. "You win, as always."

So they hurtled through the night and the stars, Ein's stomach heaving, and he came to, lying flat on his back in a little field of wild flowers in late morning. He rose, dusted off his gray pants and shirt, picked a black-eyed Susan and put it in a buttonhole, then located the path he had been instructed to follow and shortly heard the deep bass of a man singing, coming toward him. There was something very familiar about the voice.

"Orozco! I didn't know you could sing!"

"It helps pass the time. Chauffeur at your service. The MacKenzie residence—or somewhere else?"

"Just Garibaldi Square."

"You Argans! Always picking the swankiest spots!"

"I won't be there long. Then I'll just take a taxi to Horace's."

"For that you need the address and some currency. Here." And he fished in his pocket and Handed Ein a twenty dollar bill. "The address is 333 Apocalypse Avenue. We'll have lunch for you."

They drove back in town in the Impala, Orozco holding forth on the miracle of the transported galaxies.

"All the same," Ein spoke somberly, "losing an entire universe? What a cataclysm!"

"Oh yes," the policeman agreed. "We'll be feeling the effects of that for years to come."

"What do you mean?"

Orozco turned his dark, doleful eyes onto his passenger for a moment. "You don't think He sees the enemy collapse an entire reality, and things remain the same afterward, do you?"

Ein's worried gray eyes scanned the driver's lean, leathery, lined face. "How will they change?"

"How should I know? He don't confide such things in me. But I know for darn sure, things will change."

Ein exited at the elegant little park and crossed the street to the bookshop, after the Impala had driven off. Downstairs the strong, young woman with the cropped hair glanced up from her book, Dante's *Inferno*, and said, "hello, Ein—mover of planets."

"Shh," the weapons designer admonished her.

"It doesn't matter. There's only me, him and some employees in the back. Besides even if a customer did overhear, they'd think it was a joke. Go right back, he's expecting you."

"He is?"

"Yes, he told me this morning, Ein will be coming, send him back at once."

The two men shook hands in Galen's little, bright, underground office.

"So why have you come?" The old publisher asked, returning to his seat behind his gaily cluttered desk.

"I think you know."

"How would I know?"

"Well, you knew I was coming."

"Oh, all right then," the dark eyes glimmered at him with their seemingly limitless depths. "The answer is no."

"Galen, we need the guardian's flame. I already had one, back on Argas, at the lab, for project fireball. Now if we could just have it back, to take to the front."

"No."

"Just for a few months."

"No."

"Why not?"

"Because the flame is a gift to earth, for the defense and protection of a poor, harried, harassed, beleaguered, blood-stained, violent and brutal but nonetheless special world. The seraphs had to be convinced, as it was, to let us loan you one for Argas and to let us conduct our little experiments on Sere, and we were told, in no uncertain terms, not to do things like that again."

Ein's shoulders sagged in disappointment.

Galen leaned forward and said, in a low voice, "someday, my friend, within my lifetime, earth will be attacked. And we will not have cloaking devices or fireballs or fantastic Argan weaponry to protect us. I have long, long, worried over how we would survive. Now I know."

Ein glanced up. "Now you know," he repeated.

"Yes, a gift from the seraphs, a source of knowledge that is also a weapon. Something for earth and earth only,"

Galen held up his stainless steel lighter, "made from a human material, something we created, with our blood, sweat and tears, but forged by angels on worlds we shall never see. A gift from Him to us, the inhabitants of wayward earth, and when we have used it, to hold off the attack that will surely come—after that, then yes."

"Then yes, what?"

"Then the flame will pass from guardians to fighters and from earth to the front."

***

After several days in his padded room, Saltwater was told that he and Lindin were to return to the front to make their presentation to the council. Ein was away, so they could not say a proper good-bye to him, however, they hugged and kissed his wife, who was tearful and invited them back, any time, for as long as they liked. Then they took a shuttle up to the terminal, in orbit so many miles above the planet, and pressed their noses, like astonished children, to the shuttle window, to stare at the marvel they were leaving. From their perspective, though they knew there were many man-made parks, all they could see were massive buildings, the huge Argan architecture, which covered the planet. "Not for me," Saltwater said under his breath. "There have got to be other alternative conclusions to twenty thousand years of peace."

"Well, just think," Lindin spoke sourly. "Soon we'll be crappin' in an outhouse in the Great Northern forest."

"I'll take that any day."

"You're just peculiar."

Saltwater's eyebrows rose, he gestured at the spectacle of planet-wide buildings below, "you prefer this?"

Lindin shook his head. "In truth, it's not for me either. But I like my amenities. Me, I'll stick to the suburbs."

At the terminal, so vast, so busy, so many signs, gates, eating establishments, they got lost and almost missed their flight. But a fighter spotted them and approached, saying, "need help, brothers?"

"We can't find the needle to the front."

"I'll take you to it. I'm going there myself."

"How come they didn't get to their feet and applaud?" Lindin joked under his breath.

"Well, you can't travel with a celebrity like Ein every day," Saltwater replied. They sat, strapped themselves in, the machine glowed and then there, below a night sky, shone an array of needles, some having just arrived, some ready to depart, and in the distance the flash of angelic fireballs. Though it was late, the council was in session, waiting for them.

"You don't look psychotic," Ivan greeted Saltwater.

"Thanks Ivan. You look okay too."

"So you can communicate with Seymour telepathically?"

"Yes and no side effects. I trust you've all gotten to know him on computers here at the front."

"Yes," Jason replied, "and his discovery of those moved galaxies has done wonders for fighter morale. You can imagine how we all felt at first, losing an entire universe."

"Billions were saved," Ivan said. "We made sure all the fighters know that. Now if only Seymour could help us locate the enemy's death machine."

"How hard can that be?" Lindin asked.

"Hard. Enemy territory is vast, and it's a very risky business, sending spies in to ask questions about Morning Star's location." He paused to shuffle some papers on the table, gray and tired as always, but strangely elated to see Saltwater, and clearly encouraged that the implant was working as it was supposed to.

"No symptoms of any sort?" Ivan asked.

"Not a one," the pockmarked man replied.

"So we could start giving fighters the implant and then they, with Seymour, could enter enemy territory, get into those computers and Seymour could search for clues to Morning Star's location."

"I'm very nervous about being in enemy territory," Seymour piped up from Jason's hand-held computer. "What if Morning Star finds out about me? He'd make it his life's work to kill me."

"No homicidal computer life form's finding out about you," Jason replied. "We got your back."

"Don't rush things," thus Saltwater.

"Whole worlds are at stake. We always rush things," Ivan retorted.

"What I mean is test out the implant on more fighters first. And anyone you send out with it, keep them under observation for a week at first, at least."

"We can never thank you enough," Ivan began.

"Yes you can."

"No, because we can't release you."

"Why not?" The pockmarked man demanded belligerently.

"Because we were told we'd be needing you a while longer."

"How much longer?"

"At least three years." Ivan paused. "Look, you can take a couple of months in that forest you love, if Lindin agrees to accompany you. But after that—three years."

Saltwater glanced at his friend Lindin. "Three years till retirement," he said and then, to Ivan, "I'm taking that as a promise."

***

Carmella Marquez knew she had to watch her mouth. Clinging to the seraph's wings, she hurtled through space, remembering her last contact with one of the members of the Lord's hosts and the hot water it had landed her in. So she was very circumspect and asked no questions. But the angel seemed determined to draw her out. "You don't want to know why you were selected for sector 44?" He asked.

"As punishment," she thought, "from the council, for doing a good job." Aloud she merely grunted.

"Because we believe, you will be able to inflict more damage than any other pilot on the enemy fleet. And you know what that means."

"No, I'm afraid I don't."

"It would turn the tide of the war in sector 44, where the fight has been intensely dreadful for some years now."

"Yeah, a plum assignment," slipped out of her mouth, before she realized it. "Oops," she thought.

"Do not regard it as a punishment. You will be in charge of all our pilots. You will direct them, and you will train them how to use the Argan weapons. You could wind up with a promotion."

"Oh? And where would I get sent then?"

"Home."

Carmella caught her breath.

"You do not beg to be sent back home like so many of the fighters, but your quiet yearning has not gone unnoticed."

"Well, I don't know about quiet…"

"Comparably quiet. You should hear your friend Orozco," the seraph chuckled.

Carmella, astonished at this sudden confidence, asked, "he complains?"

"Complains? Every time he's called to the front, you'd think the world had come to an end."

"A not unreasonable conclusion, under those circumstances."

"But you don't complain."

"That's because I'm too scared that if I do, you'll extend my stay."

"We don't do things that way."

She wanted to snap, "oh really?" but instead asked mildly. "How do you do things?"

"Certain individuals are necessary for certain jobs. Orozco is busy most of the time running the orphanage, but for some jobs, such as liberating you and Albert and the others from that prison, he was needed."

Carmella's eyes widened in surprise. "I didn't know he was involved. The only fighter I saw was the one who sprang us—Gideon."

"Well, Orozco was part of it too, a necessary part, though on his trip to the front, he did nothing besides moan that the world was coming to an end."

Carmella chuckled. "That Rafael."

"He is a remarkable man," the seraph continued. "But for such a remarkable man, he has a remarkable number of complaints."

"Can you blame him?" Carmella asked. "The war's eaten up his whole life. He has no other life. I still find it a miracle that I got married and have kids. And the only explanation is that I married a fighter. Any normal person would have kicked me out of the house years ago. As happened to Rafael. So he lost the woman he loved, never got to have kids, never had time to get training and leave the police force—everything's the war, the death worshippers and the orphanage. Nothing else. He has no life."

"Nonsense," came the reply. "The orphanage provides richly rewarding work. And as a policeman, he's been most useful in helping to control enemy incursions into earth."

The conversation lapsed, as they spun down into a gyre, with the galaxies all aswirl all around.

"How will I know where to go?" Carmella demanded, before closing her eyes.

"Easy. Just walk toward the exploding fireballs. There are lots of them."

***

The tall, hard, angular woman, with the cheap clothes, badly cut hair and face roughened by the elements, strode into the council chamber, shut the door behind her, turned and faced the twelve men and snapped: "This is terrible news! Albert is dead. Who had the hare-brained idea of sending him behind the lines anyway?"

"He did," Jason answered.

"He should have been overruled. You were grossly negligent. Whatever could have been so important as to justify this rash, foolish and fatal act?"

"Earth," Ivan replied wearily. "We had intelligence about an enemy computer station near the front and intelligence that through those computers we could access what the enemy knew about earth. And he knew a lot. Fortunately Albert was able to alter enough material that we have effectively thrown sand in the enemy's eyes."

"How do we know this for sure?"

"We have sources we cannot reveal."

"And what makes things worse," Lontra continued, "is that Albert directed the section of the front manned by people from earth. He did that for over two decades. What will you do about that?"

"We have considered the matter thoroughly," Ivan sighed. "And come up with a replacement."

"Oh? Who?" She snarled.

"You."

Lontra's mouth fell open, then snapped shut. "No. I'm a loner, not a general. I work best by myself or at most with one other, no more. I'm not cut out for that work."

"On the contrary, given what you can do with that deadly gaze of yours, we think the fighters will be eager to follow you to the ends of the universe, if need be. And besides, you have something in common with Albert, which all the fighters appreciate."

"What?"

"The front is your home. Whenever a fighter felt sad over the life he had to sacrifice for this war, all he had to do was look at Albert. Now there was a man who had given up everything—his years as a revolutionist in Brazil, all the wealth he amassed in New York, the love of a beautiful and famous woman, his children—all gone! Gone, and for what? To rally thousands of men and women from earth, mired in mud, living in trenches, dying by the hundreds; he made the front his home for them, to inspire them, to egg them on, to rally their spirits. And you have done the same. Face it, Lontra, face what everybody knows: the front is your home. More than it is my home, or the home of the other eleven men on this council. Because we'd return to our worlds if we could. But you would not."

"If we won the war, I would," she retorted defiantly.

Jason sighed. "Ghost, we are not going to win this war for millennia, and if we don't find out why we're losing, we may lose it altogether well before then. We need you. The fighters of earth need you. Lead and they will follow. The next time there's a death sweep, turn your gaze full on it and let our side see the enemy die by the score. Even the fighters' beloved Albert couldn't do that. You alone have this capacity, which He has given you in revenge for the dreadful suffering you endured in the kingdom of night."

"I'm not up to it," she said simply. "I'm not up to replacing Albert, and the fighters will know it instantly."

"Like Jason said, you are different," Ivan spoke wearily again. "Don't try to pretend to be Albert. Of course that won't work. Be yourself, the ghost, Lontra, the woman the enemy could not kill, the woman who traded all, *all* the amenities of life on earth for the harsh environment of the front. And with you in charge, we on the council can continue our attempts to find out why things are going against us and how to correct that."

"Are you making progress?"

"Yes," several said at once.

"Then I will do it. I will take over the section of the front where earth's fighters are dug in. Anything, so that we can stop losing this terrible war."

***

She threaded her way through a cluster of low hills, keeping her eyes on the late afternoon sky and the fireballs that thundered overhead in the same direction she was walking. Soon she arrived at a wide, flat-bottomed valley, over which were spread fifty fighter jets, with numerous men and women milling about, until they saw her, stopped moving and watched her approach.

"So my guess, brothers and sisters," she said loudly, as soon as she was within earshot, "is that you don't know how to use the Argan weaponry."

A murmur went up and then one young man stepped forward and asked, "and you do?"

"Yes I do. I've used these planes to cripple five battle cruisers, but my guess is you've got more than five beyond those hills."

"More like fifty," one tough, heavy-set older woman said.

"If we take out those fifty," Carmella continued. "Will we have crippled their little fleet?"

A murmur of assent went up.

"Okay, fighters of sector 44, let's do this!"

Whereupon she climbed into a cockpit, and began explaining how to fly the jet and deploy the weapons.

"We can fly 'em," one of the men who had crowded around said. "They're just like our fighter jets, only a little more powerful."

"A *lot* more powerful."

"Well, we've flown 'em for practice, all of us. And we can operate the cloak. But we couldn't figure out the Argan rockets and missiles."

"Well, I'm shown' ya. Pay attention." And she resumed her explanations.

Another fifty or so pilots rounded a hill, detected the commotion around one jet and hurried over. Soon everyone had received detailed instructions on how to deploy the missiles.

"So we get a pilot and a co-pilot for each jet," Carmella addressed them. "Where are our targets?"

"Where do you think?" The young fighter who had first spoken said, his eyes gazing heavenward, as a fireball streaked by.

"We will hold back the fireballs until you cripple their ships," all fighters then heard in their minds.

"Let's do this!"Carmella shouted, as they clambered into their jets. The young fighter was her co-pilot. "You're ready to take over, if you have to?" She asked. He nodded. She donned her headset. "Cloak now?" And fifty cloaked fighter jets rose invisibly into the sky.

They tore forward, straight at the mass of big, black, enemy battle cruisers, looming on the horizon, then separated, one fighter per cruiser.

"Come in close, fire, then pull up," Carmella directed them.

They closed in. "Bombs away!" Carmella shouted, as hundreds of missiles exploded on their targets. The battle cruisers sank, some slowly, some quite precipitously, to the ground, exploding on impact, the sole survivors, in each case, being a nonhuman interrogator and a nonhuman commander.

"Outta here!" Carmella shouted. "Make way for fireballs." And as the jets streaked back to the hills, white-hot fireballs made contact with the nonhuman enemy, reducing all to a hundred piles of cinder and ash.

"Are those all of them?" Carmella asked her co-pilot. "All the battle cruisers on this world?'

"In this sector," he replied. "They were so sure of themselves, they didn't think they needed more'n a few dozen."

"You have crippled the enemy fleet," Carmella heard in her mind. "Now use the Argan weapons to retake the conquered territory in sector 44."

***

Horace MacKenzie sat in his high wing-backed armchair in his study, drinking coffee and studying the morning edition of *The Daily Watcher*, whose fifty-point type headlines screamed about a world-wide epidemic of graveyard, cult murderers and last minute rescues of victims by vigilantes with super-weapons. Gideon and Harry sat opposite him, eating bagels with cream cheese and also drinking coffee. It was still early morning, so they had a front window, which gave out on Apocalypse Avenue, cracked open. The warm, sticky breeze that entered thereby promised a wretchedly sultry, humid day.

"That does it," Gideon said, putting down his coffee cup. "So much for fresh air. I'm shutting it and turning on the AC." He rose, closed the window and went out to the thermostat in the hall. When he returned, cool air was already streaming into the study through the vents.

"Wimp," thus Horace.

"Hey, I come from a hot, *dry* country. I can take the heat, but,"

"Not the humidity," Harry finished his sentence for him. "I'm with you there."

"Hey, this article describes you two to a T," Horace exclaimed, then cleared his throat and read aloud: "the victims said they were rescued by two men, one in his mid-thirties, the other in his mid-forties, the younger with curly dark hair, dark eyes and a Mediterranean look, while the older had short, blond hair and blunt features. They just raised what looked like weapons at our attackers and poof! The attackers vanished. Then they cut our bonds and told us to run, to get the hell out of that cemetery as fast as possible. Which is exactly what we did.' These events occurred at four in the morning, according to the victims, who,"

Gideon let out a loud yawn and Harry followed.

"Nap time," the younger fighter said. "This coffee isn't doing a thing for me."

"Wait!" Horace cried. "Here's another story—'situation still unfolding on the South Side...swat team has surrounded a two-story dwelling...one hostage escaped...told of eleven brutal men inside, all sporting black T-shirts with white skulls printed on them...and one in some kind of trance, in an empty room, at the center of some kind of swirl."

Gideon sat up very alertly. "Where's this taking place?"

"At 1234 Armageddon Row," Horace replied.

"A swirl, hunh," Harry said. "Now where have I heard this before?"

"Come on," Gideon snapped. "You're the police. We're going there. Now. We have to shut that guy down."

"But we can't set up Orozco's machine in the window of my squad car—all the cops will see it."

"Then we'll storm the place and kill this particular fascist, before he starts transporting another army to earth."

"If he hasn't done so already."

"No, I don't believe he has," Horace said distractedly, still scanning the article. "The victim said that he saw the captor in question go into the trance at about two a.m. 'He just started chanting. Then his eyes rolled back and loose objects in the room started flying around him.'" Horace quoted.

"C'mon!" Gideon shouted at the police officer. "Hurry up!"

"Aw shit," Harry said, putting down his mug of coffee and checking on his gun. "So we storm the place and shoot the one in the trance, hunh? That's your plan?"

"You got a better one?"

"Yeah, but it involves a rocket launcher."

"I have one in the trunk of my car."

"No shit? I should arrest you right now."

"Hurry up, Harry. This guy's been at it for hours."

"Oh, all right, all right," and Harry rather unhurriedly stood up. "How many of these death worshippers are we going to have to keep chasing down?" He asked, following Gideon to the front door.

"Until we've tracked them all down," the fighter replied.

"Great. See ya, Horace. Don't let Starfield sleep past nine."

Out on the front step, a blast of hot, heavy air slammed them right in the face. "So we're off to kill a bunch of murdering fascists in 99 degree heat," Harry said, and then trotted down the steps towards Gideon's Honda. "Shit. Just another day in the run-down, second-rate, crime-ridden, East Coast city of D____."

***

He lay on the hillside, eyes wide open, waiting for sunrise. It came slowly at first, just a gold glow, and then faster, as the sun shot its rays through the distant hills, gilding them and everything it touched, but most especially the white tents, spread out below him, filling the entire valley.

"Hey, Dismal ain't such a dismal place," he said to himself and sat up, noting, in the midst of the tents, one of a different color, which had to be, he thought, the administration center. So he rose and directed his feet in that direction. Soon he had reached the tents and then, he was among them. Now and then he stopped, to open a flap and peek in at the children asleep inside. The sight of their rosy, drowsing faces cheered him, so that stretching back up and rubbing his large hands over his leathery, lined face, he murmured, "you rest, kids, you get as much rest as you want. After what you been through, you deserve it. You rock. You're the best." And so, muttering to himself in this manner, he made his way to the gray tent, in the thick of them all, where he saw two men in black cassocks, setting out rectangular tables and hooking up a sheet of burners to a small generator. As he approached, singing, shifting his knapsack and machine gun on his shoulders, one of the priests stopped, stood very still, then turned with an expression of joyful surprise on his even, kindly features. "Rafael! You've come at last!" Vivaldi cried.

"I thought it was time to check up on you, see how you're running this little operation."

"Little! I haven't placed so many fighters' orphans in all my years in the war."

"Well, what do you expect? A whole reality collapsed. And all those fighters in contested territory were lost.

Their children, I heard, had been moved far from the front beforehand."

"Well beforehand. Their parents knew that they themselves were doomed. That made them all the more determined to save their children. And they did. They held the enemy off, lots of them on suicide missions, until we got every last child out alive. And now they're all gathered here, on this badly named planet in this appropriately named galaxy."

"So you approve of Reincarnation but disapprove of Dismal."

"I have a better name for it, Rafael."

"What?"

"Alive."

The old fighter grunted. "Sounds good to me." He turned to gaze at the brilliantly white habitations that filled the valley, murmuring softly to himself, "how beautiful are thy tents." Then he sniffed, discreetly at first, then more loudly. "Potato soup?"

Vivaldi nodded.

"With onions or leeks?"

"Both."

"And carrots."

"And mushrooms, garlic, chickpeas, you name it, Rafael, we put every vegetable we can get our hands on into their breakfast soup."

A few sleepy-eyed children approached the table, glanced at Orozco, and one asked, "who's he?"

"He's a fighter, you dodo, can't you tell?"

"No, how'm I supposed to tell?"

"Well, the machine gun, for one thing."

"And what else?"

"The way he looks at us, the same way the other fighters who rescued us, looked at us."

Orozco smiled. "Like I'm here to keep you alive."

The boy nodded. "Yes, like you came to keep us alive and that's what you did. You kept us alive."